Borrowed
Horses

Borrowed Horses

a novel by Siân Griffiths

American Fiction Series

©2013 by Siân Griffiths
First Edition
Library of Congress Control Number: 2012950072
ISBN: 978-0-89823-284-4
eISBN: 978-0-89823-289-9
American Fiction Series

Cover design by Renae Hansen
Author photo by Karyn Johnston
Interior design by Richard D. Natale

The publication of *Borrowed Horses* is made possible by the generous support of the McKnight Foundation and other contributors to New Rivers Press.

For academic permission or copyright clearance please contact Frederick T. Courtright at 570-839-7477 or permdude@eclipse.net.

New Rivers Press is a nonprofit literary press associated with Minnesota State University Moorhead.

Alan Davis, Co-Director and Senior Editor
Suzzanne Kelley, Co-Director and Managing Editor
Wayne Gudmundson, Consultant
Allen Sheets, Art Director
Thom Tammaro, Poetry Editor
Kevin Carollo, MVP Poetry Coordinator

Publishing Interns:
Katie Baker, Hayley Burdett, Katelin Hansen, Richard D. Natale, Emilee Ruhland, Daniel A. Shudlick

Borrowed Horses Book Team:
David Binkard, Jenna Galstad, Megan Bartholomay

New Rivers Press
c/o MSUM
1104 7th Avenue South
Moorhead, MN 56563
newriverspress.com

For Nathanael, Gwendolyn, and Oliver

CONTENTS

I
IN THE CORNER

II
LOOKING FOR A FENCE

III
DETERMINING THE LINE

I
In the Corner

Deep in the belly of a whale I found her
Down with the deep blue jail around her
Running her hands through the ribs of the dark
Florence and Calamity and Joan of Arc

—Josh Ritter, "To the Dogs or Whoever"

The gaucho acquired an exaggerated notion
of mastery over
His own destiny from the simple act of riding horseback
Way far across the plain.

—as found by Anne Carson, *The Autobiography of Red*

Broken Down

It was Eddie, my first real riding coach, who taught me about corners. The corner is where everything happens. "By the time you reach the fence," he would say, "it's too late." I had to learn that the fence itself isn't the obstacle. The obstacle is your mind.

A stone fence should be no more difficult to jump than a piece of twine strung at the same height. Yet stone looks taller and it's all too easy to imagine its edges stripping your skin if you fail. These thoughts suck the jumper down, amplifying gravity. The trick of jumping a fence—any fence—is to convince yourself that the fence is an illusion. The jump is just another stride, taken with the same rhythm and tempo as the strides before it and the strides after. If the rider believes it, if she keeps her eyes focused on the horizon and her mind on the cadence of strides, the horse too will forget that the obstacle is solid and looming and will allow himself to clear it cleanly in one magnificent thrust of haunches and—*tempo, tempo*—move on.

Corners make this possible. In the arena's corner, the rider must both urge and check her horse. A slight pressure from the rider's legs, a fluid pressure in the hands, a confident, open chest and shoulders ask the horse to condense and collect his power. He will bring his hind feet further underneath him, coiling his body like a tightly wrought spring. Everything comes together—not only the body collects, but also the mind and spirit. Everything pulls in like water, like the tide preparing a wave. His forehand lightens and gravity loses its pull. Here, in the corner, the laws of earthbound physicality are temporarily stowed and the jumping of an enormous and all too solid fence becomes possible.

Eddie always put it more simply: "Bend the bow and let the arrow fly." He repeated this phrase, like all the stock phrases that composed his lessons, so that now, years later, I still hear his low and baritone voice in my mind. *Bend the bow, bend the bow. Let the arrow fly.*

Two miles north of Moscow on Highway 95, the engine made a guttering sound and the needle climbed from black to orange. Smoke curled from under the Chevy's wide hood, softly filling with moonlight. I pulled onto the slush at the side of the road, a single woman in the middle of the night on a road I'd never found all that lonely until now.

I took a sip of coffee from my beaten commuter mug, listening to hissing and ticks. "Shit," I whispered to myself, if only to break a little of the silence. I made it into a little song, "Shit, shit, shitty, shittily, shit."

For four days, I'd driven hard, trying to outrun New Jersey. Only the day before, I'd crossed the Bitterroots and into Idaho, which would have taxed the engine of my old truck even if I hadn't been driving fast and pulling a horse trailer loaded with everything I owned. A breakdown was inevitable.

So reason said; passion viewed the matter differently. This was all part of the larger accident, ongoing for two-and-a-half years now, beginning with the day I left Idaho and ending with a whole series of breakdowns—first my horse, then my mom, then my truck. Or maybe it started earlier than that. Maybe it started with Mom's first episode. Maybe it started in elementary school when I first met

Mouse. Maybe it happened too far back to remember, on that long forgotten day when I first saw a pony and wanted to ride.

I shook these thoughts away, zipped my checkered hunting jacket, and pulled myself out into the cold. Self-pity wouldn't get me anywhere. I popped the hood, let the warmth of the engine wash over me. The highway was black and my flashlight was in New Jersey. Kaki, the barn manager, had used it to find her Leatherman in the hayloft and I could still see it amongst the clutter on her workbench, a pulled shoe thrown across it and a bundle of baling twine underneath.

I scanned the horizon for the promise of headlights rising from any hill, but the darkness was complete. My feet breaking through the crusting slush was the only sound. It was a night for chainsaw murders and women never heard from again. I finished my coffee, watching the wafting smoke turn spectral in the moonlight. The Happy Camper Motor Lodge was a couple miles south. They'd have a phone.

I started walking, trying to whistle and make light of the situation. The last time she drove a car, my mother nearly killed me on this very highway. I'd known this road all my life and it had never been more deserted. November was too cold for crickets. No night birds shadowed the sky; no mice scavenged the fields. In an hour, the bars would close, but the drivers who'd come then would likely be drunk.

I was a hundred yards from my truck when headlights shone over the hill and leveled. The wind rose, its deep cold breath burning my cheeks and lifting the hair from my neck. The headlights traveled direct and steady, not wavering with alcohol or exhaustion. Without another thought, I raised my hand and waved.

If you'd asked me who I hoped would rescue me, I would have requested a farmer, middle-aged or older, sensible, slow to speak but quick to lend a hand, a man raised on the code that you help your neighbor. The driver slowed, pulling in behind my battered Chevy in a late model Dodge. His voice, not old but steady, called through the darkness, "Need a hand?"

"If you have time."

He emerged from the cab, tall and well-built, with a heavy object in hand that I realized, once he turned it on, was only a flashlight, splitting the darkness in two. He stepped into the headlights. His hat said Connor Construction, but it was too clean and unbattered for a workingman's cap. He looked distracted, and this comforted me. If he was a killer or a rapist, I figured he'd be concentrating on how to pull off his crime, making furtive glances, plotting.

Silently, he shone the flashlight over the engine and I lay my hand on his wrist to direct the beam. He started at my touch and looked at me.

I withdrew my hand and checked the coolant. "I'm sorry," I said. "This is probably the last place you want to be right now, right?"

"I was just out for a drive," he said.

"At one in the morning?"

"Couldn't sleep. Thought a drive would clear my head. It's been one of those days."

I smiled in the darkness. "You're telling me." I turned back to the engine and sighed. "I think I'm going to need a tow truck."

"You got a cell phone?" he asked me.

"No."

"No?"

I shrugged. I didn't make a lot of phone calls. None, if I could help it. "You?"

He pulled a smart phone from his pocket, its face a spiderweb of cracks. "I did." A smile tugged at his lips, and I laughed with him.

"What happened?"

"Accident. I've got a new one coming tomorrow. Your timing is really amazing. How do you not have a cell phone in this day and age?"

"Don't need one."

"Do now," he corrected me, smiling. "Life just changed."

I liked his easy smile and whatever trace of an accent colored his voice.

"I'm in the motel down the road," he said, "You can call from there."

"I hate to put you to more trouble."

"No trouble," he said. "I can't leave you out here alone with a broken truck. You could get killed out here."

Next to him, I didn't feel tall or strong. If he wanted to overpower me, he could. I didn't think he would, but I knew I had nothing to base that feeling on but hope. Somehow, I had the sense of being on autopilot, as if this were all pre-arranged. I climbed into the cleanest truck in Idaho and we drove.

He unlocked the room with a key on a large plastic key chain, scalloped along the edges and marked with the room number in gold paint. For all the years I lived in Moscow, I still only knew the Happy Camper Motor Lodge by reputation. You could rent rooms by the day, the week, or the month.

The hotel room told me nothing about my rescuer. A faded print of an elk looking up from the pool at the base of a waterfall hung over the bed, where an old quilt had been thrown over the edge of a floral polyester bedspread. He placed his key on a well-worn copy of *The Count of Monte Cristo* and nodded to the rotary phone.

"It's all yours," he said, granting me privacy by walking back out into the cold night.

Two-and-a-half years earlier, I left Idaho to train with the legendary Jack Stewart Flaherty, *chef d'equipe* of the U.S. Equestrian Team. Like all dream chasers, I was cocky. I imagined that he would recognize my talent and ask me to ride for him and for my country. My absurd dream almost came true. For a year-and-a-half, I spent all of my Saturdays and most of my paycheck at Jack Stewart's stable, where I trailered Foxy for lessons. I was harassed and badgered and ridiculed and, eventually, transformed from a hard-working girl with a gifted horse into a serious contender for a spot on his team.

Because everything went according to plan, I forgot that every dream relies on circumstance. On the second of October a year before, as Jack Stewart was packing to take himself and his barn full of horses off to Florida for the winter show circuit, he told me that Foxfire wouldn't be jumping much longer. The arthritis was showing, despite Foxy's attempts to fake youth and shield that hitching stride from notice. Jack Stewart told me I needed a new horse, a young one, preferably European bred, to continue in this sport—a horse that would cost, he ballparked, somewhere between $150,000 and a half million.

He was used to working with people who would have heard this advice and gone shopping. "Not enough money?" he said in his nasal upper-class Boston accent. "You're young, you're attractive. Why don't you get married?" Instead, I made a vet appointment for Foxfire and tried to plan a new attack, tried to think of any way to fight. For the next year, I rode borrowed horses, working as a catch rider, offering my services to wealthy owners who wanted trophies.

Then, my father called. His voice sounded rougher around the edges than usual, and I knew something had happened just from the sound of his "hello."

"Is it Mom?" I asked. "An attack?" My mother's MS was a constant in our lives, but a tricky constant, a constant that never let you know what to expect or when to expect it. Hot weather made attacks more likely, but even in winter, anything could happen. "How bad was it? Is she O.K.?"

"She's in a wheelchair," Dad cleared his throat and his voice shifted gears—he was a lawyer again, making a tough case, "but she's O.K. Just frustrated, you know?"

The plans I made, the owners I courted, the hours I'd spent building trust with their horses, the dream of gold itself—all of it was unimportant once I knew about the chair. "I'll come home."

"She was afraid you'd say that. Listen, Joannie, there's nothing you can do here."

"Bullshit," I said.

Dad sighed. "I'm putting your mom on."

"Wait," I said, but he called his witness and was gone before I could raise any objections.

"Joannie," my mother's voice sounded better than I expected—

there was no slurring or hesitancy as often came with a seizure. Her tone was light, even happy. "Don't listen to your father—I'm fine. I just have some fancy new wheels. Very chic."

"Mom, I'm coming home."

"Look, Joannie, you know how I feel about this. You need to be exactly where you are."

Mom had pushed me to leave in the first place. Three years before, she watched me ride at a show where I took first in every class. A girl on a skewbald cow horse had openly sneered at me from the fence rail. "Joannie Edson's nothing special. Anyone could win on that big chestnut of hers." Truth was, Foxy's power would have been too much for the girl. I'd watched her pivoting off her knee as her horse made his flat jumps. On Foxy, she would've popped out of the saddle like the cork from champagne, but there was no point in saying that. I understood. No one had beaten me in a year, and winning local horse shows was beginning to feel a bit like cheating. Mom talked to Eddie while she watched me win that final class. He said I needed to find competition.

"Seattle?" she asked. No. He suggested I go for the top as soon as possible, while Foxy was still jumping well. "New Jersey," he told her.

Mom sat me down that evening after supper. "You've gotten too big for the pond," she said, her eyes filled with both sadness and pride.

"I can't leave Moscow."

"Baloney." She looked at me and sighed. "Realistically, Joannie, what can you do? Can you stop the attacks from coming? Can you make them less severe?" She sat back and sighed. "A working body is a God-given gift, Joannie. I won't watch you throw yours away waiting after me."

Her tone was matter of fact. She wouldn't hear any arguments, and I understood that leaving her was the greatest gift I could give. She expected great things of me. That was then, when my promise as an athlete felt like a promise I could keep.

⧞

I waited on hold for AAA. My rescuer paced outside the room, lighting a cigarette, his face warmed into beauty by the match light he sheltered from the wind with a cupped hand. Trying to keep athletic good health, I'd never taken so much as a puff. Now, I wanted a drag from that cigarette, moistened by this Marlboro Man's lips. In the midst of failure, I wanted to breathe something into me that was entirely new. Something not altogether safe.

The tow truck wouldn't arrive for an hour. The man smiled an easy, sunlit smile that made me think of warm beaches and surf. "Guess you're stuck with me until then. How about a beer?"

He'd already gone to enough trouble. *No* was forming on my lips when I saw what it was he pulled from his cooler: the long brown bottle, the yellow-orange label, the blue stars of a Newcastle Brown. He cracked the top and handed it, my favorite beer, over.

"Passing through?" I said.

"Here to stay. I don't close on my house for another couple weeks, so . . ." he shrugged and looked around at the room.

"Moscow's finest."

"God, I hope not." Whatever had bothered him before seemed forgotten. "I'm Dave," he said.

"Joannie." I raised my bottle, sitting on the dark flowers of his bedspread. "Here's to wrecks."

A Little Death

"Little deaths," Mouse had told me. That was how nine-teenth-century women had described orgasm. She was always reading something. We were in high school then, but already, we'd seen enough to know those women had it right. The girls around us dulled as their boyfriends left. "To love is to kill yourself," we'd agreed.

I resisted my desires until college. Even then, my boyfriend couldn't see why I needed to go to the barn every day. As he breathed into my ear, planning a fishing trip we could take together on an afternoon, describing the love we'd make on the floor of his father's boat, the little death was almost painless, the slide of a needle under skin, a burning fluid in the vein, but I've never been prone to just any addiction.

Salamander-like, I regenerated when his promises exploded in the bed of another woman. I had revenge sex with his roommate, but it only made me feel cheap and so I turned again to the barn. I made myself the rassaphore of my passion, devoting myself to riding because I understood it as a spiritual pursuit. There was only one prayer: *Foxfire*. The blood of a horse, the body of a girl, is hard-won communion, but faith manifests in such ways.

Over the hotel bed, an elk stared from the wall hanging with liquid eyes. When the bottom drops out of faith, you can allow yourself to wash away with it or you can find a new vessel for hope. I had never believed a man could save me, and I didn't believe that Dave could, but neither would I allow myself to mope now that all my dreams were dead. It was time to try to build something new.

We talked at first to kill an hour, then we were talking because we enjoyed each other. I couldn't remember the last time I laughed so hard. He was the new regional supervisor for Connor Construction, brought up to do a job that couldn't wait for a house. I was coming back to work my old job because I had nothing better to do and because my parents might need me, though they insisted they did not.

"You like your job?" I asked.

"I hate it, but what can you do? That's everybody, right?"

"Working for the weekend?"

"Something like that."

"So what do you do with your weekends to make them worth working for?"

He held up the old book on the nightstand.

I was impressed—not many of the guys I'd grown up with would admit to reading voluntarily. "An intellectual on a construction site?"

He laughed. "You see why I hate my job."

"Oh, no," I said. "I imagine there's lots of time to swap insights about Dumas when you're putting up drywall."

He had a beautiful, easy smile after his initial shyness passed. "If only." He paused and blushed, embarrassed. "I used to write poetry, but I haven't done much of that lately."

"You should. The world needs poetry."

"I don't know. Maybe." Watching him sit back against the headboard, the buttons of his flannel undone to reveal the collar of his tee shirt, I was becoming ever more aware of just how long it was since I'd gone to bed with a man. The five o'clock shadow that played against the tan of his skin made him all the more appealing. I'd never been one for men who were clean-shaven.

It was my turn to say something, but I found myself resting my eyes on his instead, trying to find an exact word for their color. This was stupid. I was like those high school girls all over again, so easily drawn in by good looks and an easy smile. I cleared my throat. "I suppose we should check on the truck."

But when the old Chevy was pulled away, I rode back with Dave rather than going home in the tow truck. New Jersey had been nothing if not lonely, and I couldn't give up a good conversation.

Dave seemed equally eager to talk, leaning further in, becoming more animated. He'd been lonely, too, I guessed, and neither of us was tired. We opened more beer. "The guys say there's not much to do around here," he said.

"That's what everyone says, but it isn't true. They just haven't been anywhere else." His lips looked full and soft, the kind of lips that, brushing against skin, made the nerves alive and wanting. The room was cold, and I moved closer to the warmth of his body. "Other places, there's plenty to do, but it all costs money. Here, you can go to the Pritchard Gallery and see art for free. The university brings in poets and writers—also free. The summer repertory theatre is cheap. You can hike; you can fish; you can mountain bike. If you like skiing, there's mountains. If you like music, there's Jazz Fest. For a small town, we have it going on."

With his sun-lit hair, Dave reminded me more of a surfer than an intellectual, but his enthusiasm was genuine. "I can't see the guys at work going in for the culture. Maybe for the fishing."

"Yeah, well. Know your sources, right?" We were close to each other on the bed now—closer than I'd been to any person in as long as I could remember. My skin was alive with the electricity of his skin, so close to mine.

"Art, music, and poetry," his voice grew lower, deeper, turning each word over carefully in his velvet mouth. I'd named the right things. Things that connect person to person, mind to mind, heart to heart. "No," he said, "I can't see the guys at work—" Before he could finish, I leaned in and pulled his mouth to mine, tongues bitter-cooled with Newcastle Brown. He pushed me softly back, his face full of confusion and doubt. I had misread the situation.

Blood rushed to my cheeks. "I'm sorry," I started to say, but before I could finish his lips were on mine again. His hand on my cheek, my throat, the soon-bare skin of my hip was warm and soft. He hesitated, eyes searching mine, trying to read me, his body shaking as he fought his own desire. Then, his arm pulled me tight to him and all doubt vanished. Yes, we'd been lonely, but that was over now.

In the cool sheets of that dark night, I was reinvented. A girl who had never seduced a man she barely knew had become a girl who had. If that could happen, what wasn't possible?

I woke in the morning, clothed only in bed sheets, to find Dave writing in a small notebook at my side. There was nowhere I had to be: no horse to ride, no job yet started.

His eyes settled on me as I lay in the morning light. "I've never done that before," I said, apologetic.

"Done what?" He set his book and pencil down.

"Slept with someone I've only just met."

"Me neither," he said. "That's got to mean something though, right? This isn't just a one night thing."

"I hope not."

He rested his cheek against my shoulder, the stubble prickling against my skin. He stayed there for several long moments, thoughtful, his breath warm and regular. "Tell me something about you. Something important."

"Something important?" I shuffled through ideas and memories like discs in a jukebox, searching for the right one to play, something vital, something that had nothing to do with Foxfire or failure. "I love Eastwood films," I said.

"Clint Eastwood?" Dave was laughing, his fine head catching the morning light that filtered in through the muslin inner curtain. It was a far cry from art or poetry. "The Westerns, *Dirty Harry*, or the new stuff?"

"All of them," I said, "especially the Westerns." Gentle now, he rested his forearm on my bare waist, tender skin against tender skin. I kissed his strong shoulder. "You an Eastwood fan?"

The question was loaded, and he knew it. "Of course."

A misfire. The revolver clicked to the next loaded question. "Which is your favorite?"

He threw his body back against the pillows. "You want me to pick just one?"

I waited him out. This is how duels work.

Finally, "*Pale Rider.*"

"*Pale Rider?*"

"Yeah, *Pale Rider*. That's a solid choice. What's wrong with *Pale Rider?*"

"Nothing, I guess. I just liked it a lot better the first time around, when it was called *High Plains Drifter.*"

His hand traced circles on my thigh. "Isn't that the one where he rapes a woman?"

"His character's morally ambiguous."

The hand stroked now rather than circled, light against the skin. "That movie doesn't make any sense. What was he supposed to be? The ghost of some guy the town allowed to be killed?"

"Perhaps. It's never clear."

"And you're saying that's better than *Pale Rider?*"

"Clarity is over-rated."

His fingertips brushed inward. "And morality, too, I suppose?"

"Have you ever known anything to be either clear or moral?" My voice was brushstrokes. I turned, spooning my body with his.

"No." He breathed the word between kisses, working his way around my shoulder to the nape of my neck. I wanted to stay like this forever: warm and touching and talking to an intelligent and beautiful man.

I pressed myself against his chest, his hands cupped under my breasts, teasing my nipples. Talking was becoming more difficult, but I managed to whisper, "Then why would you want clarity or morality in your art?"

His lips were in my hair now, hot breath in my ear, answer enough. If I had thought that this was to be my first one-night stand, I could now see that he had no intention of disappearing into the sunrise. "Keep talking," he said. "I love the way you talk."

"I saw him once. Clint Eastwood," I said, trying to piece together words. "At Jazz Fest." It was becoming harder to be coherent. The room was ablaze with sunlight and Dave. "I only got a glimpse." I closed my eyes and saw again: the sun-damaged cheek, the curve of his ear, the sweep of his hair. I'd like to think it was respect for his privacy that held me away, but in truth, I was afraid. I couldn't see Clint unsilvered, unscreened.

Dave's hand traveled down my stomach, altogether real. He opened his lips, grazing my neck with soft teeth. Speech now was impossible. For years, only Foxy's silky nose had nuzzled against my neck. It was his way of loving me: He treated me as one of the herd. One of the *heard*: those who sensed the call of horses, of open space.

Dave moved his fingers between my legs, and my breath caught. All the things I swore I hadn't been missing thundered down on me. After all, it had not been enough. Dave held me firmly against his body with one arm while his other hand worked deeper to again find all the untouched places I'd denied these last many years. I yielded my body to the buried pleasures his fingers adeptly brought to the surface.

In college, while I was being trained in radiography, one dream had got me out to the barn on those January Saturdays when there was a fire in the fireplace and TNT's all-Eastwood weekend on TV. My roommates would be snuggled on the sofa, mugs of cocoa in hand, popcorn on the middle lap. Over by the single-pane window of that dreadful, drafty old Victorian would be me, back from working the early morning biscuit shift at Hardee's and changed into breeches, boots, and an old ski jacket that snowed its filling from the worn elbows I never had time to mend. I'd convince myself that it wasn't really that cold. I told myself that this is what riders—real riders—do. They go out, even when it isn't fun.

It's the mantra that goes right back to the Pony Express. In wind and sleet and driving rain, come hell or high water, you throw on the saddle and work. In January, the cold seeped so deeply into my feet that they exploded with pain when I dismounted. Most days, I enjoyed riding. Other days, I went because of something deeper, the wish that dare not admit itself. Dreams were earned through sacrifice. We only had one life, and we had to take what it offered while we could. My mother had taught me that.

I was eleven when she had her first attack, although at the time we didn't call it that. We were taking a family walk when my mother started limping a little. She laughed it off, saying she just had pins and needles in her leg. The wind blew loose strands of hair across her suntanned face, and she looked as healthy—no, as *invincible*—as she always had. Only later did I realize that people don't get pins and needles when they're moving. Hers lasted for two days. Dad almost convinced her to see a doctor when they went away again, as quickly and inexplicably as they had come.

I'd forgotten about the whole thing when, nearly a year later, it happened again. She woke up with pins and needles, and they lasted all day long. We didn't know then whether to worry. It hardly seemed like much.

The third attack sent her to the doctor. She was cutting carrots for soup when her hand went numb. She dropped the knife, and it missed her foot by a fraction of an inch, standing itself point down in the hardwood floor. "Enough is enough," my father had said. The shaft of the knife still shivered while he dialed the phone.

But the doctor couldn't find anything wrong. He told her to take it easy, rest up. It was probably nothing but stress. She'd been complaining about tiredness. This was just a sign that she was trying to do too much. And so it went. Different parts of her body acted strangely, on and off, with weeks or months of normality in-between. Tests showed nothing.

By the time she started falling asleep in the middle of the day, she'd seen the doctor ten times and had been sent to two different psychologists. She dreaded the appointments. "I'm not crazy," she said. Her jaw would set a full hour before a session started, and she'd come home tight-lipped and silent. She didn't tell anyone about her narcolepsy.

On my fourteenth birthday, we'd picked up a pizza in town on the way home from my riding lesson. Mouse was coming to spend the night, and we were rushing to beat her back to our house. The pizza scalded my knees as we drove up 95 on the way home, but I was never happier than I was in our old Subaru that night. I sang along to Depeche Mode when suddenly, my mother's chin dropped to her chest and the car swerved into oncoming traffic. I screamed and jerked the wheel to pull us back into our lane, but I over-corrected. We spun across the road. Even today, I can see the shining grill of the truck barreling toward Moscow as it whooshed by, inches away, neatly clipping the side mirror from the car. The sound of its horn still blares in my nightmares.

When we finally settled in the ditch facing north on the southbound side of the highway, my mother and I were both awake in the way only a near-death experience can wake you. Every sensation became crisp: the swish of passing vehicles, the strong smell of burned rubber mingling with pepperoni, the fainter smell of horses clinging to my clothes, the hum of the heater, the golden shafts of wheat bending against the breeze, everything I was inches away from never hearing or seeing or smelling again. I looked to the pines lining the hill, and it seemed each individual needle stood out from the next, under their fall dusting of thousands of individual snowflakes.

We didn't say a word on the way home. I stared out the window marveling at each small thing I'd almost lost, trying to ignore my mother's hand shaking on the gear shift. My heart rate refused to slow; every beat pulsed with urgency.

Mouse had arrived by the time we got home.

"What kept you?" Dad asked.

"Mom fell asleep on 95." My lips were strange, disconnected from the words they made. In truth, the accident had taken little actual time; it was my riding lesson that had gone long, but the lesson had been overwritten by the time that stretched between the closing of my mother's eye and its opening.

Dad turned for an explanation, but Mom had none to give.

Mouse lifted the silence as easy as lifting the pizza box lid. The cheese had slid to one side and the crust was smushed against one side of the box. She looked at me with one eyebrow raised, and the two of us both broke into laughter. It flowed out in waves, one after another crashing against that dead pizza, the night's only casualty.

As she would do so often in the months before the diagnosis when I started to believe that my mother was just crazy, Mouse pulled the pieces back together and made the world normal again, sliding the cheese back onto each slice as she served. With Mouse there laughing, it was more obvious that we had, after all, survived.

While Dave showered, I fingered the seams of his quilt. My mother had made the quilt that covered me each night. Old coffee cans along her bedroom shelf held pieces cut from outgrown riding jackets, the skirt I'd worn to graduation, my first pair of scrubs, and the assorted leftover scraps from previous quilts so that any new quilt would not depose but merely succeed the quilt I used now. All her quilts held common scraps, segues from childhood to maturity. When the time came, she'd choose a pattern to transform shed clothing into something beautiful and warm.

White sunlight flooded the room through the uncurtained window. I rolled my body over toward the bathroom door, waiting for Dave to look at me and allow me to see myself from the outside again, the view by which I was powerful and gorgeous and moved with intentionality.

What would Mouse think of Dave? I needed my high school car back to know. It'd been a small, bullet-shaped two-seater, the paint dulled long ago from blue to an ashy silver. We called it "the Pod." Mouse and I had decided it could serve as a sort of litmus test for potential boyfriends, a sort of reverse of the sword in the stone: The man who could fit comfortably in the Pod would be the man of my dreams, which safely ruled out damned near everyone. I wondered now whether Dave was the mythical man whose body would magically fold up comfortably in the torn vinyl of those small old bucket seats.

The bed was cold without him. I pulled the carefully pieced cotton over my shoulders. All quilts are displays of love. Dave's was hand-made with small, even stitches. Its pattern was a classic one, the double wedding ring. Unlike mine, the fabric looked like store-bought calico, but it was beautifully worked. I pictured its maker sewing night after night by lamplight, her fingers cramped with tedium and fine-sewing.

His cigarettes lay on the nightstand next to a large box of matches and an ashtray overflowing with matchsticks, each burned down nearly to the end. How bored he must have been, and how lonely, lighting matches to pass the time. I slid a cigarette from its paper box and set it between my lips. I imagined lighting it, burning my lungs with its smoke. Instead, I returned it to the box. Later, Dave would shake it from the box, press his lips against the paper my lips had held, kissing me by proxy, inhaling the heat.

Dave emerged from the shower, towel-wrapped and resplendent.

"Can you give me a lift to a car rental place?" I asked.

"You think I'm going to let you just rush off?" he said.

A thump at the window stayed the answer on my lips. I pulled Dave's shirt on and opened the door. At first I saw nothing. The parking lot lay cold and sterile with morning light; the highway was still. Then, on the ground, feathers caught my eye. I moved to it, the pavement slick with frost, an east wind chilling my bare legs. Dave watched me from the doorway, the color vanished from his cheek. On the concrete, a chickadee lay among its own feathers, the wind ruffling the plumage, its neck twisted unnaturally by the unseen barrier.

The Heard

No two people were ever so suited for each other as my parents. Both were retired, Mom from the Co-op and Dad from the law, old hippies finally at home in their self-created utopia. There was a great deal they'd never believed in: shoes in summer, compassionate conservatism, Walmart. My parents did believe, had always believed, and would always believe in one holy and apostolic catholic church for the forgiveness of sins, and they attended Mass every Sunday.

I had lapsed in so many ways, not only from their church but from their ideals. Not that I had totally gone in for capitalist materialism—not that I believed, as one president put it, that "America must shop." Still, I owned more than I needed, I wanted still more, and whenever I went home, I felt the weight of my guilty desires, of my closet full of boots and running shoes, of my drawers of Eastwood DVDs, and I became conscious that it'd been a long, long time since my last confession.

The fact that my parents never reminded me of this guilt, never preached or even hinted, did not make me less aware. Their confidence that I would make good decisions always baffled me.

I walked into their house, fresh from sin, unannounced as usual, without bothering to knock because they always expected me, no matter how long it had been.

"If you're staying for lunch," Dad called from the kitchen, "say so now so we can put more potatoes on."

"Lunch sounds good." I stood in the kitchen doorway to watch my father bustle from drawer to sink to butcher block and my mother wheel from fridge to counter, each getting in the other's way. I expected to be bothered by the sight of her in the chair, but instead, I seemed to breathe out a breath I didn't know I was holding, a breath I took when I left for Jersey. "Can I help?"

"We've got it," my mother said, and I could see it was true. She rolled with a practiced ease, fully able to help herself. Usually, patients take a little while to get comfortable in a chair, and I wondered if there had been temporary chairs that my parents hadn't told me about while I was gone, secret episodes that they felt would distract me if I knew. It would be like them not to worry me if they could help it—better to bear pain in silence than to drag others into their anxiety.

My parents looked more alike every time I saw them, as if they were slowly, continually morphing into duplicates of the same person. Each had an identical long, straight waist and slightly stooping shoulders, accentuated now as they leaned to slice vegetables. Their hair was frizzy and pony-tailed, hair so ubiquitous at the Co-op that I'd started to wonder whether it grew that way because of something in the sesame seeds or quinoa. Even with the chair, things hadn't changed all that much. Their hair, the earthy smell of the dark wood-paneled kitchen, the sight of Pilate curled on his dog bed in the corner: everything comforted. It might not match the pictures made in movies, but this was love.

My father didn't used to wear shoes. Ever. A southern California kid who stayed in Los Angeles through his law degree, he envisioned them as an unnecessary shackle, a signifier of materialism and what he called the hyper-socialization of Westernized humanity. To understand our world, he said, we must feel our world, touch its changes, its dust and mud, our litter, the new grass, everything, with our soles. He understood the world this way for so long that now his feet were calloused against its pebbles and thorns, and shaded with dirt so embedded in the skin that it wouldn't wash out.

He met my mother at UCLA, where she had gone to escape her parents' rigid conservatism. My maternal grandparents still live somewhere in southern Idaho, but my mother has never told me where. She can't honor a mother and father, she once said, who don't honor life, all colors of life. She's never told me that they're racists—she avoids speaking of them—but from this comment, I imagine they are. Not just talking racists, but acting racists, the kind with club memberships, the kind who organize "nigger shoots," the kind Idaho has been working hard to rid itself of. Perhaps I am wrong. There is much I will never know about my mother.

After four years of ever-changing majors and a year of dating my father, she left school and molded a life that would include all her loves: God, gardening, my father, Idaho. And eventually me, her child. I don't know how my father felt about moving to Idaho at the time. It couldn't have been an easy adjustment, and Idahoans, even in comparatively liberal Moscow, have never much cared for California immigrants. Yet now, when he sits on the deck and looks over the garden that he and my mother have planted, harvested, and planted again for over thirty years, he seems at peace.

He couldn't go shoeless year 'round here—not if he wanted to keep his toes. He bought a pair of heavy duty Sorrels, thickly lined, for winter weather. The pair that stood in the closet must have been eleven or twelve years old. There had been another pair before them, worn until they were worn through. I believe these were the only shoes my father ever owned in his adult life. Two pairs of boots: concessions.

I love watching Dad in action. I've never asked him about it, but I imagine that he could have made a fortune in some California firm, even shoeless. Maybe especially shoeless, since that was part of how he worked: lulling people into over-confidence with his rumpled suit, his frazzled hair, his apparent daffiness. People always underestimated him, revealed too much, and then my father, scratching his head, apparently confused, would catalogue the ways in which the witness contradicted himself. I loved how, even making his panther pounce, he looked so much like an absent-minded professor.

I think he could have made partner in California—made enough to buy me a stable full of horses—but I don't think he would have been happy. My mother offered him a different vision of success.

She's tough, my mother: not aggressive, but unyielding. After UCLA, I'd bet that she would have moved to Moscow whether my father had come or not, even with no job and a dozen other weighty unknowns. Or maybe this is just the story I've constructed for them, based more on the parents I know now than the kids they were then: a freshly-minted law school grad and a college dropout, just figuring out how to live, deciding when to trust love to give up one possible life for another.

We ate potato, cheese, and onion casserole in the nook off the kitchen. My parents never had need of a formal dining room. I can't ever once remember having a dinner party. Dinner was for family, which included Mouse.

I watched them, trying to figure it out, their love. What was it about my tight-lipped, wise-eyed mother that made my father give up everything for her? A few photos of her from their college days still existed, faded now and dog-eared at the edges. Clearly, she was beautiful. More than that, even. She seemed ethereal in her long calico skirts and peasant dresses. The tilt of her chin was regal even now, like the world couldn't quite touch her. And yet, she wasn't warm in the way my father was. I'd seen him chat with Moscow's homeless in the same openly friendly manner he used with the mayor or the postman. He was just one of those guys who never met a stranger. Mom was more reserved.

The potatoes were warm and silky on the tongue, cheese melting between each layer. My parents had a way of turning the most mundane dish into something sublime. When I was a kid, Dad told me that everything they made was seasoned with love. I'd always written that off as just another hokey parentalism. Now, I wondered if that was true. What my parents had was a rare thing. I'd never seen two adults with that kind of bond.

They wouldn't approve of what I had done last night, yet I did not feel sorry. In the face of despair, I had snatched back control. Like my father, I, too, could trade one dream for another. Like my parents, I took love while I had the chance.

Packing to go to Jack Stewart's, I'd asked my parents if they were sorry to see me leave. My father, for once, looked away, dodging the question. My mother smiled. "You were given this talent for a reason, Joannie." She didn't mention God, but his guidance was understood. It hadn't stopped Foxy from aging.

Red calico curtains hung in the window of the nook, the cornflower-speckled print too regular for constellations, too irregular for pattern. Mom hadn't mentioned God since I came back, but I doubted either her chair or my failure could shake her faith. She talked of a new local bakery whose bread they'd sell in the Co-op next month. Dad listened with the air of one still fascinated, the way that Dave had listened to me the night before.

My father smiled at me, benevolence in every crinkle of his hooded eyes. "Penny for your thoughts?"

I smiled back. "You think I'm so cheaply bought off, old man?"

My father laughed and winked at me. "That's my girl."

Dawn was the closest friend I had had since Mouse, but I hadn't called more than a handful of times in the years I'd been away. We were friends from the barn, and we talked in person, either on horseback or over beers, rather than on the phone. On the day Foxy was coming back, she called to ask if I wanted to grab lunch. Dick's was dark and seedy and the food was greasy, but there wasn't a cheaper beer and burger to be had in Moscow.

While I waited for Dawn, I counted the seconds between the disappearance and reappearance of the red bow of the neon "Miller Time" sign in the small, foggy window. One, two, three, cut out. One, two, three, light up. Dormancy, illumination, dormancy.

Dawn entered, parting the construction workers huddled around the unfinished plywood bar, just another Red Sea. Two watched her enter and begged her to lift her jacket so they could watch her Wrangler Ws as she walked. Dawn left them groaning behind her. I settled back in my chair, distinctly less than alluring in my hospital scrubs, and contemplated the condensation on my glass and the maps it made as it wept.

"So," she said, "where the fuck's my gold medal?" Dawn had a way of leveling conversation like a gun. She would call it shooting straight, but there was something simultaneously intimate about it, something like the connection between predator and prey. She had hunted since she was ten years old: deer, elk, pheasant, grouse, turkey. She always filled her tag, then hunted for anyone who hadn't filled theirs. Not being a hunter myself, I had never seen her in her hunting gear, so I imagined her hunting as I saw her now: a small woman with hair teased three inches high wearing red hot Wranglers, a star-spangled blouse, and an expression that dared you to mess with her.

"Gold medal? Shit," I smiled. "What makes you think you deserve one?"

"I put up with you, don't I? If that don't deserve a gold medal, I sure as hell don't know what does."

"By which, I suppose, you mean that you survived two years without me, and deserve a medal for making it so long on your own?"

"It was a pretty amazing disappearing act."

"Yeah, well, I'm back," I said and realized that for the first time, it didn't feel like defeat. Dave had given me his book that day: *The Count of Monte Cristo*, his favorite. I promised I'd read it so we could talk about it later. When his lips touched mine, there was no more Jersey, no more age, no more failure.

"Pick up any cute guys in Jersey?"

I sat back in my chair and rolled my eyes. "Two and a half years gone and I walk right back into the same fucking conversation."

"In two and a half years, any other red-blooded American woman would've had some flings. You got to give me something, Joannie. Keep the conversation interesting."

"I was a bit busy trying to earn that stupid gold medal, remember?"

Dawn rolled her eyes. "Only you see that as a full time job."

"There are always men," I said. "It's not like they won't keep."

Dawn laughed. She was the one person since Mouse with whom I could have this conversation, the one person who didn't question my sexual orientation simply because I didn't have a steady boyfriend. "If you change your mind," she said, "there's a cutie looking our way from the bar right now."

I could have told her about Dave, but I didn't. In a moment, she would've seen the hope I would not admit even to myself: two people in an oven-warmed kitchen, making a life together. Dawn would have seen the vacancy where a barn once stood.

For two weeks, I gave Dave every moment, going from night shift work to his hotel room each morning to wake in his arms as if I owned the right to them, sleeping in his bed until lunch when he came to share another hour, leaving for the barn after he was gone again and the apartment was just another empty box. Foxfire was the only truth I'd never been able to deny, but careful to give Dave no sense of my failure, I kept Foxy my secret.

At birth, a human child has roughly three hundred bones, but many of these fuse as we grow. Our adult skeleton only has 206. With age, we grow more rigid. Our underlying structure knits and sets. We begin to break more easily than we bend. I told myself that I was young still; I could still bend. I could find a way to be the Joannie he saw, the only one I'd ever shown him, the one that didn't really exist.

I watched Dave write in his little black notebook and listened as he read what he'd written, words that made me all puddled, words that made me still, words I'd somehow inspired, words that made me feel I could leap from my skin and exist in some better form, words that warmed poor, dull October into something vivid and rich. I'd listen, feeling like I only now understood what the word "amazement" meant, how it connected to puzzles and to delight.

Then, he'd crawl over the bed to me and stroke my hair until the words faded against the greater truth of touch. I sacrificed all I'd ever believed about myself, and I would have sacrificed it over and over again if only allowed to, but the gold on my false idol only took two weeks to chip.

It chipped under the blade of a word: wife.

His arms wrapped around me, Dave spoke of her, pressing his lips against my head, whispering how little she meant to him, how little he'd known of what love could be until I had taught him. His grip bruised, but I sat stricken in the headlights of another failure. All that night, he crushed my body to his as if he could prevent my escape.

Night shift: I sat in the dim light long past midnight with my humming machines. Under the weight of a heavy apron, my hand lay on my belly. I covered bodies in lead, shielding the vulnerable. I rolled them around on my cold table, positioning them under my cross of light, and took pictures of skeletons. I had to remind myself that I was no ghost. There was something solid in me. Something inflexible and unyielding. Something that, thankfully, would break before it bent.

He'd made no offer to leave her.

Dislocations, compound fractures. I have seen the body when no bones give it shape. I have felt the sag of un-boned flesh, the wobble of it like partially set pudding. It's not a pretty sight, but it's a reminder. Without something rigid at the core, a framework, we are scarcely human.

He worked for her father; his livelihood depended on her, he'd said. Excuses.

A human bone is many times stronger than a steel rod of the same weight. When a living bone breaks, it re-knits and grows whole again. The repaired bone is thicker than before, unlikely to break in the same place.

I am not a man of steel, and for this, I am grateful. I am a woman of bone.

I envisioned his wife, an Amazonian Barbie doll. She'd be beautiful, long and leggy. She'd be a woman men would swoon for, someone for whom you'd sacrifice your fondest dreams.

We are never shorter or taller than the bones we inhabit. Our secret, the skeleton, determines our life: our vantage, our carriage, our abilities. Our understanding of and interrelations with the world is determined in part by those bones. Hers would be strong and straight. She would be one of the blessed ones, the gifted ones. She would dress her bones in well-cut, expensive fabrics. She would do her hair and nails. Unlike Dave, she was not a thinker or a reader—that much, he'd told me. She had no need for poetry. She was a person for whom life's gifts came easily and generously.

I could have justified stealing the husband of a woman like that.

The door opened to a wheelchair, taking me thankfully out of my thoughts. The nurse pushed a chart at me, but I ignored him for the moment, focusing on the patient. The nurse and his chart could wait. My patient's eyes shifted around the room, and I laid my hand on her quivering wrist to soothe her. She was twenty or so, thin, black-haired and blue-eyed. Her cheek bore a long, straight gash and was quickly bruising. Too quickly, she said, "I fell down the stairs. Ice." Even her voice seemed to shake.

I didn't believe the story, but I didn't judge. "We'll get you fixed up."

Her eyes, as they met mine, were full of fear, but she sighed and became calmer. "It's my ankle."

Over the years, doctor after doctor treated my mother's symptoms, but few looked beyond the symptoms and at the woman herself. I never wanted to make that mistake. "We'll take some pictures of it at a few different angles, but I want you to tell me if it hurts to move it one way or another. I'm sure it's pretty tender."

She looked up with an almost guilty smile. "I feel so foolish," she said.

"We all slip sometimes."

The sun was rising when I got off work. I didn't want to go home to a bare apartment, but I was too tired to ride. The October morning was cool and damp, tough weather for Foxy's arthritic bones. Standing ankle-deep in wood shavings in a stall heated only by the warmth of his body, I just brushed and brushed him, focusing on nothing but the bloom of his coat, bright as a new penny.

I went home and tried to sleep, but my mind kept turning to Mouse. She'd moved to Moscow when we were in second grade. She was Jennifer then. Dad nicknamed her and "Mouse" suited her so much better that, once Dad called her that, it stuck. By the end of the year, even her teachers called her Mouse.

Her grandparents were not especially pleased to have a young child in the house but put up with her as long as she was quiet, so Mouse spent the year mostly in her room reading books, drawing, and getting fat.

Chubby girls have never done well in elementary school, and the wire-framed glasses she wore and her grandfather's job as the school custodian only made matters worse. She spent her recesses alone, avoiding notice but noticing others. All the time, she studied us in quick glances stolen in between the pages of her book. If we caught her looking, her face would break into a splotchy blush that stretched right down her neck.

I can't take any credit for our friendship. It did not start with any act of noblility on my part; I was too busy playing hopscotch and tetherball. Our friendship started with a seating chart. Seeing that we usually behaved ourselves even without his cold eye upon us, Mr. Linfield moved Mouse into my corner in the back of the classroom. For two weeks, we sat quietly next to one another without much more contact then we'd ever had. We did our math and read our stories and filled out our worksheets. Then, one day while we were reading social studies, she did something bold—something far more dangerous than I would have given her credit for. Without ever looking up from her textbook, she slid a piece of paper across her desk and onto mine. It was a picture of a sphinx, but with Mr. Linfield's head for the face, complete with his hair greying at the temples, his bloodshot eyes, and his long, crooked nose.

I looked at the drawing for minutes, unsure what to do or what it meant. If our teacher saw it, he would have said her name, "Jenn-i-fer," in that lingering, nasal way of his, and she would have missed every recess for the rest of the week and would be moved to a table by his desk. I owed her nothing, but something in me responded to the risk she'd taken, to the trust she'd shown. My eye followed the pencil lines, the soft shading under the elbows, the dark, confident stroke of the outline and facial feature. No one else in our grade could draw that well—it was like something from the Sunday paper—and yet even then I knew it was more than a cartoon. It was a test.

As Mr. Linfield turned to pace down the far side of the classroom, I quickly wrote "The Stinks" across the bottom in dark, thick, unmistakable letters and deftly slid it back. It was a calculated risk. If Mouse had laughed, if she had betrayed us with even a smile, Linfield's sarcasm would have turned on us, making us subject to public scorn that kids in our class did not easily live down. But Mouse, schooled as she was in the art of being neither seen nor heard, slid under his notice.

The first weeks of our friendship were made entirely of silent correspondence, pictures and captions. From it, I learned that she was smart, sarcastic, and generally more interesting than other kids. Outside of class, I never thought of her. I didn't give much thought to the kids who lived in town. Then one afternoon, as I was in the bus line, I saw Ben Topp in the middle of a group of boys throwing pieces of his leftover lunch at Mouse: a half a twinkie, torn bits of a roast beef sandwich. Despite her size, she looked small. I couldn't stand to see her there, fighting the tears in her eyes, trying to muster her dignity, as he called her names and flung another bit of cake. I snapped. Without a thought, I took Ben down with a flying tackle that ended in a three-day suspension and a year's worth of gossip.

By the end of second grade, Mouse was coming over to my house almost every day after school. On sunny days, we wandered the hills. On rainy ones, we searched the neighbor's barn for rat nests and snakes. Her clothes began to sag as the puffiness of a year in her room fell away, and my mother began making skirts for her as she'd always done for me. Mouse spent more time at my house than her own. I had been an only child, but by the time we entered junior high, we were closer than sisters.

Mouse lengthened into beauty, but by then she'd been discarded and ignored too long to care much for popularity. The fact that she didn't care made her more attractive still. On Friday nights when she stayed at my house, she'd talk about the guys who flirted with her. She didn't know what to say or how to act. She didn't trust their interest. They hadn't liked her when she was dull, so why would they like her any better just because she'd become beautiful?

As Mouse grew lithe and the flaming red of her hair fell down her back in a thick curtain, more and more heads began to turn our way. We remained unchanged, convinced we were better than those who had ignored us all these years. While other girls were going boy-crazy, I was fantasizing a life with horses. Mouse was talking about becoming a doctor or medical researcher to help people like my mother, who had set a place for her at every dinner table and made the guest bed into Mouse's own.

Mouse could find the underlying humor in anything. With Mom's MS, I needed that. The summer I turned seventeen, Mom had a seizure that left her speech slurred and her left side weak. I had a lesson with Eddie, and Mom insisted I go. Mouse would keep her company. I came home tired, not so much from riding but from the daily insecurity my mother's disease had brought into our home. I opened the door to find Mom and Mouse helpless with laughter. They'd been playing Canasta when Mom, who never cursed a day in her life, asked Mouse for all of her "asses."

"Aces," Mouse explained as the tears rolled down her face.

"It sounds right in my head," my mother said. Her speech was slurred and garbled by a helpless tongue but her laughter came out pure and whole, and all I wanted in that moment was for her to keep laughing and laughing and laughing, to sound again like she was unaffected, like there was nothing wrong.

After a sleepless morning, I returned to the barn and rode. My eyes burned from being open too long. Weariness seemed woven into the honeycomb of my marrow. I'd dropped my defenses with Dave. Foxfire and I strode through newly turned fields, stubbled with the shafts of harvested wheat. The ground was surprisingly soft under

Foxy's feet, the frost only on the surface. With each hoof fall, I felt it give a little, then hold. The loam's crumbling was only a way of gathering strength as the earth compacted itself: strength enough to hold the weight of a horse, the weight of its rider, the weight of any burden. I focused on nothing but that, the crumbling strength of earth, for an hour, and then I turned home, groomed Foxfire, and returned him to the lingering warmth of his stall.

Dave called and called, begging to see me. He couldn't sleep, couldn't write, couldn't *think*, he said. Self-hatred fueled my will, allowing me the coldness I needed to withstand my desire. He sounded as bad as I felt. All I had to do was give, but that I would not do, denying him even friendship.

Some days, my heart was full of birds, all flapping and trying to escape at once; other days, I could feel no heart at all. Those days were easier.

Dawn looked out from a stall as I walked in. "Well, look what the cat drug in," she said.

I didn't answer.

"How long has it been since I saw you at Dick's?" She was on the hunt. "I thought you'd gotten yourself kidnapped or caught under a bus or something."

"Night shift," I said, not looking at her lest she read more in my glance. "I'm riding in the afternoons."

She disappeared again into the stall she'd been cleaning. "And here I was hoping you'd finally gone and gotten yourself a boy-friend." She threw the words out with another pile of shit for the wheelbarrow.

I flinched, settling my saddle onto Foxy's broad back, running my hand over the cool leather that wear had made soft and pliant. I remembered again what I'd long known: human relationships are less intimate than that of horse and rider. Foxy and I operated as one body, one mind. People, even people in love, spend too much of their time moving in different directions, learning how to compromise their desires and aspirations to meet their partners half way, both suffering a diminishment. The horse and rider brought out the unthinkable in each other; as one, they could fly. Love between people was nothing but a shackle. Love was the boots you bought to live your wife's dream, or the afternoons you gave to please a lover. Love was giving up on yourself.

With Foxfire, there was never a question of equality in partnership. I was in control. He was bigger and stronger; he could hurt me, even kill me, if he wanted to. But I held the reins. In the herd, respect is hard won, a battle of teeth and hooves. Riders aren't so brutal—at least, the good ones aren't. As Eddie used to tell me, you give a command with just enough force so that you only have to give it once. You don't beat, but you don't nag either. Foxy now responded to the slightest of cues, shifts of weight rather than squeezes or kicks. Riding him was as automatic as walking, something the brain did unconsciously. I had come to move Foxy's body the same way I moved my own, as if we shared a mind. It was the ultimate intimacy.

Dave would not respond to my cues. I told him to stop calling me. I slammed the door in his face when he begged on the step.

In the silence of my apartment after each invasion, I closed my eyes and thought of Foxfire. I breathed in and out. I had to move. There could be no more distractions. I replayed horse shows in my mind, feeling again the familiar rhythm of Foxy's stride deep within my bones, feeling the dry, hot wind on my face as we galloped on, feeling the surge of adrenaline that comes with speed and the jump over the final fence. If I focused and saved every cent, if I found a young horse with potential that I could afford, I could still ride to some form of glory.

The apartment manager met me outside a new building. The architecture was boring and functional, a grey box, and the rent was cheap. From the third story, the body of a hunted deer hung, wrapped in burlap, a slow drip of blood congealing on the sidewalk.

"Oh, God," the squat man fumbled. "I'll talk to the tenant. I'll make him pull that down."

"Don't," I said. My wrist was bruised from Dave's last visit; he'd grabbed me, and I shut the door on his arm. "I don't need a tour. The place is fine. I'll take it."

I changed phone numbers, becoming anonymous again. He couldn't find me here. Dave—just another obstacle cleared.

II
Looking For a Fence

Bone and metals can be broken by repeated application of stresses that would be too small to break them if applied only once. This is the phenomenon of fatigue. . . . An athlete who runs 100 kilometers each week takes nearly two million running strides each year, stressing the tibia nearly two million times. Healing usually keeps pace with fatigue damage, but if it does not, failure or even complete fracture of the bone may result. Fatigue fractures are common in the tibia, fibula, and metatarsals of athletes. They also cause problems in horses, sometimes making them collapse with a broken bone in the middle of a race.

—Alexander R. McNeill, *The Human Machine*

But at my back I always hear
Time's wingèd chariot hurrying near.

—Andrew Marvell, "To His Coy Mistress"

Shift

While circling, the rider looks toward the first fence, establishing a course, setting its rhythm.

At first, I feared bumping into Dave, but that was only because I'd forgotten how big Moscow is for a town. Twenty-five thousand people provide decent cover. My circle was small and didn't intersect with many others, and so I made an easy slide back into invisibility. I'd passed Dave only once, going the opposite way on Main Street, each in the cabs of our separate trucks. I'd just lifted my fingers in the standard truck-to-truck two finger wave when I realized which truck I was waving to. In his turtleneck sweater and wire-framed glasses, he reminded me of a picture of Ernest Hemingway that I'd once seen on a postage stamp, only younger, blonder, and better looking. Dave had seen me at once, eyes locking on mine. His gravity exerted its pull, but I shifted my eyes, gripped the wheel, pressed the accelerator. He didn't have time to turn.

Winter passed, and spring; June built toward hotter July. The nightshift had a peculiar way of erasing time, the dark nights anonymous, one melting into another. Each patient brought a glimpse into other lives, but those moments never lasted long enough. My new apartment felt no more like home to me than my old one had. Shabby and beige, it was just another cold, stacked box nestled between others, like those of us living there were simply neatly arranged cargo waiting to be shipped and processed. Only when I was with Foxfire was there season and time: snow melt, green sprouts unfolding themselves from dirt, breeze, cloud, and at last, heat.

We rode the hills, and their trails led my mind into places I'd avoided visiting. Too soon, I knew, Foxfire would be buried in the pastures that had fed him, that had made him. In the way of natural things, the grasses would call him back, a body to fertilize tender shoots and complete life's circle. He would return to the earth's terrible womb where worms would ravage his spectacular body and those soft eyes would resolve into pits and he would be gradually disassembled. All I'd have was a box of ribbons, of trays and bowls, of cups: everything dulling in an attic corner where I would be unable to forget it.

I pressed the thought away. For now, we walked the gravel roads and looked for fallow hills. We practiced lateral movements to stretch his legs and stave off arthritis, but even so, age seemed to overcome Foxy at once. His body was a kind of clock ticking and, with each stiffening stride, winding down.

Like the marks on an unnumbered clock's face, four events punctuated summer. This was the first: one of the day-shift x-ray techs moved to Boise with her husband. The opening, the 7 a.m. to 3 p.m. shift, paid less, but taking it, I returned to life in sunlight.

Foxy and I went trail riding one day in August. Dust loomed over the roads in the hot, still quiet, pervasive as memory. My mind wandered in its motes.

In college, I'd taken exactly one road trip. The summer after our freshman year, Holly, a girl from my dorm, invited me to her family's dairy farm in New Plymouth for an August week. If the Pod could make it over White Bird Pass, it could make the whole stretch, and I needed to shake Moscow for a while, where every turn reminded me of Mouse's death.

I had a six-hour drive, a thermos of coffee, bootlegged Nirvana, a road atlas, a letter from Holly suggesting a route. Plenty. Holly's directions were comprehensive, giving the easy, straight-forward route, suggesting two possible short cuts to try, and telling me which small towns supported their police departments on speeding tickets.

The first short cut was easy enough. The gravel road cutting from one loop of the highway to the next was clearly marked and shaved a half hour off my drive, so hours later, I tried the second short cut as well, an unmarked gravel road that bypassed Payette. Holly had identified it by landmarks: a fruit stand, a Pepsi sign. I guessed at the road. Perhaps fruit was sold in the small red out-building facing the gas station billboard's sweating Pepsi bottles.

I followed this road a good way—fifteen, twenty minutes— when it tee'd and I faced my mistake. The stop sign's silvered divots told of some nameless teenager who killed time with a shotgun. In Holly's directions, there were no dead-ends.

The horizon held nothing but farmland. To go back would concede a wasted half hour. Roads, even gravel ones, are built to go places, and the most obvious place for this road to go was Payette. I turned right, crested the second hill, and the city spread before me, hazed with gravel dust. A gut decision, a little logic, and I'd found my way.

When I arrived, Holly's dad, with the thin, wry smile of a middle-aged Idaho farmer (the smile so slight it could be mistaken for a grimace) had said only, "Well, y'aint *too* dumb." I liked the man, his easy manners, his underlying grin. For him, the only serious thing in the world was the herd—and what could be more ludicrous than cows? The awkwardly angled hips, the dopey eyes, the slow-moving jaws chewing and re-chewing food for four stomachs. The life spent on mud hills, the monotony only broken by the sound of grain sliding down the chute from feed-truck to trough and the twice daily marches into the barn where metal tubes sucked their straining udders.

Now, every false turn beckoned. I couldn't see any other way to break the tedious circling (trough, mud hill, barn; home, hospital, barn). Jumpers circle to prepare for the course, bending and collecting, and I saw no other obstacle to turn to. On the silent hills, the memory of our conversations replayed. Ever since coming home, I'd lived in memories more than I lived in present time.

I halted Foxy at the hilltop and lay my chest down on his mane, stroking his neck.

We returned from the trail to find a wispy-thin blonde roughly my own age. Her thin, transparent hair poked from the edge of a shiny new safety helmet as she trotted her horse around the indoor arena. Jenny wore white sneakers and blue jeans that appeared to have been freshly ironed.

Zip had been named with a distinct sense of irony. A fat, stubborn Appaloosa whose favorite gait was standing—preferably standing and eating—he was ill-tempered and dead to the aids, whether voice, seat, hand, or leg. He ignored this girl's kicks and her pleas to "come on, can-ter." In the relative coolness of the indoor arena, she huffed with effort.

I pulled Foxy's tack, not bothering to fasten him in the cross ties. I rubbed a soft brush down Foxy's blaze, and he pressed his warm nose against my cheek, tickling me with his whiskers.

"Geez, Louise," the girl said, kicking Zip again without effect. *Geez, Louise?* Dawn would've put her language to shame with a tapestry of curse words, richer in both metaphor and vulgarity. I stroked Foxy's neck. This small blonde was a novice to this dusty order. Zip would test her devotion. I returned Foxfire to his stall.

"Need a hand?" I said.

She pulled to a halt and smiled her thanks with eyes as blue and shallow as a kiddie pool.

"I'll just hop on," I said.

"Oh," she swung off awkwardly.

"Joannie Edson," I said, taking her place on Zip's back.

"I'm Jenny Mason."

The name Jennifer always stirred memories of Mouse, plumes of dust that billowed, and then settled. I squeezed Zip forward.

He walked on easily enough. With a firmer leg, he plodded into an unacceptably slow trot, nowhere near tracking up. I asked for a canter, softly first, then more assertively. He ignored both cues. I asked again, this time with a sharp flick of the whip.

He pinned his ears and moved into a quick pony trot; he wasn't engaging behind, just moving his legs faster. I halted him, backed him five paces to bring his legs under him, and started again with a quick flick of the whip. I got a working trot this time, but he still refused the canter, breaking down again into a rush of quick legs. We halted, tried again. The third time, he gave a flat and jolting canter, his nose thrust forward like he was trying to find the bottom of a feed bag. I pulled him to a hard stop, determined to wake him up to my leg.

I've heard it argued that God made the horse for man to ride. As evidence, people cite the bars of the mouth—a toothless stretch of gum perfect for a bit—or the shape of the back and flanks, so perfectly contoured for the rider's leg. But if we're going to go there, man too seems designed for a horse. Consider the upright posture, the breadth and shape of pelvis that just spans a horse's back, the long anchors of our legs hanging either side a horse's body. Take God out of the equation, and we were still made for one another. The devout will see such things. Even so, horse and rider must study one another, read the texts of each other, to determine whether one unity can be made of this double trinity: two bodies, two hearts, two minds.

Zip had required me to prove myself. By the end of the sixth canter cue, he was bringing his legs underneath himself and balancing like the dressage horse he was.

I dismounted and handed the reins back to Jenny. "Every time you get on a horse, you train it," I recited Eddie's doctrine in his own words. "Zip's had a bunch of people on him—a bunch of kids—so he's learned he doesn't have to do what you say. He's learned that, more often than not, the rider is going to be too nice or too scared to ask him to work. He's learned he can ignore you. Your job is to train him, to remind him that he can't."

Jenny smiled warmly, accepting my unsought advice with grace. Zip turned, looking for the carrots that usually came at the end of lessons. Empty-handed, I scratched him behind the ear instead.

"Is that your horse?" Jenny asked. Foxy paced his stall, whinnying, jealous.

I nodded. "Foxfire."

"He's beautiful."

I smiled. She'd said the words that guaranteed I'd like her. It was true; Foxy was beautiful. Even still. "Have you met Dawn yet?" I asked.

Jenny's brow bent with thinking.

"On the short side," I offered. "Tall hair and tight pants—usually Wranglers. Rides a bay Quarter Horse named Sunny. Cleans stalls."

"I haven't met too many people here yet. Connie says she'll introduce me around, though."

"You'll meet Dawn sooner than later. She practically lives here. We usually meet up for a trail ride on Saturday mornings at ten. If you don't have plans, you should come."

"I've never taken Zip out of the barn," she said, doubtful.

"Dawn and I will look out for you." Jenny looked at me full of trust. How could she do anything but believe? I'd just performed the miracle of Zip.

An Eddie and an Eddy

In the dream, I was back in the cramped, century-old barn in New Jersey where cobwebs laced every corner. I stood with my arm resting on Foxfire's withers, talking to a black-haired, faceless vet in his stall. I dropped into myself from above, falling into the bones of a body already in action.

The stall was dimly lit with moonrise. Foxfire rested his head against my chest, softly pressed his blaze against my sternum, letting me share the weight and warmth of his body the way horses do. I let him rest easy there. His long ears flopped lazily to the side, ambivalent to the soft hooting of an owl outside.

"It's time," the faceless vet said, and his words had nothing to do with clocks. He opened an old-fashioned black leather medical bag and prepared a shot in a glass syringe. "You needn't stay," he said. I recognized his voice as Dave's, comforting and familiar.

"It's O.K.," I said. The words didn't feel right, like they were moving my mouth to speak, rather than my tongue and lips giving them shape. I ran my tongue over my teeth and swallowed. The vet *was* Dave now, in flesh as well as voice. I reached to stroke his cheek, but he smiled and turned to slide the syringe into Foxy's vein. As he depressed the plunger, I thought only of the way his hands once moved on my skin, when I suddenly knew what was happening.

I had to stop him. I had to pull out the poison syringe, to smash it to the ground and crush it under my boot heel, to reduce it to harmless glittering dust, but my hand fell, heavy with dream's enormous gravity.

Dave put the emptied syringe into his black bag, chuckling softly. The weight of Foxy's head pressed more heavily on me, like he was trying to push himself into my body. I could no longer bear it. I staggered back. He dropped to one knee, then the other. He groaned like he always does when dropping to the ground to roll. I reached out and eased his head to the ground.

Cradling his jowl, satin-soft in my hand, I realized we had done this in the wrong place. We'd never get him out of the stall door. Dead horses are not easy to move. The two people I'd known who had to put down their horses did it outside, right next to the grave itself. They bulldozed the body in afterwards with a small Cat. I bent and shook Foxy's shoulder to wake him like a mother trying to rouse a child for school, but his eye was distant and glassy. He was gone.

My eyes opened. Beneath my head, my pillow was hot and wet, and I was choked with the sadness of the vision of what would inevitably come to pass. I rose quickly, tearing away the covers as I wished I could tear away the dream.

I made coffee, strong and black, and washed my face. The dream gravity remained. My bones felt over-dense; my skin, too—like it was weighing against cheekbone and temple. Something as real as Foxfire could not just stop. I splashed cold water on my cheeks, rubbing it into my eyes to get the sand out, trying to wash away the vision of a dead Foxfire.

I needed advice, so I went to Connie. I'd heard her say she rode before she walked, and I didn't doubt it. She didn't look like a rider—at least, she didn't look like the riders in magazines. She was a short, solid woman whose flaming hair flew from the back of her helmet like a fox's brush. Her large, red hands were the type Palmolive calls dishpan hands, but I knew these hands were roughened by dirt, not soap—a far more respectable way to ruin your skin. We were all ruining our skin together out there, exposing our hands and faces to the harsh white sun, the chapping wind, the dust that never settled but only changed colors: the August dust turning our snot hard and black, the white snow dust of January stinging our cheeks and crusting our eyelashes. Idaho's alchemy turned skin to leather, but we were not dishpan girls.

Connie's husband died four years earlier. Pancreatic cancer. He was thirty-seven years old. Back then, she owned twelve of her own horses: brood mares, geldings in training, mostly Quarter Horses she'd trained for the hunter ring. Her husband's death left a stack of medical bills that her PacBell paycheck couldn't cover. There was nothing to be done. She sold all the horses except for a brood mare pregnant with Soldier Bill, the colt she would name for her dead brother, and Zip, the pony she'd bought for the child they had been trying for when the cancer diagnosis came. She opened the old stalls to more boarders and made Zip into her lesson horse until she realized that she didn't like kids enough to teach and leased him out instead. If her face was a little ruddier than it had been, if the Jim Beam slid down a little easier each night, not one of us faulted her for it.

Still sweaty from my morning run, I arrived before the sun had come up. Connie was in the arena working with Bill, now a lanky three-year-old and saddle-broke.

In the quiet of the morning, the barn was all her own again. Connie free-walked across the diagonal, allowing Bill to stretch his neck out and down, then collected the reins in the corner and asked for the canter at C, a pattern I recognized from a training level dressage test. When she finished the test and halted square at X, she looked over.

"I need advice," I said and told her about Foxfire, about his increasingly dangerous tripping, about how he pulled his hind legs away from me now when I lifted them to pick his hooves, about how he leaned on the bit when we worked, putting his weight in my arms, protecting his sore hocks, asking me to carry him.

Connie was one of the faithful, but the faith of riding was seldom spoken. She said, "You thought about retiring him?"

"Thought about it," I conceded.

"He's got pasture turnout. It's not like he won't get any exercise if you stop."

"If I don't ride Foxy, I can't ride at all, but you know me, I need to do more than just ride. I need to jump." I wouldn't whine—not to Connie of all people—but the facts needed to be clear. Bill stretched his nose out and shook his neck, unimpressed. He stomped his foot to shoo an imagined fly and snorted to blow the dust in his nostrils. "Anyway, I thought I'd ask you if you had any advice for me. You're the only one around here who knows jumpers, the only one who knows enough not to trash on Eddie."

"That's who you should talk to." Connie picked a stray piece of hay from her sweater. The stern face she wore when working was both thoughtful and impassive.

"Who? Eddie?" It was a strange piece of advice. "I don't even know where he is. Dawn just said he'd moved."

"Only for a sabbatical. He'll be back."

Years ago, Dawn had taken one lesson with Eddie. He'd told her she had a chair seat, her weight too far back in the saddle, and he wouldn't let her jump until she learned to balance. He made her work on basic two-point position trotting over cavaletti for the whole lesson. When I saw her later, she was fuming, ranting that he'd charged her thirty bucks for a baby lesson, teaching her what she already knew how to do. She'd been riding her whole life, and she was damned if she'd let anyone treat her like a novice.

"When's he get home?" I asked.

"I don't know. Anytime now. Julie's teaching in Southern California somewhere for a year, and the whole family went."

"Dawn told me that, only she made it sound permanent. She said he'd sold his horses."

"Leased them. One's with Pam Westerfelt in Lewiston and the other is with some woman I don't know in Walla Walla." Connie tucked one of many stray hairs back into her helmet, but it immediately sprang out again. "They would've been back already but Julie

got offered some summer course or other, and then they were traveling around a bit. Rough life, right? Those beaches? I told Eddie
not to get too tan."

It was difficult to imagine Eddie more tan, brown as he was from
a life among horses, and impossible to imagine him on vacation.

Bill turned to look back at Connie, and she rested her mild,
loving eyes on his. "They'll be back for fall term."

"I should've kept in better touch," I muttered.

"You should have. We were all wondering what happened to you
out there."

"I'm not much of a phone person."

"Or a writer."

"Yeah." I allowed my voice to drift off as I stared into the dark
corner where words and dust drifted. The silt in the corner swirled,
plumes of oracular smoke, but I had no eyes to read it.

Dawn and Jenny had already introduced themselves when I arrived
on Saturday. I did not mention Eddie or ask Dawn to tell her half-
truths. Picking that fight would only spoil a beautiful morning.

Sun-warmed horses move slowly. On the hills, green wheat
had began to dull. Soon, it would tan then fade to the ever-light-
ening blondes of Indian summer. Wind washed through the tender blades in currents and shushed the birds' morning songs. Along
the roadside, wild apple trees began to droop with porcupine and
early fruit.

Foxfire flicked an ear and a fly buzzed away lazily into the sunlight. Joan of Arc could have turned her back on angels. Instead,
the divine call to cross-dress and fight a senseless war had become a
Catholic miracle. For my mother, dreams were a gift from God, and
only faithlessness constituted failure. But Mom's calling to marry
my father and return to Idaho seemed an easy one to follow.

I had seen two visions: Olympic glory and Dave. They were
both compelling and contradictory, and each had led to failure.
Overhead, the dry heat stretched Idaho's big sky thin as muslin. Its

blue faded to a sullied white; dusty, untouchable, distant. It was not a sky to reach for. Perhaps glory was over-rated.

Looking at Dawn and Jenny on their small horses, I was thankful for the mundane and heavy things that ground us. We rode mostly on gravel roads, dusty as they were. Foxy wore shoes that summer only for this, the hammered iron easing the way for his tender feet. In fall, when the harvest's cut stubble was turned and folded back into the earth, he would go barefoot again. No need to shoe a horse that couldn't jump.

A red-tailed hawk watched us approach, wearily rising from his weathered post when we drew near. The only sounds were the flap of his wings, our idle chatter, and the crunch of hooves on gravel. I inhaled, wanting to breathe it all in, dusty as it was.

"You're quiet today," Dawn said, turning to me. Foxfire and I followed the smaller horses, allowing their gait to naturally check his longer, marching stride.

"I'm always quiet. I'm the strong, silent type."

Dawn laughed, but Jenny, bless her, said, "I thought that was just guys who were strong, silent types."

"Could be guys," Dawn said, reflecting and serious. "Could be guys, could be gals. Why not?"

Jenny looked at Dawn and me in turns, trying to determine, I guessed, whether we were making fun of her.

"I don't see why it couldn't be girls," I said. "Why should guys hold the monopoly on strength or silence?" Strength in silence, I corrected myself, a brand of silence. Joan of Arc knew when to silently don the gear to prove her point and when speech would better win the people to her vision.

But Jenny was no maid of Orleans. Over the course of a few warm, lazy days that past week, we chatted while cleaning tack, the scent of saddle soap an incense, the barn a confessional. She told me she was a "traditional" kind of girl. Born and raised outside Savannah, she married four years back, the summer after her high school graduation, to the high school sweetheart who graduated two years ahead of her. He worked; she kept house. I imagined a Ward Cleaver to her June, a slight, bird-like man with slicked black hair and a briefcase in hand arriving nightly to dinner hot on the table. He gave Jenny an allowance out of which she paid for Zip's lease, riding lessons, and the new paddock boots on her feet. I'd never thought much of that kind of life, but Jenny made not working into a full-time job, volunteering at her church and becoming a big sister to a local school kid.

Still, there were things that irritated me. Like now, always talking about "my husband." Where Dawn said "Russ," Jenny said "my husband," and I couldn't work out why. Was it reverence? Did she value his role, husband, over the man himself? Did she think we would? Was she just that formal? Or did she repeat his role, my husband, my husband, to emphasize her own place in the world: wife. I'd had enough of wives. Suddenly, I needed her to stop talking, if only for a moment, so we could enjoy the peace of the day, but she chattered on and on.

"My husband said the funniest thing last night . . ."

"My husband's been grumbling about the amount of time I've spent at the barn . . ."

"My husband's mother makes the best coleslaw you ever tasted in your life . . ."

"My husband's worried that I'm riding out too soon . . ."

"My husband says I shouldn't get a perm . . ."

Just then, a pheasant, spooked perhaps by the rocks Zip kicked when he walked his foot-dragging obstinate walk, burst from the gutter's wild wheat, all green head and brown feathers, its red-rimmed eye, its panicked *chuckchuckchuckchuck*.

Before the sight of the bird could translate into thought, all three horses spun and bolted, racing across the road, jumping its short bank into the neighboring field. Fear trumped arthritis, and for thirty seconds, Foxfire was young again. He sprang with that magnificent, powerful thrust of muscle, and I slacked the reins as if I could will it to last.

Three paces behind us, Sunny slowed and Foxfire remembered his age. Our hoof-prints marked a wide swath of spoiled crop. There would be an angry farmer. Zip, empty-saddled, pulled mouthfuls of green alfalfa.

"Shit." I jumped down to grab Zip's dangling reins while Dawn went to find Jenny. Already, I was constructing worst-case scenarios: a broken spine and life-long paralysis, a broken neck. Luminous bones hung before me, delicate as smoke against the black of film. Bodies break in ways that cannot be fixed. You could lose someone that quickly—I saw it everyday at work. I knew it earlier still. There were mistakes that couldn't be undone. Mouse's death at the end of our senior year had taught me, but I wouldn't think of that.

I mounted, ponying Zip back to the ditch. The thrill of his bolt faded, Foxy hung his head and plodded on. For yards, there was no sound except for a slight stirring of wind in grass. I had momentarily wished ill upon Jenny, just as I'd wished the worst onto Mouse in a spasm of anger a decade back, and again it manifested. *You have to be careful about what energy you put out into the world,* my mother always said. I shook off the thought, superstition, and let Foxy carry me forth. Grass blades slid over grass blades. Whispers. We'd covered some ground. Finally, the low sound of voices speaking seriously floated over the bank's edge.

Dawn was helping Jenny pick rocks out of her forearm. There wasn't much blood, just enough to make the dirt stick. The injury was only skin-deep, but the skin is where the nerves are. Jenny turned her red and burning eyes to mine.

"You O.K.?" I asked.

Dawn answered for her. "A little shook up is all. Her hip's pretty good and sore, but this," she held up Jenny's forearm, "is the only damage other than bruises."

"Thank God for helmets and thick blue jeans," I said. Jenny was drawn, paler even than usual, and terribly, terribly sober.

Like me, Foxfire was tall—just over seventeen hands. Literally on my high horse, looking down on Jenny in her ditch, I was imperious, even if I didn't mean to be. I held Zip's reins forward. It was a lame offering, and Jenny made no move to take them. "You said nothing would happen."

It was Dawn who answered. "Nothing did happen."

Jenny raised her arm, letting blood speak its eloquent testimony.

Dawn scowled. "You've got two friends at your side, your horse is caught, and you're able to ride. You're scratched, but y'ain't broke." She took Zip's reins from my hand and slapped them into Jenny's. "You're earning your stripes. You want to be a rider, then you'd better get used to it, and the sooner the better."

There was no arguing with the jut of Dawn's pointed chin or the flame in her eye. Jenny took the reins, and heaved herself back into the saddle. She flinched as her arm grazed the pommel, but she said nothing.

This was why I loved Dawn, though I had been on the receiving end of her diatribes myself. Her fire never lasted. The love I felt for her moved through my skin, St. Elmo's fire in the rigging, heating it instantly as a blush. Dawn had a particular brand of charisma.

Jenny muttered, "My husband's going to kill me when he sees this. He always said riding was a dumb idea."

I was prepared to let the comment slide. Dawn was not. "It ain't his call, now, is it?" Dawn's thin, shrewd face dared Jenny to contradict her. Russ called her "Spitfire" when she got like this, his eyes brimming with love and admiration. I felt it, too. At five foot ten, I was a head taller than either Dawn or Jenny, but I only noticed it around Jenny. Dawn, the shortest of all of us, always seemed to be looking me right in the eye. "You want to ride, then damn it, you ride."

"It's his money," Jenny shot back, her own chin up and eyes flashing, showing there was hope for her.

"Don't you ever believe that." Dawn didn't advise now; she commanded. "You keep his house, you fix his meals. You earned that money. Those are your wages and you'll spend them as you like. Don't you let him forget that." There was now an added edge in Dawn's voice. We were on the grounds of a fundamental belief.

At the house, Connie helped Jenny from Zip's back and folded her under her wing, cooing to her like some awkward, over-sized bird. She took off Jenny's helmet and stroked her hair with a rough, ruddy hand while her own frizzled hair lifted on the breeze. Jenny ate it up, leaning her head on Connie's broad shoulder.

I ponied Zip to the barn and waited for Dawn to condemn Jenny, but she didn't say a word. The horses were eating hay in their stalls when Jenny returned to the barn, arm neatly patched. From the tilt of her smile, I guessed Connie had offered a few nips of something "medicinal." Dawn put her hand on Jenny's shoulder. "Feeling better?"

"Connie says I owe you all a beer." Jenny's voice was bright now. We'd been forgiven.

"Hey, that's right," Dawn said. "I always thought that was a raw deal—the one who falls having to buy the round."

Jenny shrugged, and just that quick, she was one of the gals. "What are y'all doing tonight?"

"I don't know," Dawn said. "Eat leftovers and rent a movie?"

They turned to me, eyebrows raised. "Shit," I said, "same thing I do every night: buy food, watch TV, and contemplate my total lack of social life."

Jenny tilted her head in triumph. "Then I say we all meet at El Mercado's at six, Budweiser all around."

It would be Bud, it was always Bud, but my spirits rose in response to Jenny's. The beer was an olive branch not to be turned down.

"Good," Jenny said, seeming to grow a little taller. "That's settled." She smiled serenely when a new thought set her eyes dancing. "Hey, Dawn, I'll get to meet your Russ, and y'all will meet my Dave."

"Dave?" I asked.

"My husband."

A Story to Regret

The Count of Monte Cristo lay on top of the television. I flipped through its soft pages, wondering why I kept it. Each page wore the history of its reading. Page 146 had a grease stain. Perhaps Dave had set a cruller there, a temporary bookmark, while he got a fresh cup of coffee. Page 352 was flecked with blood—a paper-cut. All were browned at the edges where the oils of his palms had permeated the paper's fiber. I, too, was marked. Nothing obvious, nothing you'd notice on the surface, but there was something essential from him that I'd absorbed. I was browned and softened and stained.

I put the book back and told myself that it wasn't him, that Dave was a common name.

I tried to imagine him with her. Did the stubble of his five o'clock shadow rub Jenny's cheek raw when he kissed and kissed her? Did his one hand slide over her hip as the other clasped her neck? Could he feel that same passion for her? Could he love this woman? I shook myself. *It wasn't him.* My Dave wouldn't dole out an allowance. He'd have no patience for a woman who would expect one. My Dave wouldn't have left books and school and all he loved—*he* wouldn't work construction for a woman like Jenny.

Russ and Dawn were waiting for a table. In the dim light of the vestibule, Dawn's hair was a stiff blonde cloud, with the lights from the restaurant illuminating her hairspray to a tangle of silver lining. Russ's crew cut stood in salute. The style suited his broad, smiling face. He'd look the same at sixty as he did now. A little greyer perhaps, more sun-lined, but his denim work shirt would always drape the same broad, sturdy shoulders. His eyes, the same shade as the denim of his shirt, would always shine with laughter. Russ was an immutable force of nature. Time didn't touch him.

Jenny and Dave—her Dave, my Dave—arrived, diving together through the thin drizzle under an old letterman jacket that Dave held to shield them. The hostess called us to our table. They'd been laughing at a shared joke when he saw me. Jenny, slightly in front, didn't see him go dumbstruck, but once we were at the table, her eyes never left him. "Dave," she nudged him, her gaze puppy-like with the sick adoration of a love-struck woman, "these are the girls from the barn."

He gave a weak smile. "She never mentioned your names," he said, as if Jenny weren't standing right next to him. "You were always just, 'the girls at the barn.'"

"Well, she talks about you all the time," said Dawn, causing Dave to look right at me, his eyes trying to plumb mine.

"But until today you were just, 'my husband,'" I added.

"That's not true. I said your names," Jenny said, her southern accent thick and sweet as honey.

Dave hung his jacket on the seatback and sat directly across from me, his toe brushing mine under the table as he pulled in his chair. Not a quick, accidental touch either, but a long, slow slide, making my breath catch. That settled it: I'd be getting drunk that night. My fingers gripped the side of the table. Dave was still looking at me. In my confusion, I'd dropped my guard.

Mariachi music pumped from the speaker above our table. The waitress came, a short woman who would have been slender except for her large, pregnant belly. Jenny asked for a pitcher, and I ordered a margarita with a double shot. Dawn's "yahoo" in response to my drink order turned heads at nearby tables; Dave's face broke into a wide grin. "Have you and Joannie known each other for long?"

No one had introduced us by name yet, but I was the only one who noticed that Dave used mine. Dawn said we'd met years ago when Foxy and I first came to Connie's. "She was so quiet and, what with her riding *English* and all, at first I thought she was a spoiled bitch." Dawn smiled lovingly at me. "Just goes to show, first impressions are *always* right."

I blew her a kiss. "Thanks, Love."

"You bet."

Dave's foot traveled up the inside of my calf. I faltered only a moment before drawing my legs well underneath me. He was being too obvious, but Jenny was clueless. "I told you these girls were funny." She put her arm on the jacket that hung on Dave's chair, droplets still shimmering in its burgundy-colored wool.

My margarita arrived, and I drank while she rubbed Dave's shoulder. She leaned into him and kissed his cheek. I flagged down the waitress to order another before this one ran out. My bed was empty, but an empty bed can be all the loving arms a drunk woman needs, and I loved the way margaritas felt on the back of the throat, the way they scratched at places otherwise untouchable.

I don't remember who started talking about the subject of regrets, but the subject itself arose from my drink order: stories of worst hangovers leading us naturally to regret. It became a sort of party game; everyone going in turn.

Dawn began with the story of an early hunting trip. She'd just gotten her first gun for her birthday—her sixth. She been on hunting trips before, but this would be the first time she went armed. Her father had talked gun safety, and they'd shot paper targets for weeks. She hadn't tried to kill anything yet, and she was itching to. A picture of her cousin stood on the mantel, a grouse gripped by its legs in his tiny fist, his first kill. She was eager to have her picture next to his, so when she and her father went in the woods that day and she saw a chickadee flitting in the branches of a hawthorn, she asked if she could shoot it. Her dad laughed. "Sure, Baby Doll," he said.

She pulled the trigger and hit her target. It fell quickly and without struggle: one shot, one kill. "Immediately, I knew I'd done something wrong," she said. "Knew it without looking at my dad or hearing his low whistle. It looked like an exploded golf ball laying there, not a bird. I'd done that. I turned to Dad so he could tell me I'd done right, but I could see by his face that he was shaken. He said, 'hot damn,' and his voice was unsteady. 'I didn't think you'd actually hit it.'" She'd said it looked smaller than it had in the tree. Not meat, not threatening, just a small innocent thing she'd killed to prove she could.

Dave interjected here. "You were too young to know."

Dawn sized him up with her gaze. "I don't know about that. I knew I could hit it, or at least, I was pretty sure I could. And I knew I shouldna done it. It seems like I could have put two and two together before pulling the trigger."

My teeth felt like they were beginning to float in my mouth. Our waitress came and wrote our food orders wordlessly, and I thought about my father. When he was nine, he'd found a nesting seagull in some rocks on an ocean cliff side. Practicing for the baseball team, he decided to test his aim by throwing rocks at the bird to make her fly. He'd thrown wide at first, but when she didn't move, he threw closer. Then, a rock went a little off from where he'd meant to throw and hit her squarely in the head, which instantly dropped. He knew he'd killed her and her unborn chicks in their eggs. He watched and waited until the sun set, praying constantly that she wasn't really dead, but prayers aren't so very strong.

The waitress waddled off to the kitchen, and Dawn continued her story. "Dad tried to make me feel better about it when we got home. We even took the bird to show my mom. It was so light when I picked it up, but in the truck home, it seemed to get heavier and hotter. It itched in my hand. Dad took my picture with the Polaroid, me holding it up by its little foot, and he stuck the thing in the freezer so I could show my cousins at Sunday dinner."

At the head of the table, Russ was unable to stay serious any longer and sputtered something incoherent about bird-sicles. Soon everyone, Dawn included, was laughing. Dave caught my smile and held it. For the hair of an instant, I wondered what would happen if I responded to his desire. "That damned Polaroid is still on their mantel," Russ said as soon as he was able to get the words out.

Dave volunteered Jenny to go next, putting his hand on her shoulder as he did and letting it sit there. My jaw clenched and I tilted in a little margarita to loosen it. My foot could reach forward—I could touch his toe—instead, I reached again for my drink.

Jenny stunned no one with her totally lame regret: "I regret cursing my father."

"Fuck me if that counts." Dawn reeled back in her chair. "I spill my guts about shooting a poor little baby bird and the best you can come up with is cursing your daddy?"

I regretted taking Jenny, so inexperienced, trail-riding and getting her hurt. I regretted swiping Lemonheads from Rosauer's and cheating on my U.S. history midterm in high school, though I never got caught at either. I regretted leaving my mother for New Jersey.

"No," Jenny looked wounded, "come on. It counts. It was serious—you don't know how close my dad and me were. We had a really close relationship, and I almost wrecked it."

"Key word: 'nearly,'" said Dawn, but she sat back and let Jenny continue.

"It was back when I was in high school. My dad and I had always been really close, like I said, because mamma died when I was just a kid." Dawn's hard stare softened. "It was always just the two of us. We'd do all sorts of stuff together that dads and daughters don't normally do: go shopping, make cookies—he even helped me learn to put on make-up and choose a prom dress." She looked at Dave and smiled here, and I had no doubt who her date had been. Numbness spread through my cheekbones, tequila's anesthesia. "But Daddy was never quite sure about Dave."

"That's putting it mildly," Dave said. "Her old man hates me."

Jenny laughed this away. "He never *hated* you. He just wasn't sure. And think of things from his perspective: he didn't want to give his baby to just anyone."

I could see Dave fighting with himself a little here, wanting to say, I imagined, that he wasn't "just anyone," but he merely smiled at her, making Jenny's eyes dance again. *I still regret you, Dave,* I thought. *I still do.*

"Anyway." She turned back to the table at large. "Dave gave me a promise ring my senior year, and my dad hit the roof. He said there was no way he was going to let me marry Dave, and that Dave couldn't offer me the emotional and financial stability I deserved. That's exactly what he said: emotional and financial stability." She gasped, as if astonished afresh by her father's words, her eyes wide and blue. "We kept at it, saying things we shouldn't, until I told him that I was eighteen and an adult and he should mind his own f-ing business."

"Only you didn't say f-ing?" Russ was grinning.

"Right. I didn't say f-ing. My poor dad. I thought he'd explode or something, but instead he got real pale. I'd thought for a moment that I'd killed him, he was so pale—like he'd had a heart attack or something. Then, he just got up and walked out of the room and I swear to God I've never felt so alone in all my life. Dave was back at college, and my dad didn't say a word to me for weeks. I started to think he'd never talk to me again. I begged him to forgive me and to give Dave another chance, but it was like he couldn't even hear me." Jenny stopped. No one said anything.

Three guys had ever seen me naked, and I was sitting across from one of them, and he was rubbing the shoulder of my friend, his wife. Every time Dave glanced over at me, I felt naked again. Naked and angry and wanting him nonetheless and not wanting him anywhere near me.

"Eventually he started saying little things," Jenny said. "'Pass the salt,' or 'are you taking the car tonight?' That sort of thing. A little more every day until it was almost like normal, but sometimes I feel like that f word is still sticking between us, like, like," she turned to Dave, "what's that thing you wedge in a door frame when it isn't right?"

"A shim."

"Yeah, like a shim. Only instead of making us right or true or whatever, it took something that was true and pushed it out of place and I can't make it right. Eventually, Dad seemed to settle himself to the way things were. I think he hoped that Dave would get so into college that he'd never come home, but we got married the next summer, and then Dave went to work for Dad, and now everyone's happy. It all worked out in the end, but I still wish I hadn't said that word to my dad. I wish I hadn't hurt him like that."

I regretted selling the Pod. I regretted my last fight with Mouse. I regretted not visiting my parents more often. I regretted not calling regularly when I was in Jersey. I regretted the last pair of shoes I bought. Tomorrow, I would regret drinking these glasses of Budweiser—but not the margaritas, never the margaritas.

I didn't ask how Dave came to work for the man who so hated him—that story seemed to tell itself—and no one asked Dave if everyone was really as happy as Jenny claimed. I wondered if their marriage was an act of nineteen-year-old rebellion or a way for Dave to prove himself, to prove her daddy wrong at all costs. Or maybe Jenny was more powerful than I'd credited her, able to construct her own happiness.

When I was four, I had my own moment of animal cruelty. We had a cat, a stray my mother had fed. We named him Rumpelstiltskin, but we called him Rump because, as my father always said, he was a pain in the rump, pissing and scratching and spraying. I decided one day that he needed a collar, something to show he was owned and loved. We'd never kept cats, though, and the puppy collars in the drawer were too big. I found instead a thin blue rubber band, slid it over his head, and forgot about it. A week later, Rump's neck started oozing, the stinking green and blood-streaked goo of a festering wound. The vet washed her way through the pus-matted fur to find the band. It wasn't until I saw it that I realized it was my fault, that I had almost killed Rump. Even then I didn't understand; it had slid on so easily, so slender and stretchy, so innocuous. My mother and the vet were outraged, blaming the rubber band on the cruelty of local teenagers hopped up on AC/DC and God knew what else. I sat silent, turning over this new reality in my head: I had very nearly killed.

It wasn't regret exactly. Rump recovered and, over the years, fully paid me back for that rubber band with a series of dead birds on my pillow. I woke, over and over, to staring rubbery black eyes, stray feathers, and open yellow beaks. My arms were covered with parallel tracks of slender scabs written in claw, and at seven, I got cat scratch fever, making my armpits so sore I could not lift my arms. Infection for infection, quid pro quo.

Dawn turned to Russ. "Your turn."

"Mine's easy," he said with the broad, class-clown grin so typical of him. "I regret not nailing Brittany Anderson back in high school."

The table erupted with shocked laughter except for Dawn who scowled. Everyone was starting to feel further away, even Dave, whom I could look at now through the visor of margarita armor. Jenny said, "If my cursing my dad doesn't count, than that one doesn't either."

"Clearly, you never saw the rack on Brittany Anderson." Russ held his hands in front of his chest, pantomiming copious handfuls. "Back me up on this, Joan."

Russ had also gone to Moscow High, but he was two years ahead. For me, Brittany was little more than a blurred memory of black hair, dark eyes, and pouting, frosted lips, but the memory of her impact on the guys at school remained, even through alcohol's fog. "She was pretty hot," I said.

"Pretty hot?" Russ rolled his eyes. "That girl was totally amazing." He leaned across the table toward Dave and lowered his voice slightly, as if giving him a hot stock tip. "She was supposed to be totally easy, too."

"Hot, yes," I said, "but honestly, when did you ever have a shot?"

Now it was Dawn's turn to laugh. "You better cough up a real regret."

"O.K., O.K." Russ shot a pseudo-glare my way, then paused and grew somber. "I don't regret Brittany Anderson, but I do regret Melanie Richards."

"Another hottie?" The word sounded funny coming from Jenny, but no one took notice.

"No," Russ's voice was lower now. "No, no one ever called Melanie Richards hot. They called her many things, but never hot. We teased her relentlessly. Actually, teased is too weak a word. We tormented her." His eyes pierced the fog, "You remember Rhonda, don't you, Joannie?"

I shrugged helplessly. "Doesn't ring any bells."

Russ sighed. "I guess not a lot of folks would. Rhonda moved away before junior high, but back at Russell Elementary, she was the shit. Melanie moved here at the start of fourth grade. She was a nice enough girl, just small and quiet, but Rhonda must have seen her as some sort of threat. Or maybe she was just an easy victim. Good sport. Melanie wore these really ugly glasses, those big round kind with the thick frames? And she had thin, gawky, bird legs that were white even in summer. Otherwise, she was cute enough. For whatever reason, Rhonda hated her. She said she was a weird little freako and that her clothes all came from the poor box at their church, blah, blah, blah. Maybe it was true about the clothes. Rhonda said she smelled like brussels sprouts and started calling her Mel the Smell, but that wasn't true. Melanie was always clean."

"La Cucharacha" trumpeted through the speakers, with its rolling, celebratory brass.

"Pretty soon, everyone hated Melanie for no other reason than that Rhonda said we should. Even the girls who'd been Mel's friends at first wouldn't be caught dead with her, all so worried about what Rhonda would say."

"There was a girl just like that at my school," Jenny said quietly.

"Mine, too," said Dawn, "I guess every school has a Mel and a Rhonda."

Russ continued. "Rhonda made rules for the playground: only girls wearing this kind of jeans or that kind of tee shirt were allowed on the monkey bars this day or the swings that. She made charts for the girls she liked so they'd all know what to wear on certain days of the week: the cool kid uniform. Things could change hourly—only Rhonda ever knew the rules. Then, Rhonda started in on me, asking me to flirt with Melanie and stuff, just as a joke. She'd found out that Mel had a little crush on me or something. I hedged a bit and tried to get out of it, but Rhonda started hinting that I didn't want to do it because I really did like Melanie and that maybe she'd tell the whole school that I was in love with Melanie Richards.

"I should have let her say what she wanted. Looking back, she wasn't so tough. If she'd gone up against me, I don't think my friends would've ditched me as quick as they'd split on Melanie. Shit, I could've been the breaking of Rhonda McMillan, but instead, I did what she said, writing these notes to Melanie with Rhonda at my back, telling me what to say, how much I loved her, dumb little poems, how hot she was in her glasses, how I dreamed of her during math. Finally she told me to write one asking Mel to meet me at the flagpole after school so we could kiss. She showed up, and all the kids just laughed and laughed." He looked up, shaking off the memory. He swallowed and ran a hand through his flat top, all the laughter gone from his eyes. "That's my regret."

I knew the rest of the story, but I wasn't going to make Russ tell it. I may not have remembered Rhonda, but everyone remembered what happened to Mel the Smell. It wasn't uplifting. It was an everyday story, a story everyone knew, a girl driven so far down she couldn't possibly recover. Her mother had found her one afternoon in her bedroom closet. Mel's body hung from her father's tie. She left no note. She'd been quiet to the last.

The waitress broke into our darkness with sizzling plates of fajitas, chili Colorado, carne asada, and a fresh margarita; it didn't lighten the mood.

"I feel bad watching her carry all that food," Jenny said. "She shouldn't be carrying a heavy tray in her condition."

I searched for something to change the subject, something to steer us away from regrets in general. The topic was too damned depressing—it'd even brought Russ down. "You know in Jersey they charge extra for guac?" I said.

The rest of the table stared at me and for a minute I thought the ploy could work. "It's, like, two bucks extra." I closed my eyes. Margarita danced in me: Rita Hayworth and Chaquita Banana. Her close-fitting yellow dress, rimmed along that exposed and perfect leg with frothy layers. The sequins shone like crystals of salt. Sex and alcohol, she seduced from the hips, sliding them loosely in undulating rhythm to canned mariachi.

"Two bucks?" Dawn said. "That's fucking ridiculous."

Russ was giving me that man-are-you-*wasted* look, but Dave was smiling. For him, I could make even avocados charming. The map of digressions stretched forth in my head, the possible trails leading us away from regret. That's what going to New Jersey had been all about: all the little differences that made me realize that America there was not the same as America here, despite the McDonalds, the Walmarts, the Banks of America.

Jenny foiled my plan at a stroke. "O.K., Dave's turn. What's your biggest regret?"

You're looking at her, I wanted to say. The words itched like an infection wanting to be lanced. Dave looked at me from under his hair and gave a half-smirk, then pulled the beer mat from under his glass and turned it over and over in his hand, thinking. Margarita moved my foot forward, the heat of her desire burning in my mouth and enflaming my lungs. If he'd only reach, and he'd touch me; I offered my long, seductive limb. Margarita. If he had the balls to spill it all, I'd take him back. We could still have the life I'd once imagined for us.

His hair shone gold in the restaurant's mellow lighting, a golden man: Tequila, triple sec, ice. And I, like all backward-looking women searching for life in remembered times, was salt. I didn't know it then, didn't feel its crystals threatening to grow in my heart, becoming more pillar the longer I looked at Dave. I merely stared, urging him to touch me, to take me away.

But the eye has no power after all. Dave spoke, "Mine is back from my first year in college."

The quality of my stare shifted. I was not his biggest regret. I shoved a spoonful of rice down, hoping to stop the turn of my stomach. It should have been me. Instead, Jenny sat there at his side, not even looking at him now as she mindlessly picked at her food. My margaritas were finished. Beer filled my cup, and I drank deeply.

"My mom called one night early spring semester. Her sister, my aunt Ruby, was dying. Stomach cancer. Doctors gave her two months." He paused. I shoveled in more food, barely tasting it. "My mom and she were always close. They were twins, and I guess what they say about twins is true, how they feel each others' pain, because when I went home that weekend, Mom looked rough. It was like she was sick, too. She talked to me about when we'd fly up to Baltimore to see Ruby—that's where she was living. Where she was dying." He laid the mat flat and put his beer back on it, staring intently at the glass.

Jenny put her hand on his shoulder, rubbing it, and he darted a look at her, and a small smile. Within, Margarita slowed her dance. I pieced in what I knew: they'd still been dating when this was going on; he'd leave school for her at the end of that year.

"My mom wanted to fly out right away but I dug in my heels. It was stupid, but I had this job at a little junk shop downtown. The owner was cool—just a nice, nice man. Really easy-going about working around my school schedule and stuff. He even let me do my homework there in-between customers. I never had to worry about trying to fit my schedule around work, the way a lot of my friends did. I knew that he couldn't spare me more than a couple weeks. It was simple economics. And I would have to drop all my classes for that semester. My teachers weren't going to let me miss that much time—not if it ended up being a month or more. I kept thinking about the money I'd spent on tuition and books, the loan money I'd have to repay, the money I'd lose in that job. I figured I could take a week off, maybe two, but no more.

"I was so worried we'd end up in Baltimore for months. People are always saying that the doctor gave someone three months but they lived for another year or more. My mom was broke. She couldn't go back and forth, couldn't risk her own job. I made the practical, the stupid choice. I told her we'd wait a month. We'd go later, I said, those final days, when she'd really need us." He stopped and looked at me, like he earnestly needed me to understand. "I don't even think I realized she was dying, if that makes any sense. I didn't realize how precious our moments together are, and how fleeting." He held my gaze another long moment, and something deep in me seemed to reach for him, even then. For that brief instant, there were only the two of us.

He dropped his gaze and spoke again. "I loved Ruby. She was so enthusiastic about everything she did. She was an avid reader and every time she talked about a book, it made you want to run to the library so you could read it, too. She was like that about everything—the food she ate, the last show she'd seen on TV. She loved life so deeply, and she made you love it with her. She didn't seem like someone who could die."

We're all dying, I thought. His letter jacket at his back, Dave was another person here, not my young Hemingway but the high school football star Jenny fell in love with. So many selves fly around inside us; they were flying around in me. I felt the need of a shotgun or a pile of rocks. Some of those birds would die that night.

I grabbed the pitcher and refilled my cup.

"We called Ruby that Sunday. She sounded tired, but that's how you expect a woman with cancer to sound. I told her that Mom and I would be with her in just a few weeks. I could tell she was disappointed because it took her a long time to say anything, but she didn't ask us to come any sooner. She just made me tell her about college, what I was studying, what my professors were like, all that. I went back to school that night and it still hadn't all sunk in. Then my mother called that Thursday and told me Ruby was dead." Jenny reached her arm around him and squeezed his shoulders. The gesture strengthened him. "We were the last thing she was holding on for, but she couldn't hold on that long. My mother was shattered. It was my fault. I'd been so worried about all that stupid shit that didn't mean anything. Like there was some rush to get through school—I mean, Christ, I didn't even end up getting a degree anyway."

We were silent under the heavy pall of Dave's regret. His story had us all beat; he'd won. *It's not a competition*, I told myself, but everything is a competition.

Of course, I could still win. I could tell them about us, our two weeks together, him sleeping in my bed, his confessions of love. That's the regret everyone would remember for the night, the only trump, the queen of spades. They'd never speak to me again—maybe even Dave wouldn't speak to me—but it would be honest. I'd win. My tequila-thick tongue was fat with stories and alcohol, but my plate was empty.

Dawn looked at me. "Well? You're up. Last regret of the night." Her hair, intentionally sprayed on end, danced with lights reflected from her beaded shirt. Russ's arm rested against hers. Jenny's eyes were bright and encouraging. Each girl paired. Dave didn't look at me now. His shaggy hair curled protectively around his ear while he traced images in the mist of his glass. I loved them all, in one way or another. I could devastate them.

I took a long, steadying sip of Jenny's crap beer, letting bubbles rush cool against the back of my throat. "I regret nothing." My voice was raspy but firm and unslurred, like some salty sea captain's.

Dawn clapped the beer she'd been lifting back on the table. Jenny said, "You can't regret nothing." Dave's eyes locked on mine and a blush came to his cheeks. I held his eyes briefly before he turned away, stunned, incredulous, trying to decipher the code I offered.

"I regret nothing," I repeated, staring at each in turn and daring them to contradict me. "Everything I've ever done has led me to this moment, so I regret nothing." Everyone was finished eating, and the pitcher was empty. I raised my glass. "To friendship," I said, and in the chink of thick bar glass against glass, I was off the hook.

The drizzle had been short-lived and the air felt like something I could lie across and swim in. I concentrated on my feet, watching as they went fat, thin, fat, thin. Dawn and Jenny both offered rides, but I needed the walk. Their trucks rumbled off in the night leaving nothing more than the red glow of taillights. I wouldn't sit in the middle of either happy couple this evening. *Joannie the lonely*, I thought, and now that I was away from Dave, that seemed right and good. Like Joan of Arc. Powerful and solitary.

Summer heat still radiated from the sidewalk, though the rain had made the air cooler. The sky was cloudless now, yet the glaring streetlights hid all but a few stars. How difficult it was to see things clearly.

My limbs floated and tingled but my feet were club-heavy at the ends of my legs. Adrift on *déjà vu*, I crossed another street. Nine months ago, I'd slept with Jenny's husband. He was a good man— even his choice of regret spoke for him. Little kept me from him now. The eyes of the stars were on me, though I couldn't see them. A sudden breeze seemed to bring forth a long-ago conversation with Dave, the morning he'd come to me and kissed me in his Hemingway sweater, back when there was no Jenny.

He'd asked if I believed in love at first sight. "I'm not sure I believe in love," I'd said, "first sight or any."

He weighed my words, his hand moving along my back against my skin. "Bad experience?" His ice-colored eyes warmed oceanic.

"No experience." I shrugged. "A crush now and then, nothing more."

He moved closer still, his breath moving the strand of hair that hung loose along the side of my face so that its ringlets kissed me with each of his exhalations. "And you don't think it's out there for you?"

I was dizzy. The carbon-dioxide, I thought, but it was more than that. My faith in solitude was slipping; I was drunk on his breath. "Honestly I don't know." My voice was husky and foreign. Disembodied by his nearness, I wanted him closer. His body could displace my body, inhabit my space. He could absorb me entirely. I wanted him to.

"You'll find it," he said. "A girl like you? I'm surprised you haven't already." He leaned in and kissed me and I was gone, replaced by the vision he had of me, a vision I preferred to the failure I was. He kissed the long, curving line of my clavicle, and it became a blade cutting into me, a surgeon's scalpel reshaping my flawed self. He said, "You're different from any girl I've ever met."

"It's not intentional," I whispered, but what I wanted to say was that I was wrong about love. Erased by his presence, giving myself entirely over, this was love at last.

The Man with No Name

Clint Eastwood is as beautiful a creature as God ever created: the lash-fringed flint of his cold-stare, the lean length of him. Who else could make a poncho look so damned *tough*? And the way he sat his small, grey horse, not so much balanced as melded. A perfect rider.

The new guy working the express lane at Rosauer's was similarly beautiful, though there was little apparent likeness. Maybe it was his eyes, something Clint-ish about them. His were almond-shaped. Hazel, I guess you'd call them, though their lightness reminded me more of gold-littered creek beds, undisturbed and cool. They danced with audacity and intelligence. He looked to be, not so much predicting your next move, as knowing with absolute certainty what you would do.

Long, slender sideburns framed his face. His hair was dark in a way "brown" doesn't describe. There was more luster, more darkness, more richness. There was a shine, a crow-feather quality to its shifting color. On his neck was a tattoo of a salmon in mid-jump, styled like a totemic figure. The guy was young, like me, but he seemed time-mellowed. His stare had none of Clint's sneering calculation. Where Clint would scowl, this guy smiled.

Perhaps it was the tall-thinness, the bootcut jeans, the clean flannel shirt faded past the point of being any recognizable color. It would have been too hot outside for this shirt, but here in the over-air-conditioned store, it wasn't out of place. The shoulder seams lined up perfectly with his own shoulders, as if it was custom made for him, or he was made for that shirt. The two belonged together, just like flannel seemed to belong exclusively to the Northwest. Its soul lived here, cotton-soft, multi-hued, and complicated. And yet this guy didn't quite have Clint's cowboy swagger. He wasn't "cowboy" at all, but I couldn't say why. It was something more than the absence of hat or horse.

His name tag read Jed, but I knew Jed and knew his tag, with its pink smiley face sticker partly obscuring the bottom curve of J. The new guy must have borrowed it. He chatted easily with the customers in front of me, with too much confidence for someone new to the job.

Not-Jed turned to me, and I looked quickly away, aware that I'd been caught in the act of staring, of trying to find a word for the color of his hair. His eyes were unreadable. "You finding everything all right?" he asked, his rogue smile all confidence and knowledge. He'd seen me looking at him, but I determined not to blush.

"You're new here," I raised my chin, trying to fake a calm I didn't feel.

"Sure am."

Around us, people talked, registers scanned and beeped, lights hummed, but when he spoke to me, those noises receded. I found myself wanting to become small, to curl myself up in the curve of his soft, warm lip, to rest there, like the child cradled in the moon in the old cross-stitch my mother hung over my childhood bed. "Got a name, 'Jed'?"

"Yep." He smiled again, that damned Clint Eastwood smile, so devilishly delighted with himself. It was the smile I watched over and over in all those films—the smile I waited for every time—the magical smile that required me and anyone else who saw it to smile in return.

I couldn't help myself; I grinned. "Going to tell me what it is?"

He narrowed his eyes, sizing me up. "I'll make you a deal. I'll tell you mine if you tell me yours." He typed in the number for lettuce without bothering to look it up, totally at ease. "You first," he said.

"I'm not that curious." I looked out toward the automatic doors, posing indifference.

"We'll keep it anonymous for now, then."

"Fair enough."

"$7.09."

I pulled exact change from my wallet and placed it in his cupped hand, smiling directly and defiantly into his eyes.

"Have a good day," he said, nodding to me.

I nodded back and picked up my groceries, thinking about his cool, silky shock of hair and how it must feel against skin.

Even after all the beers and margaritas at El Mercados, I'd woken feeling miraculously good, no trace of headaches or queasiness. Now, I felt even better, like something that had been washed in pure water and dried in sunlight and air.

The lightness carried me home. Inside, the red flash of my answering machine blinked a warning I should have known to heed. Dave's voice rose at the press of a button. "Joannie."

He'd found me.

That night, I had my recurring dream. Mouse and I were in the Pod together, cruising around as we so often did in high school. It was a soft June night, and the Milky Way shone in all its glory despite my headlights. Mouse was reciting astronomical facts, as she often had. "The earth is, on average, 93.2 million miles from the sun," she said. "Do you think we'll ever reach the stars?"

The question hung in the car, as it did in every time. Knowing what was coming next, I tried to warn Mouse, but the truck hit before the words could form. We spun a disrupted orbit around the semi's fender. I, the center of the vortex, gripped the wheel and remained still, but at the edge of our circle, Mouse flew. Her white dress flapped around her. I sat, watching, screaming to her, and she silently sailed away from me toward the too-hard earth.

I woke in a sweat and rose from bed, mad at myself for still being shaken by the same relentless vision.

✎—✎

Dawn was cleaning stalls and I was giving Foxy a post-ride rub-down when Jenny walked in. "Hey, strangers!" she chirped, all pertness and smiles. We hadn't seen her all week.

"Hey, yourself," Dawn said and laid another shovelful of manure on top of the pile in her wheelbarrow.

I nodded, brushing the sheen into Foxy's smooth, summer coat.

"Dave totally loves you guys," Jenny said. I cringed. Foxy bent his long neck to look at me, as if he knew the whole story.

"We'll have to do it again sometime," Dawn said.

Jenny stood in the middle of the aisle, apparently in no hurry. "We'd love that. Dave can't stop talking about you two. He said you were sassy, Dawn, and he called Joannie fascinating."

Dawn's hoot of laughter filled the barn. "Jesus, Joannie—even drunk you manage to get 'em. Watch out, Jenny."

I would have given Dawn a dirty look if she was in eye-shot, but she'd ducked into another stall. Instead, I closed my eyes and tried to look persecuted.

Jenny only laughed. "I'm not worried."

My mind wandered outside, to the hills, and then into town, into Rosauer's, to the man with no name. He was a challenge, that one. Worse, he had everyone in on the joke, maintaining the secret of his identity. Old reliable Dale wouldn't tell me the guy's name even when I offered to double my usual order of brats, and Alice openly laughed at my casual attempts to find out as she sliced the Swiss.

A snort of hot breath on my thigh broke me from my thoughts. Foxy's clear, brown eye was on me, looking for the cause of the carrot delay. He was expectant and impatient as Dave on the answering machine, saying only my name and waiting for me to give whatever he asked. As if that's all I was good for: filling his needs. "What makes you think you deserve carrots?" I muttered.

Dawn's head darted out of the stall, the keen hearing she'd relied on when hunting caught my every word. "Don't tell me Foxy acted up?"

"Never," I said, reaching for the bag.

Once in my truck, the emptiness of the passenger seat struck me with renewed force, and I drove to my parents' house to check in on my mother. She was reading the paper when I walked in; Dad was nowhere in sight.

"Oh, good," Mom said, not looking up as she finished the article, "you saved me a trip. I was going to have Dad swing me by tomorrow to bring you these." She nudged a brown paper bag on the coffee table, brimming with the first of her zucchini, tomatoes, and summer squash.

"You sneaking Miracle Grow on these?" The zucchini were as big as my forearm.

"That's all organic." She looked up from the paper and smiled. "Great compost this year. Speaking of which, can you bring some more manure when you get a chance?"

"Sure." I was my parents' horse shit connection.

Pilate walked up and pushed his head under my hand, asking for love. I settled down on the braided rug and stroked the silk of his ears. Pilate was never a licker, but on rare occasions he offered a tiny kiss, his tongue barely touching the skin and then disappearing. He gave me one now.

"Watch out, Mom. I'm going to steal Pilate and take him home with me."

"And violate your apartment's no pets policy?" She smirked, an expression I recognized as my own. The left corner of her mouth lifted and creased, and her eyes danced. We were good smirkers.

"They'll never know, will they, Pilate?" He looked at me with steady, quiet earnestness. "Where's Dad anyway?"

"Oh, wandering somewhere." She didn't look at me.

"Without Pilate?"

"Your dad's walks are a little long for Pilate now."

Pilate, the dog who once went on Mom's walks, Dad's walks, and any other walks offered. Pilate, the inexhaustible. Now, he collapsed on the rug next to me, rolling halfway onto his back, his paw lolling lazily in the air as I rubbed his chest. I felt coming loneliness lapping at me even here: Mom in her chair with vegetables from the garden she could no longer tend, Foxy and Pilate dying in increments.

Mom and I made falafel while we waited for Dad. I chopped tomatoes and mixed cilantro yogurt, wondering if Not-Jed liked cilantro, wondering if he ever held it to his nose as I did now, to inhale its pungent freshness, or if he only knew the number to punch into the cash register. It was an important question.

Dave called me at work Monday. After months of carefully constructed privacy, he had taken the home and work numbers listed on the emergency card outside Foxy's stall—a card I'd never before seen as a vulnerability.

He wanted lunch. His voice was upbeat and hopeful, like there was nothing strange in this. "No," I whispered into the all too public phone. Cheryl kept stealing glances at me.

He paused and the edge of urgency sharpened his voice, "You said, 'I regret nothing.' I can't stop thinking about that, about the way you looked at me when you said it. I know what that look meant, Joannie." He waited for a response I wouldn't give. "Joan, I need you in my life. And you need me. You don't regret our time together, and neither do I."

"Having no regrets doesn't mean I'm going to make the same mistakes twice." I let that sink in. "Having no regrets also means I don't regret ending it with you."

That stopped him for a moment, but he rallied. "Listen, I understand what we did was wrong. Maybe we can't be all we were before, but I need you as a friend at least. Please, Joannie. Don't deny me this. Don't deny me a chance to redeem myself."

The words were a trap; there could be no friendship. If I slipped out of Imaging on that slow afternoon, whose foot would be the first to touch the other's in the darkness under the table?

Cheryl, making a pretense of filing old paperwork, was listening to every word. She was never so busy as when there was a phone conversation she could eavesdrop on.

"I can't take personal calls here." I let the phone drop heavy into the receiver, wanting him to understand the finality of that conversation.

Cheryl gave me a conspiratorial smile. "He sounded cute." She winked a heavily made-up eye.

"Not my type."

Apparently hoping to draw her into this conversation, Cheryl turned to Doreen, the other receptionist in Imaging, but Doreen continued to stare, bored, out the door. Cheryl turned her red smile on me again. "Well it sure sounds like he thinks you're his type."

"He's wrong."

Doreen stood up. "I'm going for a cigarette."

"Those things will kill you," Cheryl chirped after her. Cheryl waited until Doreen was not quite out of hearing and stage-whispered, "I hate to see a young girl like that throwing her looks away." Cheryl took a lot of care in this regard, with thickly applied make-up and Coke can curls. "Those cigarettes will turn her skin grey— I've seen it happen before—makes them look like ashtrays."

I shrugged, "She's fine."

Cheryl pursed her red lips a moment. "Are you, a medical professional, honestly telling me that you think that she's not hurting herself smoking those cancer sticks?" She smiled again, to show that she wasn't serious, but I could already imagine how she'd twist my words.

I attempted some triage. "Well, obviously, smoking isn't good for you, but she's young and smart, and I'm sure she'll quit when she's ready." Even as the words floated from my mouth, I could see them swirling like smoke rings, bending into Cheryl's words. She'd lean toward Doreen like a co-conspirator. *You know Joan says that, if you're smart, you'll stop smoking.* I never seemed to be able to find my feet when talking to Cheryl. I decided to escape doing any further damage. "There's a new article on head trauma imaging I want to check out. I'll see you later."

Again, she smiled that red grin, "Don't wait for tall, dark, and handsome to call again before you come back up here. You'll go stir-crazy in that room all by yourself, and you know how I enjoy our little visits." I turned away before she finished, but her words followed me down the hall. "And don't worry—I won't mention that you're getting personal calls at work. It's hard enough to find a man once you reach a certain age. That old biological clock, huh? Our looks can't last forever."

A Silence

B renda was stocking produce. She was Dale the butcher's daugh-
ter and had inherited his sloping shoulders, but she wore them
differently. On him, they looked resigned; on her, jaded, set low
by the tremendous weight of a world designed by adults. Her hair,
dyed black to contrast her pale skin and the burgundy of her lipstick, fell in backward-bending spikes, as if they too were tired of
fighting gravity and other inexplicable forces. Brenda was a shy girl,
for all her bold appearance, and I had always liked her.

I tore off a plastic sack and sidled up to her, thinking I had
perhaps found the perfect co-conspirator. Brenda, a high school
student, walked the same halls I once walked. We had an understanding.

Casual as could be, I picked an orange from the pyramid she
was reconstructing with the meticulous slowness of those paid
by the hour. "Scorching hot lately," I said, trying to stall while I
thought of tactics.

Brenda, speaking with the same slow care with which she
arranged her fruit, said, "Before you get any further," she said, "I
think it's only fair to tell you that I'm under strict orders not to
reveal any names."

"Brenda," I said, picking up another orange, "I'm hurt. Really. I can't believe you think that the only reason I'm talking to you is to find out that guy's name."

"No, of course not." She smiled but didn't look at me. "You have a deep and abiding interest in meteorology and wanted to compare notes on the day's heat. You're right. Scorching hot," she glanced at me slyly, "like some checker we know?"

"If I were to agree to that remark," I said mimicking the mock-serious tone she'd adopted, "I suppose said acquiescence would reach the ears of said anonymous someone, thus building on what is obviously an over-inflated ego." I plucked another orange from the pile. "No, I reveal nothing."

"Whatever, dude," her quiet voice was light with restrained laughter.

"O.K., O.K.," I said. "But, seriously, who is this new guy? I mean, what the hell? I've been shopping here for years, and you all take up allegiance against me? Take us, for example. You've known me for months, and your father's known me since I was a kid shopping here with my parents. You guys are deserting me for some fly-by-night checker? I'm hurt, Brenda. Really hurt."

Brenda shrugged. "Store loyalty, man." She looked at me, then laughed softly with the air of a much older, more experienced woman resigned to the foibles of life and humanity. "You guys sure have a weird way of flirting." Before I could object, she gave me a parting smile and pushed her plastic cart toward the Red Delicious.

I had six oranges in my sack—when was I going to eat six oranges? I grabbed a head of Romaine, and a six-pack of Newcastle.

My luck with the bakery was no better. Arlene stonewalled me before I even had a chance to ask if they had any loaves of wheat still available. "No names," she called to me as I walked up. "Otherwise, I'll get you whatever you need."

"Where's the loyalty?" I asked. "Where's the love? I'm like family to you people."

"Tough love, darlin'," Arlene said. "Can't ask for more from a family than that."

"Tough love's supposed to prevent bad things from happening. You think this new guy . . . what'd you say his name was?"

Arlene only smiled. She held up a loaf of wheat and raised her eyebrows. I nodded. She put it through the slicer.

"You think he's that bad?"

"Honey," Arlene said, "he'd be the best thing in the world for you, and I'm still not going to tell you his name."

I groaned. "That doesn't make any sense. Besides, this isn't about romance. This is a quest. You've got to help me win. We're both women, right? We can't let these guys beat us."

"No dice." She turned to a birthday cake she was preparing to decorate. "See you, Joannie."

"Hey, not so loud. You at least haven't told him my name, right? Right?"

Arlene didn't answer. There was nothing left to do but pay. I hoisted my basket and resolutely made my way toward the checkout.

He looked away and sighed as I reached the front of the line. "Not you again," he said. "Don't you work? I mean, really. Get a job."

"Early shift," I said.

He scanned my cheese and held it up. "Oregon Blue. Don't you worry that this'll make your breath stink?"

"It keeps the vampires away."

Judging his face, I'd say he was baiting me, testing me, and for a moment, I thought he'd add another remark. I noticed that he hadn't commented, for instance, on whether or not he liked cheese. Instead, he scanned the oranges.

"Hmm. Either you love fruit or you have a visitor who does."

"Good work, detective," I said.

"Which is it?"

"Just me and the oranges," I said. I raised my chin and looked him in the eye. "No name tag today?"

"Not once I saw you in my line." He met my gaze unflinchingly. "$24.97."

I handed him a twenty and a five and his fingers brushed my palm as he placed the three pennies in my hand, resting lightly there. "Normally," he said, "this is the part where I say come back and see us again." His fingers hadn't moved. "But with you, that seems totally unnecessary, so I'll just say, 'scram.'"

"Thanks. Very good business sense you have there."

We were looking at each other a little too long in a store where everyone knew us. I let my hand drop. "See you tomorrow?" he said.

"Let's leave that a mystery. Give our lives some suspense."

He laughed and turned to smile for the next customer.

The waning moon rose in the twilight. Heat still radiated from the asphalt, though the air itself was cooling toward night. He hadn't called me by name; the game was still on. I wanted to be angry with myself, to remember Dave and complications, but somehow the brush of fingertips on my skin pushed all other memories aside.

Saturday, the girls and I saddled up early. The still quiet of that peaceful morning imbued itself in us, and there was little other sound except the clink of stirrups against girth buckles.

Once astride, Dawn and Jenny chatted softly about their husbands, and I allowed Foxy to fall back. Russ had been complaining that Dawn and he never had pancakes on Saturday mornings anymore. Eyes flown wide, Jenny looked shocked that Dawn wasn't at home making breakfast. "What'd you tell him?"

Dawn slumped back in the saddle like an old cowboy. "I told him his options. One, he could get his lazy ass out of bed earlier and we could have pancakes; two, he could fix his own damned breakfast; or three, he could have pancakes with me on Sunday."

"What'd he say to that?"

"He whined a bit." She leaned over and plucked a piece of wheat to stick between her teeth. "Men always whine."

Jenny laughed. "Dave complains sometimes, too," she admitted. "It's weird. Sometimes he's all supportive, saying maybe he should buy me a horse of my own so I wouldn't have to lease Zip. Other times, he says I spend too much time at the barn. He hasn't been like this since we first started dating. Back in high school, he'd barely let me out of his sight. He'd get so infuriated if I went off with my friends. So jealous. Like I was going to flirt with other guys when he wasn't around." She laughed at this. "My friends said he was too possessive—Daddy, too—but they never understood him."

I wished the wind would blow their words far from me, but they seemed to float in the still air even longer than the dust we stirred. Nine months ago, he hadn't wanted to let me out of his sight either. Again, I felt the pressure of his grip on my arm as we parted.

Jenny turned again to Dawn. "It's like he's jealous of the horses or something."

Dawn nodded. "They all get jealous. You read the riding magazines, they're all full of advice columns on how to make your husbands and kids feel better about your riding. I understand it, though. I'd be jealous, too, if I lost Russ every weekend to some hobby, and it isn't exactly a cheap sport. If you're not a rider, it's tough to understand the time and money."

The hooves made soft crunches in the gravel of the road. Foxy snorted, clearing the dust from his nostrils. The late August sun was growing quickly hotter.

"Dave did the funniest thing last night," Jenny said. "There's this guy, Rick, who's been annoying him at work, and you know what Dave did?" Jenny waited only a minute, knowing full well we wouldn't guess. "Dave stole Rick's hat and burned it in our kitchen sink." She laughed at her own story.

"Uh oh," Dawn said. "A man's lucky hat is a sacred thing."

"I bet Rick's wondering where on Earth he lost it. Dave looked pretty pleased with himself—at least while it was burning. We laughed and laughed."

My mind wandered. As a kid riding the bus, I used to dream of the day I would finally own a horse. I'd lean against the square windows each school day morning, watching the green hills pass outside, imagining galloping across them, my horse's stride keeping pace with the yellow bus and jumping the wide creeks in amazing bounds. Now, riding my horse, I watched the hills around me and thought of the anonymous checker and imagined walking these fields hand-in-hand with him. We strolled along slowly, him stopping to pick a wild poppy. He'd smile quickly and say something ironic and witty as he slid the flower behind my ear. I'd lean in and rest my forehead against his tattoo, pressing the length of my body to his.

Dawn turned to me. "You picked out a man for yourself yet?"

"Picked out?" I said. "What? Like found one on the shelf at the man store?"

Dawn turned to Jenny. "She always denies it, but Joannie's got her pick. Guys always love her. *Why* they do beats the shit out of me, but they do. And she just walks away like she couldn't give a damn about any of them."

"You two have been bitching all morning about your men," I pointed out, "and now I'm supposed to feel like my life is incomplete without a guy of my own?"

Dawn rolled her eyes. "You sound like a fucking feminist."

"That's rich coming from you, Miss 'Fix-Your-Own-Damned-Pancakes.'"

Jenny looked from Dawn to me, clearly concerned.

"Don't worry," I said. "Dawn and I always talk like this. In a previous life, we were married to each other. It's all love."

"Which brings us back to the subject at hand, Joannie. What's the fucking story? I want Russ and I to be able to go on a double date with you before we're all too old to walk unassisted."

"Yeah, all right," I admitted, just to get her off my back. "There is one guy who looks kind of interesting."

Dawn pulled Sunny to a dead stop. "Holy shit." She stared at me for a moment, jaw dropped. "Jenny, this is a fucking first. I have been asking Joannie about men since I first met her, and this is the first time she's so much as mentioned a fleeting interest."

"Don't get too excited," I said. "I don't even know his name."

"Tell me what you do know."

"Tall, dark, handsome. Sarcastic, funny. That's all I know." I didn't mention the sideburns, tattoos, or Clint Eastwood.

"Where'd you meet?"

"In the express lane. He works at Rosauer's."

She paused, considering. "You should ask him out for coffee."

"I don't even know if he drinks coffee."

"He lives in *Idaho*. Of course he drinks *coffee*. You're avoiding the point, Joannie."

"What if I don't want to ask him out?"

Jenny, silent and perplexed by our conversation so far, asked, "You want him to ask you out?"

I shrugged. "I don't know that I want a boyfriend."

Dawn groaned. "Always the same thing from you. I don't need a boyfriend, I don't need a boyfriend." Her voice, mimicking me, was high and false. "No one *needs* a boyfriend. You have one because they're fun, if infuriating, and because you can't spend all your life at work or the barn."

"Sure I can," I said. "It's worked well so far."

Again, Dawn rolled her eyes. We'd had this talk nearly once a month as long as we'd known one another. "You said yourself that this guy looks interesting."

I didn't answer. The truth was, I didn't know what to answer. Dave's arms around me had felt so warm and natural. Foxy couldn't fill that absence.

Jenny and Dawn had forgotten me, talking about some romantic comedy my story had recalled. I was happy to fade quietly into their wake, absorbing the sunshine. I was getting strong again— strong in a way I hadn't been in the dark of El Mercado's.

Back at the barn, I shoveled up buckets of manure for my mother's garden, turning down Jenny and Dawn's offers to help. I wanted to be alone, and odd as it may sound, I relished this work. The sun beat down across my back, but my back was strong and equal to it. I felt the skin warm against the damp cotton of my shirt, my back contoured by the flex of muscle as I shoveled. In this world, nothing was wasted. It could be as true for me: I regretted nothing. Dave was a shitty experience but a necessary one. I'd learned, grown. "Black gold," my mother called her compost. Shit and refuse fertilized. Connie's brother had died for the other black gold over in Iraq. His body was composting a small square of land on the other side of the country in the silent graves at Arlington. Everything seemed connected, light fractured by a prism. Soldier Bill grazed in the next pasture, strong and black in the golden sunlight. Behind him, the Bitterroot Range stood immovably blue and distant at the edge of the horizon, a natural border to the sky.

I picked another forkful. In spring, I would turn this manure in with the soil of my mother's vegetable garden, seed it for her and weed it for her, taking my turn feeding our family with produce that wasn't trucked miles across the country with the oil that men were dying for. Filling this bucket was a small act, physically and politically, but it was satisfying and purely good. My thoughts meandered as motes in light, pulverized dust looking to become part of the whole again. Land, silence, and time offered solitude without loneliness. They always had. If I could make myself believe that the time spent with Dawn and Jenny had not somehow made this moment possible, I could give up all desire for love and the company of others.

That Sunday morning, I made my manure delivery and ran Moscow Mountain, enjoying the familiar roads and the cool air of a mountain morning. The crunch of each footstep on gravel brought memories of my first clumsy attempts at running, all those years ago, back when my mother was in remission and I had nothing to worry about except my calculus homework and the sudden loneliness that came when Mouse started dating that guy. The pain of running was infinitely preferable to the loss of my closest friend. Out there, only my own body could betray me, and I soon found that it would not. Once I'd built a little leg and lung strength, I was good for miles. Foxfire too was young then, and together we made a strikingly athletic pair.

I drove back to my apartment tired, planning to spend the afternoon watching television, but once I showered, I was restless again. I wanted to ride—to jump. I could almost feel the measured cadence of Foxy's collected canter, the power collecting, ready to explode in flight, but that feeling was no longer possible. Bored, my mind wandered to salmon swimming upstream, the explosive power of their bodies jumping against the current: I'd crack that puzzle of a man.

Clouds lined the horizon and hid the mountain, but I was too stir-crazy to drive. I walked through the old part of Moscow where a few Victorians still stood, painted conservative greys and tans that obscured the gingerbread and lace of their architecture. Between them, newer homes had sprouted like mushrooms in subdivided lots. Mouse had lived in one of these—a post-war bungalow that her grandparents sold years ago. Mouse and I had often walked this stretch together, complaining about our government take-home final or laughing at Vince Johnson, an MHS linebacker, whose eyebrow had been shaved off one night when he fell asleep on the return trip from an away game. I hadn't thought of him in years. Rumor had it that he'd raped a girl at an Idaho State frat party his freshman year—'roid rage, I'd been told—but I hadn't seen him since the night we tossed our mortar boards and marched into our separate futures.

A summer breeze and the rumble of thunder brought me back to myself. Maples leaves danced around me, losing their green but not yet yellow. An older couple cleared up from a yard sale, tarnished silver and a broken Remington still on the card table. On the corner, lanky kids with flopping hair pushed skateboards, trying to jump the curb. They failed. Over and over, they failed, laughed or cursed, and made another doomed attempt. Jumping against the current. What strange creatures we are. I crossed the rim of broken down apartments, old sheets serving as curtains, to Main Street.

My checker was not working today. Instead, I waited to buy elbows and Tillamook cheddar in a line made long by the slowness of another new checker. She was a blonde ringleted, pudgy girl who giggled and chatted constantly while she looked up code after code to peck into the register.

Her face lit up as she turned to my groceries. "Mmmm, macaroni. You're totally making me homesick—all I can make is Stouffers, which is O.K., I guess, but it isn't like homemade." She didn't stop for me to agree. "Man, my mom makes the best. All creamy and cheesy, you know what I mean. Oh, and she'd always slice tomatoes on the side, fresh from the garden. There's nothing in the world like a home-grown tomato, especially with macaroni and cheese." Even if I could find a pause in her mac and cheese monologue, how could I segue to Not-Jed? "I could go for a huge bowl right now, but like I said, all I can do is frozen. It comes out all gluey, you know? Even the expensive kind. The one in the black box?" She talked on and on, but in the wrong direction. "Hey! Now that I work here, I bet the deli ladies would hook me up, don't you think? They seem nice, and the stuff in the case isn't bad. It's still not Mom's, is it?" *The name?* I wanted to blurt, but her thoughts trundled one into the next unceasingly, a current I couldn't fight. "Real cheddar, browned crust. All I've got today is PB and J, but I just don't think it's a PB and J kind of day."

The name! The name! She was ruining it. I couldn't get a word in; she didn't even pause to give me my total but seemed to slide it in edgewise as she prattled on. I stood there, slack-jawed and un-speaking in a sort of verbal hypnosis. She'd handed me my change and turned to the next customer. I hadn't uttered a word and felt no strength in this silence.

The First Showdowns

Monday was back-logged with pre-op patients awaiting x-rays of their barium-white guts, mixed in with assorted surprises: a hung-over city worker who'd slid off a pothole's metal ladder for a compound leg fracture; an adulterous Deary man who drove himself to the hospital with a serrated bread knife in his thigh to the hilt; a two-year-old who'd tried to swallow his brother's race car, which was now lodged between tooth and palette. I did my best to soothe each as I moved them under the lights with a firm but slow touch, attuned to feel the smallest flinch, listening for the faintest catching of breath. They'd come to me hurt, but I would not add to their pain if I could help it.

I gave attention to each person, a far more important part of my job than aiming machinery and pushing buttons. It was too easy to allow a patient to become a name on a chart or a diagnosis to be treated. As I met them, I tried to gauge what else they needed besides the x-rays. In the case of the city worker, he needed his shell of silence preserved. Rather than chat or smile, I kept a hand on his shoulder each moment I could. The Deary man, on the other hand, flirted continuously but seemed reassured when I laughed off his advances. He needed to know he was still a man, even if it wasn't the time for a fresh romance. The child needed a good view of his mother at all times and a lot of soft touching and smiles, and his mother needed my good cheer, optimism, and sincere confidence that everything would be all right.

For each patient, experience helped me find the type of treatment required, but when Dave walked into Room One, I was at a loss. Cheryl should have stopped him. He had no right to be there, disrupting the flow of the sick and injured. He paced a full minute before speaking.

"You found someone. Jenny told me."

Under the door, a shadow slid across the narrow band of light. Cheryl.

"I'll leave Jenny," Dave said, his voice breaking.

I felt hit, gut punched. Dave's breath filled the silence. I couldn't seem to breathe at all. If there was a word to offer in return, I was not capable of voicing it. This reality cleaved from the one I'd known, in which such things didn't happen. And yet, I understood why he was here, because in that hotel room and for the weeks afterwards, I too had been as happy as I'd ever been before.

Silence made him desperate. He sank down to a crouch, pressing his hands against his face as if that was all that would hold his head together. "I need you, Joannie. My life is empty without you." His haunted eyes never moved from mine.

Audacity. Audacity! The thought grew from my feet upward, bringing me back into myself. I was no counterpart. I was no missing piece. A woman is an entity unto herself, and I had already rejected this as a possible life. I would not waste myself spackling the gaps of an insufficient man.

I wanted to kick, to punch. My hands balled to fists, the skin stretched taut over a ridge of knuckles, fingers kneading my palms. To fight would be to unleash a passion I could not stem. I met his gaze, and my anger melted, leaving only pity. "Dave."

His eyes dropped, a small but consequential victory.

"I don't even know the guy's name."

He looked almost gaunt in the dim light of Room One. "Talk to me," he pleaded. "Tell me that there's a way out of this."

"You're married," I said, as much to myself as to Dave.

He seemed to come to a little, looking around at the machines, "You must think I'm totally psychotic, coming here." I didn't, though; I saw him only as a failure. I was a failure myself.

"We'll talk later," I tried.

"It will only make it worse." He turned and paused only briefly before pushing through the door and walking away. I stood for a moment, staring at the space where he'd been, before signaling for the next patient.

I struggled for focus. Doreen led in a wire-haired woman who scowled, holding her wrist. I attempted a smile. In her faded floral shirt, she looked like a farmer's wife with little patience for hospitals. "I'm betting this is the last place you wanted to be today," I said, laying a hand on her shoulder. She grunted in reply, but already her expression had softened.

Half an hour later, Dr. Rivers stormed down the hall, white coat billowing in the wake of his self-important striding step. "I need a word with you, Joan," he said. I was in reception, helping an eleven-year-old girl back into a wheelchair, but he did not wait for the nurse to wheel her away.

"Yes?"

"I understand you had a personal visitor this morning."

The child's mother looked from him, to me, to the nurse, who gave a little start and suddenly remembered to push the chair back toward the emergency room. The mother hurried behind them, gripping the plastic bag that carried her child's shoes.

Dr. Rivers wasn't my supervisor; he took Glenda's job upon himself—all in the best interest, he felt, of keeping a smoothly running hospital.

"It was not my intention to have any visitors," I replied. Anger clipped each syllable between my teeth.

Dr. Rivers ignored the words, tone, and defiant stare. "This area is for patients only, not your current lover. People here are in critical states, and we have to be ready to serve them."

Current lover. If I had felt indignation at Dave's assumptions, it was nothing to what now seethed. All morning, I had been quickly, efficiently, and most importantly, *caringly* serving patients. How long had I served them, without ever having a visitor so much as ask for me?

The gold clip of the Montblanc pen in his pocket flashed under the fluorescent like the shining saber of his self-righteousness. What moral high ground could I claim? I'd slept with a married man.

My jaw locked tight. I determined to stay silent, to have this done with quickly. Dave had been there—my mistake—the rubber band collar I'd pulled over my own neck, now festering.

Dr. Rivers crossed his arms in front of his chest. "Frankly, I'm beginning to wonder if your personal life is beginning to affect your job. Moving one place, then another, your mind someplace else, always distracted."

I broke. "You think all this is affecting my work?" I glanced at Cheryl as she feigned deafness at her keyboard. I wondered how much she'd heard, how much she'd constructed, and what picture of events she'd offered.

"I am wondering if it might," he said.

"This is horseshit."

Cheryl gasped at the reception desk, but I didn't acknowledge it.

Dr. Rivers' lip curled into a sneer. "I hope you don't use that language around our patients."

"And I hope you don't reprimand all hospital professionals in public when they have patients to attend to."

Dr. Rivers' cheeks burned red, a stark contrast to the gel-slicked hair starting to turn prematurely grey at his temples. He was no more than five years older than me—still very young for a doctor—but that was easy to forget.

I quivered with ill-suppressed rage. "My radiographs are good—better than good—and you know it. Clear, detailed. Without them, you'd only be guessing at ailments I let you *see*." I paused there, letting him remember that. "I most certainly do not invite people back here to visit. I never have. The man who came by today was particularly unwelcome, as I made clear to him. I asked him to leave, and he did. I hope the visit will not be repeated. If it is, I hope someone," I shot a glance toward Cheryl now, "will do her job and call security."

Dr. Rivers, now confused, looked from me to Cheryl. Whatever she'd told him, this wasn't the cast she'd put on the affair. I could only imagine her story: me and my lover in the darkness of Room One doing Lord knows what on the x-ray tables. He cleared his throat and said, "As long as we're on the same page."

"I believe we are." I stared, unflinching, daring him to say more.

He put his hand on my back, guiding me into the darkness of the x-ray room. Once there, he said, "Joan, I'm sorry I didn't talk to you privately. I should have." His silvering hair looked darker here, erasing the illusion of age. Here, he looked sincere and incredibly young. Liable to make the mistakes we all make.

My anger gave a little. "It hasn't been an easy day."

"No," he said, "not for any of us." His eyes dropped and his smooth brow creased in thought. He turned and stepped quickly away.

As I closed the door, I heard him ask Cheryl if she'd have a word with him in private—only a small measure of vindication. It hadn't escaped me that he'd chastised me in public but apologized in private, and the sting of his insult remained.

III
Determining the Line

Think only of the jump, I implored her, as if I had put the whole of my money on her back; and she went over it like a bird. But there was another fence beyond that and a fence beyond that.

—Virginia Woolf, *A Room of One's Own*

Love-making mimics the act of departure, moonlight drips from the leaves. You can spend your whole life doing no more than preparing for life and thinking "Is this all there is?"

—Terrance Hayes, "Lighthhead's Guide to the Galaxy"

Timothy Like the Grass

Years ago, I broke my collar bone. Foxy had stopped on course at a cross-country event I'd entered on a whim, and I flew head-long into a solid log vertical.

To this day, I don't know what caused him to stop. We were still drenched from the water obstacle—the only fence that I'd worried about—and were galloping along at a pleasant pace. Water flew from my boots at each stride; his cadenced hoof beats seemed to thunder the announcement of our coming victory. Perhaps I took my leg off, perhaps the shadows shifted, perhaps a mouse ran along the round gap between logs.

At a vertical no different from those we'd jumped a dozen times, Foxfire folded his haunches beneath himself in a magnificent sliding stop, raising clouds of forest loam that rode the breeze to settle where I was flung.

The pain of the break was so overwhelming that, at first, I felt nothing. My mind seemed to fill with the dust floating around me. All I could hear was sliding hooves, long after the slide had stopped.

Foxfire approached and lowered his nose, blowing at and sniff-ing me. It was as if he breathed the hot pain into me, each snort bringing another surge.

The pain of losing Foxfire was strangely similar to the fracture; it was a sharp, internal hurt, inexplicable to those in the smooth functioning, external world. Then, as now, I knew exactly what was happening to me, yet I was powerless to fix it. This is how pain works: the mind's clouds rolling in and then away. It felt like losing Mouse all over again. Each sight of him breathed both pains alive.

The image of Dave hung before me all afternoon, his desperate appeal echoing. I could not see Foxfire that day. I couldn't have my escape route, my solace, my barn, blocked from me by knowledge of his aging. Even if I was able to swallow the ever-more apparent fact of his limits, the barn was infected with Dave; Jenny, his vector. Instead, I went to buy groceries.

The man with the sideburns was back in the express lane. For once, I hadn't tried to learn his name. He picked up my frozen noodle bowl and regarded me. "You don't look like your usual feisty self."

I didn't answer immediately. The scanner beeped, and the price of dinner flashed on his screen. "Bad day."

"Want to talk about it?" He scanned milk, looking at me with concern, and I stared at the salmon on his neck, thinking of currents, of muscle and perseverance, of instinct and fate, of tired fish and waiting bears. How did one go home?

"Not here," I said. "Maybe over coffee." The words seemed to come from nowhere; I hadn't thought to say them. The thought Dawn planted somehow came out, though I didn't know it was growing. The words had merely appeared in my mouth, a cartoon bubble she had shaped for me and inserted between my lips.

He paused a moment. "I'd like that." The lady behind me shifted her groceries on the long belt with obvious impatience. "My name's Timothy, by the way. Timothy like the grass, not Tim." I dropped my gaze. He had not removed his name tag.

The lady behind me huffed, and noisily repacked her items into the plastic basket, heading for another line.

Timothy glanced at the now empty spot behind me, then smirked and looked again at me. "And you're Joan." The way he said my name implied he'd always known me, only now he had a label, a signifier to tag the substance.

I pulled my self together. "Someone ratted me out."

He handed me my receipt and smiled—that whole-face grin he shared with Clint, that all-conquering smile you had no choice but to return. I'd won that smile from him, and he won my smirk. He said, "I'll never reveal my source."

I took the receipt and scribbled my name and number on the back. "For whenever you want that coffee."

He looked at the number for a moment, then folded the paper carefully and put it in his shirt pocket. Each move was methodical, thoughtful. He looked back at me, challenging me with his eyes. I held his gaze. Something elfish flickered there. Something not entirely safe, but too playful to be malignant either. The sands were shifting, the gold sparkling. He said, "Why not just set it up now? How about tomorrow?"

I nodded thoughtfully. "The Beanery, then. Two o'clock."

I arrived early and bought my own drink. The hot paper of the cup warmed my hands, the coffee strong and black. No flavored syrup, no foamed milk, no cream or sugar. I savored the honesty of its hot and oily bitterness.

It was a good day for coffee. The rain promised by yesterday's clouds fell steadily, and a table of farmers sat in the corner, tipping cup to mouth under the sweat-blackened brim of old caps: John Deere, MacGregor, Caterpillar. College kids huddled in the private glow of their laptops. A lady in a jingle-belled tunic made her way through the tables to meet a bearded mountain man in the back.

This was what I loved most about Moscow, the way it contained all these people, the way they not only tolerated but grudgingly enjoyed each other as they leaned from separate tables to speculate on presidential politics and Super Bowl contenders. I'd never seen another place quite like it. When I left, it seemed so colloquial and small; now it seemed Utopian. Neither view was accurate, though both were true.

Outside the plate glass windows, a small pickup truck sat in the parking lot, several rectangular forms giving shape to the blue tarpaulin tied down over them. A student moving in. An old dresser, some cardboard boxes. A young guy walked out, steaming paper cup in hand. I found myself suddenly nostalgic.

Mostly, I hated moving. Hated packing, hated unpacking, hated finding another beige apartment, hated final inspections. But the move itself—the fleeting moment when everything I cared about fit in the back of my pickup and everything I didn't care about was disposed of—had a liberty offered by nothing else. Solitude was freedom. With the Chevy's dual fuel tanks full and the key in the ignition and the truck pointed to the unknown future, there was nothing but potential. A leap into the darkness. Flight.

And then, Timothy walked in. Rain streamed from his jacket, an impervious pelt, and I was aware of a subtle wildness in him— not the lame wildness of studs and leather, but the wildness one meets in deep forests. Rain simply could not matter.

"You ordered without me," he said. The ghost of his smile played about his lips, but it did not break. He checked his watch. "I'm five minutes early."

I shrugged. It wasn't an apology; I hadn't wanted him to buy my drink. What was I doing here? An object in motion doesn't get coffee. Dave had called again that morning, reminding me that things were easier to start than to stop.

Timothy set down his rain-soaked backpack and left to order, returning with not only a steaming cup but a large slice of coffee cake and two forks. He slid one to me, his eyes steady on mine to gauge my response. I let the fork rest for now.

"What's in the bag?" I asked.

"My deepest, darkest secrets." He leaned across the table toward me like a waggish conspirator.

"Ah." I nodded. "Mystery man."

"Of course." He looked me dead in the eye. "Let's hear about this bad day of yours."

All offerings cost, this much I knew, so I said, "I'm supposed to spill my guts an you won't even say what's in your backpack?" I cocked and eyebrow and glanced at his bag. "I don't think so, hot shot."

"She wants to play hardball."

I made no comment.

He unbuckled the flap of an old-fashioned rucksack to reveal textbooks. I gazed at them, their spines neatly lined up.

"A student. Figures."

"Guilty as charged."

"Is that Geology? You taking rocks for jocks?"

"Actually, it's pretty interesting."

My radiography coursework had revolved around anatomy and physiology—internal landscapes. Timothy buckled the flap back in place. My look inside was over. He laid his arm across the table, his fingers inches from my own. "Your turn," he said.

I let the coffee's bitterness wash over my tongue. I wanted and did not want to be honest. I couldn't tell him the truth. I couldn't say I'd been the other woman.

"I have a horse." I said instead and let that sink in, trying to read his response, trying to determine what course to take from here, constructing a trajectory. His face was open and unimpressed. "Foxfire—my horse—he's getting older now. We used to jump." I wanted to back up, to start over. "You ever ride?"

"Just around the backyard at a friend's house, an ancient old pony, but that was in grade school."

"I wish I could explain what jumping is like. You fly for this one little moment, and even though it's almost immediately over, it isn't. That feeling of flight stays with you. You can carry it for hours, days sometimes."

I looked for traces of the tell-tale sneer, the disdain for a girl who never got over the pre-teen infatuation with horses, but I couldn't see any judgment in his open face. Even stranger was that, as I spoke, I realized that I wasn't evading the issue at all. Dave was only an obstacle, and I was a jumper. Obstacles surely couldn't bother one who spent her life charging down the nearly impassable.

Again, the familiar yearning yawned within. To jump was to become a cyclone. Energy coils dense and dark inside us; a horse allows it to touch down and explode. I had none.

"The problem is, Foxy is getting too old to jump. It used to be, I had a bad day, and I had somewhere to go. Foxy was the ultimate listener. I never spoke a word. With horses you don't have to. They know whatever you're feeling. They absorb your emotions, and you absorb theirs. It's a depth of communication I don't think people can have, and it's been hitting me lately how much I'm going to miss it. Now, I have a bad day at work, and there's nothing I can do about it. I can't jump it away."

"Where do you work?"

"The hospital. I take x-rays."

He brushed his hair from his eyes. "You must see some pretty gruesome stuff."

"It's not so glamorous. Sometimes I get a really nasty case, but mostly, I do pre-op stuff; nothing too gory. Just a lot of people in a bad mood from drinking a quart of barium or whatever. They're rightfully unhappy, and I just try to help them get through it all. The secretary is the only real horror. Even so, there are some days I just want to forget about it, and there are days when I see things I wished I hadn't. Sometimes, I just don't want to think about anything. Horses give me a space to not think, but not feel vacant either."

He took a sip from his cup and leveled his gaze on me again, waiting for more.

"I've always ridden competitively. I spent the last few years in Jersey, training with the Olympic coach." I turned the empty fork in my hands, studying the dents that marked it, thinking of the way time turns all silvered surfaces grey.

"You were going to ride in the Olympics?"

"No," I sighed. "Maybe. Foxy had the talent. Had." Some time-marred objects remained useful; others did not. "Even when we were there, he was slowing down, and I can't afford the type of horse that can jump the big stuff. Foxy was a total fluke. A gift from God if you believe my parents. Catholics. But, if he was a gift from God, then I wasted the gift, because all that time and effort didn't amount to jack."

"That's no different from me, really." He stopped himself. "Well, I mean, you were doing something a lot bigger than me going to college, but in some ways it's similar. I'm spending all this time and money, and I can't say my life will be any better for me having done it. No one at home thinks it's worth it. I can hear them now: *You get your degree and so what? You think anyone's going to hire some half-breed? Then what? You work in a cubicle and get ignored by white people? All to chase some white version of success?* To them, I'm just another superfluous reservation dreamer, and they can't wait to see life beat me back down to Earth."

He smiled, and the devil was in his grin again. He said that I was doing something bigger than him, but from where I sat, it didn't look that way. I was just another white girl with a pony and a selfish dream. He was trying to find the fulcrum and lever with which he could move his world. He sipped his coffee.

"Sad thing is, they're probably right. I mean, the education I got on the rez didn't focus on college prep. Half the books we had were falling apart, missing pages, and everything was out of date, so I'm playing catch-up most of the time. It's not practical that I'm here, but I came anyway, and I'm going to stick it out."

"No one can take that horse from you." I said it under my breath, looking away from him.

"Damn straight," he said, and his voice too was low but firm. "No one can take that horse from you."

Solitude was freedom. If you were alone, you could travel anywhere your heart led. Dreams came at the price of love. We shared this, but sharing it was a bar between us.

He looked to the wall for a moment then leaned in, taking me into an alliance. "When I was in high school, my buddy and I got into science—mainly because if there is one thing an Indian is not expected to be, it's a scientist. We were a couple of jokers, but we were angry jokers. We'd look at the people around us and just get fed up with the ambivalence. Things should *matter*, so we decided to shock them out of complacency—almost literally. We'd tie a copper wire to a shoelace and throw the shoe so that the wire arced the power-lines. The pop was so loud, we'd have to yell for the next hour to hear each other. People jumped out of their dark houses, trying to figure out what happened while we hid under the shrubs and tried not to laugh our asses off. We called ourselves the Electron Liberation Front. Our ideals, of course, were impeccable: We wanted people to question their dependency on the white man's power, to see how they paid for it and enslaved themselves."

"You were a punk."

"All Indians are punks; some have just forgotten to show it. Anyway, anarchy looked a lot cooler when we were sixteen and heavily under the influence of the Clash."

"And now, you're getting your degree to join the Establishment?" I shook my head in mock despair.

He grinned broadly. "If you can't beat them, join them, right?" The coffee cake sat uneaten between us. "Actually, I like to see it as unseating the power from within." His smiles had a gravity I hadn't noticed until now. I couldn't see him giving up school for a girl the way Dave had. Timothy's eyes did not blaze when he spoke either of college or of anarchy—there was nothing there to ignite or quench, only the steady determination of one who would not be fucked out of his goals by someone else's ideas of how life worked. I liked that. I recognized it.

He said, "You went all the way to Jersey and came back, huh?"

I nodded to the tattoo on his neck. "I guess even though salmon leave for the ocean, they all come home in the end."

"Not all of them," he said. "Some get eaten by bears."

I laughed. "That's uplifting."

"Honest, at any rate."

"And how *does* a salmon avoid being the one who's eaten?"

Timothy gave this more serious thought than the question deserved. "It can't. It just swims fast and hopes."

I picked up the fork again. The coffee cake was raspberry with slivered almonds, and so good it made me catch my breath. Timothy smiled as he watched me eat a bite, then another.

"So, you grew up on the rez."

"Sort of. We moved there when I was in junior high. Before that, I lived in Spokane."

"But you went to high school on the rez?"

He nodded but said nothing more. I didn't want him to stop, but I needed an offering, a *quid* for his *pro quo*. "My best friend in school was a girl named Mouse." For years, I'd kept the story of Mouse carefully locked and guarded. I hadn't spoken of her in years—not since the accident itself. Timothy's grief made mine easier to confess. The flood waters of all those years broke and words poured out of me. "Actually, her name was Jennifer, but everyone called her Mouse because she was as quiet as one—but that was only if you didn't know her. If you did, you realized she was always saying quiet little things, and that she was smart and funny. Best friend isn't strong enough description, really. From the time we were little, she practically lived at my house. No one ever knew me so well. When my mom got sick—she has MS—Mouse was the only one who knew what I felt because she was feeling it, too. I didn't have to say a word. It had always been that way. We never finished a sentence when we were talking to each other. We never had to. I'd start saying something, and before I finished, Mouse would know what I was going to say and would reply. I'd do the same. It used to drive our other friends crazy. The weird thing is, I never felt like I didn't say my whole thought. I never felt like she was cutting me off. That was just how we talked, 50 percent speech and 50 percent intuition."

Timothy nodded. "My brother and I used to be like that."

"Used to be?"

"He moved to Chicago, got a job as a garbage man. Now, when he comes home, it's different. There's a space in the conversation that didn't use to be there. It's cool and everything. We still get along and all. Everyone has to grow up. Actually, I hadn't thought about it in a long time, but when he first left, I remember thinking that there was something precious lost." He took the fork and ate a bite of cake.

"I lost Mouse even before she died." On the wall hung a painting: two purple figures sculling across green water. The artist had laid sheet music over the canvas, and Mozart's notes showed through the oil paint. "I can't believe I'm telling you all this. We had this huge fight over her asshole boyfriend. More than one fight actually. It was more like a series of yelling matches. I couldn't keep my mouth shut. Maybe it was jealousy—that's what people said. I loved her better than he did. Not in a sexual way, you understand, but who else would be there for me if she wasn't? I knew it wasn't my business, but her boyfriend was such a jerk, and I couldn't understand why she didn't see it. Then, when she died, it seemed like it was my fault because I couldn't make her see it. I couldn't make her stop seeing him."

"What happened?"

"Car wreck. He was driving. They were coming home from a kegger just before graduation. Happens all the time, right?" If I knew one thing, I knew that I was not going to cry in front of Timothy. I took a big swig of coffee to steady my voice. Outside the window, the rain droned on. "The more I bitched about him, the tighter she clung." I skimmed the surface of the problem, sculling the time-muddied waters. "Maybe, if I'd just shut up, she would've seen him for what he was. If I'd actually been there for her, instead of antagonizing her, maybe she wouldn't have felt so alone. Maybe that would've given her strength to leave."

Timothy pushed his cup in circles on the table, staring at it intensely. "The problem with maybes is that you can get trapped in them. Sometimes things just happen and there's nothing you could've done." He stopped moving the cup and looked up. "You ever read Cormac McCarthy?"

I shook my head.

"Well, I can't quote him exactly or anything, but he said that the problem with using history as a guide is that there's no control in its experiment. We never know what would have happened if everything hadn't worked exactly as it did. *All the Pretty Horses.* You should read it." He took a sip. "Maybe it's the chemist in me, but I always loved what McCarthy said about history needing a control. We really can't learn any truth from it. If it's interesting or revealing, it is for other reasons. Like you and Mouse, it speaks a lot about you."

"Nothing good," I said, uncomfortable with having shown so much of myself so early, and with not showing enough to cast any kind of true light. He wouldn't feel so kindly if he'd known how I'd acted, if I'd told the long-silenced story of the night before the accident, if I'd spoken the cruelty of which I'd proven capable.

"On the contrary." He didn't elaborate, except to smile. His eyes had a softness to them lent by their golden gleam. They were quiet eyes; he didn't spook easily.

Losing Mouse had to mean something; it made *me* have to mean something. I thought again of Foxy; the thought carried a familiar ache. Maybe history had no control, but this much, I'd learned: Life could not be wasted. "I shouldn't have said all this."

"Actually, I was just thinking it was nice to have a real conversation with someone."

"As opposed to a fake conversation?" Here I was with a man in a coffee shop, not riding. I had learned nothing from my history and experiments.

"As opposed to a plastic conversation: pleasantries, the weather, what's on television, the price of gas. All the stuff I talk about all day with customers and classmates."

"Honesty doesn't get you anywhere."

His skin was smooth and clear. I wanted to press my face against his as he smiled, yet I loathed myself for the desire. He raised his cup and finished his coffee, thinking for a moment before saying, "It depends on where you want to go." He stacked his cup in mine and slid his hand again toward mine, brushing the skin lightly with a gentle touch. "Me? I could go for a movie."

This was the moment. I could make him need me as I had made Dave need me. He would stroke my hair. He would brush my cheek with the back of his fingers, cup his hand around my neck, draw me in for a kiss. He would hold me in the darkness. The darkness would recede. But darkness is solitude, freedom, and drive.

Foxfire. I had committed heresy against myself once. It would not happen again. Timothy was right: Life had to *matter.* No more distractions. No more wasted time. In that moment, I saw the next fence and aimed for it. My throat closed around the words that must be spoken, but I forced them out. "I'm sorry. I have a boyfriend."

Looking at me steadily but mildly, his eyes narrowed slightly, trying to work something out with that unreadable Eastwood gaze.

❧

Emptiness filled me with its surprising capacity. I dropped Timothy and his ten speed at his apartment and spent several hours at the barn alone with Foxfire. I had lied in order to maintain myself. Without a horse, who was I?

It was late when I finally drove home. In the dark, the answering machine's red light flashed its warning. I didn't want to touch the button, sure that once again Dave's voice would come out of it.

I was the epitome of privilege, a white girl with a horse. Timothy was an anarchist against privilege. I'd seen it in Jersey. The money, the entitlement. I was only on the edge of that rich man's world, but it stained me nonetheless. And hadn't I envied that wealth? Even still, didn't I want the horse it could buy? Timothy's intelligence, his calm, even his way of looking and seeing all seemed like an invitation, but how could he want me? He was above me, beyond me. I was silent. He was a man who could arc wires and make the night echo with a booming electrical thunderclap.

I reached to the machine, and Eddie's voice unspooled from the tape. Eddie, a part of the determined course. My breath left me in a long, steady exhale.

"Joannie," the recorded voice said. "Sorry not to call sooner. I got back last week, but things were crazy with the move. Anyway, I heard you were back and so I thought I'd see if you were interested in doing some riding. Give me a call."

I closed my eyes and breathed, the old relaxation technique from the show ring. The red light was not the lighthouse flaring the news of rocks, but the lifeboat bobbing on the wave: Eddie. He was a drill sergeant of a trainer with a meticulous eye and a demand for perfection. There was no way to hide sloppiness from him—no way to hide days when you skipped the barn, or trained less hard, no way to hide today. He could see work that hadn't been done, muscles that hadn't been trained, and he'd have none of it. He was precisely what I needed: a reason to go back to the barn again, a reason to ride, even if I couldn't jump.

Tomorrow morning, as soon as it was a reasonable hour, I would call Eddie and set up a lesson schedule, and then I would ride. I would ride like I used to. I would ride like I meant it.

Cheryl typed away, back toward me, the tilt of her head dour and disapproving, as I made my overtly and unabashedly personal call. Eddie's "hello" was as warm and comforting as the smell of the pipe smoke that clung to his clothing. I said, "I want the very first lesson you've got open." He laughed and gave me a Thursday.

"Eddie," I said, hesitating. "Foxy's not jumping anymore."

His *hmmm* offered neither sympathy nor surprise. "I picked up a new horse in California that might suit you," he said. "For the time being, anyway. She's a bit rough yet; I'd been planning on working with her for a while myself before I put anyone on her, but what with trying to get the boys to school and soccer, I'm not sure I can give her all the time she needs." He was silent for a moment, thinking. I held my breath to give space for his decision. "I'll tell you what. I'll bring her Thursday and you can have your lesson on her, then tell me what you think."

Cheryl didn't turn to look at me. She hadn't spoken to me since Dr. Rivers chewed her out. I offered her my brightest smile; I didn't miss the conversation.

Timothy smirked at me when I came through the checkout that night. "Man, haven't you had enough of me yet?"

"Now, that's a charming greeting."

"I'm a charming guy."

I was glad for the return of light banter, glad to know we could get back there from yesterday. No trace of anger or woundedness hovered around him. He looked genuinely happy to see me.

"Do you always shop for just one meal at a time?" he asked.

"I never know what I might feel like eating," I said, only partially honest. The truth was, it was something to do when I wasn't riding or working.

"And this stuff is for . . ."

"Fried rice. Why? You want some?"

It was meant as more banter, but the air felt suddenly stiff. The reserve he hadn't had tempered his smile and he seemed to suck back into himself. "I would, but I've got an essay due tomorrow," he said. The words weren't especially formal, but they felt so.

The boyfriend I didn't have might as well have been standing at my side, waving a fist at him. *It's better this way,* I thought. *No one gets hurt.*

Riding the Zephyr

Eddie's battered blue Ford was already in the parking lot when I arrived, the rusty door of his mismatched stock trailer left open and swinging in the breeze. Odd: the open door. Carelessness wasn't like him. Latching it, I noticed fresh scratches marred the paint, the angry glare of silver.

Eddie's voice drifted out the barn door. "Sit back, back." The words were slow and decisive and commanding. He was giving a lesson.

I stood a moment, eyes adjusting to the barn's darkness. "A little leg," Eddie said.

"I don't have any leg left." Jenny giggled, plodding along on Zip.

"Come on. No rest for the wicked." How many times had Eddie said that line to me?

Zip picked up the pace. He was moving better than he'd ever moved for Jenny. His hind legs stretched forward underneath him, almost tracking up. Jenny squeezed her leg again, and it all came together. His hind feet filled the hoof prints left by the front. Zip was moving like a dressage horse again. I heard my words again in my head, *I want the first lesson you've got.* Yet here was Jenny.

"There it is," Eddie said. "Do you feel that?"

"Feel what?" Jenny bounced lightly in the saddle, though Zip's trot was smooth. She had to unlock her lower back to absorb the motion, but she couldn't do that until she released the tension in her legs. "I feel like we're trotting a million miles an hour—is that what I'm supposed to feel?"

"Fast, yes, but not quick. You're moving forward because he's engaged behind and pushing off like he should instead of giving you that little pony trot you were doing before. We've got nice, long strides now."

Jenny beamed, but the rest of the lesson went downhill quickly. Her hip remained rigid and her lower leg flopped as she tired. Again, she began to tilt forward in the saddle, out of balance.

"That's enough for now," Eddie said. He watched Jenny circle for a moment, Zip on a long rein. "Your homework is more of this—much more. Next week, I don't want you pooping out on me. I think I'll probably take your stirrups away."

"Take my stirrups?" Jenny blanched, but Eddie only smiled. She took heart and asked, "When do I get to jump?"

"Your leg is too loose right now, and you're struggling with balance, but don't worry. We'll get there. You do your homework; it won't take long. Just keep working. There's no substitute for work."

I smiled, thinking back to Dawn's response to the same advice. He hadn't let her canter either. "You want thirty bucks for that?" she'd said. "For trotting me in circles and telling me to keep my leg on?" Eddie had only shrugged. He never argued his methods. You worked his program, or you didn't train with him. That was all.

He turned. "Well, hey there, stranger."

"Hey back." Hearing my voice, Foxfire nickered from his stall, pressing the pink tip of his velvety nose between the bars, nostrils flaring to catch my scent.

"We'd about given up on you coming back. It's good to see you. You learn anything new in Jersey?"

"Learned I couldn't afford the board there and that it pays to be rich."

"Ah," Eddie waved these words from the air. "No bitterness. That'll get you nowhere."

I smiled weakly and fiddled with the strap on my helmet, its old, sun-bleached velvet worn through at the edges. "Just answering the question. Jack Stewart helped me with my hands a bit, too."

"Good. They needed helping."

I didn't take offense. My hands had never been bad, per se, but I tended to carry tension in my elbows and shoulders, stiffening at times, especially in shows. Decent hands, but not great.

Eddie looked me over, appraising me as he might a horse, checking my conformation and fitness. The skin around his eyes was slightly more wrinkled in spite of the ever-present ball cap. He wore the same damned cap as when I left, a freebie that came with a grain purchase lord knows how many years ago. The tee shirt, too, looked familiar, though who could tell one faded Mariners shirt from another? Perhaps it was the way his slight paunch hung over his jeans that made all shirts look the same. Yet like me, he had a good build for a rider: long, straight legs and a shorter waist than most men. Even aged and paunched, he was a force to be reckoned with, but he'd always preferred working with green horses to winning competitions.

"You look good," he said. "You're keeping in shape."

"Trying to."

"Good. You're going to need all you've got today."

"Lazy?"

Eddie barked a laugh. "No, if there's one thing she's not, it's lazy. The reverse, if anything. She's ex-track with a bit of a mean streak."

I looked him in the eye. "Define 'a bit.'"

He looked away, and I remembered the gouges in the trailer door. "Maybe it's better if you just meet her," he said.

"Shit."

"You might say that."

I cast one last look at Jenny, but she just brushed Zip, apparently too exhausted to listen to our conversation. "Where is she?" I asked Eddie.

"Back pasture."

I matched my stride to his as we walked. Rounding the barn, she came into view. The mare's coat was a dull, lackluster grey. To say she was thin was an understatement. Her ribs were pronounced as fence rails, her hips angular and jutting, no neck to speak of. Everywhere, her un-muscled, un-fattened skeleton was visible. She was a living anatomy lesson. "Jesus."

"Yeah." Eddie tugged at the greying hair that curled over his ear at the edge of his cap, a gesture I recognized from past moments of tension: jump-offs, injuries. "I ran across her one day just as we were packing to come home. Tiny paddock grazed down to dust. She lost weight being shipped, of course, but she was rough to begin with. More than rough. I think the previous owners tried to starve the spunk out of her." His hand stilled, and he smiled. "It didn't work."

My sympathy for the mare was short-lived. We hadn't gotten the pasture gate closed when she lunged at us with sudden fury, teeth snapping. "Whoa! Easy, girl," I said, ready to jump back out of the pasture. Eddie stopped and stood, and we watched her put on her show. With a whole pasture to run in, she wasn't running. She was stomping, rearing, tossing her head, and through it all, she was watching us and gauging our reaction.

Eddie stood, the calm before her storm. He held out his hand sideways, two fingers raised, a signal for me to hang back. I needed no prompting. He never took his eyes off the mare, approaching slowly and cautiously, pausing frequently. The air was warm and dry around us; only her antics broke the stillness.

He stood at her shoulder for nearly a minute before slipping his arm around to catch her with the halter. They were testing each other, and I wondered how long it had taken to get this response, how many times a day Eddie had caught her in her pasture to show that no harm would come of it.

"She's a mare all right," I said.

"An alpha mare," Eddie said the words softly, like he was wooing her.

"Fantastic."

He handed me the lead and I walked her into the barn and cross-tied her quickly, eyes never leaving her mouth. As I brushed her, she swung her body alternatively away from me and suddenly toward me, trying to pin me against the wall. When I approached to pick her feet, she cow-kicked at my head. "Quit," I growled, drawing the single syllable long and low in my mouth. Her joints showed excellent flexibility—I'd give her that. Even starved, she was an athlete.

Foxfire was growing ever more anxious at the end of the barn. Upset that I hadn't come for him, his welcoming nicker had changed into a more insistent whinny and was fast becoming a scream. The shuffle of his hooves filled the barn with noise and dust as he paced the front of his stall, increasingly frantic. I should have moved him—that was clear now. I would have, if I'd realized how upset this would make him.

How many times had I hurt him? How many times had he hidden the lancing pain of a jump's landing just because I'd pointed him at a fence and asked him to go? If he'd stop for a moment, I could clear my head. Everything was loud and swirling. The mare kicked again, barely missing.

"Just go slow," Eddie said. The horse rammed her flanks against me, scrambling and tossing her head against the ties. The bolts shuddered in the wall as Foxy screamed on. Noise filled the barn, echoing from the rafters.

I had wasted my life, wasted it! How had I fallen from jumping Foxfire over five foot fences to this—a broken-down mare who wanted to kill me? There was no future offered here, and I'd turned Timothy away. There had never been such an idealistic fool, such a girl of insupportable pretention, as I was.

The mare kicked again as I layered on saddle pads—stacking them to make up for her thinness. She shrank from the saddle it-self, first crouching low, un-horselike, then springing sideways and slamming me again into the wall, her bones crushing against mine through the too thin flesh. "Jesus, stop!"

She was Eddie's project, not mine. Foxfire screamed and screamed his rage, pawing at his stall door. My betrayal, my infidel-ity turned him into a crazed animal. He reared and struck the stall door, the metal bars singing with the hoof strike.

The mare kicked again as I passed the girth under her belly. Her hoof clipped the side of my hand, leaving a circular indent that bruised instantly. Stifling a yelp, I shook my hand as if pain was a spider that could be shaken off. The barn was full with Foxy's screaming, crowding out any rational thought. He had to stop. If I was going to stay uninjured, I had to *think* my way around this mare.

Eddie just nodded me on. I gritted my teeth and tightened the girth, stepping out of the way of the hind hoof as once again it flew. "Stop, God damn it."

The larger accident had all come to this moment: fate in the form of an angry grey bitch of a horse. Every muscle of me tensed—a surge of adrenaline that prompted no instinct to flee. I wanted to hurt something.

Eddie held a bridle to me—an old-fashioned hunting-style headstall with broad, flat leather pieces long out of fashion in the show ring. He wasn't risking nicer leather, but he'd fitted it with a fat loose-ring snaffle, an optimistically gentle bit for this horse. As I came to her side, she snapped at me five times in quick succession. The halter and the cross ties gave her no real range, but I would have to free her to bridle her.

The bird bones of my hand throbbed where the iron shoe hit. I tried to think, tried to find a way to slip the headstall on. One moment of silence, and I could bridle this mare, but Foxfire grew more panicked. My head was a ringing bell. Every muscle rigid with his screaming, every bone vibrating like the metal bars he struck. Foxy the rock and this mare the hard place, like Dave and Timothy, like Cheryl and Dr. Rivers, like all the things I was trapped between.

God damn it all: This horse wasn't going to take me anywhere. With this behavior, she deserved to be junked. I had no hope, not even the sliver of a hope, of ever riding for Jack Stewart again, and yet I turned Timothy away. A bridle in one hand, and nothing in the other. All the eggs in my basket broke under these iron-shod hooves.

A stand-off: The mare and I watched each other. The broad muscles of her shoulder and haunches quivered as she watched me. Fire burned in the core of her unblinking eye. Her ears were pinned so flat against her head she appeared not to have ears at all. The mare's flaring nostrils counted the seconds.

Vigilant, vigilant, I gripped the halter firm in hand and unsnapped one side of the cross-tie, but the mare was strong and she was quick. Her teeth locked like a vice around the denim of my jacket, clamping onto the skin beneath in a vicious bite. I tore my bruised arm from her teeth, wheeled, and before reason could stop me, I punched her in the face.

I'd hit her hard. My knuckles ached with violence, the bone of her skull as flat and unyielding as brick. I barely had time to register shock when she lunged at me, teeth stretched for anything to get hold of. She was not a flight animal either, this one.

I staggered back as rational thought returned. I had hit a horse. The only thing that kept her from me was the nylon halter that held her in check. I fought to make sense of what had just happened, but Foxfire's screams were still ringing through the barn as he struck and struck at his door.

Eddie laid a hand on my shoulder, stepping past me to snag the mare by the halter. He didn't say a word, but stood there stroking her neck until she relaxed ever so slightly under his hands. It took a while. Her eyes stayed white at their rims, watching me. Eddie slipped on the headstall.

I couldn't meet his eye. "That will never happen again." My voice was rasping. Tears threatened, and I braced my jaw against them. This was no time for weakness, and tears had never won sympathy here.

Eddie didn't respond, but he didn't have to. Self-loathing welled. I sunk back against the wall, disgusted with my behavior. "Get up," he said, his voice firm but not unkind. The offered reins, a second chance. The ghost-grey horse stamped, and Eddie pulled me to my feet. "What happened in Jersey is over. This is Idaho, and you have a horse to train."

I took the reins. Foxfire shuffled and called from his corner stall, eyes rolling, pausing now and then to rear up, arthritic hocks forgotten in his madness, and looked over the tall bars of his stall. I hand-walked the mare once around the arena's perimeter, introducing her to its mirrors and dark corners. She spooked at nothing.

I hopped quickly into the saddle as the mare ran from the weight of my body. I pulled the reins hard against her mouth to slow her canter, but she simply threw her neck back and ran, her head practically in my face, her gallop wild and hollow-backed. I worked the reins: pressure, release, pressure, release, but to no effect. I found the second stirrup with my dangling foot and pulled her sideways into a tight circle, her nose to my knee, until she slowed, dancing in all directions.

"She's a little sensitive," Eddie said.

"Track horse, track manners."

"Not so skittish as your run-of-the-mill track horse. She's not even listening to Foxy down there, which is more than I can say for her rider."

I frowned. "Should we move him?"

"Leave him. You need to get over this," Eddie said. After a moment's consideration, he added, "next time, we'll move him."

Next time. I couldn't believe he'd want to put me near this horse again.

I hadn't realized that Jenny was still there until I saw her from behind the fence rail, pale and watching. How much had she seen? The lesson was ugly, and I felt foolish under her gaze. Zip was gone, and I tried to remember if she was out putting him to pasture when I had snapped. Jenny smiled to me as we passed, and the mare kicked at her. How her image of me must have shifted: no longer the riding expert on the fine horse but just Eddie's awkward student fighting for control.

"Relax, relax," Eddie said. Jenny waved and left. "Where are those good hands I heard about?"

My shoulders and elbows were marbled with tension, unyielding as rock. I breathed, trying to release them. It'd been easier to relax on Foxfire, who invited my contact, who if anything, leaned into it. The mare held her head high and back, evading any contact with the bit. Eddie drug out poles for her to trot, but she jumped them. There was a moment of relaxation before each leap, and she stretched round and forward, but then she landed and tensed again. The moment was so fleeting it might have been imagined.

It was a short lesson—she didn't have the stamina for anything more, despite her bravado. When I dismounted, she again ran from under my weight, breaking one of Eddie's reins and dancing at the end of the one that remained intact. An angry red stripe crossed my palm where the pebbled rubber of the rein chafed it.

"Well, what do you think?" Eddie watched me with his ever-appraising eyes.

"You don't want to know."

"You could learn a lot from this horse." He stroked her under-muscled neck, and she allowed him to do so. "You've been spoiled by Foxfire, and you know it. You won't luck into another one like him."

I looked at Eddie more closely: the battered cap, those quick, shaded eyes. "You're not trying to *sell* me this animal?"

"No. No." He laughed as he said it, hands open wide to stop that thought as he would have stopped a runaway horse. "I'm suggesting that I could give you free lessons on her if you'd be willing to put in some time, say three days a week, training her. I'm going to winter her here at Thornfield—Connie and I have already talked." After what I'd done today, he had to be desperate.

"Connie know about her manners?"

"She's met her." He smiled again in that small, private way of his. "She wasn't thrilled, but she's agreed to let the mare have the back pasture. With winter coming, I need an indoor to get her in shape."

"You'd be working with her, too?"

He nodded. "The other three days. Lesson day, we work her together. You in the saddle, me down here. She needs consistency. We need to work as a team."

"I don't know." Her head hung in the cross ties, finally showing her exhaustion. The flop of her ears was pitiful. I ran my eye over the perfect angle of her shoulder, pasterns and knees. Her bones were impeccable, but bones alone did not make a horse.

"We have to go slow with her, of course, but I think she could show in the spring."

I laughed. "You're insane," I said, but the promise of horse shows was tempting, and Eddie knew it. I took a step toward her to stroke her neck as Eddie had. Immediately, she sprang, eyes white, legs shuffling, and teeth snapping. "Give me some time to think about it."

"Call me this weekend and let me know."

I watched her another moment. "What other horses have you got right now?"

"None. They're all leased out."

"I thought that was just for the summer."

"I extended them. Everyone's getting along well. In fact, I'm hoping Pam's going to buy Winston at the end of the month. Hansel's with a girl in Walla Walla, but he can't jump more than three feet any more. He'd be no good for you even if he was available."

I gestured toward the mare. "It's not like she's jumping."

"Yeah, but that's only a matter of time. You need to learn how to handle a difficult horse."

I walked up to her and ran my hand over the dull fur of her throatlatch. Her eyes never left mine. She was quivering under my touch. "So it's this horse or Foxfire?"

"Unless you can borrow something else. And let's face it, Joannie, Foxfire isn't an option anymore. You know your flatwork. You need a jumper, and with the boys in soccer, I need someone to give this horse some time."

I picked up a dandy brush and flicked dust and sweat from her coat. "She have a name yet?"

"Her registered name is 'Luckstar's Last Zephyr.'"

"Oh God."

Eddie snorted. "I know. Someone got a little too creative. She's by Mesrour out of Luckstar—those are good lines for jumpers, but her owners must've been quarter horse people to come up with that name."

Eddie picked up a soft brush and ran it slowly over her face with a mother's care. "I've been calling her Zephie," he said.

Zephie. As if removing an r could remove her bite. I picked out her last hoof and set it down. No sooner had it touched the aisle than it sprang back as if the floor had been electrified, swinging out to catch me hard in the thigh.

I fell against the wall, biting my lip to keep from reacting. *Deserved*, I thought. We were even now: a blow for a blow. We would start fresh if we started at all.

Over the next week, the bruise would darken into a blue-purple U, like something mimeographed, like something branded.

The Next Storm

I n New Jersey, I never saw the weather coming. The horizon was
tree choked, and the clouds gathered quickly. At the small stable
where I could afford to keep Foxy (not run down but running), the
barn manager heard it every time. Kaki was a petite woman with a
harsh voice and mannish walk. We'd be in the arena, Kaki barking
instructions at one of her never-ending string of lesson kids, when
suddenly she'd call for everyone to stop. She'd twist her face against
the stillness of the sky, listening, then, "Everybody in. Now."

It wasn't thunder she heard, but the wall of water approaching.
The storms came so fast. One minute we'd be working away in the
same old thick mugginess, and the next, sheets of rain rolled across
the arena, instantly soaking everything. We'd watch from the sliding doors of that ancient stable, pleasantly dry amidst the deluge,
the heady scent of straw made pungent by rain. Five minutes later,
maybe ten, it'd be over, and we'd make our way out through puddles
quickly draining from sandy footing.

The sweat and mustiness of another gym workout didn't quite wash
away in the shower: that mirrored box of a room, those weighted

bars, the heavy stares of men strutting from bench to bench, puffing their chests. Soap and water had made the deep purple of my bruises shine darkly. It'd been four days since the lesson, but Zephyr's teeth marks were crisply individual. The circle of teeth seemed to have that permanence.

I didn't want a new horse, and I didn't want my horse, old. I'd given up two offers of love and now, worse still, my mother had relapsed again, her hands too numb to feel. I'd gone home Saturday to help, but my parents, anxious to show they could cope, wouldn't let me lift a finger. I stayed late Sunday anyway, and I felt more tired than I would have been if I'd cooked full meals all weekend, washed every dish, and scrubbed the house from top to bottom.

I was in a bitter mood, frustrated at the disease I couldn't fight. Rather than allow myself to displace anger onto my patients, I hated my apartment. From the beige walls that I was under contract not to paint to the scratching of the cheap, synthetic carpet to the vinyl blinds bending in the morning sun, smudged by the greasy hands of some former tenant and now impossible to clean, this was no place to live. Upstairs, someone had turned the stereo up and now the beats of some unidentifiable song vibrated in the door frames. I was getting too old for this. I stared at the clock while my coffee brewed. The phone's ring was one straw too many.

"Yeah?" I said, both dreading and hoping that it was Dad. Instead, nothing. I was about hang up on the silence, muttering, "Fucking telemarketers."

"Um, sorry to call so early." It was Jenny.

"Oh." She'd never called me before. "It's O.K. I've been up for a while." I paused, waiting for her to explain, but there was only silence. "How are you?" I asked.

Another moment's silence. "Not so good."

I ran the finger over the dust on my dresser, drawing stick figures on its cherry surface, then hanging them on stick figure giblets like the victims of unguessed words. They stood out bright and clear, though I'd dusted Saturday morning before my dad's call. Dust gathered quickly in the dry air. "What's wrong?"

Jenny ignored my question. "Are you riding today? Can I come home with you after?"

"Sure." I stopped doodling. For once in my life, I seemed to hear a storm in the air. "Do you need to come over sooner?"

"No. Just this afternoon—if it's O.K. I'll be at the barn at four thirty. I have to go."

She hung up before I could reply.

There is an art to taking a good radiograph, to dosing the radiation, to timing the millisieverts. When I look at a body, when I adjust its position, I estimate mass and density, fat and muscle, so I can get the best picture in the fewest tries. Because I'm good at this, I've been cross-trained in CT and MRI, but x-rays remain my favorite, so this is where I stay. Despite the speed and economy of computerized radiography, I miss the old gelatin and silver film that I first learned to shoot, the satisfying heft of the white plates we slid into the table, the flop of developed film, all the tangible artifacts of my art.

That day seemed to be one chest x-ray after another, reminding me that the heart was grey and bulbous, just another ghostly cloud of organ through the lens of my machine. I spent the day telling people to take a deep breath and hold it, and I seemed to be holding my own, thinking of Jenny's tense voice on the phone, and her tenser silences. Did she know about Dave and me? Had she guessed? Had he told?

I beat her to the barn by a good hour and a half. I walked to the back pasture and stared at Zephyr for twenty minutes or more. No x-rays were needed to see her bones: She wore them, or they wore her, or they *were* her—not much else to her. But I could see what Eddie saw in the composition of her bones. The angles were all precisely right.

She'd been starved though, and her bones were surely weakened by malnutrition. Jumping was one thing, landing another. If it was too depleted, that perfect canon bone might shatter on the landing side of the first big fence she took.

My fingers traveled again to the lump of pain where her teeth had latched on. They'd been strong enough.

Foxy saddled, I rode the hills, wandering their gentle ups and downs. Jenny had arrived by the time we got back. She said nothing to me. Only the redness in her eyes spoke, but I could not translate the language of color. I wrapped Foxy's hocks with magnets and brushed him leisurely, appreciating more than ever how quiet he was. I picked his hooves and, as always, he turned his large head to me, brown eyes softly asking for the carrots in my brush box. I broke each in half and held the pieces first back by the girth, then low between his hooves, making him stretch for each. The research was mixed on the effectiveness of carrot stretches, but if they bought us even one more day, I'd do them.

Foxy back in his stall, I returned to Zephyr, still turning the puzzle that was Jenny over in my head. Did she know? About Dave and me?

I could confess. Before she said anything, I could tell and ask for penance. But she couldn't know, could she? Why now?

Zephyr grazed, ignoring me completely. Not even an ear flick. I was invisible, unworthy of notice. I picked up a stone and tossed it at her feet. Foxy would have galloped across the pasture at that, but Zephyr just turned away, pointing her ass at me, lazily swatting at flies with her thin tail.

I had not called Eddie that weekend, and I had not called Timothy. Mom's relapse had pushed everything else to the back burner.

I sighed. "Why should I make anything of you?" I asked the mare. "What's in this for me? More fucking bruises?" I snorted and watched. A breeze tickled the loose hair at the back of my neck. "You don't even want to be a show horse anyway, do you? Not that you know what it's like, there in the ring with everyone watching. Everyone cheering."

A cowbird settled on the mare's withers. Grasshoppers jumped away from the scythes of her teeth. I thought of all the ways she could hurt me. A hoof to the arm, a broken bone, and I'd be out two months or more. A hoof to the gut, intestinal damage. A hoof to the head? I didn't want to think about that. Retardation? Death? I'd heard the stories. Yet all were better than the blow to the heart that love inflicted.

A second cowbird joined the first. Zephyr ignored them. She looked so tranquil like this.

"I don't hit horses, you know." My words evaporated in the arid afternoon. "Only you. I'm not sure I like what you bring out of me." I closed my eyes and let my mind stray. Timothy's hair, dark as mink, begged petting. Around him, I wanted to be soft, but softness was for the weak. Weakness led to errors in judgment. Softness had led to Dave.

Zephyr turned and bit at a fly. The snap of her teeth, the only sound, was quickly consumed by the summer's still.

"Oh, to hell with you," I said, but I kept standing there.

Moments passed. Nothing was my fault, and it was all my fault.

"If I work with you, you'll only make my life hell. Frustrating me, biting me. I can't even jump you yet, your flatwork is so bad. If I'm going to get stuck doing flatwork, I might as well be stuck on Foxfire, a nice horse."

Zephyr walked a few paces to a fresh patch of grass. I threw up my hands and walked away.

When I walked in, Jenny was just finishing off Zip, wiping his face with a soft cloth to remove the sweat marks where the bridle had been. "How's Zip coming along?"

Jenny didn't look at me. "All right, I guess. Still a pain in the butt"—she blushed and hastened to add—"not like Zephyr, though."

I tensed against her judgment. "Do you want to just follow me home?" I asked.

In my rearview, Jenny's Taurus wound over the gravel roads. She was a safe driver. I slowed to adjust to her.

At my apartment, we ordered pizza and turned on Monday night football. We sat back on the sofa, me with a beer, her with a pop, both of us waiting. The sofa's loose spring dug into my shoulder, but to move away now would be to fail Jenny again.

Jenny stared at the screen impassively, uncharacteristically somber. Glum. Her silence baffled me. I focused again on the game. "Come on," I said, "that was flagrant." The holding went unpunished.

The pizza man left us our dinner.

"Dave might call." Jenny's eyes never left the screen.

"O.K.," I said. I picked my slice, pulling the cheese apart with quick fingers. "Are you guys O.K.?"

She still didn't look at me. I tore off my crust and ate that first. For a full minute, I was convinced she knew everything and was giving me a chance to apologize, but no, I decided, I was being paranoid. How could she know? Why would she be silent if she did? The Eagles kicked a field goal. Finally, she said, "He's mad at me, but it wasn't my fault." Her voice was matter of fact. She didn't whine. If anything, she sounded tired—exhausted.

Relief flooded in like oxygen after a held breath. It wasn't my fault—she didn't know. *He* was mad at *her*, the hypocritical bastard. I wanted to laugh. I nearly smiled before I remembered that, for her, nothing had changed. "What happened?"

Jenny sipped her pop and watched a couple of plays before answering. Dallas's running back juked and darted but failed to make a first down. After the punt, a foot cream commercial came on, and Jenny spoke at last. "We had some money sitting in the bank. Money market. Whatever." Her eyes didn't leave the screen. "We talked to the financial advisor last month and he wanted us to put it in funds, but Dave never gave the go ahead. The guy kept calling, and I kept trying to talk to Dave about it, but he always said he was too tired to think about money."

She sighed and looked at the ceiling, and tears wavered at the bottom of her eyes, but she refused to let them fall. "His job's tough. I know that. I know he doesn't get along with everyone, that they blame him for not working his way up, but the money was just sitting there, and something had to be done, so I did it. I told the guy to move the money." She sipped her Coke again and returned her eyes to the screen. The tears had vanished. Her eyes looked vacant now, like those of a dead woman's. "When I told Dave, he hit the roof. He said it wasn't my money—said I didn't know crap about money, and even if I did, I didn't have the right to touch it."

I sighed and watched as the Eagles made a first down. "What a jackass."

"Maybe I shouldn't have moved it."

I tried to imagine my way into her problems—too much money and questions of how to invest it. A problem I could only wish for, yet here she was with tears sliding down her face. "Was Dave planning on spending it on something?"

"I don't think so. We've got a savings account for stuff like that." She blushed. "You know, the liquid funds."

I didn't know. I reached for a second slice of pizza, conscious that Jenny hadn't even offered to split the bill or pay the tip. It probably never occurred to her. The Eagles rushed for fifteen yards. "Why didn't you come over here first thing this morning?" I asked. "You know, if Dave's being a jerk, you always have a place to stay."

"I had some stuff to do first."

I looked over and raised an eyebrow. She met my gaze with a darting glance of her own baby-blue eyes. "The house was a mess," she said. She was smiling now, embarrassment pinking her cheeks. "Mondays I vacuum, clean bathrooms, and wash the whites."

"You cleaned the house?" An interception, but I ignored the TV.

"And I made dinner." Jenny looked over at me again quickly and then feigned at watching the game.

"You knew you were coming here."

"Dave's dinner." She laughed at herself as she said it, and there was more than a trace of embarrassment in her voice. "It's in the fridge with a note on the door telling him how long to cook it."

I smiled, remembering how much I liked her. "Un-fucking-believable."

Before Jenny could respond, the phone rang. Dave's voice was low and steady. "I need to speak to my wife." Not Jenny but my wife. Possessive.

I held the receiver to my palm but didn't bother to lower my voice. "It's Dave. You want to talk?"

"Should I go home?"

"Hell no. Not if you don't want to. Stay as long as you need."

Jenny held out her hand for the phone, and I slipped through the vertical blinds and walked onto the balcony, shutting the glass door between us.

Twilight. In the parking lot below, a girl in an Arby's polo hurried from her car, pulling a grease-stained visor from her hair. I'd been that girl, just off dinner rush and hungry for quiet. Her door slammed and she was gone. She would shower away the itch of grease and microwave a frozen entree, turn on the television and watch its flickering light alone. Even now, was I so different?

In the stillness of the evening's warm gloaming, night really did feel like it was falling, like the impossible sky above lowered closer to Earth to cover us like a blanket, falling slowly but unstoppably, dark as molasses, falling like I imagined one fell in love.

In town, no crickets sang the sky down, and the leaves were, as yet, too green to rustle in the slight breeze. The stars remained cloaked by townlight and the lingering light of dusk. I wondered how my mom was doing.

The door slid in its tracks behind me. "I told Dave I wasn't ready to come home. He didn't apologize."

I nodded.

"After the game, I'll probably go."

"You don't have to. If he doesn't cough up an apology, you stay here." Dave was alone, like I had been so many nights. He could stay that way.

The night's quiet filled the spaces where speech had been. The ghost boxes of apartments sat squat against the sky. Jenny said, "No, I should go back. I just want to see when he'll apologize."

"When? Not if?"

"He will." Jenny picked at the peeling paint on the railing, flicking a chip over the side. As hard as I looked at her, I couldn't tell what she was thinking. The thought surfaced again: What if she'd known about Dave and me this whole time? What if she was just one of those women who swallowed infidelity as a part of marriage? I swallowed the last sip of my beer. "Well," Jenny sighed. "I guess I'll go watch the rest of the game."

I stayed at the railing a moment, the empty bottle heavy in my hand. I wanted to fling it over the railing, to watch its glittering arc as it condensed and distilled the glow of the distant streetlight, turning end over end. I wanted the violence of its final smash as the spray of shards skittered across asphalt. It's what we were heading toward, Jenny, and Dave, and me.

But I recycled the bottle, like any good Northwestern girl, and opened a fresh one. Puddles of cheese grease congealed on the now cold pizza. Jenny and I didn't talk. We ate and watched as each team strategized, threw, darted, ducked, did all they could to move toward their goal, only to punt in the end.

When Dave called midway through the fourth quarter, he apologized. Exiled to the balcony once more, I surveyed the parking lot again while he and Jenny talked. I lived among students. Rows of old American cars sat idle, dull and unwaxed. In the building across the parking lot, two guys came out to drink coffee on the deck. Their soft laughter floated toward me. I stood silent and alone and thought of Timothy and how much I would rather be sharing a pizza with him. The softness of his shirt might brush against my arm, a warm thought.

All thoughts seemed to circle back to the brush of flannel on skin. Jenny and Dave talked and talked, and the night grew cooler. My jacket was only on the other side of the door, but I couldn't open it, couldn't again wedge myself into their intimacy, however silently. I looked again for stars I couldn't see, as if they could provide a navigable direction.

Finally, the door slid open behind me. Jenny smiled sheepishly. "I'm heading out."

"You know you don't need to," I said.

"It's O.K. He said he was sorry."

Yes, I thought, but not sorry enough, not sorry for me. "He was wrong," I said. "He should be more than just sorry."

She looked at me oddly. My tone was too harsh. Her tears had long dried.

"Or go home," I said. "You know him best." She didn't know him at all. "Just remember that while there are women in Idaho—me, Connie, Dawn—you always have a place to stay."

Jenny only nodded. "It's time. I appreciate it, though. Letting me come by and all."

"Any time," I said. If she hurried, she'd be home before the two-minute warning. I crammed the pizza box into my fridge, and settled back into my easy chair. It smelled faintly of moss and earth. How well it curved to fit the contours of my back. As I finished my beer, Dallas threw an interception and the Eagles scored. Life was better alone. I needed money and a horse; that was all.

Bodies in Motion

September rolled on, and the mornings grew cool. That morning, I pulled on my old sweatshirt and soccer shorts, laced my shoes, and hit the road. The grasshoppers were almost gone now, but birds still sang. It felt good to run that day, a way of exorcising something, sweating it out. My legs and lungs felt endless. I could leap tall buildings, I could stride out and out. The early air was clean and pure. Thank God for this. For actions without words. For my moving body. For a space where I could exist alone in the world. Thank God. I was powerful; I was in control; I was a runner.

I turned down Mountain View and lengthened my stride on the long straight stretch of road. A man on a bike pedaled toward me, his cardinal red windbreaker flapping. He slowed as we drew close, a shy grin spreading over his face. "Good morning, Joannie," he said, the metal tap of his clipped shoe on the pavement punctuating the sentence.

I stopped and looked closer at the man under the helmet. Dr. Rivers—only, I barely recognized him. His greying hair, always slicked and greased at work, now curled from the edges of his helmet. He looked young out here. In the sunshine, without his white coat, his skin had a healthier glow, but there was more to it than that. I stammered a "hello" and apologized for not recognizing him under his helmet. "I guess I was in my own world," I said.

"That's the whole point of being out here, right?" He actually smiled. A real smile. With teeth. "No patients, no roommates," he grinned again, "no Cheryl."

I tried to think of something to say. Dare I agree? I looked down. I was wearing the old navy-blue sweatshirt Dawn had given me for Christmas four years earlier. In large orange block lettering, the words "EAT SHIT ASSHOLE" were spelled across my chest.

I crossed my arms over the words. "Nice bike," I said. It was, too—front and rear shocks, gears and gears, rapid fire shifters. The paint was well and truly scuffed; this bike had been on the mountains. The image of Dr. Rivers recklessly barreling down a steep decline didn't square with anything I'd ever thought about him. "I didn't realize you were into biking."

"And I had no idea you were a runner."

"I'm more of a flopper. But that's only two steps below 'jogger,' so I'm not without potential."

Dr. Rivers laughed, and his laugh seemed authentic. "I don't believe that." He was real out here, and the hospital version of him was only a ghostly replicant. "You seemed to be trucking right along."

I didn't know how to respond. Language failed me. I wanted to say something witty or sarcastic, but my mind was void except for wonderment: He'd just used "trucking" in a sentence. "Trucking" was a part of his working vocabulary. Even his smile was natural here. Lines I'd never noticed on his face before indicated that he'd smiled before—that smiling was actually something he did when he wasn't wearing a white coat! And then there was the sight of his legs in shorts, scarred but tan and knotted with muscle. None of this squared with the Dr. Rivers I thought I'd known.

He seemed to want to say something else, but no words were coming to him either. His smile fell, and he picked absent-mindedly at an old scab at his knee. We were mired in silence. The pause was just becoming palpably uncomfortable when he said, "I'll let you get back to it then. It was good to see you, Joannie."

"Have a good ride." I breathed and turned, relieved to be able to run away.

And yet, I couldn't seem to find my stride again. My legs were awkward now, my knees ached, and my arms were in all the wrong places. My running shoes no longer seemed to absorb the road's shocks. My shorts rode up my thighs. I stopped again and ripped off my sweatshirt, but my rhythm did not return. The scars on Dr. Rivers' legs told of mountains and endurance—an entirely different story than the one told by his gleaming Montblanc pen and white coat.

I lay foot in front of foot, slapping the pavement down, trying to outrun the thought of infinite spaces. It was a policy of mine to avoid the terrifying thought of things going on forever: space, time, the soul, the emptiness where Mouse had been. It was too much like the old puzzle from sophomore geometry, can a line run along the side of a plane?

My mind could not make room for endless things. The idea of time stretching on forever always made me feel like my heart was dropping out from under me. It was all too much. The mind needs edges, containment, limits. The mind needs a fence.

Wednesday evening came, and I was once again seeking refuge in the barn. I had called neither Eddie nor Timothy, though I'd had a phone message from both. Connie came in as I finished with Fox. "You talked to Jenny lately?" she asked.

"Not today. Something wrong?"

"No, not wrong. She's looking to buy a horse, it seems. She told me today that her husband is, and I quote, *letting* her buy one."

Connie's face was impassive. I turned again to Foxy's coppery flanks as if it was possible to brush even more bloom into them. Jenny had gotten her apology all right.

Connie said, "I've got a couple geldings in mind, but I'm going to talk to Eddie first before I make any phone calls. He'll have some thoughts."

"It seems so fast. She's only been riding a couple of months." Jealousy rose as a lump in my throat.

"That's more than most people who buy horses. And she's got Eddie to help her."

"I'll have to call her tonight and say congratulations."

"Too bad Foxy's not jumping any more. Two or three years ago, he would've been perfect for her."

I stiffened. Two or three years ago, he was jumping grand prix fences in Jersey for Jack Stewart Flaherty. "I'm not selling Foxy," I said, not trying to keep the anger out of my voice. I slid the bolt home on his stall door and glowered at Connie.

She simply held up her hands and laughed it off. "I know, Joannie. Glad you're looking out for him in his old age. Besides, I don't think you could sell him now if you wanted to."

I turned away from her. The knowledge that Connie was right didn't make her words any easier to hear. As far as the market was concerned, Foxfire was worthless. Mild manners and gentleness, a heart of unparalleled size, all that meant nothing. No foot, no horse, as they say. Foxfire was losing his legs, and a horse without legs is barely a horse at all. By those standards, my mother was worthless, too. Tears pricked at my eyes but one fierce blink cleared them away.

"Well," Connie said, "keep your ears open for decent starter horses. Something sane and reasonably talented. It sounds like she's got some money to spend."

"Will do," I grumbled, still unable to look at her.

I put my stuff away and climbed into my truck. I didn't open the windows or start the engine right away. Instead, I sat in its warmth for several minutes, thinking, allowing the truck's trapped afternoon heat to seep into me. The dry, purifying heat helped stave off the chill of Connie's news. I drank tepid water from a plastic bottle, opened the window, and turned the key.

At home, I lifted the receiver and dialed. When a male voice answered, I spoke. "I'll work with Zephyr."

"Joan?"

"You offered her to anybody else?"

"I just didn't know if you'd made up your mind."

"It's made up."

"O.K." He hesitated as if he was thinking about asking a tough question, but, if so, he didn't ask it. "Good. We'll do your lesson on her tomorrow."

"That's settled then." I hung up before I could say another word.

The Calm

Timothy was ending his shift. Having made my decision, it was safe to see him again. I caught his sleeve just as he headed behind the Employees Only sign.

"Joannie," he said. "I thought you'd dropped off the face of the earth or something."

"I did, but I'm back now, and I could kill for a burger." He raised an eyebrow, but wheeled his bike out and hoisted it into the back of my truck. He watched me as we drove, but he didn't ask for explanations. I wanted to give him something, an offering of sorts, anything to pay for this patience.

The flowered and flounced curtains in the windows of Eric's Café were grey with grease and dust, and the walls, once white, were scarred black where chairs dug gauges into the plaster. The tables wore waxy green and white checkered tablecloths, but though wiped continually, they too collected grease. What Eric's lacked in atmosphere, it made up for in straw-bendingly thick milkshakes and emu burgers.

Between mouthfuls, I recounted the week: the decision to ride Zephyr, the strangeness of Monday night. When I told him about Jenny cleaning and cooking for her husband before coming to my house, Timothy nodded a single, curt, appreciative nod. "Strong woman," he said.

My jaw slackened. "No. Weak woman. I can't believe she did that, like it was the 1950s and she was Donna Reed."

"Don't you see, though? She put her anger aside and did what she thought she had to, what she thought was her duty."

I stared into his calm eyes gazing at me under the casual flop of hair. They betrayed none of his secrets, none of his unfathomable history. I needed to know if this was really what he expected from a woman. "She made his fucking dinner like some galley slave. He didn't deserve that."

"That's why it's so tough. She didn't do the work because he deserved it. It wasn't about him at all. She made that dinner for some other reason."

"What other reason?"

Timothy dipped his curly fry into fry sauce. "No clue," he said. "Duty? Pride? Whatever it was, you can bet your ass it had nothing to do with him. He doesn't control what she does. That's a strong woman."

I was not convinced. Mayonnaise, tomato, and burger juices had began to run down my hands. I fumbled to pull a napkin from the over-packed dispenser and almost missed Timothy's quiet words. "My mother was like that."

"Sorry, what?"

"Before my father died. She was one of those housewives from the old school of housewives. She had this regimented list of chores. Got them done every day—and best not get in her way if she had a mop in hand." He smiled and laughed, but I noticed the past tense.

I let her past go and asked the safer question. "When did your father die?"

"When I was thirteen. That's when we left Spokane. Why we left. We just couldn't afford to live there anymore, so we went to my mom's family on the rez. She sold tourist stuff at the trading post on 95, and we lived with my grandmother in a HUD house that was falling down around us. It was all a bit of an adjustment." He smiled. "Anyway, housecleaning after a fight? That's something my mother would've done."

"But your father must've expected it, right?"

Timothy snorted. "My father wouldn't have noticed if he had to wade through a pile of dirty clothes to get to the table. His mind was always back at the shop—he owned a shoe store, Llewellyn's Fine Footwear, and he was there practically every waking hour. If I learned one thing from my father, it was never to own your own business. It ate him alive."

I smirked. "So you went into chemistry?" The science professors I'd met worked ridiculous hours. Twelve-hour days during the week, several more on the weekend, always trying to finish the experiment or write the results for one deadline or another.

Timothy smiled and shrugged. "Before Dad died, my mom was every bit as much of a workaholic, even though she never left the house. You should've seen her hands and arms; they were all corded with muscle from scrubbing. And the look in her eye when a stain wouldn't come out? I've never seen anyone look so fierce. I used to think that's how eagles looked when they saw a fish: all hunger and ruthlessness."

The flounced curtains hung limp and pathetic with the weight of grease. Beyond them, the parking lot was full of shoppers walking in and out of the mall. "I never would've thought of a housewife being like an eagle."

"Sometimes people are tougher than we give them credit for." He shrugged. "Sometimes they're weaker." He paused again. An unexpressed sadness hung momentarily in the air, but he smiled it away. "Sometimes they're both." His expression was soft as he said all this, but I imagined he'd inherited his eyes from his mother, the golden brown inflection of an eagle's stare. All around us, tables of people were having their own conversations, laughing at their own jokes, but Timothy's words seemed to weave a cocoon around us so that even in the midst of all these others, we were protected and private.

He pulled a paper napkin from the dispenser and began folding it into triangles. "You know, when we moved back, I heard a lot of gossip about my mom. People said she didn't really want to be an Indian. They said she married a white man because she thought

141

she was too good for her own people, but they were judging her based only on what they could see on the outside. She wasn't one to wear her ethnicity on her sleeve, but she was proud for all that." He unfolded and refolded the napkin, aimless origami, I thought, until he set it up on his plate, a little paper pyramid, a fragile house of secrets. "If they could've seen her like I did, I think they would've stopped talking. She was more Indian before my father died than she ever was once we moved back. When we moved into my grandmother's house, it wasn't my mother who came. It was her husk."

We were silent for a long while. I didn't know what to say. I wanted him to keep talking about his mother, his childhood, about life on and off the reservation. I wanted to know where he'd been and what he thought. I wanted to know him. Talking was like crossing one fence, but one fence alone is easily crossed. It is the combinations, the patterns and their related distances, that create the challenge.

Timothy smiled again and picked up his pyramid, crushing it and wiping his mouth.

"I don't think Jenny's an eagle," I said.

"Ah, but she got her husband to apologize, and even when she was gone, the house was still her dominion." He shrugged. "I've never met her of course, so obviously, I could be wrong—probably am—but from what you're telling me, she's tougher than you're giving her credit for."

"Yeah, well, no man of mine better expect his dinner from me if he pisses me off," I said.

Timothy looked at me with his laughing eyes. "But you never put your identity into your house. Your domain is in the barn, and I don't see your boyfriend keeping you from it."

I winced and looked to the curtained window before he could read my face.

Housewives and eagles—the comparison would have seemed laughable to me an hour earlier. I pictured Jenny, thin and wispy, leaning on Dave's arm and looking at him reverently. There was no power in that portrait—not as I understood it. I couldn't see her becoming fierce at the sight of a stubborn toilet ring. I couldn't see her fragile hands forcefully gripping a soapy rag. And even if she did, could such a meager scope of power really be considered power at all?

But Jenny was getting a horse. She'd married the man she'd chosen and secured them both a decent income, even though her father had hated Dave. If strength was measured in goals met, then Jenny had me beat.

Dr. Rivers hovered all day, seemingly on the verge of speaking. I'd never known him to stay silent when he wanted to speak, and his quiet bumbling made me suspicious. Cheryl was forever raising a single painted eyebrow at any eye she could catch. He had no reason to be around. I waited for his pager to call him back to the ER, but it was unusually slow. It seemed like every few minutes, he was back in Imaging, fingering through filing cabinets, "making sure everything was all right."

The straight-forward problems of the barn were a welcome relief: the teeth I knew were coming, the hooves sure to kick. Dawn was crossing the driveway as I pulled in, an unopened bale of alfalfa in the cart she pushed. A shit-eating grin stretched across her face when she saw my truck. She rested the cart as I got out. "Heard you're riding Zephyr."

"Yep." I squinted off toward the pasture where the mare grazed peacefully. An Eastwood kind of stare. One meant to read, "This conversation is over."

"That horse is wound up tighter than a gnat's ass stretched over a skillet." Dawn was clearly enjoying this.

"She's a little tense."

"A little tense? She charges me when I go into the pasture with her God-damned grain."

I let the words drift into the warm silence of evening, unanswered. Foxfire, on hearing my voice, stuck his head out the stall's outer Dutch door and nickered at me. "Speaking of tense, is there anywhere I can put Foxy during my lesson?" He threw his nose up and down impatiently, and I smiled. "He's a bit jealous."

"Shut the barn door and lock him in his stall run for an hour. That's what I do when I clean his stalls, or else he paces all around me and drives me 'bout crazy."

"I guess that would work, but you know he'll still hear us in the indoor and pitch a fit."

"If you want, I can throw him in Zephyr's paddock once you get her out."

"That might be better. Give him a chance to move, too."

Foxy was listening to us, ears straining toward our voices. Dawn laughed again. "You've got the only horse who gets jealous of work."

"It's not the work he misses," I said. "It's the attention."

"Because you spoil him?" Dawn was forever trying to get me to admit that point.

"I just treat him like he deserves. Anyway, it's not *my* attention that he misses—he's still got that. It's the ring: the silence when he jumped his round and the applause when he went clean. All those admiring eyes. Work is just as close as he comes to that feeling now." And as close as I came.

"Shit, you're depressing."

We stared at Foxy a moment longer. I said, "How much do you reckon it would be to get him cloned?"

"What, you mean like in a test tube? That's fucking creepy, Joannie." She looked at Foxy skeptically. "Not cheap, I bet."

"They cloned some mules at U of I. Racing mules. Now they're winning all these stakes and derbies."

"Yeah, and I'm sure the guys that done it are getting flooded with requests from every rich bitch with a favorite cat. Can you make me a new Cleopatra? I simply can't bear to part with this one." Dawn drew her a's long and round, as if all rich people spoke with bad British accents.

I should take her to Jersey and introduce her to some real money, I thought, but said only, "You're probably right. Still, if I could have him as a six-year-old now, imagine what we could do."

"You don't clone God's fucking work, Joannie." Dawn lifted her cart. "And I told you once already to stop being so God-damned depressing. I'll get Foxy out for you. You go get Zephyr. Maybe that mare'll knock some sense into you. Just as long as she don't knock too hard." Dawn muttered the last words as she walked away.

"Thanks," I called to her back.

She lifted her middle finger and kept walking, not even turning to look at me. It was a gesture of love.

The grey of the mare's coat had gained a faint luster after a week of the high fat, high protein grain Eddie had put her on. It gave her a sheen that, with the lightness of her coat, seemed almost ghostly, as if she was more air than flesh.

There was nothing ethereal about her viciousness. As I unlatched the gate, she spun and ran at me. I swung the halter in a wide arc, defining a boundary she could only cross by taking a blow. She halted just shy of it, tossing her head and rolling her eyes. "Easy now," I said, throwing the lead around her neck to catch her, keeping my elbow cocked and ready in defense.

Zephyr came out of her pasture all hellfire and bone: the bone of each hard tooth, the coffin bone within each ironclad hoof pointing to its target like a driven spear. She danced on the lead rope with athletic grace and balance. I had to convince her to use that athleticism for rather than against me, but I had no clue how to pull that off. Already, the edges of my patience began to crumble. "Walk like a normal damned horse, please," I said. No reaction.

Tugging her would be useless. Thin as she was, Zephyr outweighed and out-muscled me. If we fought a battle of physical strength, she would win. Our battle would be one of wits and strategic strikes. I gave the lead a modicum of slack and then yanked it hard, popping her on the nose to correct her poor ground manners.

Zephyr pulled back against the halter. I let her drag me a little, balancing like a water skier against the rope and raising the spare end of the lead threateningly when she tried to rear. The gravel rolled underfoot, then stopped. She stood, and we regarded each other, standing there in the parking lot, each waiting for the other's next move.

After a moment, Zephyr's head lowered almost imperceptibly as a measure of tension relaxed. "All right," I said, going again to her side, her eye following me. "Let's try again. Walk on."

Zephyr took one step and then threw her body back, sitting on her haunches and tossing her head high.

Again, I held the rope against her struggle, giving nothing. I thought of Clint in the final showdown of *The Good, the Bad, and the Ugly*: the dizzying camera work, the increasingly claustrophobic close-ups, the dirt, the burning cigarillo, the watching eyes. The wait, the wait. The quick draw, the response.

She stood; the dust settled. Again, we watched each other. "You done?" I said. She merely stood, her head stretched high, her breath coming in snorts like some dragon that couldn't get the fire to come but kept trying nonetheless. Behind me, I could hear Dawn chuckling inside the barn door, and behind her the distant mumbling of Eddie's voice directing Jenny's lesson. I said, "I can wait all day, horse."

Truth was, we had twenty minutes to tack up and I needed to get her in the cross ties. I'd timed this as if I was getting out Foxfire. Each fallen dust mote was a second hand ticking. Zephyr's nostrils flared and relaxed, flared and relaxed. Her ears unpinned, flicking forward to catch Dawn's laughter.

"She's laughing at you, you know," I told Zephyr. We continued to stand another moment. When her head dropped a little again, we walked on. For a moment, she was a picture of good manners, but her rebellious eye was on me. We almost made it to the barn door when she spun against the halter, the lead rope burning across my hand as I clamped down on it to stop its slide. I cursed myself for unconsciously relaxing. I dropped my guard; I'd forgotten to put on my gloves. Everyone was right—I was spoiled by Foxy.

Dawn stood at my shoulder and patted me on the back. "Good luck." Her voice was light with choked-off laughter. Zephyr relaxed as Dawn walked away.

"What the hell happened to make you so ornery?" I whispered. Zephyr's eye rolled white and she pulled her head high again, but it didn't last. We walked into the barn.

She managed to grab a piece of my forearm as I snapped her into the cross ties, hard enough to pinch and bruise and graze the flesh. I pulled a jumping bat from my brush box and dealt her one good pop on the shoulder. *Quid pro quo.* The thwack of its broad leather topper was loud and startling, though it had no real sting. The sound was enough. Zephyr shuffled in the cross ties, looking for an out. I aimed the crop at her, like Patton delivering a point. "Don't bite and you don't get hit."

She quieted slightly as I tucked the bat into my tall boot where it would be close at hand. She stayed well back, the cross ties straining in their bolts. I caught hold of her halter and moved her a step forward. "We'll be O.K., as long as you learn some basic manners. Biting me is no good. That's rule one: no biting, no kicking. Got it?"

I glanced at Eddie and Jenny in the ring, but neither appeared to have noticed Zephyr or me. Eddie had laid poles out, and Jenny was trying to coax Zip into a more forward canter so that they'd make it from pole to pole in three strides instead of four. She was getting about three and a half, and that half an ugly bumpy little stride Zip snuck in just before the rail. Under his ever-present cap, Eddie was frowning. "Tempo, tempo," he said in a deep steady voice which tried to mask exasperation as he clapped his hands in the rhythm he wanted to see.

I smirked and grabbed a dandy brush, full of memories of Eddie and me. Zephyr pinned her ears at each stroke, the tossing of her head synchronous with the movement of my arm. When she tried to kick again, I called her "bitch" and swatted her, once, with the bat.

Our lesson was composed in endless circles. One direction, the other: figure eights, voltes, serpentines. Transitions to trot, to walk, to canter, to halt. It was simple stuff, but not dull—Zephyr made sure of that, worming and wiggling under the saddle. Circles, if done well, take the full concentration of both horse and rider. There were glimmers, moments when she actually stretched for the bit. Then she'd remember herself, throwing her head up and back so far it was practically in my lap. Eddie's voice droned through it all, steady and calm. "Half halt. And again. Little more leg. Relax those shoulders, Joannie. Relax. You've got to trust her." His watching eyes never left us. And suddenly, she'd be there again, a horse I'd want to ride. And then it'd be gone, her head up and trot jarring.

"More of this, all week," Eddie said when we finished. I nodded from the saddle, accepting my homework assignment. Zephyr turned and grabbed the toe of my boot between her teeth. I yanked free, inadvertently kicking her hard in the side as my foot sprang loose. She grunted with the force of the kick, but she neither reeled nor reared nor bolted. The mare had guts; I'd grant her that.

Eddie tilted his head, watching it all. "Maybe next time we'll add some trot poles, but for this week, I want transitions. Let's see if we can't get her to trust our hands a bit more and accept the bit." I nodded again and swung down from the saddle. My toes ached against the pressure of my weight and the soft footing.

Eddie walked me to the cross ties. "Short rides, still. No more than a half hour while we get her fit. And *your* job is to focus on your elbows and shoulders. I want much more relaxation out of you. You need to learn to trust her as much as she needs to trust you."

"Whenever I give, she bites my toes." My voice was low, but I knew he heard.

"Give, but watch out."

I sighed. "Constant vigilance."

"Right. Constant vigilance."

I looked at her. "I hate to admit it and Dawn certainly never would, but she actually looks better already. She's got a long way to go, but she's a little less . . . hollow."

Eddie nodded. "She's getting stronger, too."

"Great. That's just what we need."

"Once she gets some muscle over that topline, she might not shrink from the saddle like she is now." He watched me as I removed the old hunting bridle and Foxy's saddle and began to brush her down. His gaze was soft and wise and amused. I picked Zephyr's hooves out and moved to clip her lead on.

"No carrots?" he asked.

"You want me to put my hands near that mouth? Those teeth?"

Eddie laughed. "You need to treat her like any other horse. Treat her like you treat Foxy."

"Foxy is not 'any other horse.'"

He smiled and took the carrots from my box and snapped one in half to offer her on his flat palm. She jerked back in the ties as if he'd struck her, rolling her eyes and pinning her ears at the treat.

Eddie dropped his hand and walked to her side, his eye on hers. He walked her up a few steps and let her stand. Slowly, he raised the carrot in his left hand, stroking her neck with his right. He touched the carrot against her jowl and moved it toward her nostril where she could smell it. Her eye whitened again and she jerked away. "Hmph." (Eddie's short snort.) "She doesn't know what it is."

I shook my head. "A horse that doesn't know what a carrot is. Just 'like any other horse,' huh?"

Eddie ignored me. "We'll put this one in her grain tonight and let her figure it out. She didn't know what apples or sugar cubes were either, but I hadn't tried carrots yet."

I lead Zephyr out. Exhausted, she walked quietly enough now, though her ear and eye stayed trained on me until we reached her paddock. Foxy was running the fence-line, screaming, and Zephyr looked at him with what could only be seen as disdain. I led her in and got him out as she grazed her way toward the back. I mounted Foxy and rode him bareback over the soft loam of the hills, guiding him with nothing but his halter and shifts of my weight. The twilight deepened around us as we returned to the barn. It would become our routine, the post-Zephyr unwinding.

Forge

Timothy had left a message on my machine. Punk chemist indeed; I appreciated the way he challenged a fence.

When I called back, he answered on the second ring. He said, "I'd called to see if you wanted some dinner, but when I didn't hear from you, I figured I'd better just go ahead and eat."

"I was at the barn late tonight. A lesson." It was eight o'clock and I had no food that I wanted to eat. Someone said hunger is the best sauce, and maybe it is, but no sauce can save the limp peppers of a frozen rice bowl.

"How was it?" Timothy asked.

"What?"

"The lesson." There was a smile in his voice.

Where to begin? "I'll tell you over dessert, if you're still interested, but I've got to eat something."

Timothy laughed. A gentle, intimate laugh. A laugh as warm as the receiver pressed against my ear. My smallest bones reverberated, waking the tiny forge in my ear: hammer, anvil, stirrup.

"Where to?" he asked.

"Shit, I'd even eat McDonald's at this point," I said, but quickly feared he'd take me at my word. "No, strike that. I'm not that desperate yet."

"Gyro and baklava?"

"*Yes.*" The man had taste.

"I'll be by in ten minutes," he said, and hung up before I had time to ask for fifteen. My skin was dry and powdery with barn dust and my nose was lined with a hard black crust of dirt-hardened mucus, but he'd left no time for a shower. I washed silt and sweat from my neck, face, and arms. Rivulets of grime coursed down the drain. I'd just had time to pull on jeans and shove a ball cap over my head when he knocked.

The crow-feather hair that flopped over his eyes picked up a hint of starshine. He said, "You changed already?"

"You sound disappointed. I'm sure I still smell like horse shit. Surely, that's worth something."

He laughed again, that lovely sound. "Let's get you fed," he said.

I thought back on our dinner the next day at work. There, amidst my humming machines, I thought of the way he leaned on his hands and watched me eat, waiting to eat his baklava until I'd finished my gyro. His imagined presence, the remembered conversation, the taste of seasoned lamb, feta, and cucumbers warmed the sterility of Room One.

I had told him about Zephyr and showed him the bruise on my arm, the broad red where she'd first gotten hold of me, the thin blue line where her teeth had pinched before I'd yanked my arm clear. He had laughed, the glint again in his eye. "Tell me again why you like this sport?"

I had smiled the question off, then was startled to realize he was waiting for a reply. The flip answer was at my lips, but I didn't want to push Timothy away with insincerity. I paused before answering, "It makes me feel real."

"Real?"

"In touch," I tried. "In my body." I shook my head. "I can't explain it." I looked away from him, pretending to study the invented hieroglyphs that decorated the walls of Mikey's.

Timothy didn't drop it there. He was really trying to understand, but how does one explain obsession? How does one explain faith? He asked, "Real or corporeal?"

I met his gaze. "Is there a difference?"

Now, Timothy paused and reflected. "The difference, I think, is passion."

The hieroglyphs were painted in browns and blacks, as were the pseudo-Egyptians marching around the room. I'd always found them comfortingly amateurish—the proportions off, even for primitive figures. There was no message in their movements, nothing offered in their empty hands. "Real, then, because that's the passion part, right? That's the part that's more than just physical."

"Like the difference between sex and love," he said. His voice had been smirking, but I couldn't read the smile on his face.

He was baiting me. There could be no unthinking conversation between us. I let baklava honey rest on my tongue, and raised my guard.

"Tell me about your boyfriend," Timothy said.

"Not tonight."

Again, he regarded me, at once calm and thoughtful. The challenge in his gaze latent, but there.

Sitting in the dark of Room One, this was what haunted me. Instead of building truths between us, I had been constructing more walls. Joan of Arc: castles and keeps. I had made a fortress of myself. For what?

There weren't many patients that day. Some stomachs early in the day to prep for surgery, an appendix, three knees. Herman Kraus was in the ER again with another possible heart attack—the fourth chest x-ray I'd given him this year. He got crankier every time. Having four x-rays apparently entitled him to tell me how to do my job; he instructed me how to line up the portable unit and complained about everything: the weight of the apron as I swung it on (*Christ, Joannie—are you trying to sterilize me? Damned if that wasn't dead on the nuts.*), of the nurses' slowness (*Did they forget to brew the coffee today, ladies?*), of the lack of attention with which he was served (*Hello? Ladies?*), as we all buzzed around him and attended to his comfort. Outside ER, I knew Kraus to be a nice guy—a retired insurance man. I'd often passed him in the afternoons as he walked his Bichon Frise, the small white poof of a dog that was his only family. Pain brought out the ugly in some people.

Just before the end of my shift, Dr. Rivers walked into the lab. For once, he hadn't slicked back his hair. Its relaxed wave framed his forehead, styled as if for an L.L. Bean catalog, with none of the ease or naturalness that I'd seen on the morning of the bike ride.

"Joan, I was looking for you."

"You found me."

"Ha, yes." He ran his hand through his hair, then fiddled with his name tag, straightening it although it was already straight. "Nothing pressing. I'm having a small get-together tomorrow night. Bread, cheese, a little wine, that sort of thing. I, um. I thought you might want to stop by."

He straightened the expensive pens in his coat. "Sounds nice," I lied, wishing for a ready excuse.

"Great." He took out his prescription pad and scribbled his address and phone number on the back. His hand shook as he wrote. I wondered if all the gel and stiffness was just an attempt at self-protection, a layer of veneer to protect himself from the pervasive miasma of sadness that floated around the hospital, mingling with the scent of disinfectant. It didn't make him any easier to take.

"What time?" I said.

"Eight-ish?" He held out the small square of paper.

"O.K." I looked at the slip. "Good lord. Don't you doctors ever break stereotype? Is this a four or a nine?"

He moved to look over my shoulder and held my hand within his warm hand, turning the scrawled writing toward him. I couldn't remember him ever touching me before, even casually. His fingers were soft, long, straight, and slightly feminine, tipped with clean, manicured nails—perfect for surgery or playing piano.

"Four," he said. "And no, we don't ever break stereotype. Bad penmanship is part of the Hippocratic Oath. In the footnotes."

Without cracking a smile or waiting for a laugh, he removed his hand from mine and walked out of the room.

In the morning, I ran. If there is evidence of the existence of God, it is the human foot. My vertical tower of not quite six feet of moving flesh and bone should not be able to balance on that meager foundation. When we run, an area the size of a dog's paw contacts the earth. It defies physics and exists well beyond our own rational thought or intentionality. In a million thoughtless adjustments of muscles, the spreading and unspreading of toes, shifts in weight, we not only stand and walk but run. No merely human inventor could manufacture so finely tuned an engine.

In high school, I'd once argued with Mouse's jerk boyfriend about whether horses or motorcycles were a better all-terrain vehicle. He'd said that motorcycles don't buck off their riders. "Sure they did," I'd replied, "but when motorcycles put you in a ditch, they don't head back to the barn to let people know you're hurt." Horses jumped walls that stopped a bike, and they did not poison the world with toxic fumes or deafen their riders with their noise. The engine of the horse was more sublime.

But thinking of the human foot, I realized that neither horses nor motorbikes were as versatile, as adept, as capable as an unaided human. Neither could climb a tree, or scale chain link, or rappel down a sheer face of rock. With time and stamina enough, I could traverse just about anything.

I reminded myself of all this that morning, trying to convince myself that getting through Dr. Rivers' cocktail party would be no big deal. At the moment, I'd rather prepare for an Everest climb than find clean and presentable clothing to wear. My arms, covered with Zephyr's bruises, would have to be covered.

I was terrible at these things. The first cocktail party I'd been to in Jersey, the barn's Christmas party, was a lesson in East Coast formality. I'd gone in jeans and a nice sweater and arrived to find myself amidst the sequined and silked; a duckling amidst swans. I felt destined to make a similar gaff tonight.

I arrived a half hour late, but only three couples were there so far: an OB/GYN and her husband, an older couple I recognized from photographs of the hospital's board, and a small tan man and his wife who introduced themselves, immediately, as being from Nepal. They did this repeatedly through the evening, each time one of them met a new person. *Hello, I'm Janak and this is my wife Melina; we're from Nepal.* I came to think of this as their function at the party: to be the couple from Nepal. To be glamorous. To be exotic. To show how kind Dr. Rivers was to have invited them. What an open-hearted man he must be, their presence said. He'd met them on the Wheatland Express, the bus linking Moscow, Idaho, with Pullman, Washington. They'd "hit it off," he said.

And what demographic was I representing tonight?

I balanced a heavy crystal goblet in my hand and tried to think of anything to say that would make me appear intelligent and funny, but the familiar tension had settled into my shoulders. Eddie would tell me to *relax, relax.* How I wished he was here—how I wished anyone was here whom I could talk to. I asked the couple from Nepal how they liked it here, realizing as soon as I'd said it that the question left them no choice but to say they liked it a lot. "You don't have to," I said, trying to break from the conversation's script into something more natural. "I don't always like it here." The couple looked at me oddly, and I suddenly felt myself a spoiled American, complaining about an idyllic land where I held crystal goblets and ate proffered Stilton and grapes. They edged away from me.

The house was beautiful. Along one wall, paintings hung, spotlit by recessed lighting. They were real paintings—not prints, but oil on canvas. I tried to picture the artists who created these modernistic pieces, full of color and movement, but I couldn't see any suggestion of the creators in the created. Along another wall, stained glass windows, apparently recovered from demolished churches, hung on invisible wires. Overstuffed sofas, overstuffed chairs, overstuffed ottomans were placed to allow conversation, their patterned cushions coordinated with the intricately patterned rugs that lay at angles on the gleaming cherry wood floors.

Everything was the essence of good taste: old fashioned glamour toned down with burnished bronze mood lighting. Coltrane slid from speakers I couldn't find. The walls themselves seemed to be speaking in jazz. Had Dr. John Rivers chosen the ebony elephant on the mantle, pearls for eyes and tusks that might have been real ivory for all I knew? Was it an antique store find, or had he haggled for it in some dusty foreign market, or was it simply mail-ordered from the latest issue of some catalogue for the fashionable wealthy? My favorite orange easy chair would have been rejected here, too old or not old enough. It wouldn't withstand the rigorous attention of spot-lighting without revealing itself to be what it was: shabby. Yet at that moment, I would have taken it over all the too stuffed, too perfect chairs in this trophy-case of a room.

I drank my glass of Shiraz too quickly. The weight of the empty goblet hung on my hand. Obvious and pathetic, I stood alone without a soul to talk to. Even the couple from Nepal was doing better than I was. They chatted amiably with a small woman whose frizzy hair was poorly contained in her French twist. For lack of anything better to do, I moved toward the oil paintings, pretending to examine them with something approximating interest. The paint had been laid on thick—too thick, I thought, for the lightness of the moving swirls of color. I wondered what Dave would have thought of it.

"Enjoying yourself?"

I hadn't heard Dr. Rivers approach, yet he stood at my shoulder, watching me examine his painting. His amused smile struck me as self-satisfied.

"You're out of wine," he said, taking the glass from my hand. "Let me get you a top up." He left me again, alone and awkward, only more so now—abandoned. There was no one here I knew. No one from my station.

Dr. Rivers was back with a full glass and a plastic plate with fresh mozzarella, basil, and tomato stacked on melba toast, an appetizer so ubiquitous at New Jersey doctors' parties that even here it struck me as cliché. I took the glass and plate and thanked him. The fresh mozzarella was as bland and pretentious as everything that surrounded me.

"I'm glad you could make it, Joannie."

"Why?"

He laughed, and this time his laugh was genuine. It was a laugh that dismissed my question. I'd become merely original: clever, rather than sincere. He patted me on the shoulder, and let his hand linger there a moment. I looked at him, trying to work out what this all meant. Dr. Rivers did not like me; that had been a cornerstone to our relationship since I first started at the hospital. I'd been hired fresh out of school, and he'd immediately disapproved, constantly finding fault with my work, which even early on had been better than average.

"Well," I said, "I know you've got a lot of important people to mingle with. I won't take up your time."

He looked stung, but he didn't say anything as I turned from him.

As a child, I had played the game of opposites. The opposite of up is down, in is out, black is white. If there was an opposite to a barn, it was this party. I missed the silence and sincerity of horses.

I stood at the edge of a circle of surgeons telling familiar jokes. Lawyer jokes were a staple of hospital life. They were all too predictable to laugh at, but plied with good wine, the surgeons were practically doubling themselves over. Without a scalpel in hand and a body to save, they moved with more ease, joyous in this freedom.

I finished my second glass of wine as quickly as the first. The alcohol was starting to work on me—I hadn't realized just how large the glasses were, how very much they had held. I went into the kitchen to put my glass in the sink and slip out. This room was built for beauty as much as function. Long granite countertops gleamed along the walls under rich cherry cabinetry and brushed steel lighting. The man himself leaned against a Viking stove, casually chatting with members of the board. Dr. Rivers was so relaxed in the midst of it all, smiling warmly, his wine glass in hand held as casual as an afterthought.

The clouds of alcohol were rolling in, and I wanted to get home. I caught Dr. Rivers' eye, waved, and mouthed "thank you," trying not to disturb what I imagined to be an important conversation.

"You're not leaving?" he said, interrupting the board member's wife in the middle of her story. If she was offended, she hid it behind a red lipstick smile.

I shrugged and mumbled something about being tired.

"Do you know Joannie Edson?" he asked the couple, waving me into the group. "She works in Imaging—takes the x-rays that let the surgeons know what we're getting ourselves into."

"I just do my job," I said, embarrassed.

"Best x-rays I've seen—better than we'd get when I interned in Seattle—and I can't tell you how much we rely on those pictures. We almost lost her to New Jersey. Did lose her, I should say, for over two years, but I think I speak for many of us when I say we're grateful she's back."

I didn't know what to say. He'd never been so forthcoming with praise, but we'd never talked about my x-rays in front of people he needed to impress.

"You ever think about going back to school, Joannie?" the woman asked. "Medical school, I mean."

"You could go into radiology," her husband added.

"Don't you two give her any ideas!" Dr. Rivers said. "We just got her back, and now you'll have her leaving us for school." They all laughed.

I was superfluous to the conversation, a topic rather than a participant. Perhaps they hadn't meant to patronize me, but it chafed. I put on a smile. "I'm sorry, but I really do have to go. Thanks again for inviting me." I turned to the woman smiling at me. "It was a pleasure meeting you."

But I hadn't met her, not really. I hadn't even learned her or her husband's name. Nor had they met me. The person they met was a cardboard cut-out of Joannie Edson, a life-sized paper doll skillfully cut for their amusement by the good doctor. I'd done my job: as always, I'd provided the picture that was needed.

Phantom Actualized

Sunday morning, my mother's hands regained feeling. I stayed for an early breakfast and left when they went to church. I hadn't known how much I had worried until that worry was removed. Now, I thought I might go see Timothy.

My eyes never left him as I waited in line, so I hadn't seen Dave walk up with his case of Bud and bag of Cheez Doodles. I didn't know he was a step behind and listening as I asked Timothy if he wanted lunch. I didn't see his face blanch, then purple.

Timothy saw it all: an unknown man setting down his groceries and turning on his heel, pacing a moment at the aisle's end, as if looking for a manager, and storming off. I merely saw Timothy's eyes move in that direction and then return to me while I counted the dark eyelashes that framed each eye. He'd smirked. "I can get a break in a half hour." The phantom lover could waft into so much smoke and mirrors. The wall I'd built could crumble. I peeled the Butterfinger I'd bought as an excuse to stand in Timothy's line. Life could be as sweet.

Dave sprang on me as I walked out into the sunlight; the candy bar flew from my loose grip and broke against the pavement. The grip of his fingers on my forearm pressed deep into Zephyr's last bruise, spinning me on my heels into his close face, twisted in rage. "Who the fuck was that?"

I still reeled in his grip. "None of your business."

For a moment, Dave didn't speak. The veins, already visible, grew larger and deepened their hue. "You think it isn't?" His voice was closer to an animal's growl than anything human. Zephyr's bite throbbed under his hand as he pushed the bruise in deeper. A middle-aged woman in a faded "Yellowstone" tee shirt looked at us through photo-grey spectacles, their dark glass beginning to lighten under the shade of the awning. She hurried into the store, while Dave pulled me out into the sun, into the fire lane, into the parking lot, muttering, "You can't do this, Joan. You can't."

"Let go of me."

"I fucking love you."

"You're married." I hissed the words, conscious of the stares upon us like we were playing out some twisted episode of *Mutual of Omaha's Wild Kingdom*: The lion claims his mate by grabbing her by the nape.

"Yeah, and you're messing with her head, too."

Dave's shag of hair hung over savage, brutal eyes. I'd never been so aware of the sheer power of him—how tall, how muscled. My heart beat against my ribs as if I'd been sprinting for miles, but I knew the ways of animals. The battle does not always go to the larger or more powerful. I made my eyes harsh, generating a sneer of unforgiving disdain. I settled my weight into my feet, centering my balance. I found my teeth and claws.

His fingers dug again into the meat of my arm as if he meant to tear directly into the muscle itself, and he pulled me again, dragging me through the parking lot. In a not small but small enough town, this was exactly the type of thing that could get back to his father-in-law and to Jenny.

"Let go of me." As I struggled, his fingers only dug deeper between bicep and triceps. My skin stretched and burned. I tried to kick but lost my balance, feet skating on the blacktop skree. The new security guard ran from the store and toward us, a blur of tan polyester.

Dave flung open the door of his truck and tried to stuff me into the seat, as if I were a sack of meal to be thrown over a mule's back. My head cracked against the door's frame, and I felt the warm ooze of blood. The world was suddenly blurry and distant and slow-moving, but the door had bounced on its hinges as Dave had flung me in, and had hit him in the shoulder. More acting than thinking, I grabbed this moment of divided attention and kicked him in the balls with every ounce of strength my leg had to offer. Not an upward kick but almost a stomping motion, a mule kick.

I hadn't kicked a guy there since grade school when it was little more than a game, an anatomical curiosity. How the boys would crumple at the slightest blow! They, who lorded their strength over us, were so easily defeated. It had all come back as I watched Dave fall. My head rang, aching where it hit the door frame. "Don't you ever touch me," I said, my voice choked and guttural.

I stepped over him, fetally curled and rolling on the asphalt in his sad little letterman's jacket. Once he was a man to admire, a man with potential, now he was grasping at straws and missing even them. The security guard slowed, arriving late and now unsure of what to do or who to help.

"My fiancé," I said, unsure what possessed me, "didn't like the cake I picked."

"Oh," he said, staring. My eyes were elsewhere. The cloud-free sky stretched high and far beyond him, beyond the square brick solidity of Rosauer's. The autumn winds were starting to gather and gust, rattling the drying leaves on their trees and lifting them free.

I got into my own truck and drove home. My heart would not stop its terrible beating, and yet I now felt no fear. It pounded within; a primal drum, a cadence.

My head throbbed. This would kill Jenny if she knew, and she would know. I had no doubt of that. Maybe not today, but if Dave couldn't keep quiet any better than this, she'd know someday. I paced my blank apartment, drinking cup after cup of black coffee. I should have met Timothy hours ago.

Bars of late afternoon light stretched through the vertical blinds and across my living room. Light and shadow only, but bars nonetheless. I was caged.

I filled a bag of ice for the lump on my head and lay on the sofa, staring upwards, fighting to find my bearings, my sense of self, hating my weakness. Dust clung within the crevices of the cottage cheese ceiling. A long fuzz-coated strand of old spiderweb hung from an air vent gently waving in the seemingly still air of the apartment, marking time like an odd kind of metronome. If dust is mostly made up of dead skin particles, whose shed body clung to my ceiling? Was it my own dead body I was staring at? The metronome continued to swing.

It was after five when Timothy came, his face a shadow behind his wing-black hair. "Jeff told me about the parking lot."

"Jeff?"

"Security."

For a long time, neither of us spoke. We sat listening to the ambient noise of the parking lot, the distant clatter of pots in the apartment above, the lives unfolding all around us with their own private triumphs and disasters. We were small in the world; little more than specks of dust.

Timothy didn't look at me when he spoke. "So that was your boyfriend."

I didn't answer. I was looking at the sweater he wore: khaki green with patches on the shoulders, an army cast-off. Dave's clothing read as costuming. With it, he created the person he wanted to be. There was always the element of construction. Timothy's clothes were at once more and less personal. Shirts fit him as perfectly as if they had been tailor-made, but the clothes didn't make the man. An old army sweater might have looked gimmicky or self-conscious on anybody else—a persona adopted. On him, it was only functional and appropriate. Like his tattoo, it suited him and offered a suggestion of the man inside, but only a suggestion. More was concealed than revealed.

"I'd half hoped," he said, then stopped. He started again, his words coming more slowly and carefully now, as if he was hand picking each from a garden of words, not wanting to bruise them with rough handling. "I half believed," he looked at me with a penetrating gaze, "that you'd invented the boyfriend."

I sat up. Timothy should not have come. Dave was crazy, and I was a head-case inventing boyfriends out of, what? Stubbornness? Fear?

Timothy's gaze challenged mine; there was strength there. If I could trust it, if I was willing to combine it with my own, if I was willing to partner with him as I had with the strength of Foxfire and now Zephyr, then maybe I could navigate a way through this mess. But Timothy was a man, not an animal to be harnessed.

I looked away from his fierce, intelligent eyes to the salmon that jumped on his neck. He said, "The rumor at the store is, you're going to marry that guy. They couldn't stop talking about it. Your secret lover. They said it was typical of you not to tell anyone, but I still can't make myself believe it. That you'd marry that guy."

I never could tolerate being told what to do. Dave had tried, and now here was Timothy, judging me for what he decided were my bad decisions. "Why shouldn't I, if I love him?"

"Do you love him?"

"Shouldn't I?" I watched Timothy's eyes, looking for a flinch of pain. "He's good looking. He's got money." I wanted to see him feel something about this, but his gaze merely rested on me with their same relentless calm. "I can handle him."

"Your soul can't possibly respond to his."

Again, he'd surprised me. Who, aside from the religious, talked about the soul? It was a word even more mistrusted than the words "God" or "love." I disowned that piece of the trinity of self. Body and mind were easier.

Timothy studied the door. "To marry him would be to degrade yourself."

"Let's assume Dave—his name is Dave—could buy me a horse to carry me to the Games. Would I still be degraded in your eyes? If, by marrying him, I could actually ride in the Olympics and represent my country, then I'll have done something I couldn't do in any other way. Is it strong or weak, making a choice like that?"

Timothy met my stare, absorbing my words as steadily as if they had no power against him. His shoulders neither slumped nor tensed. His brow remained unwrinkled by anxiety or frustration. He shook his head. I'd laid down a dare, yet he wouldn't speak. I thought, *He communicates a passion his lips will not speak, and I respond.* But how could I be sure of that? It was a stupid thought, a silly, romantic thought. If I could know he was willing to risk that passion with me, I might have braved all Dave's psychotic rage to claim Timothy's love.

I was being foolish. He didn't speak, and I'd been wrong about love before.

Timothy said, "I have to leave Moscow for a few weeks." The words were bullets to the gut. "My mom's sick. She called me just after I spoke to you; it's why I was so long in coming. I'm driving up tonight."

"Don't go," I said before rational thought could stop me. All the lies I told about marrying Dave had come out in a strong, true voice, but now, my voice was little more than a whisper. My head pounding, all I wanted to do was to be weak. I wanted to crawl into his arms and forget about horses and Dave and my mother's next unpredicted attack.

Timothy said, "You don't need me here."

"What if I said I did?" The words were selfish and I immediately regretted them. I couldn't see Timothy dropping everything for any sickness. If he was dropping everything mid-semester to go see her, it had to be something serious. Before he could answer, I said, "No, you need to go." I took his hand and squeezed it, "Just promise you'll be back."

He nodded, his hair once more shadowing his eyes so that I could not read them. He did not look back at me as he rose to leave, my own lies winging him from me.

IV
Lightening the Forehand

Maintaining the horse's natural balance is of primary importance in riding. This in turn depends on the rider's ability to bring his own center of gravity into synchrony with that of the horse. The rider's position, as well as his weight, must be adjusted to the horse's movements; usually by the rider placing his body directly above or ahead of the horse's center of gravity, depending on the horse's velocity.

—Bertalan de Némethy, *Classic Show-Jumping*

When the blackbird flew out of sight,
It marked the edge
Of one of many circles.

—Wallace Stevens, "Thirteen Ways of Looking at a Blackbird"

More Rivers

The autumn winds began to blow; they were early. Water had made the Palouse, flooding from Montana when the Ice Age's glaciers broke, carrying the silt of Lake Missoula westward in a sudden, unforgiving sprint to the ocean. The wind has been shaping it ever since.

All that week, Dave's truck had been parked at the end of my block when I got home. I watched him watching me. It was pointless to move again or change my number. The new address, my emergency contact information, would always be posted on Foxy's stall.

Because the world was rich with danger, I tacked up Zephyr rather than Foxy that Sunday. The mare was becoming subtle in her violence, and the rate at which she learned was frightening. She was a more intelligent horse than Foxfire, a difficult thing to admit. It was becoming easier to betray him. Yet unlike Foxfire's intelligence, Zephyr's worked against our training. She thought to find the best evasion or to discover a moment when my guard against her savagery was dropped.

Taking her out of the barn was reckless, but I was feeling reckless. I wanted to test her, to see what she'd do. Afraid that Eddie might disapprove, I hadn't asked permission. If nothing happened, he couldn't object. She needed training. And if she laid me out on some field? So be it. At least that was a problem whose solution was clear.

We had made progress. Wednesday, I'd managed to give her a carrot without losing any fingers. She'd taken it with a quick dart toward my hand, then pulled up and away, carrot still held between her teeth, as if I'd follow the treat with a blow. She'd hold it there five seconds, ten, like an orange cigarillo, before finally drawing it in and eating what my hand offered. It frustrated me, her reaction. I wasn't asking a lot of her, just a little speed and power. In return, I traded grain, carrots, a pasture to run in, a good and easy life. I would pick the shit from her hooves and wash it from her tail. All she had to give me was an hour of control, an hour of her power and speed.

Foxy screamed when I lead Zephyr in. Dawn just looked at me, sighed audibly, and resumed grooming Sunny with a dramatic show of resigned tolerance. Jenny was too absorbed in her own excitement to notice Zephyr or even, more incredibly, Foxfire, who was now rhythmically pawing at his stall door. Listening to him broke my heart, but what was his agony to her? She'd be trying out a potential horse that afternoon.

Zephyr added a fresh bruise to those already marking me. The saddle brought its usual reaction; she shrank and sprang.

We were no sooner down the road than a combine crested the hill, harvesting directly along the roadside. Dust and chaff spewed forth in a dense brown fog. Dawn turned, wide-eyed. Sunny and Zip had grown up around farm equipment, but Zephyr had not. It churned toward us, looming ever larger, shining dazzlingly in the morning sun.

I nodded Dawn on, and she and Jenny were consumed by the dust cloud. Zephyr stopped and snorted, then reversed quickly, scooting straight backward while still facing the machine. I pressed my calves to her flanks, and whispered in a low tone that was at once menacing and taunting, the voice the devil speaks when he wants your soul. "I thought you were brave. Come on, now. You can't let Sunny and Zip show you up." Zephyr stopped backing, but she was shivering violently—for the first time, she was afraid. Her breath came thick and fast and she raised her head up and back toward me. I held the reins firmly against her neck and kept my leg on. If she was going to run, it must be forward. She twisted her raised head against the rein, turning to look me in the eye. Hers was white with terror. I stared at her utterly calm. She crouched so low on her haunches that she was practically sitting. "Zephyr," I said, reminding her of who she was. I took my eye from hers and looked down the road for Dawn. The thick and billowing dust advanced, the red block of the combine moving steadily closer.

The moment I looked forward, Zephyr sprang. Pelted with wheat chaff that stung like hail, she ran blindly through the cloud as if it were some plague of locusts. For Zephyr, there was no end in sight. Entering the cloud, we sprang into blindness. We'd bolted directly into fear.

The horses were stopped twenty yards up the road. Zip pulled stray grass from the ditch. Zephyr and I flew through the cloud, but on seeing them, she slowed. We drew up next to them and she blew the dust from her nostrils and shook it from her coat like a retriever shaking off the lake.

"She came through," Dawn shook her head. "I thought sure you'd have to take her back to the barn and get Foxy."

Foxy had never entered my mind. Even in the thick of it, I'd had no thoughts of wanting to be on any other horse but Zephyr.

The horses ambled up the road, all the excitement over. Zephyr insisted on being in the lead, and for now, I let her. Once in front, she relaxed slightly. Her ears still strained toward every sound and her body felt as tense under the saddle as twine stretched to the snapping point, but she didn't dance and didn't spook. Even when a quail dashed out from a small cluster of pine and practically under Zephyr's hoof, she merely snorted and stomped her foot down, sending the bird in a wobbly sprint back to the ditch. Focused on the outside world, Zephyr forgot our antagonism. She worked the bit between her teeth and tongue, salivating like a dressage horse.

Dawn looked at her, shook her head, then looked at me. "You ever ask that grocery store guy out?"

The world seemed to fold inward; I was the center of its crushing origami. "No." I willed myself the calm he held in his gaze, the steadiness in his voice. "He must have switched shifts. I haven't seen him."

"You're a bad fucking liar," Dawn said.

I didn't comment.

"He sounded perfect for you," Jenny said.

He was, but I couldn't see how anything I'd said could have told her that. "Keep clear of her feet," I said.

She moved Zip over. "Even Dave's been asking about you. He said he couldn't believe you didn't have a boyfriend, what with how pretty you are and how smart. I was sure that guy would turn into something."

Dawn looked at me with her hard, appraising gaze. No matter how I tried to lacquer my face in indifference, she could always see through it. She'd see the pain now in my hard stare.

"I like being single," I said.

"Bullshit," Dawn said, under her breath. Then louder, "People like being single because they can date and have fun. You haven't had one date since coming back from Jersey, and don't tell me there haven't been opportunities."

"What the fuck do you care?" On television, girl talk was light and fun; it didn't hurt like this.

Dawn turned to Jenny. "You go out with her sometime and watch how the guys react. The men throw themselves at her, and does Joannie notice?"

"They're an unnecessary distraction," I said.

"From what? You going to the Olympics on that?" She gestured at Zephyr and snorted. "Face it, Joannie, you're using horses to dodge out of living your life."

"Horses *are* my life," I muttered. "If I meet a guy who makes me feel what they do, I'll be the first to let you know."

"You did, Joannie. You should have seen the way you lit up when you talked about that guy. You know you can't shit me."

"Yeah, well, it didn't work out."

"Fine. Just don't lie to me, Joannie. You lie to me and next thing, you'll be lying to yourself. Maybe that'll work in Jersey, but it don't slice mustard with me." Already, the red was draining from her face.

"I'm sorry," I said. "You're right." We paced on a bit. Jenny looked confused. It was unfair to talk like this in front of her, putting her on the outside. I said, "What's this horse you're looking at today?"

"He's a Quarter Horse out in Lewiston."

"Color?" said Dawn.

"Bay."

"Wait," I stopped and turned to Jenny, "Hobbes?"

"Yeah, you know him?"

"Good horse," I said. "Sensible." I hadn't realized Pam was selling him. He was perfect for Jenny. A blood bay with gleaming flanks, though built a bit like a fire plug, at least compared to the lithe elegance of Foxy and Zephyr. He'd be thirteen or fourteen now, and would reliably jump three foot six or more. Pam had ridden him in third level dressage before I'd left, and he'd be doing at least fourth by now. She'd be asking a high price, but Jenny would be hard pressed to find a better trained horse in Idaho.

This must mean, too, that Pam was buying Eddie's Winston. Or, worse, that he was setting her up to buy Zephyr. A sudden surge of possessiveness surprised me.

"Is Dave going with you to look him over?" Dawn asked.

Jenny's faced blanched. "Dave," she cleared her throat. "Dave's been acting a little weird lately."

"Weird how?"

"Oh, I don't know. It's probably nothing. He's been sneaking cigarettes, again. I found a fresh pack of Marlboro's in his work shirt this week, but his shirts have smelled of smoke this past month, you know? More than if he'd just been hanging out with other guys who were smoking on their break. He knows I hate it when he smokes. And last Sunday, he went out to get some stuff for the football game and came back in a *mood*. Said some guy cut him off on the road, but he didn't have any of the stuff he was supposed to pick up. He just sat there all afternoon lighting matches and letting them burn to his fingers. I haven't seen him do that in years. Now he's making comments about how maybe we can't get a horse after all, but I know him well enough to know he won't go back on that promise. If I mention it to Daddy, he'll set him straight." She paused and blushed, aware perhaps that she'd said too much. "I doubt it will come to that. He's probably just angry at one of the guys at work again. He'll come around. He always does."

The conversation buckled in as tight as a straight-jacket, a sudden vision rose before me: Dave and Jenny in bed together, her legs wrapped around him, her fingers in his hair, drawing his lips to hers. His hands, the ones that had stroked my own bare hips, crushed her to him. I could still taste his unlit cigarette in my mouth, but it was Jenny who got what she wanted in the end.

I don't want Dave, I reminded myself. Sunny swung a little close, and Zephyr aimed a kick at his side. It missed, but barely. "I'm going to run her a bit," I said. "See if I can't get some of the piss and vinegar out of her."

Without waiting for a response, I asked for a canter, and after three good, balanced strides (the best I'd felt on her), we turned to jump the bank paralleling the road. It was a relatively short bank, a little over two and a half feet at that point, but we cleared it at an angle with feet to spare, a powerful, round, perfect jump. Dawn's faint "yahoo" followed us over the bank, and then all I could hear was wind as we galloped the field, a true hand gallop.

My God, she was fast! A blood horse, a racing thoroughbred. Her legs extended themselves in impossible strides. Zephyr, indeed; we were the wind. I looked to the horizon, ever-distant but now seemingly attainable. Zephyr's breath came in oxygen-rich snorts, cadenced to her stride. Our fused body was something mythological, something more than centaur; an unwritten thing, beyond physical possibilities: wind and blood and bone without corporeal limitations. We flew, all four hooves seeming to hit the earth simultaneously in the incremental nanoseconds between our stretching bounds. We skimmed through air along the earth's uppermost crust like angels of the Apocalypse, traveling at the speed of God. Ethereal.

I squeezed the right rein slightly, turning her uphill. My own breath came in gasps, the muscles of my legs working in time with hers to maintain my balance. My lungs burned in my chest as if my legs were the ones doing the sprinting. I gently reined Zephyr in as she slowed with the incline of the hill, remembering only then to fight a little, tossing her head against the bit. Up the steepening incline, we went from gallop, to canter, to trot, to jog, then turned and walked back to the girls. I gave her a long rein and she dropped her head low, sides heaving under my thighs.

We'd covered a startling amount of ground, and it took some minutes to get back in sight of the girls. I waved when I saw them trotting over the field toward us. They waved back and I could make out their faces, smiling—no, beaming. I, too, was smiling uncontrollably. This was joy; *this* feeling.

Jenny was laughing. "I've never seen a horse move so fast!"

My cheeks hurt with grinning. I only nodded. Adrenaline pounded within, capillaries expanding with its surges.

"No shit." Dawn's voice was pitched high with her enthusiasm. "She's a bitch on wheels—but damn, what wheels!"

Zephyr snapped at Zip, whose head was nearly in range of her teeth, but the snap was half-hearted. I turned her, both of us still panting, and we continued our ride. Though we never went faster than a walk all the rest of the way home, I floated on the power of that round jump, the rhythmic pull of those enormous strides. Talent—Eddie was right. This horse had something, if we could get to it, if we could make her trust us. This horse could be my ticket. I didn't ask to what.

The combine was on the other side of the field when we arrived back at the barn. Zephyr didn't deign to even look over; she merely snorted her disdain and walked on. My hips dipped and swiveled with the movement of her back, and I pushed her from one leg to the other, asking her for the leg yielding Eddie had assigned as this week's homework. She moved grudgingly, walking sideways but trying to lead with the shoulder rather than truly curving around my leg. For two strides she got it, and I called it good enough.

When I pulled off her saddle in the barn's cooler air, steam rose from her back. The muscles were filling in over her withers and haunches. Foxy paced as the aisle's end, nickering now as if pleading for me to get him, his nickers hoarse from his earlier screaming.

Eddie pulled in as I led Zephyr out. We walked up to his open window. He would notice she'd been worked hard. Despite careful grooming, her fall-thick coat showed sweat marks, the rippling of drying salt that my damp cloth hadn't totally erased. "How's our girl?" was all he said.

"She's good. Better than good." Best to fess up. "I hope you don't mind, but I took her out in the fields today."

Eddie was impassive. "And?"

"And we should work her out there more often. It's good for her. It's like, with so much else to look at, she stopped worrying about me so much and actually yielded a bit."

Eddie looked at his mare.

In my excitement to tell him of our success, I was holding her on a loose line, as I would have led Foxy. She hadn't bitten me. Instead, her ears were perked and her gaze was off on the hills behind us. "I'll put her back," I said. "We can talk more if you want."

Eddie shook his head. "I've got to get our Miss Jenny up to Lewiston to check out this horse." He settled his eyes on mine, commanding my full attention with that look. "I'm glad you took her out; you two have made some progress today. But next time, you call me first."

"Sure thing." I understood perfectly: she was his horse, and I wasn't to forget that. "I'm sorry I didn't call this morning. A split second decision."

Eddie merely nodded, and I led Zephyr back. Even after everything, the world was still permeated with the euphoria of that ride. I'd hoped to stretch it with an easy ride on Foxy, but he felt old and stiff in the cool of that morning, his legs stocked up from a night in the stall. His arthritic trot was becoming more jarring. I slowed him to a walk and closed my eyes, remembering how he used to move. His canter had been as comfortable and rhythmic as a rocking chair. Strangers used to come up to me at shows and say they liked even *watching* him move, his textbook stride: his canter so good it gave a vicarious thrill. Now, he leaned and tripped in that gait, guarding his hind legs from pain. I hadn't asked for a canter in weeks.

I was folding laundry when the pounding began, the fist on my front door, the monosyllable of my name moaned long, "Joooan, Jooooan." Dave lowed the word like an ailing cow.

I slid on the chain and unlocked the deadbolt, realizing as I did so that it was the first time I'd ever used the chain on that door. As I turned the knob, his weight flung the door hard into my hand in a movement so sudden that the chain sparked as it went fast. Every link strained against him. How thin and flimsy that chain looked against his strength.

"What's your problem?" I hissed.

He laughed mirthlessly at this. "You. I can't stop thinking of you. I can't get you out of my brain." Bourbon and cigarettes hung in the air like a halo around him. "It hurts, Joannie. It needs to stop hurting like this."

I edged back. His face, pressed through the narrow space in the door's opening, was speckled with gold light, the reflection of the chain stippling him like a trout. Timothy's fish was more permanent, I thought. Timothy's fish was no fool's gold. "This is sick."

Dave's eyes were somber now, and held the sadness of an unbearable wisdom, the desolation of a prophet who knows his truths will not be believed. "Don't you remember what it was like?" His breath was molten: slow, dangerous, burning, inevitable. "You understood me. You could talk about intelligent things. Politics, literature. You'd listen to me. You respected me. No one does that now." He pulled back from the door slightly, and I lost his face to shadow. Not seeing him was more terrible than seeing him in pieces. I stared, mesmerized, pulled by his strong gravity.

"What about Jenny?" I said, my voice little more than a whisper.

Dave's voice was thick with alcohol and warning. "You don't know a thing about Jenny."

"I know she's sweet and beautiful. I know she dotes on you."

"I'm just a tool to her. A way to get money out of Daddy."

"That's unfair."

"Is it?" His face illuminated again as he pressed it forward, twisted by the seething cocktail of whiskey, anguish, and rage. "You think *she* could work as Daddy's foreman? You think he'd have that? You think I'd still be around if she could?"

"She worships you." It was taking more will now to force the words out. I tried to think again of Timothy, but he was far away. "You're all she talks about."

"Yeah." He gave a low, mad laugh that went straight through my spine. "I'm all she talks about at home, too. She doesn't have another thought in her head. Do you know how boring that is? Or she talks about you and the horses. I don't know which is worse torture." He punctuated the words with a blow to the door that jerked the chain and made it hum. "I never wanted this life."

"Bullshit," I said, but my voice was low and soft, its edge blunted by sympathy. I tried again. "Stop feeling sorry for yourself. If you hate your life, then do something about it."

"Don't you see, Joannie? That's why I'm here. I've got a bag in the truck and I'm ready to go, but you have come with me. We can start a new life. I'll go back to school. I'll do my life over again, the way it should have been."

"You don't need me for that."

"Don't I?" He paused a moment to let the smoke clear from his voice. When he spoke again, his words were clearer. "If you're not there, then what's the point?"

I tried to think of a way through this spinning logic. "It wouldn't work."

"We could both be so happy."

"No," I said. "We wouldn't." It helped to speak the words. Hearing my voice speak them made me realize they were true.

"Yes," he groaned the small word big.

"People aren't happy. Maybe they are for moments, but it doesn't last. That's just how it is; we always end up wanting something more. You were happy with Jenny once, and now you're not. It would be the same with me."

"You don't believe that." The chain was level with my eyes, straining on its bolts, one slip away from everything changing. I could slide it backward, slide backward with it.

"I don't love you," I said, trying to reduce everything to one simple truth. The gold flecks played over Dave's tan face, and I thought again of Timothy, wondering if he'd ever feel the love for me that Dave felt now. What would he do to love me, if he decided to love me?

Dave's eyes were half-hidden in shadow. "Unlock the door."

I backed a step but said nothing.

"Sometimes, I want to hurt you, Joannie. Sometimes, I want you to feel just a little bit of the pain I'm feeling. Just a taste. Then you'd understand. Then you'd come with me. That's fucked up, isn't it? But sometimes that's how I feel."

I did not know which way to move. I'd felt that way myself. I put a hand on the wooden door between us, heavy with the weight of him. If I were to let him in now, would it lessen the guilt I carried from losing Mouse?

"I thought I could live with it," he said. "With our affair being over. At first it seemed like the weeks we had might be enough. Like I could live on the hope for little moments like those."

The jumps in the course, I thought, *the temporary flights.*

"But then, when I saw you again that night at dinner, when you were so close again, right within reach, and then hearing about you from Jenny all the time, and about the new guy you're seeing, something had to change. Every day is worse than the last."

But this wasn't about me at all; it was about a way out. I was only the thing he equated with freedom. He'd made me into a pair of wings.

"I could buy you a horse," he said, the desperate or despairing words rasping in his throat. "You don't need anything that's here. All we need is each other." Each word was quieter and less convincing than the last.

The door started to shake on its hinges; he was sobbing, the muscled bulk of him resting on that too thin door. No sound escaped him now. He wouldn't let me hear his grief.

And then, the chain went slack. It took me a full minute to realize he was gone. When I did, I fell into my orange armchair, letting its protective arms curve around me.

I stared at my hands, far at the ends of my arms: their dirt-stained calluses, their pronounced whorls, the bitten and broken fingernails. The knuckles showed sun damage, the elephant skin of a lady far older than twenty-seven. If destiny was in the hands, no palmistry was needed to make mine clear. These were not hands formed for love.

I rose and went to my truck. The whining roar of the aging belts as the engine turned over was a cry I felt but would not voice. I drove to the barn, empty of all but the horses now, and I groomed Foxfire. At every stroke, his coat burned redder, rich with oils, burnished.

He leaned into the soft brush, then rested his broad skull against my chest while I stroked the brush behind his ears. The long-tailed star on his nose resembled nothing so much as the star that hung over that long-gone manger and gave it place. I knew then what I'd always known: When a horse trusts you enough to rest the weight of that skull against your chest, you can't help but be changed. Your heart absorbs the warmth of a creature of the land, and that warmth spreads within your arteries and veins, and your feet relate to the soil on which they stand. Not everyone who rides can love a horse, but you can see this understanding in those who do, those elect whom the horses choose.

I moved to Foxy's side and he rested his heavy head on my shoulder, his windpipe against the side of my neck, our jugulars communicating warmth as his hot breath wafted over my back in its ancient rhythm. One of the heard.

Leaving the Comfort of Fire

My parents had a fire going in the wood stove, warming the house. Mom had wheeled her chair next to the sofa we had forever. The patchwork slipcover she made years before was soft with time and the slow wear of bodies. It was threadbare at the seams, the batting visible through thin fabric—particularly in the corner under the lamp where she had spent so many nights sewing. I collapsed in her old spot, tracing the pink vines of a favorite bit of calico with my hardened fingers. I hated to see her in that chair.

"You look tired," she said.

"Tired of this town." My tone was too harsh, but the knitting needles stayed busy in my mother's hand. How often I'd seen her just like this, inscrutable, her wild hair frizzing and glowing with fire. She'd never aspired to anything more than this, but the chair was never part of the dream. I stared hard at the wheel inches from my leg. I said, "I'm thinking of moving again." I realized even as I said it that I was testing the idea out, that I needed to know if that escape was still possible.

"Back to Jersey?" Her knitting needles kept going, but in the flick of her eyes, I knew she was reading me, my expression, the slope of my shoulders, my casual hands.

"Maybe not so far." I hadn't understood Jersey, and it hadn't understood me, but maybe Spokane or Seattle had something to offer. Her chair was every reason I had to stay and a good part of the reason I wanted to leave. She'd learned to do everything without me. She wanted me to succeed where she could not. If I was going to have a shot at success as an athlete, hadn't I better find a way to that success? Wasn't that what my mother wanted?

But even as I'd said I might go, I knew I couldn't. Not now. It didn't matter whether Mom needed me. I needed her, and I needed Dad, and I needed Idaho. I needed its coldness and its open spaces. I leaned back and stared at the fire flickering in the grate. "It's just tiredness talking. I'm not going anywhere."

"If you need to go, you know you can." She stopped and looked at me, assessing, then returned to her knitting. For now, at least, her hands were working. MS was fickle. She stopped and laid a hand on mine. "Either way, you'll make the right decision."

"Which decision is the right one?"

"The one your heart tells you to make." Souls and hearts: She was as bad as Timothy. She patted me on the shoulder and wheeled away to help my father in the kitchen. My heart was silent on the matter.

I traced the stitching on the sofa arm. My mother spent months piecing the squares: driving her slender silver needle through all these hearts and roses, stabbing the iconography of love to make something real and functional and lasting.

Pilate nudged his cold nose under my hand, and I slid to the floor to pet him. His fur was soft and clean as always, but it had grown coarser with age. I remembered the loft of his first fuzzy puppy coat, and the silk that grew in its place, and it seemed unfair that I should witness the whole of his life, that he should age so much faster than I.

Dave talked of my intelligence. If I was so smart, what the hell was I doing?

Pilate looked at me with absolute adoration and trust, like he knew I'd always come back to love him. His gaze was wise and patient. The white blaze that ran down his nose reminded me again of the miracle of animals.

I hoisted myself up. In the kitchen, Dad was layering lasagna noodles with his famous spinach, tofu, and feta blend and ladles of thick marinara. Mom grated mozzarella and Parmesan into a steel bowl in her lap.

My father glanced at me. "You want garlic bread?"

"Do you really need to ask?"

Dad nodded to a stick of butter, bulb of garlic, and a homemade baguette. I smashed a dozen cloves of garlic under the flat of my knife with a fist as swift as justice, peeled them, and diced them into a pulpy mass. It was good to smash something. I beat it into the softened butter and added salt and pepper. The bread knife slid through the loaf with the ease only a good knife can provide. I'd been wrong to think Jenny's choice of life at home was necessarily that of a caged bird who doesn't know how to stretch her wings. A house isn't always a quiet prison. My mother looked at me and smiled. Housewives and eagles. She'd found all the food she needed in this small habitat.

This is what "home" offers: a tattered quilt, a warm dog, the functional violence of cooking.

My routine swallowed each day, chewing through the hours with the patient persistence of a grazing horse; it should have been easy to forget Timothy. He owed me nothing. I had made sure of that, putting Dave between us, building him rail by rail, a wall so thick that he couldn't see through.

But, by God, Timothy *did* owe me something. If souls could connect, like he said, then surely ours had. And if he couldn't feel my need, then all his soul theories exploded. Romantic pap and bullshit. Hearts and flowers—the things that die.

I rode Zephyr more in his absence. I needed a good dose of Zephyr. If nothing else, the mare knew how to protect herself. She knew how to persist. Whatever they'd done to her, her previous owners had eventually given up because she simply and forcefully refused.

All in all, she was coming along well. We stayed inside and did our homework as instructed: circles, transitions. Her bones were becoming less visible now that muscle rounded to cover them. With the added strength in her back and neck, she'd began to round up into the saddle rather than shrinking from it, and she gave to the bit for longer stretches. Her trot was becoming steady and scopey, her legs reaching endlessly forward with each stride. If she didn't succeed as a jumper, she'd have a decent shot at dressage. Her athleticism and movement suited that disciplined sport, even if her temperament did not.

A series of sounds wafted through the open barn door with fall's crisp breeze: heavy wheels crunching the gravel outside—a truck, weighted. The engine cut. Car doors. Voices. The long, complaining screech of metal doors opening. A horse trailer. Hooves and feet scuffling. Light and shadows poured through the barn door.

Eddie led Hobbes in, followed by Jenny.

"Hey there," I called.

"Hey yourself," Eddie called back. "And how's our girl today?"

"A champ. You know, I doubted you when you said she'd show by spring, but I'm converted."

"Ah, Joannie," he smiled under his mustache. "Your faith in me should never falter."

I did a few more transitions. I said, "She's smart, this one."

Eddie snapped Hobbes into the cross ties while Jenny ran to tell Connie that her new horse had arrived. Zip would return to pasture now, and Hobbes would take his stall.

"Vet check done already?" I asked.

"This morning," Eddie said. "Pam offered Jenny a two-week trial, and we decided to go ahead and start it."

The gelding was looking better than I remembered. Even after a half hour trailer ride, his coat shone deep red, lustrous as mahogany. If we did show in spring, I was looking at the competition. The realization came like a pistol report, sudden, arresting: I might lose to Jenny. Jenny! Only months ago, I showed her how to ask for a canter, but Hobbes would soon carry her over the same rudimentary fences I would have to train Zephyr to cross. In her custom boots and new breeches, Jenny looked like a winner.

I cued Zephyr to halt, then canter. She sprang like a coil, driven by the haunches. *We wouldn't lose. Not if I could help it.* But no sooner had I thought this than Zephyr planted her front feet and ducked her head, nearly succeeding in dumping me. I slid onto her neck, but grabbed mane and kept myself from being pitched headlong.

At that moment, Jenny returned with Connie. "What are you doing?" Jenny asked, laughing, as if this was some crazy new drill she hadn't run across yet. My cheeks flamed with anger and embarrassment, the grasped handful of hair the only thing that had kept me from the dirt.

Eddie only chuckled. "Dropped our guard, did we? Keep that leg on."

I shot him a nasty look but didn't comment. Zephyr trotted off and I slid back into the saddle. "How was the vet check?"

"Good. She said he'd popped his left splint at some point, but she and Eddie said that's nothing to worry about."

Connie laughed. "You're starting to sound like a real horsewoman. Popped splint. Doc's right—that's nothing. Half the horses in this barn have a popped splint, including Foxfire if I'm not mistaken."

I nodded, irritated that I had, once again, to concede that Foxy was anything less than perfect.

Point Hobbes at a fence, and he'd find the distance and make the jump. Jenny had months to build the balance and strength to hang on. While I was slowly building Zephyr's fundamentals, Jenny would be clipping along on her living hobby horse, collecting blue ribbons. It was a lesson I learned in Jersey: Money always beats talent.

"What's the scowl about?" Eddie was smiling.

"Nothing."

Transitions. Trot to halt to canter. Canter down the long side. Extend the stride. Think of Timothy—the death of his father, poverty, the childhood on the reservation, the quiet fight for an education, the channeled rebellion. Halt. Transition to walk. I had nothing to complain about. These were only fences to cross. Half halt to collect, and canter. Extend across the diagonal. Watch for Zephyr to plant herself. Hear her thinking it. Flick the whip when she does.

Zephyr reared in response, but I kept my seat this time. Eddie watched from fence-side, his eyes crinkled with amusement and pride. "Very good. Remind her now so she keeps going forward when the fences come." We trotted, and walked. I gave her her head.

She had the bone structure; she had the bravado. If she knew she could jump a big fence, would she? If so, how long until she was out of my hands and on the market, priced where I couldn't afford to dream of her again?

Jenny brushed Hobbes and led him into Zip's newly vacant stall. Out with the old, in with the new. I was as bad, putting Foxy out in Zephyr's paddock so I could ride in peace.

Eddie unlatched the arena gate and walked over, patting Zephyr on the shoulder. He looked her in the eye, then smiled and looked up at me. "How are things?"

"With me or Zephyr?"

"I already asked about Zephyr." He smiled and shook his head. "You're scowling again."

"Things are fine."

He looked at me sideways, determining his line. Finally, he said, "Still too much tension in the shoulders and elbows. Keep working on that."

Zephyr wouldn't love jumping like Foxfire did. That part of her heart was too scarred to beat again. Maybe she was never that kind of horse. Instead, I hoped she'd see each fence as an affront and jump it with the disdain it deserved. I hoped she'd see herself as better than all of it, constantly proving herself superior to the striped wooden poles, to wooden boxes painted to look like brick or stone, to artificial flowers, and to shallow blue liverpools. I wanted to harness her anger and put it to work.

All that week, I dreamed of Mouse, the same recurring dream. I was alone, sitting in the passenger seat of the Pod, a seat that, in the entire time I owned the Pod, I never sat in. Its worn vinyl seats were cool to the touch, its blue dashboard dulled with sun and dirt. Timothy pulled the latch to the driver side door, and had just moved to climb in when Mouse appeared, stepping in front of him and pushing him back. She turned the ignition and the car purred with life.

"Let him in," I said.

Mouse turned her smile on me, each tooth a shining bone. Underneath her skin, the death's head of her skull was momentarily evident, then vanished again. "He's not part of the journey." She pressed the gas. In the rearview, Timothy stood with Dave and John Rivers. In front of us was a brick wall.

I grabbed for the steering wheel, but the distance grew longer than my arms could reach. I screamed for her to stop. When we hit the wall, she flew. The wall evaporated, and her thin cotton dress carried her like wings across the surface of the earth, while I lay in a heap, powerless to fly.

At work, Don Bridges, the local rep for Jackson Medical, was the only excitement. He was a salesman to the core, but we all looked forward to his rounds. His voice brought me out of my cave to the reception desk.

"Joannie, Joannie," Don beamed. "Still single I suppose."

I shrugged and smiled.

"No young man with a twinkle in his eye?"

One young man with too much twinkle, one young man without enough. I only shook my head.

"Great looking gal like you? What is this world coming to? Never would've happened in my day." He reminded me of my grandfather, my dad's dad. "I thought for sure you'd find some hotshot surgeon back east and we'd never see you again."

"You sorry I didn't?"

"Me?" He looked at me with gentle but distant eyes. "Nah," he said. "You three gorgeous gals are the best part of my rounds."

Cheryl's eyes shone with the compliment. She'd been carrying a torch for him for years. "Don," she said, "are you flirting with us?"

Tread lightly, Don, I thought.

"Now you know I can't say that I am, not with all this sexual harassment hooey, so I'll just say that you three make it hard on an old man, looking more beautiful every time I see you."

"Boy," I laughed, "you must be selling something *really* expensive today."

Don smoothed his neck-tie, over-playing being offended to show how little offended he really was. "Joannie, I'm hurt you'd think I'd stoop so low."

I was about to retort when Dr. Rivers appeared. He turned to me as if about to say something, but appeared to think better of it. "Don, you must be looking for Nathan."

"He just popped over to accounting," Cheryl said. "He'll be back in a tick. No need to rush off."

Don looked at Dr. Rivers and then at me, smiling slyly. "Any twinkle there?"

I shot him a nasty look. Dr. Rivers looked at Don, then me, and cleared his throat. "Well, I'm sure we've all got work to be done."

"Right," I said, and slumped off back to Room One, trying to decide if it was a cave or a chrysalis or merely a stall.

In the late afternoon, light slanted through the barn door. It gleamed in the dust like gold, like the color of Timothy's eyes.

Hobbes trotted along obediently, mouthing his new Herm Sprenger KK Ultra loose ring snaffle bit, which cost triple the price of my best bit. No amount of money could still the bounce of Jenny's inexperienced hands and the meaningless Morse code they sent to Hobbes' sensitive, knowing mouth. He carried himself anyway.

I brushed at the manure stains on Zephyr's sides with the quick hard strokes that she'd grown to enjoy. Why did all greys roll? Hobbes rocked into a perfect canter. Jenny beamed from his back. "Why didn't anyone tell me riding could be this easy?"

Because it's not, I wanted to scream. *You didn't train that horse. You aren't the one who made his neck arch, who helped him learn to reach underneath himself behind, who taught him that carriage and confidence. You only paid for it.*

At a slight pressure, Hobbes transitioned from canter to trot to halt, his feet perfectly square underneath him. A dressage judge would salivate over such perfect foot placement. A solid eight, if not even a nine. I could see their scores adding up, the tests they would have.

Zephyr kicked me, the hoof deflecting off the leather of my half chaps. I glared at her and swung the saddle pads on her back as she danced below them, snorting and tossing her head. We would work outside; I wouldn't talk to Jenny that night. I would simply wave as she drove out, smiling as if I meant it, pretending I felt no jealousy, riding in the darkening light. I wanted my barn back. Jenny could go to hell; she could take Dave and Hobbes with her.

At home, I chopped vegetables for stir-fry. I made extra rice for easy leftovers, and foresaw a future of forever eating alone. *Fine,* I thought. Look at what reaching out had done: the trouble with Dave, and now with Jenny. Zephyr and I had a bad ride. She took advantage of my distraction to remind me of all the reasons we would never be a team. I was foolish to put my hopes on such a horse. I could already see us lined up in the ring, being placed by the judge; Jenny in first; me, empty-handed. "No one ever told me it was so easy," I mouthed. A summer in the ring, a pocketful of cash, and she'd be the one with the blue ribbon flapping. She, who'd never sacrificed a day in her life, who bitched and moaned when Eddie had her ride without stirrups, who'd never broken a bone on a fence, who'd never taken an iron-clad kick and stifled pain in a clenched jaw, who pouted over that tiny scratch she'd gotten on Zip, *she* would be serious competition.

I pulled a partially frozen steak out and began my ferocious slicing. The hot oil seethed in the skillet. I'd worked too hard for too long only to be back at the bottom. The knife clip, clip, clipped against the cutting board, neatly cleaving each slice under the pressure of my hand. Flesh divided. What I had put asunder, let no man join together. I dropped a handful of beef in the skillet and began slicing the remaining half, listening to the crackle and hiss of ice in oil. Dave would have bought a winner for me, if I'd asked him too.

Love was a promise for idealistic fools. The knife, keen at hand, cut on sure and steady. I'd made my bed. I'd chosen my course and would not diverge. Dave was a madness, a sickness to excise. I threw my palm into my work, the blade sharp and true. Hobbes' burnished coat hung red in my glare. It colored everything.

I couldn't say whether it was the ring of the phone that caused my hand to slip or whether I simply misjudged the final cut. The two things seemed to happen simultaneously. The knife was deep before I felt it: a long cut down the inside edge of my index finger. The callus built from years of reins against skin along with a good bit of the flesh below it now flapped loose, exposing the finger's meat as hundreds of capillaries opened at once. The phone rang again. I watched the finger bleed, my stomach collapsing. I was lucky to have missed the joint. I was lucky not to have cut fully through. I'd severed the finger nail and the top edge of my finger cleanly in a cut that ran from nearly the center of the top of my finger and down to the edge of the first knuckle leaving only the scantest bit of skin. I had no memory of stopping the knife short of its job, but I must have.

The phone rang again and I picked it up with my good hand. I couldn't feel its plastic in my hand. Only my eyes told me I held the receiver.

It was Timothy. "I just got back into town," he said. He was far away. He wasn't a real person. He was a specter I'd conjured.

My mouth worked, but I couldn't call a word to mind. I gripped the side of the counter. "Hello," I managed, but the voice was not my own.

"Joannie, are you O.K.?"

"Not," I said, but I couldn't think of a word to follow it. I stood for a moment, then moved the phone to its cradle. Was that right?

The world folded in again, full of smoke and hissing. I pushed the chunk of my finger that had hinged away back into its place. Blood coursed down the side of my arm in a narrow stream. I tried to focus. I ran the hand under water, every nerve objected to the sting. I grunted and flinched. My ears were full of ringing phones.

With a sheet of paper towel, spattered with hot oil, I pressed the finger closed again. The white bloomed geraniums of blood. My hand pulsed and my stomach fell. The kitchen I stood in was distant and falling. Tiles receded under foot; the counter swung away. I caught at it, the trailing edge of paper towel picking up the flame of the gas stove. The fire leaped up at me, and I fell, my knees failing. I stomped at the paper towel with my paddock-booted foot, but I misjudged and crushed my hand with the flame, smearing dirt and horseshit into the wound.

I couldn't stifle a cry. The scarred linoleum tiles refused to steady themselves beneath me. The blood was lurid in the kitchen's florescent light, but my head was wrapped in cotton. It fogged my vision and muffled sound.

I closed my eyes, swallowed hard, and waited for the white fog to roll away, but it persisted. My finger throbbed, the paper towel wrapped around it now blood soaked. My legs shook as I tried to stand.

In the fog, Timothy stood before me. For a moment, it seemed I dreamt him there.

"You're white as a sheet," he said, holding my arm in his warm hand. He led me to a chair, then faced the kitchen. He pushed the skillet off the burner, turned off the stove, and opened the window, fanning away smoke from the burning oil. "What happened?"

My whole body felt cold and I couldn't trust my voice.

"How long have you been bleeding?" His eyes traveled the paths of dripped blood over the tiles.

He was so far away. "It seems like you're coming from a whole other world," I whispered.

"I am." A rueful smirk played over his face, then vanished. He peeled the paper towel back; already it had began to stick.

A moment later he was patting my face. "You still with me?" He smiled as my eyes opened. "You fainted," he said.

"This is ridiculous." I was shocked by the quavering weakness of my own distant voice. "Blood doesn't bother me."

"This is your own blood. It's different." He rose and soaked a new paper towel, gently sponging it around my wound. "Shit, Joannie. It's like you took off half your finger. We'd better take you to the hospital."

"No," I said. Dr. Rivers would be on shift. I looked at the ceiling and took in a deep breath. Pride pushed back some of the clouds. "Butterfly closures," I said.

Timothy's eyebrows rose. "Are you serious?"

"There's a first aid kit in the bathroom. Under the sink. Blue tub."

"Joannie."

"I know what I'm doing." I smiled weakly. "Trust me."

Timothy emerged a moment later carrying the familiar plastic box. He pried open its scuffed lid and shifted through tubes of bacitracin, packets of sterile non-stick pads, assorted gauze, rolls of ace bandages, various widths of medical tape, and boxes upon boxes of bandages. His lashes lay dark against his skin as he dug through the neatly ordered boxes.

"Stop, stop." I pushed him gently aside. "There's a system." I plucked the butterfly closures from their dedicated position and shifted the other boxes back into place. The work helped; it was as if putting the box in order helped order my thoughts as well.

Timothy was smiling, though worry still hung about his eyes. "Does one person really need this many bandages?"

"You've obviously never been to a horse show." I ran my hand under water, gritting my teeth as I again rubbed soap into the door of flesh that swung obscenely open on the skin. I felt stronger. Timothy's hand on my back gave me strength. My finger bled, but that too was good. Blood would clean out bacteria; the body's logic working when the mind failed. I squeezed a bead of ointment in. It was easier to work, now, almost as if someone else's hand was at the end of my wrist, and I was merely its doctor. Timothy handed me clean towels, and I daubed as he taped me shut with the small white closures.

Timothy looked at the open box and sighed. "What next?"

I handed him a non-stick pad, a thin roll of gauze, and white medical tape.

"I can't believe that you of all people won't let me take you to the hospital." He applied each with the speed and skill of a field doctor.

"How's your mother?" I said. "Better?"

"My mother is dead," he said, low and matter of fact. "To tell you the truth, it feels like she's been dead for years. The only difference is, now, we can bury her." His face was dark, and he didn't meet my eyes. This was forbidden ground.

"I'm sorry." I had taken a wrong turn; I wanted to back up. "I didn't realize."

He cut the last strip of medical tape and gently smoothed it down. The throbbing pain spread into the entire hand: too much blood. When he looked up, his face had grown still darker. "How are the wedding plans?"

I didn't answer.

He sighed and held up my finger, turning it to inspect the bandage. "You sure you don't want to go to the hospital?"

"They'd just do the same thing you're doing, only they'd charge a few hundred for it."

He sighed. "He's not your equal."

"I know."

"So why marry him?"

"Who says people marry for love?" I thought of Jack Stewart's words: *You're young, you're attractive* . . .

Timothy still wouldn't look at me. A ball of twine was lodged under my ribs in place of a heart; a single strand of twine connected it to a ball lodged under his ribs. Now, as he pulled away from me, the string sung with tension. It strangled the ball in my ribs, pulling it hard and tight as a fist.

If I completed the lie, I would live with that rock of broken string within. It would be the ultimate freedom. I need never feel guilty for not coming straight home from work to see him or make dinner, or for staying in a cramped apartment while I frittered away money on horses. There was power trading a heart for a fist of string.

But when Timothy turned, his eyes were no longer cool water. "You don't feel that way. You can't. I've seen you speak of horses. You couldn't submit to a man like that. You can't tell me you'll be reined and harnessed. I don't buy it."

"Timothy," I said, but nothing followed. I was empty of language.

"Joan." He pulled a chair in front of mine and held my hand in his, examining the fresh bandage. "I have no right to say this, but you owe it to yourself not to marry that guy."

"To myself?" He needed to give me more than that. "I owe myself a horse and a shot to ride against the best."

His eyes flashed like light on steel. "You're not one for the easy path."

"No," I said quietly. When it came down to it, we were, both of us, punks. That was fundamental, and what was fundamental about us understood what our surface refused.

"I can't sit by and watch you do this and say nothing." His wing of hair folded over his eyes, but still I could see them blaze. "It's like watching a piece of myself be bought and sold."

A piece of himself. He'd finally spoken words that mattered. "Where are you going?"

He said nothing but grabbed the doorknob. My finger throbbed with a thickening pulse, but I laid that hand on his arm. "I'm not the one who should be here," he said.

"If not you, then who?"

He was silent and unmoving as stone.

"Do you really still believe there's someone else? It was a lie built up with stupid rumors. I don't know why I let you believe it. Maybe because I couldn't believe you actually would." The words rang with reprimand. No one else had ever looked at me and seen a love of horses and knew what that love meant. If he could read me so well, how dare he think I'd stoop to Dave?

And then, I remembered. "You didn't, in fact. You told me so when you first saw Dave. Until then, you had never believed I had a boyfriend. You'd seen the lie for what it was, and you saw me." He'd known me better than I'd known myself.

Timothy's eyes were still clouded with doubt.

I softened, feeling the tears at the corners of my eyes and refusing to let them fall. "I protected myself with that lie, and I protected you. I'm always going to put horses first; I don't want to put you second. You deserve better than that, better than me."

"You let me decide what I deserve." He swallowed and turned his fierce gaze on me. The fish on his neck seemed to move as if slipping a net. His face held incredible resolution, incredible strength, but in that moment it struck me that it was not a strength that would be used to trap me. He was an outlaw. He was a cutter of nets.

Wreck

Car wreck: five people from a head-on on 95, just north of town. The truck had jack-knifed and its driver was bloodied but was able to drive away. The four family members in the passenger car that hit him weren't so lucky.

The father and toddler were on the right side of the vehicle and fared best. Her booster seat had held up well, and though she had minor abrasions and her neck had already began to tighten from whiplash, she would be O.K. Her healthy screams echoed off the walls of the ER. The father, too, had whiplash and lacerations, and had broken his wrists bracing against the dash. The mother looked battered and broken everywhere. Their six-year-old's seat belt, not fitted to his small body, had failed him. His arm was severed at the shoulder where he'd wrapped the seatbelt under his armpit to keep it from rubbing on his neck, and he'd been tossed around the car as it ricocheted off the truck and swerved over the road. The EMTs clamped the axillary artery, but that only slowed the flow of blood and he'd lost so much. A steady drip puddled on the gurney sheet next to his body where his arm should have been.

He was my charge. I lifted him, gently pulling the sodden bedsheet up to slide x-ray plates under his body. He felt invertebrate, a jellyfish. His face was swollen and full and dangerously pale from lost blood. My cut finger pounded under his weight, though his body felt bird-light. I lowered him onto the plate, careful to move around the arm he no longer had, as if touching its absence could cause him more pain.

Our senior year, Mouse was wheeled into this very ER to breathe her last breaths. Her casket had been closed. Some long-gone tech had lifted her body, some since-retired doctor had tried to close her wounds, but the floor on which his blood puddled was the same. She would have been heavier than this boy. She had longer to grow.

I blinked away the thought and asked the nurse to dim the room lights so I could better see the positioning light and maneuver the portable unit quickly in the race against his fading pulse while they prepared another transfusion. The glass imbedded in his skin and blood-stiffened hair made him shimmer. His hair could have been any color: white blonde, red, black. The darkened blood removed even that small marker of his individuality. He was anybody's child. This wasn't Room One. There were no individuals here, only bodies to treat. That's how we made the ER bearable.

I adjusted the machine. Had Mouse's hair been as stiff and un-readable? Clavicles, sternum, ribs, face, spine: We would focus my machine first on the core, locating lung-puncturing bone shrapnel, giving the doctors in OR a map of his internal terrain so they could plot their course. I took my pictures and jumped out of the way to allow the doctors and nurses to go to work, but not before seeing that the boy had began to cry blood. The red hemorrhaged from his tear ducts over his eerie, still face. I hoped he was not inside that shattered vessel, feeling this pain. I wished his soul reprieve from its body.

Timothy would be in class now. P chem. What knowledge was there to cope with this?

The sister's wails rung against the walls. She formed her sobs around calls for her mommy, her daddy, her brother. The cries went straight to my bones, ringing them so that I felt like shattering as well, collapsing internally, like a glass in response to that perfect, terrifying note.

Dr. Rivers leaned over the boy. He paled at the sight of his patient, and his face set with resolve. His hair, stiff with gel, gave him uncompromised vision. Stony-eyed and unflinching, he looked more like an automaton than a feeling human being; he worked with inhuman precision and speed.

Primeval groans from the boy's father echoed off the walls behind the curtains that hid his son from him. *He can feel the loss of him. He can feel him dying.* It was not a medical thought, not a professional thought. "You need anything else?" I asked.

Dr. Rivers gave a curt shake of the head. They would send the father up once they'd given him painkillers and cut off his shirt.

Mouse's grandparents hadn't arrived at the hospital until her pulse had stopped. We got there right after them, but no one would let me see her. It made me crazy to be forbidden. I had cursed them all—my parents, her grandparents, the doctors and nurses—but I couldn't make them let me through.

I walked out of the ER, concentrating on my sneakered feet not running as the weight rolled through them with each step, crossing the waxed floors silently. My nails, raggedly short as they were, bit into my palms. I focused on inhaling steady lungfuls of antiseptic air. *Relax,* I told myself, *relax,* but all I could see was the glass-glimmered child who would not make it: the softness of him where bones should make him hard, the bruises purpling, blooming larger with transfused blood. The mortician fixes what the hospital can't repair, but Mouse's casket had been closed.

I dashed to the bathroom and vomited the toast and milk that had been my breakfast, fighting to remember that the boy might not die and that Dr. Rivers, for all his personality glitches, was a damned good doctor. If anyone could save him, he would. Where there was life, there was hope. All the clichés.

I rejected this softness in myself. I cupped my hands under the faucet to rinse my mouth and realized that I still had my gloves on. I stared. I couldn't believe I'd forgotten them—I should have torn them off when I was done with my patient. It was so old a habit, I usually did it by rote. It wasn't like I'd never seen an accident victim before.

Anger began to flow, building low in my knees and washing upward, hot as blood: anger at the kid for being in the wrong place, anger at his parents for not making sure he wore his seatbelt properly, anger at the mother for forgetting her car was a lethal weapon, for letting it drift. For God's sake, a twenty dollar booster seat might have saved him! It was stupid fucking waste, that was all. Just like Mouse. Their lives were blank: the outlines of promise that would never be realized. My mother would have pointed out the joy they brought, the way their love affected the world, but I couldn't make the equation of love and loss balance. It would have been better if they had never been born to the world at all. The love they created only made the pain more searing for those who lost them.

I stared at the wall, and willed myself to be as hard and blank and impermeable. Anger was better than sadness. Angry, I could work. I set my jaw and wiped my eyes to prepare myself for Room One and its everyday miseries, its stream of complaining patients unconcerned with the fact that I was trying to help.

I tore the purple gloves from my hands. The boy's blood had stained my bandaged finger through a pin-sized hole in the glove. It wasn't much—barely enough to notice. I squeezed my hand into a fist. I would carry those cells, that microscopic part of that boy, with me.

I glared at my image in the mirror, tucked a stray hair back, and returned to work. Anger hardened around my eyes into a decent mask.

Patients crowded the waiting room, grumbling over their wait. Cheryl sat at her desk examining her nails. My jaw clenched, and I pulled on a fresh pair of gloves. What a waste of space that woman was! "Sounds like a bad one in ER," she said.

"Yes."

"We won't be seeing Dr. Rivers today then." She sighed audibly. "Too bad—you'll miss him."

I knew I shouldn't bother, especially in front of patients, but I turned on my heel and walked back to her, leaning so that my face was inches from hers. "Would you care to explain what you meant by that?"

She didn't look at me. She just patted the back of her lacquered curls. "Nothing. Just, you two seem awfully close."

"I just came from a room where a family is fighting for their lives." My voice was a whisper, my face inches from hers, trying to retain the last shreds of my professionalism. "If you want to sit here and make idle speculations about some perceived attraction between me and another employee of this hospital, then that's your deal, but I am not in the mood, so keep your comments to yourself."

Cheryl turned to Doreen. "I must have been awfully near the mark to get that reaction," she said, tittering like an over-aged girl to show there were no hard feelings.

"Just send back a patient," I said, turning away. I would have slammed the door to Room One if it could be slammed. Instead, it heaved a heavy sigh behind me as air left the tube that slowed its shutting. I rubbed my forehead, feeling where my mask had cracked, where emotion had spilled out in spite of my resolve. My finger stung under the pressure.

My namesake was a warrior, a sword in her hand, shining plate armor. I wished I could channel her courage and will. Doreen opened the door and a boy hobbled in, clumsy on hand-me-down crutches. He moved tentatively, hopping forward rather than trusting the crutches with his weight. I looked at his chart: possible fracture of the ankle. If it was broken, he'd soon be used to his crutches. Follow-up patients swung their bodies in graceful arcs, pendulums to their own personal clocks.

Near the end of the shift, Dr. Rivers slipped in. His eyes were sunken, the circles underneath an unnatural purple. Wraithlike, he moved as if he'd had to will each step forward. His twenty-four-hour ER shift should have been over hours ago, but I knew why he stayed, and I knew it wouldn't be compensated.

"We just lost the boy," he said.

I sank onto my small stool and looked at him, standing there in his limp coat. It looked as if even his clothing were exhausted from the effort to save that child. "There was never much hope, I guess."

Dr. Rivers looked at the ceiling, struggling with all the emotions he barred while working with the child as they now surged in. "I thought maybe if we could ever get him stabilized, we could airlift him to Spokane."

Though it was time to leave, the dim light of this room seemed more appropriate for this conversation than the stark white light outside. "And the mother?"

"She'll be in surgery at Sacred Heart within the hour. No guarantees, but she has a decent chance."

"The others?"

"We set the father's wrists and gave him a sedative. The little girl will be just fine once the swelling in her neck recedes. They're waiting for their ride downstairs now. The father," Dr. Rivers paused and cleared his throat, "the father thanked me for all I'd done." His voice broke in spite of himself, and a tear slid from his eye. He brushed it away with the sleeve of the white coat he'd pulled on over the scrubs.

"You did all that you could—more than most doctors could." The words were stupid and mechanical; I had no real comfort to offer. He was exhausted. "You should go home and get some sleep."

"The rest cure," Dr. Rivers snorted a sarcastic, mirthless laugh.

"You know as well as I do that there is no real help for this."

"That's honest, if nothing else."

He looked like a haunted man. I understood. The weight of the boy still hung in my shoulder joints, the sadness of losing him making the bones heavy. His small, shattered face was in front of me again, the thin blood tears.

Dr. Rivers lifted his hand toward me, paused, then ran the back of his hand down my cheek. There was no mistaking that gesture: its tenderness, its hope. I knew the loneliness that generated it. You can't watch a person die and not want someone to cling to. I swallowed and turned my face away, just enough to slip from his caress.

"A bit of a cold fish, aren't you, Joannie?" Dr. Rivers dropped his hand. "I'm sorry. That was inappropriate. I don't know what I was thinking coming here."

You weren't thinking anything; you were feeling. I could have said something to comfort him. Perhaps I was a cold fish.

He was no better, no less awkward, at love than I. He, too, had forgotten how to reach out. His house was lavish but empty. I, at least, had Timothy. "It's been a long day all around," I said. "I'm sorry." I hoped he heard the finality in those words that I intended.

"It was wrong for me to come in here. Please forget all about it."

"It's forgotten."

It wasn't the answer he was hoping for. He reeled from me as if I'd slapped him.

"I'm sorry," I said. "That's not what I meant," but he was already gone.

I looked at my watch, 4:15. I should have been on the way to the barn by now.

Cheryl's chuckle slowed me. She'd stayed past quitting time, gossiping with Glennis, the night receptionist, just to have this opportunity. "I see I shouldn't have worried about Dr. Rivers not getting a chance to stop by. Room One's turning into our own little tunnel of love."

I stared at her, unbelieving. I was used to trying to read through her innuendos, but she'd laid all her cards on the table. "Dr. Rivers just came up to let me know about the patients we treated earlier. The boy died. He was six. His mother was just airlifted to Spokane, and we don't know if she'll make it either. There's a little girl downstairs with her father whose lives have just been blown apart. He's going to have to raise her by himself for a while, which will be tricky since both his wrists are broken. Does that satisfy you?"

The smile had dropped from Cheryl's face. Her mouth worked, but no words were coming out. Glennis, sitting next to her, looked wide-eyed from Cheryl to me. Cheryl said, "No need to get snippy, Joannie. It was just a little playful teasing to pass the time."

She is expecting an apology now, I thought. That would be the kind thing to do. They say that kind words cost nothing, but I'd never bought that. To be kind to Cheryl would have exacted a great cost, the words coming at an expense I was not willing to spare. Instead I leaned in so that not even Glennis would overhear. "Do me a favor and go fuck yourself," I whispered, then turned and left: cold fish indeed, swimming away.

V
Finding the Distance

Stasis in darkness,
Then the substanceless blue
Pour of tor and distances.

—Sylvia Plath, "Ariel"

But please, just let this long light be garlanded by birds
and the garrulous, sloe-eyed toad.
Let the mare scratch her ear all the way down the length of me.
Let her breathe where the lick of memory wants.

—Robert Wrigley, "Clemency"

Dream Girl

The blood was the boy's blood. I did not go home and change the bandage. Instead, I pulled on riding gloves, letting the tender deerskin press the stained tape to my skin. It seemed the least I could do.

Every toss of Zephyr's head sent a searing reminder through my cut finger that the world was a different place than it had been this morning: One of its small ones was gone, and my time, like everyone's, was limited. I took Zephyr into the hills, neglecting again to ask Eddie's permission. We jumped banks; we galloped. She'd started to know me, and I was more subtle with my aids. We were coming to terms, defining boundaries, learning how to stay out of one another's way. It was a crisp day. Twilight was already well advanced. We kept it short and raced dusk home.

Back in the barn, Dawn had arrived to clean stalls. "Damn," she said. "You know I hate to admit it, but Zephyr's actually starting to look like a half-decent horse. Her hip bones don't look like they're going to poke straight through her skin anymore."

I patted Zephyr on the shoulder. "Good grain and good work."

"I still say she's a waste of pasture space. Hounds could get some good eating off her now, though, if Connie'd take my advice and send her for dog food."

Zephyr yanked the lead across my lacerated finger. The pain brought me back to myself and to what I had to do; I had a life to get on with. The time had come to confront all the disasters I'd tried to avoid with lies and sidestepping. I said, "Been a while since we all went to dinner. What do you say to getting everyone together again at El Mercado's? Maybe Friday night?"

"Suits me down to the ground." Dawn paused pre-toss, holding a shovel-full of piss-sodden chips forward as if offering them to me. "You asked Jenny?"

"Not yet."

She pitched the shovel-full into the barrow. "I've got to call her tonight about getting together for a trail ride. I'll tell her."

Zephyr faked a spook as Dawn lifted the wheelbarrow to push it outside, bringing the lead rope once more against my finger. I jerked her back, popping the halter on her nose to stop her nonsense. "You've never been afraid of anything in your life," I said to her. Dust rose under her shuffling hooves, and the warmth of blood oozed afresh under the bandage. *It's time to grab a hold*, I thought, *even when it hurts*. The clock was always ticking. I stroked Zephyr's nose, and she stood, nostrils flaring.

"Waste of pasture space," Dawn called again.

Timothy was on his bike outside my apartment when I arrived home. "Thought I'd missed you," he said. "You hungry?"

"Starved."

"You look it; your face is so pale." He walked me up, carrying his backpack of groceries. "It's kind of giving me *déjà vu*."

"Yeah?"

"Yeah. To back when I first met you. I had the strangest dream." He paused a moment, his hair flopped down over his eyes to hide his thoughts.

"Was I in lace or leather?"

His faced broke into a smile. "Not quite. Nothing so expected, actually."

I unlocked the door, listening, not daring to interrupt.

"I half don't want to tell you," he said. "It's all so hokey."

I raised an eyebrow.

"Fine," he said. "But don't take it as some Indian vision thing. I don't believe in that stuff, and I never had a dream like this in my life."

"Other people dream too, you know. Indians don't have a corner on the market."

"O.K.—but don't forget that." He took a deep breath, glanced up to read my expression, and continued. "It started with just me: I was out in a freshly plowed field at night. The moon started getting brighter and brighter, and I had to walk north. For some reason, I knew that, like it was my mission or something, but the moon was so bright, I couldn't see the stars. I was looking hard at the sky, trying to figure out where Polaris would be, when a cold nose nudged my hand. This huge black dog was standing next to me. If you believe in omens, a black dog should be one, right? Isn't that out of mythology or something? But this one just seemed big and goofy— you know, one of those big dopey dogs that smile all the time. I kneeled and started to pet him. Then the moon went out, and there were no stars, only darkness, and the sound of horse hooves."

I liked the way he told a story. Together, we pulled bread and cold cuts from his bag.

"I stared into the darkness and began to see, though there was no light. A big grey horse and rider were galloping right at me. I don't know why I didn't move. The dog was so big and smiley and unconcerned, it seemed like everything was just O.K., but all of a sudden, I realized the horse was going to run me down. I started to move, and that's when I saw it wasn't a normal horse at all, but one made of bone and fire. It balked when it saw me, throwing the rider into the dirt. 'Catch my horse,' the fallen rider said, but I couldn't catch it. It was a wild thing. The rider started laughing, and I looked back. It was you, laughing at me because I couldn't catch your horse. You whistled, and the horse ran right to you where you sat. You handed me its reins to hold, and I helped you stand." He paused and looked at me, a bottle of Shiraz in hand. "Corkscrew?"

"Second drawer on the right."

"Your foot was hurt, and I offered to give you a leg up, but you said you didn't need my help. You just reached out and grabbed a rib of the bone horse and swung yourself up onto the saddle, laughing again. The moon came back on when you mounted, like you'd thrown the switch. 'Hand me my whip,' you said, and I cut a switch from a tree branch and handed it to you. The horse tried to move away, but you held it. I looked into its eye, and it was full of flame. Without making a sound, that flame spoke to me, like Moses and the burning bush or something."

Timothy looked at me, like he was unsure if he should keep talking, then he smiled at himself. He poured liberal glasses while I sliced the crusty bread, careful of my cut.

"'Mine,' the flame repeated, low and steady. 'Mine, mine, mine.' The word sounded like a bell tolling—you know, how the toll seems to hang in the air long after the bell is struck. I looked up at you to see if you heard. The smile on your face was all mischievous. A coyote howled at the new-lit moon. 'Guy likes you,' you said, nodding at the black dog. He licked my fingers, and I stroked his big, soft, dopey head. 'Ride with me,' you said, but when I approached, the horse bolted, and it was just me, the dog, and the echo of your laugh as you rode away."

I was spellbound.

"See what I mean?" he said. "A stupid dream, but it's kind of stuck with me ever since." Timothy sliced tomatoes, and I tried to laugh off the strange sense of premonition. What stunned me was how thoroughly he knew me right from the start. I was exactly the person he just described—someone not to get mixed up with, someone who would leave him and ride on alone. I didn't want to be that person. Not to him.

Timothy smiled and handed me a glass of wine. "I didn't even know your name yet, but I was already dreaming about you. Weird, huh?"

The day had been full; its edges pressed on me. I said, "A boy died in the ER today."

Timothy had been about to take a bite, but he stopped and laid the sandwich down. "Are you O.K.?"

There was no way to begin to answer that question. "Death makes you think." I held the glass of wine in my hand, its glass resting against the bandage. "Mostly, I've been thinking about how we're always dying. Did you know your skeleton is always breaking down and being rebuilt? No matter how old you are, there's no part of your skeleton that's more than ten years old. Whether you're fifteen or eighty, your skeleton is the same age. Our skin's always sloughing off and re-growing. Maybe that happens with our minds, too. We're always dying. I think of who I was in high school and who I am now, and the person I was then is dead." I saw myself dressed in a stiff black skirt at the side of Mouse's coffin. It was the last time I could remember wearing a skirt. "I don't think there's a single molecule of myself left from then, except maybe the blue-prints that give me shape. Like how, once we stop growing, our bones stay the same length even after they've been rebuilt over and over." I spread mayonnaise and layered cold cuts to feed the body I both loved and couldn't trust. "I've been thinking how we're always dying, only some people don't get as long to die as others."

Timothy let the words hang in the air a minute before he spoke. "Maybe that's what we should celebrate, though. Because at the same time we're dying, we're also building, right? Like how you said the skeleton is always getting remade, we're always dying but we're also always being born. Maybe the big death is also another kind of birth."

I smiled. "You sound like my parents, all faithful and optimistic."

He shook his head. "I don't know what to believe, but it's too easy to be depressed. I've seen people doing that all my life, deciding not to fight. But nothing's ever really simple. Maybe the birth and death are a necessary balance."

"Or maybe death just reminds us to live while we can." I took a bite of what was quite possibly the best sandwich ever. "Do you want to go to dinner with me and some friends on Friday?"

"Sure." He looked at me again, sideways this time, appraising. "There's something you're not telling me."

"What? I'm supposed to reveal all my mysteries now?" I tried to smile like a sprite, like the dream Joannie. "I thought you just said you like complications. Besides, I'm the nameless woman with the bone horse, remember? Secrets are part of my charm."

He laughed. "You're my *femme fatale*. I'd better be careful."

"That's right." I kept my tone light, hiding the worry I felt. He *was* right. I thought of Joan of Arc; I thought of Eastwood. The time had come to prepare for battle.

After Timothy left that night, I went running. The November air was invigorating, so crisp and so dark. I imagined turning the moon on and off, riding a horse of bone, a fire burning within. The image lifted me onward. A thin mist moved across the street, slicking it with the beginnings of black ice. I placed my feet carefully and focused on balance.

I inhaled slow, deep breaths that cooled my tongue and throat. My warmth was more powerful than its freeze. I moved between the halos of light dropped by street lamps, half in love with the rhythm of my feet, the way my heels absorbed weight with each stride, the roll toward my toes. I could run for miles like this.

A cloud rolled over the nearly full moon, silvering its edges in light. Frost-crystallized, the neighborhood glimmered like the glass boy whose blood I still wore. My parents would see him as a good soul awaiting the opportunity to sing in heavenly chorus, but I could not see that as a hopeful vision. Surely, there was more to life than earning your place in eternity. I imagined his days, being hurried to Cub Scouts and soccer, arguing with his sister, avoiding his homework, trying to get in another race on MarioKart rather than setting the table. An American boy's life was no preparation for Paradise.

A breeze picked up and tickled across the hairs on my neck. On a night like this, could heaven offer any improvement on Earth? Was there air like this in heaven? Was joy possible without a body to feel it—without these legs striding, these lungs breathing, this mouth tasting sweetness in the frozen mist? The silence, broken only now and then by the rare, low hum of snow tires on pavement, was a music in its own right beyond that of any faith-invented choir. If Earth could be this good, what's a heaven for?

These were the attitudes that had shocked my CCD teachers when I was a child. Training for confirmation, I'd asked for evidence that the Bible was divinely inspired. The teacher, so bent on his mission to fill us with the sweetness and light of his hopeful imaginings, had melted down completely. His skin had reddened right to the bald spot in the middle of his thin red hair, and he quivered within the thin madras plaid of his Sunday shirt as he answered in barely controlled rage. I'd been pummeling him with questions for weeks. He talked about what a big, long book it was, how impossible its creation would have been for mere mortal men had the mind of God not touched them. *Bullshit*, I thought.

My mother let me stay home from church after that. I've long wondered whether my own inclination toward faithlessness was by then supported by the CCD teacher, who saw me as a corruptive influence. What conflicts I must have created in him . . . though certainly no more than the conflicts I felt in myself. My parents believed that to keep me in church against my will would only strengthen my resolve against it, barring me from ever taking God willingly into my heart. They were right, yet even having my way, I'd never come around like they'd hoped. Now, we simply avoided talk about the state of my soul.

My legs felt tireless this evening, like they had a marathon in them that wanted out. I ran past my old high school, three stories of Depression-era brick built by the CCC and ornamented with concrete. It was annexed later with the functional but imagination-deprived architecture of the nineteen sixties. The only ornamentation there were brown squares of . . . what? metal? plastic? that sat at the top and bottom of each window. I wondered if the same shades still hung inside—the long rolls vertically striped in circus colors: turquoise and lime green in some rooms, orange and red in others.

Mouse and I had owned those buildings while we were there. I could still feel the hardness of the brown vinyl-tiled floor in front of her locker, where we ate our packed lunches. We were always too good for the cafeteria, though even we would occasionally deign to purchase one of their freshly made maple bars. We spent our days laughing at everyone: the teachers who thought they were smarter than we were, the peers who knew they were cooler. I imitated Madame Beauclerc's histrionics at another sample of my poor handwriting; Mouse mocked the girls in the bathroom fretting over the state of their mascara.

I ran on, feeling like the last one standing. In the dark stillness of night, the high school was as still as a mausoleum. Tree branches and moonlight threw shadow lace across my path, patterned like the cast-off veil of a communicant. The breeze had picked up, blowing steadily through my fleece. My body was too warm now to mind the cold. Stopping to wait for the light of a cross walk, I imagined what I looked like to the passing car, the steam rising through my stocking cap alight with moonlight, stretching out and dispersing.

I thought of Mouse's last birthday. Seventeen. We had the party on the Mountain, inviting everyone, even the kids we barely knew. The Hoedown Jamboree, we'd called it, a loving tribute to rednecks everywhere. Mouse and I wore matching trucker hats and form-fitted flannel shirts. Half the school showed up, hicked out in impromptu costumes, chewing straw and tobacco, cheap illegal beer tucked casually under arm: Oly, Hamm's, Milwaukee's "Beast" by the case. Rumor had it that Chad Johnston brought a sixer of Rainier (still cheap, but a significant step up), but if he did, I never saw it. In the boom box, we alternated bootlegged tapes of classic country: Kenny Rogers, Patsy Cline, Johnny Cash. When we knew the words, we belted them out; when we didn't, we danced like fools.

It would have been a historic party, one to be written about in yearbooks and talked about at reunions, if only its honoree had lived. It'd been that night that Mouse had first flirted with the bastard who killed her. I hadn't paid much attention at the time. I'd been flirting too. Flirting had seemed like harmless entertainment then. I flirted to feel my own power, seeing how badly I could make someone want me, then disappoint him. I was as chaste as I was naïve. Mouse, I felt, was the same: untouchable.

Later, when the party was winding down, Mouse and I lay on the hood of the Pod, reclined against the windshield drinking warm cans of Schmidt's, "the every other letter beer," and watching the horizon lighten against the pines. She talked about her plans after high school. She was set to be our class valedictorian with letters in track, cross country, and soccer, and lately she had spent her nights filling out applications to big schools in glamorous places: Berkeley, UCLA, NYU, the University of Chicago. "Get the hell out of this town," she said, like we all said. She was going to do something major.

I'd been quiet. I had no plans then. All I cared about was riding Foxy, my new horse. It was weird to think of him that way now, of not knowing him precisely. I'd taken riding lessons for the past few years, but I'd only just met Eddie. He didn't train high school students as a rule—*kids*, he'd called us, his tone implying that nothing more need be said on the matter. Connie had talked him into giving me a trial. I could still remember how he watched me that day, his eyes wary and grudging, looking for the first sign of flightiness, loudness, disrespect, lack of commitment. Rebellious, I refused to play into his stereotypes and became the only student he had under twenty-five.

He'd taken me on more for Foxy's sake than from any early indication of talent on my part. Eddie liked Foxy from the first, commenting on his confirmation and carriage. He couldn't believe my parents had found him in a neighbor's yard, an out-of-shape pet trained for Western pleasure and not showing a great deal of aptitude. He was too leggy, they'd complained. He didn't "jog." Eddie immediately asked to be allowed to train Foxfire to jump, and my parents agreed to the price. He was a far more demanding trainer than I'd ever had, and my parents liked the determination and focus they saw him creating in me.

I ran on, refusing to slow until the last quarter mile, when I broke stride to begin my cool down. My breath was deep and rich. I shook warmth into my hands. Looking back was a way to avoid looking forward if all that was forward was darkness. I had set wheels in motion that I couldn't control.

The phone rang as I let myself in. "Joannie," Eddie said, "I'm calling for two things. Item one: I'm thinking of taking Zephyr to Deep Creek Saturday morning to train on some cross country jumps before it freezes. You interested?"

"Yes." It hadn't required a moment's thought. "Is she ready?"

"I think so. She'll respect those fences more than the ones we can set up in the indoor, and you're right about her working better outside. Still, we'll work some cavaletti this week. Meet me at the barn at seven on Saturday morning. Item two: There's a new boarding stable in Lewiston, and they're putting on a winter schooling show. Some New Year's thing—first of January. If things go well tomorrow, I want to put Zephyr in it."

"Are you offering me the ride?"

"If you're interested and aren't going out of town."

"Do you even have to ask? When have you ever known me to pass on a show?"

"Good. One more thing then: I think Jenny should show Hobbes, but I don't want to put him in the same trailer with Zephyr."

"She'd kick the shit out of him." The thought came with some little pride.

"Exactly. It's not worth the risk. Would you mind pulling him in your trailer if we can talk Jenny into showing? He shouldn't give you any trouble."

I began to rub the calluses on the sides of my finger, an old nervous habit. The sting from my cut jolted me back, and I inhaled sharply.

"You O.K., Joannie?"

"Yes, sorry. Yeah, I'll haul Hobbes."

"Good. I'll see you Thursday for our lesson. We'll do a few small fences to get Zephyr thinking about jumps."

The still green numbers on the microwave's clock preserved the notion that time was not ticking. The digital numbers composed themselves of fences and walls, loose boxes and pens.

Showdown

I couldn't decide what to call Timothy, how to name the role he filled. "Boyfriend" was wrong; it smacked of high school and the girls I'd ridiculed for making zit-riddled, hormone-driven adolescent boys the center of their existence. "Lover," too, was wrong; that was what Dave had been. Lovers were exciting because they were illicit. Love had very little to do with lovers. Timothy took things slow. We had not so much as kissed yet, though I felt as close to him as I ever had to Dave. Still, I seemed to be assuming too much to call him any of the usual names. Timothy was my corner: the place I went to when I collected my strength.

On Friday night, he came to the door with his hand deep in his pocket, hiding something. He brought it out with a flourish; a single large bulb rested in the middle of his palm, with all the romance of a brown turnip. He tossed it to me. "It's an amaryllis," he said. "Fill a jar with gravel and bury this halfway in. It should bloom around Christmas."

A few unpromising strands of dark fiber hung from it. It reminded me of root cellars and darkness. "Will it be beautiful?"

"Time will tell." Clint Eastwood was haunting his sly smile once more. His bike rested against the railing behind him, and his face was pale with the night's cold. "You should see the frost," he said. "The moon is full, and the ice crystals are acting like natural prisms. There are tiny spectra everywhere if you look for them."

I put the bulb in my coat pocket, and we, my body in his body's nook, walked together down the icy street crushing rainbows under foot. "Dave will be there tonight."

"Dave?"

"The guy who famously drug me out into the parking lot at Rosauer's. He's my friend Jenny's husband."

Timothy considered this. His jacket was too thin for the night, and I wondered if he had a warmer one, or if he'd simply learned to live with cold. He held his head proudly, or obstinately, in the face of winter.

I said, "Aren't you curious about why he did that?"

He stopped and looked at me. "Do you want me to know?" Softly illuminated by moonlight, his eyes rested on me with absolute trust.

"Eventually," I said.

He wrapped his arm around me, strong inside its thin jacket. Though I was shivering inside my heavy wool coat, Timothy's arm was steady. We walked on together through the darkness.

The mariachi music from El Mercado blared through doors shut fast against the Idaho night. Walking in was like crossing a continent in a step. In the tropical heat, a man speaking heavily accented English asked if we wanted a table for two, but Dawn had already spotted us and came to fetch us to the table.

Dawn's smile stretched so broadly that I was immediately embarrassed by her joy. She asked the waiter to add another seat to the table, then nudged me in the ribs mouthing, "Is this him?"

I stood by Timothy as we waited for the extra chair. "This is Timothy." Jenny and Dawn exchanged smiles.

"And do you work with Joannie?" Jenny was fishing. Dave looked Timothy over once, up and down, then stared like a stoic out the glass door that fronted the restaurant, his face unreadable. He wore the Hemingway sweater again.

"I work at Rosauer's," he said. Dawn was almost bouncing in her chair. Timothy's hand brushed the edge of mine. All I had to do was take it.

I shot another glance across the table at Dave, but he wouldn't look at me. "We're friends," I said. I regretted the words as soon as I said them. I'd come to set things right, but I'd ducked out around the first obstacle I came to.

"Friends?" The word dropped from Dawn's mouth like something foul-tasting.

"Good friends," I added lamely. It wasn't enough. Timothy raised an eyebrow at me but said nothing.

The table wobbled, and Dave disappeared underneath it to shove beer mats under the high leg. Refried beans and Spanish rice filled the air, their warmth couldn't fight the coldness in my belly. I had dodged the fence when it was time to jump. I had run out.

Dave checked for stability, and sat up. Whether the sudden rush of blood to his face was anger or simply the result of sitting up, I couldn't tell. He began folding the corner of his napkin. The action chilled me—among all the possible reactions I'd imagined, the calm folding and refolding of a napkin was not among them.

Timothy had asked Russ where he worked, and the two began comparing past jobs in construction.

"I didn't know you'd worked construction," I said. I pictured Timothy in an orange helmet and vest, driving the roller. It fit. I pictured him in a tweed jacket teaching a class of college students, and that fit too. I could as easily see him in a suit and tie, arguing a case to a jury in the style of my father, or working the register at my mother's co-op like he now did at Rosauer's, or in a lab coat dosing liquid from pipette to Petri dish. "What's the worst job you ever had?" I asked, wanting to know what he couldn't do.

"The casino," he said. "No contest."

"I thought casinos paid well," Dawn said.

"Yeah. I was the whitest Indian on the place, so I got plenty of tips, but I hated taking people's money—which I guess sounds funny from a guy who works as a cashier, but at least at Rosauer's, they're getting something out of the deal. And I hated watching people lose. I knew too many of the ones losing."

Jenny reached her hand across the table and squeezed his hand, a gesture of comfort which made Dave flinch.

Timothy turned to me. "What was your worst job?"

"Hardee's, hands down."

"Always fast food," Dawn sneered. "That's everyone's worst job."

"Actually, that isn't what made it bad," I said. "I worked 5 a.m. to 1 p.m., but getting up early never bothered me. The job itself was kind of fun. I had the corner where I made biscuits all to myself for the first few hours, and then, when the manager pulled me over to flip burgers, I'd just shoot the shit in the kitchen with the boys, making the sandwiches and putting down fries. It was the manager who was the problem. He was really sleazy. Nothing I could prosecute or anything, but he was always untying my apron strings while I was cooking and standing way too close to talk to me. He even invited me to his house a few times, but I wouldn't go."

"Trying to get in your pants," Russ laughed.

"Yep."

"You should've worked that shit for some raises."

Dawn slugged Russ in the arm and rolled her eyes. He looked entirely pleased with himself.

"What's your worst job?" I asked him.

Russ leaned back and stretched as he pretended to think. "I'm going to go with Bonanza."

Dawn yelped in protest. "That's where you met me, you fucker."

He turned to me, eyebrows raised. "Need I say more?"

Jenny had never had a job, and the server came to get our drink order before we got to Dave. I doubted he would have answered; he hadn't said a word all night. Margarita called, but one would lead to more, and I needed a clear head. "Water," I said.

Dawn stared.

"Eddie and I are taking Zephyr to Deep Creek first thing in the morning."

"You *do* have a death wish," she said.

The boys ordered beers, but Dawn surprised me by ordering water and Jenny, not one to break from what other women were doing, followed suit. I turned to Dawn. "I know why I'm not drinking," I said, "but I never thought I'd see the day when you didn't order a Bud."

Dawn tilted her chin down and smiled toward Russ. "We've got some news to share."

I looked at Jenny to see if she knew anything about this. Her face was blank at first, but almost immediately she flushed and smiled. "You're pregnant!"

Dawn's smile turned beatific.

Jenny squealed and clapped her hands while I sat there absorbing. "You never told me you and Russ were thinking about kids."

Jenny launched into a barrage of questions. When was she due? How long had she known? Were they going to find out the baby's sex? Did Dawn want a boy or a girl? What did Russ want? How was she feeling? Then suddenly, she paused, and her smile fell slightly. "You won't be able to ride now."

"Like hell." Dawn scowled.

"You can't ride pregnant."

"You bet your sweet ass I can."

"Isn't that a bit, well, dangerous?"

Dawn's eyes narrowed. "Are you saying I can't manage my horse?"

Jenny hadn't ever dared Dawn's ire since her fall from Zip, and she didn't know what to do in the face of it. I merely smiled encouragingly. It was Dave who spoke, like a forgotten giant everyone had come to mistake for a mountain. His voice was barely audible, each word filled with ice. "Aren't you two supposed to ride tomorrow morning?"

Jenny looked from Dawn to Dave, then gazed, pleading with her wide blue eyes, at Russ. I waited to see which would win out: Dawn's adamancy or Jenny's mewling persuasion. Russ wouldn't meet Jenny's eyes. He just stared at the table smiling, and in the moment I saw his smile, I knew the victor. Jenny was up against an army. Dave, dark with treason, would be no help. Jenny had never won a fight on her own. She'd always had a man to enlist, but her father was not here.

Dave's question hung unanswered in the air. It was Dawn who spoke, "Damn it, yes we are."

Jenny again looked to Russ who was shoving a lime section down the throat of his Corona. When he finally looked up, it was not Jenny but Dawn who smiled on. It was the final blow. Jenny said, "As long as you think it will be all right, then I guess we can go."

"Have you ever seen Sunny spook?" Dawn asked.

"You told me all horses spook."

"They do," I said. "But you've got to let Dawn decide her own way. Right, Russ?"

"Boy howdy."

Timothy, meanwhile, was reading the menu and staying well clear of this discussion, a sensible course. I put my hand on his thigh, rubbing the soft cotton of his worn blue jeans. He glanced up at me and gave me a sliver of the warm, slightly surprised smile that first drew me to him. Desire stretched like a sun-warm cat along the inside of my thighs.

Dave broke a tortilla chip in two, and I jumped. His eyes locked on mine as he scooped salsa onto a single half and tossed it back like a shot of bourbon, crushing it between his white teeth. I had been wrong to think that his eyes were the color of ice. Their clarity had gotten me, had made me think in terms of refraction and of depth. Fixed by them now, I understood that they were the color of a magnifying glass when it tilts to the sky to catch the sun and blister an ant. And I, for all my bold bravado, looked away.

Dave could do nothing to me, I reminded myself. He was just a man, only a man, but now, fear sprouted within me. Our showdown would not be here, and I would not decide its terms. The sun was hours from high noon. When Dave was ready, he would pull it off the horizon. God damn it, where was the cowboy in me? Where was the Clint? Why hadn't I found a better word than "friend"?

Dave didn't break his gaze. I took a long slow drink of water. They were only eyes. Why was I so afraid?

"Where are you guys riding tomorrow?" I asked.

"Over the hills, wherever." Dawn snuck a sip of Russ's beer and Jenny made another little yip. Dawn rolled her eyes. "One sip ain't going to hurt anything. Joannie's the one you should be worried about. Deep Creek on Zephyr?"

"Thanks for the vote of confidence." The waitress passed plates of food.

"Foxy's going to be a mess when he sees you hauling off that mare." She turned to the table. "You never saw a horse so attached to anybody in your life. It's crazy."

"Foxy loves Joannie as much as she loves him," Jenny said, all sappy. Dave snorted. "A horse can't love."

Timothy's eyes rested thoughtfully on him, but it was Dawn who spoke. "If they can't, then Foxfire sure puts on a good imitation."

"We've been together a long time," I said. The words were dishonest in their insufficiency. I owed Foxy more than that. "He's always been the one great love of my life." Dave's face darkened and his lip curled in a sneer; Timothy's was unreadable.

I looked away. In the corner, a green plaster parrot perched on a brass ring, the hard gloss of its plumage reflecting the track lighting with gaudy brightness: heavy, flightless wings. Its beak curled to a sharp yellow point. The beak would never open to speak or bite. I needed to be like that: hardened, content to perch in the center of a small, reliable circle.

Jenny broke the silence. "I can't believe you're going to have a baby. I've been trying to convince Dave that it's time to start a family, but he wants to put it off." She shot him a sly glance. "Maybe this will change your mind."

He said, "Having kids isn't something you do because everyone else is doing it."

I flinched at his cruelty, but Jenny showed no signs of hearing it. She slid her hand into the crook of his arm. "He thinks we need to build our nest egg up before we have kids."

"Getting you a horse was supposed to put a stop to all this baby talk," Dave muttered.

"He's always so practical." Jenny's lipstick cracked against a smile pulled so tight. "Did I tell you I trained Fritz and Shirley to run on the treadmill?"

Timothy looked to me. "Fritz and Shirley?"

"Her basset hounds," I said. Jogging along on the treadmill, they'd trip over their own ears as they paddled along on too short legs. Was it funny or tragic?

Russ cracked jokes about doggy aerobics. "Your dogs could be the next Jane Fondas."

"Shit, are you out of touch," Dawn said. "Jane Fonda hasn't made a tape in years."

Russ ignored her. "How long does it take to get a basset hound in swim suit condition?"

"They could make pin-up shots," Timothy suggested. "Maybe a calendar."

"They could go into adult film!" Russ shouted, causing Jenny to blush from the roots of her thin blonde hair straight down her neck. "Can you imagine the titles? Tits and Bassets. Doggy Style."

"Rabid Love," Timothy suggested. Why on Earth had I said we were just friends? I wanted to turn back; I wanted a do-over. Mouse and the glass boy hovered before me: There is only ever one chance.

Russ was laughing too hard to speak for a moment. Dave, on the other hand, shoveled his food in with steady, mechanical diligence. Jenny looked desperate. I changed the subject. "Eddie call you?"

"No," she said. "I haven't seen him since my last lesson."

I ate *pollo asada* to postpone the words I couldn't believe I was actually going to voice. The charbroiled chicken rested on my tongue, the taste of mesquite smoke. "There's a schooling show in January. If you want to show, I'll haul Hobbes."

"A show?"

"It's just a small one."

"Would I have to jump?"

"There's flat and jumping classes. Don't you want to jump?"

"I've only done cavaletti so far."

"If Eddie didn't think you'd be ready, he wouldn't have suggested it." They were the words I expected a friend would speak. "It's not until the first of January. New Year's Day. The new barn in Lewiston. There's plenty of time to decide. Just think it over."

Eddie would make her jump. Now that she had Hobbes, there was no reason not to. The fences would be small. All she had to do was stay in the saddle and remember the order of the fences. For me, on the other hand, a lot depended on tomorrow's ride. I ran my finger over the week-old laceration; the flesh had began to knit under fresh bandages. The bandage with the boy's blood was in the drawer of my bedside table, close at hand if I needed it.

Jenny said, "Are you thinking of Foxfire?"

I started. Dave's lips stretched into a thin, terrifying smile.

"Are you wishing you could show him there?" Jenny asked.

"No. We won't show again now. I'm going to ride Zephyr for Eddie."

"I'd love to come and watch you," said Timothy.

"Zephyr's a waste of pasture space," Dawn added. I ignored her.

"I'd love it if you came," I said.

The smile still hung on Dave's lips, but it was a shark's cold, joyless smile.

We paid our checks. Outside, the icy air cut into our lungs. Timothy and I broke from the others, waking toward home. "They're nice, your friends."

"Yeah?"

"Yeah. I like Russ and Dawn a lot. They're real easy-going."

I nodded, pleased.

"Jenny's cool, too. I thought she'd be worse from your description."

"Too harsh?"

He shrugged. "One night isn't enough to judge. Dave, though. I don't know what to think of him. He looked like a guy who is," he paused, searching for the right word, "unhinged." He put his arm over my shoulder, allowing it to rest loosely there, but his gaze stayed fixed forward.

For several paces, he said nothing. I waited. Along the edges of the sidewalk, I saw the tiny rainbows in each frost crystal that Timothy had said would be there, if I looked.

"Joannie, I won't ask what happened between you and Dave, but where do we stand? *Are* we just friends?"

I hadn't meant to stop, yet I found I had. His arm dropped away and he turned to face me, his features chiseled into marble by moonlight. Silence hung in the frost-crystal trees. He didn't know, even now, what he meant to me. Why, for God's sake, couldn't I find the words to tell him? He looked upwards toward the moon a moment and back again. "Forget I asked," he said.

Deep Creek

The alarm jarred me from sleep into the sudden cold of the room. My window blinds hung closed and still with secrets. I stuck a granola bar in the pocket of my coat and, no time to brew fresh, reheated a mug of yesterday's coffee.

The white pre-dawn light showed the cars and trucks that stretched across the parking lot and along the curb, but Dave's late model Dodge pickup was not among them. Of course. He was with Jenny. Dave was just a man, no more.

Even so, he haunted me. I dashed to my truck and locked the doors once I was inside. The engine was cold and reluctant to turn over, the starter chugging weakly. The world was shadowless in the ubiquitous grey light. "Crank, damn it," I whispered, and the Chevy roared into life. The heater whirred, and any lingering fear faded into the noise from the early morning farm report. I pulled out, the old shocks bouncing over the uneven pavement. This was what I was born for.

Eddie was waiting for me when I pulled in, though I was early. He'd already loaded my tack, and Foxy had began screaming. "I was going to see if I could get Connie to help us load," Eddie said, "but I can't rouse her."

We both knew what that meant. She'd been on a bender. They were less frequent than they had been, but every few months or so, the memories would be too much. Connie would come late to feed, making her rounds green-faced, her head tucked low into her jacket, wincing against the broad daylight.

Zephyr came to Eddie's whistle and ate a handful of grain from his hand as he haltered her, but when she saw the trailer, the old Zephyr was back. It took us over twenty minutes to get her within five feet of the trailer. Every forward movement was made with painstaking slowness on our part and frantic spooking, fretting, and skittering on hers. Eddie and I did our best to remain unfazed. Frustration would only add fuel to Zephyr's fire, and it was blazing away nicely without that.

When she finally put her first hoof in, the sound of her shoe against the wood sent her into convulsions. I expected her to rear or fly back, but she merely stood and shook violently, snorting the air inside. Eddie stood next to her, his left hand on a grain bucket several inches in front of her nose, his right holding the folded end of the lead rope and a dressage whip. He shook the grain bucket now and clucked to her, then gave her some time to think about this. When she didn't move, he added the lightest touch of the whip. I worried as he did so that she would spook and jump, banging her head on the trailer's ceiling and undoing all the work of the last half hour, but instead she hurried on, stomping her feet on the floor boards as if to show it who was boss. I swung the door mostly closed behind them while Eddie tied her.

Eddie's truck was already running. I peeled off my gloves and held my fingers in front of the heating vent. Eddie's hands rested lightly on the wheel. "We'd better add trailering to our list of things to work on," he said.

"We're going to run out of space on that list."

Out the window, the fields rolled by. Compared to facing Dave again, the solid fences of the cross country course didn't bother me, which was crazy. Riding is statistically one of the most dangerous sports, and eventing is perhaps its most dangerous discipline. Dave, on the other hand, had no stats against him. *He's all grimace and growl. I'm making a problem where one doesn't exist. Remember the stone wall. Remember that height is mental; you hit the fence only when you stop believing in flight.*

"How are Hobbes and Jenny getting along?" Eddie asked, breaking me out of my thoughts.

"Swimmingly. She says, and I quote, 'no one ever told her riding could be so easy.'"

"You sound bitter, Joannie."

"Riding isn't easy."

"It was when you had Foxfire."

"I *still* have Foxfire, in case you've forgotten."

"I haven't forgotten. I don't think Fox will let anyone forget him today. That's quite a show he puts on."

"I'd pasture him, except the girls are riding out today, and he'd just run the fence the whole time. The last thing I need is for him to panic and tangle himself in a hot wire."

Eddie flinched. Years ago, his champion mare, Talullah, had gotten caught in a fence. The wire wrapped around her leg, every thrash drawing it deeper. It cut into the hock, into the tendons and ligaments. I heard the blood was everywhere. Connie said Eddie's shirt looked like you could wring it out, and the ground where she lay was dark for months afterward. They hauled her to WSU's vet school, speeding the whole way, but the damage was done. He hadn't showed another horse since putting Talullah down.

"I'm sorry," I said.

His eyes were hard on the road. "You're right. You don't want that to happen to Foxfire."

"I haven't ridden Fox this week," I confessed. It depressed me to ride him now. Once the weather had turned, he was noticeably stiffer. Riding Zephyr, I could see glimmers of improvement. Riding Foxfire, I felt the gulf between what he was and the champion he had been. "I know he wants me to ride—you've seen him when I get Zephyr out—but he moves so stiffly now. I can't bear to feel it."

"That's only natural."

Is it? I didn't ask. Love is natural, and love should have gotten me in the irons. I changed the subject. "Jenny's going to kick my ass in January's show."

Eddie shrugged. "Anything can happen at a horse show; you know that."

Back in high school, Mouse used to say the same thing about backgammon, but she still beat me nine times out of ten.

We rattled along in his old green Ford, silent for the rest of the trip, each lost in our own thoughts. The day bloomed blue and cloudless. The sky itself was open with unfettered possibility. I was free and I had a horse to ride—a borrowed horse, but a horse none the less.

Under a blue and endless sky, I tacked up at the trailer's side and mounted. On opposing horizons, the Bitteroots and Cascades did not look so much like mountain ranges as simply more stone walls we could jump if only we opened our strides enough. Zephyr took her first jumps clean and round, though she struggled deciding where to put her feet before each jump. Distance was something only experience could teach, but she had strength and agility.

We pulled up to get some instructions from Eddie, whose words kept getting lost on the wind. "These must be the New Jersey hands I heard so much about," he said. "You're finally starting to let go of that shoulder tension."

The breeze blew a loose strand of hair across my face. I tucked it behind me ear. The best part of a good ride was how everything apart from your body, your horse, and your obstacles faded from your mind. There was only the moment, and the moment was enough. Zephyr covered the ground with her large, powerful, cadenced strides, relaxing forward into the mote-filled sunlight.

"Do the cross-rail to the log again," Eddie said. "Only this time, I want it in eight strides instead of seven."

Zephyr fought me as I checked her, sticking in an awkward stride and jumping flat-backed and hollow. The hard landing jolted up my spine and rang in my ears.

"Again," Eddie called. He counted our strides, clapping in time from cross-rail to log. "Stop her," he called when she again sped up instead of collecting. I pulled her to an awkward halt inches from the fence's base. She tossed her head, snorted and offered a small rear, and I backed her several paces. "O.K.," Eddie said. "Trot her forward and let her jump it now. Let her know there's no rush."

She popped over it this time as if she had springs in her legs; another jarring landing.

"Again," Eddie called. "And think about your center of gravity. You're getting defensive again. You've got to let that go, Joannie. Allow her to jump. Relax your weight down into your heels."

Zephyr listened this time as I checked her, only tossing her head once before collecting and giving me the round jump we'd been looking for. She landed clean, then shot out her back leg to give the fence a good kick before moving on. Eddie and I shared a quick smile.

"Again. In seven." He began calling numbers, how many strides he wanted. Happy with that, he pulled a cavaletti from the bed of his truck and set up some shorter related distances.

For all her inexperience, Zephyr did well. She even seemed proud of herself. "I think she's found her calling," Eddie said, patting her neck at the end of the lesson.

"Pretty good day for a waste of pasture space. Wish Dawn had seen it."

"She'll have her chance. We'll do some more jumping this week."

I dismounted and began to untack. The earth felt strange underfoot after such a ride, like some strange mythic reality you dreamed once but hadn't truly believed. Zephyr and I were not terrestrial animals. We were creatures of the air, landed.

Zephyr turned quickly and bit my arm, but it was a strange bite. Her teeth held my triceps, but she didn't bite down. She looked me in the eye with a direct, steady gaze, as if there was something she would have me remember, and then released me before I could wheel and strike back.

I can't let anyone else have her. The words came into my head as her teeth gripped my arm, and though I tried to shake the thought, to dismiss it as a moment of weakness after a good ride, the thought had come, and it wouldn't go. It bloomed into conviction. Her next rider wouldn't understand her. Not like I did. Her next rider would wreck everything we've built, would violate every bit of trust she'd put in me. I owed her this. I owed myself.

Even the forty-five minutes she took to load seemed, now, a point in her favor. She was all unfinished potential. Every roughness, every unknown brought her closer within my price range. "What do you think Zephyr would fetch if you sold her now?" I ventured.

"Tough to say." Eddie swung the door to the trailer, and to the conversation, shut.

I climbed into the truck. The seats were stained with coffee and everything smelt of straw, but it felt warmly secure after the open fields of Deep Creek. I let the subject drop while we ordered drive-through roast beef sandwiches. The curly fries weren't quite ready, and Zephyr kicked the trailer sides as we waited. The truck shook with each pounding hoof. If I bought her now, I could stay close to my mother without guilt, without the feeling I was wasting my life. I wouldn't have to give up her or Timothy. I'd been stupid not to see it before. Zephyr—*Zephyr* of all things—wasn't a problem but the solution to my problems. She wasn't perfect because no real solution ever is, but I could finally see a way clear. I tried again. "She's got a lot of rough spots, still. She's never going to totally train out of them."

"Probably not." Eddie shoved a mouthful of sandwich in and chewed thoughtfully.

We turned onto the road and moved toward the ribbon of high-way that would take us back to Idaho. There was no way to ease into this subject. "Would you sell her now, if the right buyer came along?"

Eddie frowned, but did not look at me. His eyes were trained down the road's yellow stripe. Even now, aging and slightly out of shape, he was a consummate rider, always looking at the course ahead. He squinted slightly. When he shot a glance my direction, I felt the first hope that I might convince him. "Do you have a buyer in mind?" he asked.

"You know I do."

Eddie's face relaxed into a smile. "Yes, I know you do," he said, "but why rush into this? You had a good day today, but as you said yourself, she's got a long list of problems."

I didn't speak.

Eddie's smile dropped, and he sighed. "If we could work her out of even half of her faults, this mare could be worth a lot of money, Joannie." *This mare,* I thought. He was reminding me of her potential as a breeding horse as well as a jumper.

"You don't want to sell her to just anyone," I said. "She's got to have the right rider."

Eddie was slow to respond, and I forced down a few curly fries. "The boys are headed to college in a few years. I need to think of them as well. There are good riders in Seattle and Portland, ones with money and trainers to work with." He looked at me apologetically. "And can you really afford two horses? Two board bills? Two farriers? Two sets of blankets? Two vet bills?"

"I can make it work for now. Foxfire won't be around forever." I wanted to bite back the words as soon as I'd said them. Foxfire deserved better. "Just think about it," I said, the voice rough in my throat. I ate my sandwich mechanically.

The memory of this morning's jumps should have kept me floating through the day, but I'd been set roughly back on Earth. The promise those jumps held was a promise I would not be allowed to realize. Always, always, it came down to money. Frustration balled in my throat, but I swallowed it with lumps of sandwich and chased it down with Coke.

For the next hour, we were silent. I watched the hills roll past as we threaded the barren highway between them. Occasionally, we would pass a house with a horse or two in the yard, plain, stalwart animals that wouldn't spook if someone shot a twelve gauge off their backs. I fought against bitterness. Eddie didn't owe me this.

The sky was hazy over the horizon near Moscow. "Brush fire," Eddie said.

"Weird time for one." We'd had rain only a week ago, and snow was again in the forecast.

Eddie and I watched through the windshield. The smoke grew thicker, spreading dark fingers across the sky, blotting out the sky. The air was dusk-filled. A mile from the barn, ash began to fall on the hood of the truck.

We pulled on, over the crests of the hills and into the ever-thickening haze. The air smelled strange and unnatural. "I hate to think of Foxy breathing this shit in all morning," I said.

Eddie was silent, his face set and immovable. In his silence, the first seeds of panic germinated. I said, "You don't think this is a barn fire, do you?"

Eddie ignored the question, slowing to a stop as the flashing lights of a police car permeated the haze. They had blocked the turn to Connie's. An officer approached the car. He was young. Too young, I thought. His face was a maze of popped pimples. Eddie nodded to the trailer. "I'm hauling a horse to Connie Thornfield's place."

"Sorry, sir." The young officer's voice was surprisingly deep. "No horses are going there today."

My heart beat against its cage of ribs. The policeman looked back to the trailer, which jostled violently as Zephyr shuffled and kicked.

"What happened?" From under his beaten cap, Eddie watched the boy, sizing him up, figuring out exactly how much he could ask.

"We're not sure yet."

"Barn fire?"

"Looks to be."

"Any horses killed?"

"I'm sorry, sir. I'm just here to direct traffic."

I stared at the boy-man, the unused walkie-talkie strapped to his shoulder. "My horse is there," I said. "Can't you talk to someone? Give us more information?"

"I'm sorry, ma'am."

I stared at him, but he stayed impassive. Eddie turned to me. "We'll take Zephyr to my place and come back with the trailer. If Foxy needs a place, he's got one with me until Connie can rebuild."

The *if* did it. It was Connie's place, and from what we could see, no horses would be staying there. That much we knew to be fact— there was no *if* about it. The *if* was for Foxy. *If he survived.* "I'm sorry, Eddie," I said, then turned and jumped from the truck. Around me, officers shouted for me to stop, but what would they do to make me? Pull their guns? I hardly thought so. Foxfire was all that was on my mind. Though ash drizzled from the sky, the burnished copper of his coat blazed in my mind's eye, pulling me through the disorienting smoke.

I ran without looking back, daring them to hold me back. Panting in the choking air, I sprinted across the road, or tried to. My feet sunk deep into the gravel. Recently and thickly resurfaced, the road gave under my feet like quicksand. It was like running in a nightmare, going nowhere.

My lungs burned by the time I crested the hill. My fleece had gathered soot and turned from blue to grey. Through the smoke, I could make out the shape of a woman pacing behind the fire trucks, Connie. The blackened frame of what had once been her barn teetered. One charred rafter swung and fell, pulling the next five with it. Cinders flew upward like New Jersey's summer fireflies. "Connie," I called, but smoke ate my voice. I stood next to her. Black lines ran down her face where tears mixed with ash. "Joannie," she said, "it's gone."

Gone was a flimsy word. Her husband was gone. Her herd, gone. Her brother, gone. Now the dream she'd spent a life building was only as a blackened skeleton.

But a barn was only a building, one she could rebuild. I needed to know that Foxy wasn't included in all that was gone, but the words clung to the ash that lined my throat. I tasted burnt hay and wood and other things I couldn't name. Sunny and Hobbes ran the fence line of their pasture; Bill and Zip ran theirs. "Fox," I finally managed.

Connie, turned to me, the loss of everything hanging on her face.

"Just tell me he was out to pasture," I pleaded. "Tell me someone got him out." Fire trucks blocked my view of the stalls.

"It was burning already when I got up."

"Dawn got him then. Someone got him. Please, Connie. He wasn't in the barn. Say it." Tears were welling in my eyes and panic edged my throat, but I blinked them back. This morning, he'd screamed when I left him, and those screams, the last sound I heard from him, echoed in my ears. "Just say he's O.K. That's all. He's in a pasture. He's a little shook up, but he'll be all right. Jenny got him, maybe. Someone got him."

Connie's shoulders seemed to collapse, and the sound she made was more than a sob. I left her standing there, facing the horses, and went to her house. Through the haze, I found the phone and called Dawn.

"Joan." The way Dawn said my name crushed all hope. She'd always called me Joannie.

I shook the tone of her voice away. "Tell me what happened," I said.

"I came and saw Connie hadn't fed, so I threw Foxy some flakes of alfalfa. He was still a little anxious, but he was settling down. The hay seemed to help. I figured I'd wait and give him his grain when we got back, and we rode out. We were only out about twenty minutes when I saw the horizon. Joannie, you know we rode hell bent for leather when we saw that smoke, but everything was on fire." She paused to still the quiver in her voice. "I banged on Connie's door until she woke up, and we called 911. I rode around until they came, looking for any sign of him. I mean, I knew the stall door was shut, I knew there was no way out, but I wanted so bad for it not to be true. When the cops got there, they made us get out. Said it wasn't safe to be around. Probably right, too, cause I can't stop coughing, but Joannie, if they'd a let me, you know I'd still be out there looking, just in case."

The world was spinning. No one had even been close enough to hear his final screams. And me? The one who owed him everything? I'd been the farthest of all. He'd given me a distraction from my mother's sickness, and he'd offered my life a purpose after Mouse's death. And I deserted him on one day he'd ever needed me.

How would I endure a world without Foxfire?

I hung up. There was nothing more to say. Wisps of smoke curled from the timbers, but the fire was out. The firefighters coiled their hoses. They were surreal in their blackened yellow coats, the bands of reflective tape glittering strangely in the half-light of the smoke-filtered afternoon. It seemed again that I was walking through a dream, but I wasn't so lucky. The two far corners of the building still stood upright, the siding melted. On the side closest to us, the side where Foxfire's stall had been, only a few blackened beams and rafters remained, crazed black, smoking in a heap where they'd fallen. Woodchips, hay, and dry manure. All excellent tinder.

Men in uniform were beginning to look around the exterior of the building. Connie turned to me, dashed tears from her eyes, and cleared her throat. "We saved your truck. Dawn parked it behind the house."

My keys would still be dangling from the ignition, right where I'd left them. Still, I found myself stepping toward the barn. One of the firefighters put his hand on my shoulder. "I'm sorry, ma'am. It's too dangerous to go any closer. Hot spots." His kind eyes, soft and brown as melted chocolate, rested on me. Soot drew dark lines in every crease of his face, aging him beyond his years.

"My horse was in that barn."

He paused, his hand still on my shoulder. How odd that the gloved touch of a stranger could give so much. "I'm sorry."

I turned to leave. Images of Foxfire were coming thick and fast: Foxy screaming for me became Foxy screaming in a burning barn with no one to save him. Foxy's beautiful coppery coat became charred flesh. Foxy's soft eyes melted into black pits. I had to get away, but there was nowhere to go.

An inch of ash covered the truck's hood. I cleared the windshield with an ice scraper and cranked its reluctant engine, driving away as if there were a destination anywhere that could take me out of my head.

I pulled into my apartment and walked to the door with my head down, afraid I would see Dave's truck, afraid he'd be watching. Home was empty with Foxfire gone, the walls bare, the furniture tattered. Home is where people who don't have horses spend money.

The house was silent, but the noise wouldn't stop. I remembered the first jump I ever took. Foxfire was young and talented but totally inexperienced. Eddie had us on a lunge line, the whip in his hand to coax Foxfire on, but Foxy only needed coaxing on the first jump. Several paces out, he gave one little stutter step, and Eddie popped the whip in air behind him. Foxy's ears swiveled from the sound forward, trained on the short cavaletti, and he moved into the collected powerful stride I would recognize so many times before a fence. He jumped the one foot obstacle clean and round as if it had been two feet higher. The jump seemed to last for minutes, not seconds. I just held on and smiled. When we landed, I gathered the reins in one hand to pat his neck, but he needed no praise. The jump itself had been enough. He circled 'round again to it, confidently this time, and from that day until his first run-out in New Jersey, I'd never worried about him stopping at a fence. No matter how tall, how wide, or how solid the obstacle, Foxfire jumped because jumping was what he loved.

There would never be another Foxfire. Once, I turned him out in the arena where Connie had set a course. I hadn't had time to ride that day. Mom was in the hospital, and I wanted to let Foxfire have a quick run around the arena before spending the night in his stall. I never thought for a moment that he'd jump the fences, but once he saw the standards, they became a game for him. He made his own course, prancing at the end of combination, nickering to make sure we'd seen.

I heard Connie whistle from the cross ties. "I'll be damned," she said. "I've worked with horses all my life, but I've never seen anything like that." It was Foxfire all over. He was never just an ordinary horse. He was born for greatness, then tucked into an Idaho corner where I was lucky enough to find him.

I remembered, too, the last jump we'd ever taken, the bank he'd jumped after spooking at that autumn pheasant. It was the last time I'd feel that round, raw power, the jump that was Foxfire's and only Foxfire's.

There were calls to be made, people to tell. How could I tell my mother? My father? How could I say that the horse they bought to distract me from her disease was dead? To say it seemed to confirm that all hope was gone. I couldn't do that. I couldn't betray him one more time. I lay on the couch, my face pressed into the throw pillow, willing the world to stop, to change the rules by which it worked. Willing time to reverse itself and let me have Foxfire back.

Truth, Will, Out

On the morning of Mouse's death, we'd had the worst argument of our long friendship. The night before, she and her boyfriend sat three rows ahead of me at the basketball game and never even noticed I was there. My mother, recovering from another attack, insisted I go out, and for the first time, I'd gone out alone. Mouse hadn't returned my call. Now, I saw why. They were utterly absorbed in each other, pumping their fists as they chanted the fight song, but looking more at each other than at the game on the court. Birds and spiders filled me. I seethed and stared, choking on a cocktail of self-pity, jealousy, and scorn. Mouse had always been there. I needed her. Who else could help me when my mother had another attack? Who else understood?

When he got up in the third quarter to get Cokes, I followed him. Standing behind him in line, I ran my finger around the back pocket of his jeans. He turned to me, confused by my small act of seduction. It was the first time I felt the full scope of my power: the power of an attractive woman to stop a man in his tracks and against his better judgment. I held him with tiger-bold eyes. I moved my body up against his, laid my hand inside his thigh and stroked it up toward his penis. He closed his eyes and shivered, and when I pulled his mouth to mine, his kiss was hungry for me. There were maybe twenty people standing around. Two would have sufficed. By the end of the game, there wasn't a person in the stands who wasn't talking about it. I hoped to hurt Mouse as deeply by my betrayal just as her desertion hurt me.

Had she forgiven him, or had she merely washed her anger down with a fifth of vodka? She could barely speak through her rage the morning she called. "Cunt," she'd said. "You fucking cunt." She hung up with those words ringing in my ear, the last she would ever speak to me. She'd gone back to him in spite of me. *To* spite me.

My head was splitting. The one and only thing I wanted was to ride Foxfire, and it was the one thing I could never do again. I'd never been so alone. He'd known every emotion I'd ever felt. Who else in the world had felt the depth of my sorrow when Mouse died? Who else knew my guilt? Who else could hold such a loss of the one I now faced?

I ignored the ringing phone. I ignored the knocks at the door. Sorrow pushed outwards on the boundaries of my body. I ached at my seams. Foxy carried me through my mother's illness and Mouse's death. He even carried me through his own decline. Foxy always carried me.

When the front door opened, I didn't turn. I hadn't fastened the locks. Dave, I thought. It didn't matter. Even he couldn't make this pain worse.

The couch sank behind my back, and warm hands turned me to face things. Timothy didn't ask what was wrong. The moment I saw him, all the tears I'd tried to hold flooded out in a moment. He held me as I choked out the rabbits of story that crowded inside my throat, pushing for exit. They ran in all directions, but they kept coming back to the same emptiness.

I was cold and paper-thin. Timothy wrapped me in his soft flannel shirt and listened as I coughed up story. I talked and talked until there were no words left, until all I could do was stare at the squares of the flannel, trying to find order in its time-worn geometry, soft as Foxfire's coat in spring. At some point, Timothy pulled off my boots, washed the soot from my face, and made coffee. I sat up. The mug in my hand was warm, and its warmth helped. When he looked at me, I could believe that he understood the depth of my pain. Had he helped his mother in the same way after his father's death, wrapping her in flannel and feeding her coffee?

There was a knock at the door. "Stay put," he said. "I've got it." He returned bringing with him a large man with a badge.

The man barely looked at Timothy, coming straight to where I sat and making himself at home in my chair. "Ms. Edson, I'm Detective Floyd Watson." The words came from a mouth hidden under a thick brush of mustache that looked as if he could use it to strain soup. He shook my hand and sat down. "I'd like to talk to you about this morning's barn fire at Connie Thornfield's."

"She's had a rough day," Timothy said. "Can't this wait?"

"I'd really like to talk now, if she's able." His bald head expanded at the neck into a massive body, and he reminded me of nothing so much as a walrus, but the small eyes that looked at me were bright rather than piggish. His eyes, I realized too, were not unkind.

"Did you find Foxfire?" I asked.

"Her horse," Timothy said. "We think he was in the barn."

"I'm afraid he was trapped in his stall," he paused, turned on his belt audio recorder, then added, "I'm very sorry for your loss."

"It," I stopped a moment and gathered my voice. "It couldn't have been any other horse? I mean, you can't be certain it was Foxfire."

"I'm afraid there is no doubt." He seemed at a loss to know what else to say. Timothy sat on the couch next to me and rested his hand on my knee.

Finally, the detective began again. "Ms. Edson, we're investigating this as an arson case."

I looked at him for a moment, then shook my head. This detective didn't know shit. "If you're thinking Connie did this for the insurance money, you're way off. She loved those horses, and the barn was her life's work. Her dream. If you think this was arson, then you don't know Connie. This? This was an accident." I wanted to give her a better alibi, but I wasn't sure it would help her case if I said she was passed out drunk.

He opened a small notebook and flipped through a few pages. "Do you know anyone who drives a large, late-model Dodge pick-up?"

I stared at the man, trying to make sense of his question. "Dave?"

He flipped through the notebook with pudgy fingers, but didn't seem to find what he wanted.

"Dave Mason," I said, impatiently. "Jenny Mason's husband."

"Through the VIN, we traced the truck registration to Connor Construction."

"Jenny's father owns the company. Dave worked for him."

He fixed me with a penetrating gaze. "Ms. Edson, do you know of any reason why Mr. Mason would want to harm Mrs. Thornfield's property?"

I shook my head. I didn't want to make sense of this.

"Is there a reason why he would want to hurt your horse?"

I brought my hands up over my face and rubbed my forehead. "No," I managed. I could feel the sadness swelling in my throat but I swallowed it, unwilling to show any weakness in front of the detective. Dave had found the ultimate way to hurt me. I could not answer without telling the whole story. Timothy moved his hand to my back. "Do you want me to go?" he said.

I dropped my hands and opened my eyes to the ceiling, trying to decide how much to say and how to say it.

"What exactly was your relationship with Mr. Mason?" the detective asked.

"I shouldn't be here." Timothy moved to stand, but I stilled him with a hand on his leg.

"No. If anyone deserves to know, it's you. I should've told you weeks ago." I looked at Timothy only, willing him to understand. It didn't matter what the detective made of all this. I needed Timothy to know. "Dave and I had a brief affair. I'd just come back from New Jersey. When I found out he was married, I ended things with him. He wouldn't leave me alone. I moved apartments. I thought I'd managed to lose him, but then Jenny started riding at the barn, and he found me."

The man scribbled a few short notes in his book, the fat of his neck shaking as he wrote. "He approached you?"

I wanted to say no, but I wouldn't lie to Timothy again. "He's been watching me—his truck sitting outside my apartment. He tried to get me to leave with him. Move somewhere. Start a new life."

"Did you ever think of getting a restraining order?"

I shook my head. "He was a little desperate, but I didn't think he'd hurt me." Memories of Rosauer's contradicted me, but that had only been one day.

"When did you last see Mr. Mason?"

"Last night."

"Here? Just the two of you?"

"No. We all went to dinner: Dawn and Russ, Jenny and Dave. I wanted to introduce them all to Timothy." I waited for the detective to finish writing and look at me. "I wanted Dave to know it was over. That I'd moved on."

"And how did he react?" He sounded like a doctor, asking questions with that disinterested tone as if nothing important rested on my answer.

Timothy's face was smooth and calm as unbroken water. I said, "Dave didn't really react at all. I chickened out—I don't know why. I wasn't scared of Dave, exactly, but instead of introducing Timothy as my boyfriend, I told them he was my friend. I don't think I fooled anyone, except maybe myself. They know me well enough to know what bringing Timothy to dinner meant. How big a step it was for me. Dave was silent and sullen, but he didn't say much. He didn't explode."

"Was that what you were expecting? An explosion?"

"I didn't know what to expect." These questions were stupid. Last night was an eon ago. I tried to reconstruct it, and suddenly remembered the conversation. Foxfire, my one great love. Bile rose in my throat. I had suggested Dave's revenge.

The detective ran his hand over his scalp, as if he were polishing it. He had worn no coat. Perhaps he carried enough heat within him. Now, in the small warmth of my apartment, he'd began to perspire. "Ms. Edson, do you have reason to suspect that Mr. Mason was more than normally smitten? Did you ever consider him dangerous?"

"He said he wanted to leave his wife and run away with me, but I never thought he was dangerous. Only unhappy. He felt trapped in his life, and he saw me as a way out."

He looked at me, waiting to see if there was anything more. I didn't know what he expected me to say, but at last, my silence seemed to satisfy him. He sighed. "Mr. Mason's truck was found inside the barn, along with human remains."

I sat very still, trying again to understand, frustrated that the detective didn't talk straight. "Are you saying Dave is dead?"

The detective flipped his notebook shut and returned it to his pocket. "We have not identified the remains. It would be premature to assume that they are Mr. Mason's. We'll know more after the post mortem." The detective rubbed his palm over his head again, then dropped his hand and stood. "This must all be quite a shock." He shook hands, first with Timothy and then with me. "Thank you, Ms. Edson. You've been very helpful," he said as Timothy let him out.

I sat on the sofa, staring at the floor. *You've been very helpful*, rang in my ears. "What have I done?"

"You told the truth." Timothy looked too calm. He hadn't said "finally." He hadn't implied it in tone or look, hadn't suggested it with even the most minute gesture, but I heard it nonetheless.

"Dave was a little crazy, but not like this. This makes no sense." My hand shook, and I set my empty coffee cup down, then picked it up and again went to pour another cup. He rose and rifled through cabinets. I listened to him clanging around my kitchen for a while, cooking.

Memories flashed before me like poorly spliced film: Dave stepping into the beams of the headlights the night the truck broke down, Foxfire's last jealous scream, lunch at Mouse's locker, the urgency in Dave's kiss, Zephyr's power at Deep Creek, Jenny in the ditch holding her arm toward me, the Pod driving away when I sold it, the first time I laid eyes on Timothy. I wrapped the flannel shirt more tightly around my shoulders.

Timothy returned with a bowl of chicken and dumplings. I sipped the broth. Food should have been inedible. My throat should have constricted at the mere thought of eating; instead, the herbed broth warmed me. I broke the clouds of dumplings with my spoon and swallowed them quickly, their steam scalding.

He waited quietly while I ate, but his eyes rested on me thoughtfully under the flop of glossy black hair. I watched the small movements of his tattoo as the muscles of his neck tensed or relaxed. I couldn't imagine what he was thinking. His gaze reminded me of Dr. Rivers' when he was looking into the blank eyes of new ER patients; it had the same penetration, keen as a scalpel's edge. He took my bowl and refilled my coffee. When he did speak, he said what I least wanted to hear. "Joannie, I think I should give you some space for a while."

I stared, choking on all the things I wanted to say. He couldn't care for me and feed me soup and coffee and then vanish. He picked up his coat and kissed my forehead, hesitated, then put his lips against my hair and rest them there.

"Please, Timothy. I'm not strong enough for this."

"You've always been strong enough."

I looked at my hands, powerless. "I need you."

His lips curled into a smile that seemed both proud and amused. "You've never needed anyone."

"You're wrong." I thought of Mouse and of Foxfire. I had never faced any loss alone. I didn't know how to begin.

He turned away, then paused. His black hair curtained the eyes that did not meet mine. "You see, what I can't quite work out is, did you bring me to dinner to drive Dave away or to bring him back? I'm not totally sure you know the answer to that question either." He pulled on his coat. "Perhaps the question is unfair. It's a moot point anyway. You're a tough woman, Joannie. Even stronger than you think. You need some time right now to find your strength again. You need to heal, and I don't want to be part of the scab you shed when this is over." He tucked the hair behind my ear, his fingers gentle and loving. "When you're ready, I'll be waiting. You know where to find me."

Again, he kissed me, his lips soft on my forehead. I closed my eyes and leaned in, willing him to stay. For a moment, he leaned his forehead against mine and the breath between us was warm with the home-rich scent of dumplings, but he quickly turned and left without looking back.

VI
The Jump

If I moved out of my own mind, I'd wager something would still func-
tion. Some awful perfect part that would inflate my lungs and pump
my heart out to my extremities. I wouldn't be sharp then.

—Kirsten Kaschock, "DNR"

If you are going to win any battle, you have to do one thing. You have
to make the mind run the body. Never let the body tell the mind what
to do. The body will always give up.

—General George Patton, 1912 Olympian

Dark and Bitter

You've always been strong enough. My small room was infused with vapor and mist. Dave and Mouse had filled my dreams. Phantoms glimmered dust in the slanted morning sunbeam. Flesh and bone were mirages, things we believe in to make it through the desert. Touch, smell, sight, sound, taste: just so many fired synapses, electrical currents, nervous energy that we foolishly mistook for a soul. I couldn't trust my hands to feel.

I smoothed the quilt across my bed and showered, concentrating on each hot needle of water on my skin.

Foxfire burned constantly before me, running endless circles in his inescapable stall, mane and tail ablaze. There was no escaping the searing tongues, and I was always too far away. The vision exploded in cinders. "It wouldn't have been like that," I said, needing to hear the words aloud. I hoped lack of oxygen had knocked him out. I needed to believe in smoke.

I didn't want another thought. If there was a way out, the way was through the body. Screw the mind. Its thoughts only hurt. I made eggs and watched the Mormons walk from their apartments to the Ward. I went running, then showered again. I couldn't get rid of yesterday. I couldn't sweat or wash or distract it away.

Dawn, Connie, and Jenny came in the afternoon, each carrying a casserole dish. "Figured you'd need some company," Dawn said.

My tongue lay like a slug, fat and numb, in my mouth. I couldn't believe they would want to see me. Why wasn't Jenny at home with her family? She should be the one getting casseroles, for God's sake. Why did she look so composed? I pressed my thumbs into the calluses on my hands, but there were no reins there to stop this.

They fluttered around me. Connie collected the casserole dishes and disappeared into the kitchen, Dawn poured coffee, and Jenny hugged me, the tears wet on her cheek. "I'm so sorry about Foxy," she said.

I started and pulled back from her hug. Connie and Dawn were back. "You don't know. The police officer didn't tell you? The detective?" I looked at each of them.

"I told the police I couldn't talk to anyone yet. It's all too sad, losing the barn and everything," Jenny said. Dawn handed her a mug.

"It's my fault. Foxy's dead because of me." I stared at Jenny, unsure to believe she knew as little as she said.

Connie stared. "Detective Watson didn't say anything like that to me."

"Are you sure you're all right, Joannie?" Dawn said. "You sound kind of crazy right now."

I closed my eyes. Not seeing them made it easier to speak. I tried to put my thoughts in order, but they flew from me as I reached for them. "New Jersey was a disaster. Mom was sick again. I was in bad shape driving home. I wanted to leave it all behind, and I pushed too hard. I made it here, but the Chevy broke down the next day. Water pump."

"Joannie, what does this have to do with anything?"

"A guy stopped to help me, and one thing led to another. To an affair. For two weeks, things were intense. Maybe unhealthy, I don't know. I thought it was love. We spent every moment together."

"Joannie?"

"Then I found out that he was married." An oily swirl twisted on the surface of my coffee. "That Dave was married."

The room was incredibly still. For the first time in our long friendship, I'd surprised Dawn. Jenny's knuckles whitened, gripping her coffee cup as if to choke it.

"I didn't know it was your Dave then. I didn't meet you until another couple of months later. As soon as I found out he was married, I broke things off. Only." I paused. There was no easy way to say any of this. "We met again at El Mercado's that night after you fell in the ditch, and Dave started calling again. I told him to stop, but he wouldn't."

I told the truth, but not all of it. I didn't tell them I'd had to change apartments, or how he'd followed me to work. I tried to cause only the necessary pain, but that did not dull the blades in my mouth. "Then there was Timothy the other night. I set that up. I just meant to end things, for it to be over. I never thought this would happen. Dave set the fire. He burned down everything because of me. To hurt me."

Jenny's skin glowed livid but she wouldn't look at me. She stared off into the corner at the blank television set. "It's a lie," she said, her voice shaking. "Dave never cheated on me. Why would you say that?"

"Jenny, I'm sorry."

"That's all you can say? After all you just said? Sorry?" Jenny wouldn't look at me. Instead, she kept staring at that damned blank television where we'd watched the Eagles play the day she and Dave had quarreled.

I had hurt her enough. There was nothing I could say now. Dawn and Connie would comfort her.

Quite suddenly, she walked out. I followed her into the kitchen. She tossed the nearly full cup of coffee down the sink. Her face was white as she carefully washed and dried her mug, refusing to acknowledge me. She returned it to its place on the shelf, positioning its handle to be exactly in line with the sole remaining cup. What had she thought when Dave didn't come home last night? Had she told Dawn or Connie? Wiping the counter, Jenny's hand knocked the amaryllis bulb. She picked it up with the towel as if it were something toxic and looked at it only briefly, scornfully, before throwing it in the garbage. She dried her hands and folded the dishtowel into perfect thirds to hang neatly over the oven door handle. I'd always kept my house clean, but now it was immaculate. She was better at this than I was; that was her point. Her wrath was bound in dishcloths. Whatever I had given Dave, it was not a perfect house.

She picked up her coat and turned to me, face set into a porcelain mask. "I'm glad Foxy's dead," she hissed under her breath. She walked out, pulling the door softly but firmly shut.

For a moment, I stood stunned. In her words, *I'm glad Foxy's dead*, I felt the first surge of hatred rise.

Connie and Dawn stood at my back. "She didn't mean it," Dawn said. I had never seen her so lost for words.

"She meant it," I said.

"Not what she said about Foxfire. She couldn't have meant that. It's just shock." Dawn was trying to convince herself. She wasn't even looking at me, but at the door Jenny had refused to slam.

Connie's face was grim. "I've got to get out of here," she said, as if her anger too would erupt like vomit.

I hadn't apologized to her. Now, it seemed too late. "Where are the horses?"

Dawn answered. "We hauled them to Eddie's. Looks like we'll be trail riding for a while." She paused, and her face seemed again to screw up in confusion. "You didn't tell me any of this? Not one word until now? This way?"

I looked for an olive branch. "I can call some places with indoor arenas, see if I can find a place for us to ride."

Connie shook her head. "You really are unbelievable, Joannie Edson. You think those barns would do *you* a favor? You've never been one for winning popularity contests. You were too busy winning horse shows." She said it with a scorn I didn't expect. "You've beaten their best at every show, and every one of them thinks that if they'd had Foxfire, they'd be the ones with the ribbons. If I want an indoor arena to ride in, I'll call. I could use something to do." She walked out, holding the door for Dawn.

Dawn hesitated only for a minute. "You couldn't trust me with even a word of this?"

I had no answer. Dawn waited a full minute, staring at me before closing the door between us. I thought I'd prepared myself for their anger until I actually felt it. I'd never expected that they wouldn't forgive me. Not Connie and Dawn.

Alone in my prim kitchen, I sat absolutely still. There would be no more sympathetic visitors, no more casseroles, no more coffee made. Now, it was simply up to me to see if I could pull together a Joannie out of all these pieces.

I dug the amaryllis bulb out of the garbage and pulled out a mason jar from the box under the sink. Outside, I gathered stones.

It was only after I watered the jar and went to put it in the living room that I saw what Jenny had been staring at on top of the dead television: Dave's copy of *The Count of Monte Cristo*. It'd been collecting dust there for so long, I no longer noticed it. I flipped through the pages, taking in the loamy scent of a dying paperback. Its pages were brittle and brown as fallen leaves. I could tear each page one by one, light them in the gas flame of my stovetop, and pretend I'd made a pyre.

Instead, I crammed it into the glove box of my truck where I could lock it away, where it couldn't taunt me with the memory of the one person who had, again and again, refused to leave me.

At my parent's house, I dropped onto the patch-worked couch. I told them about Foxfire dying in the fire and how a man had killed him to hurt me. My father laid down his paper and looked over, and my mother rolled her chair in from the kitchen with her coffee balancing in her lap. I fingered the familiar seams. I felt hot under their eyes as they stared at me. There was an awkward pause that was never there—not at home, not with my parents. I called Pilate. Outside, an early flurry had begun. The flakes were small and stung as the wind pelted them against my skin. I turned my collar up and trudged over the hills, Pilate trotting by my side.

I stopped at the truck on the way back in and pulled from it the box of ribbons, of cups and bowls, of all the prizes Foxfire had ever won. I gave them to my parents. Hugging a woman in a wheel chair has an awkwardness I would never fully learn to overcome, but I hugged my mother long and hard that night, hugged my father, too, thanking them for Foxfire.

The shadows of the next afternoon were long when the detective's knock startled me from my thoughts. I turned on my living room lamp and let him in. "Do you have a few moments?" he asked. "We know a little more about what happened."

I led him to the kitchen where I could brew more coffee for both of us. He turned on his belt audio and flipped through his notebook briefly. The coffee maker gurgled while I waited for what he had to say. He sighed and ran his hand quickly from the back of his skull to his brow as if he might squeegee his thoughts forth. He looked at me. "One of the benefits of living in Moscow is that we don't have many crimes with fatalities, so we were able to get a post mortem pretty quickly. I have confirmation from the dental records now. The remains are indeed Mr. Mason's. The truck pointed us that way, but of course we had to be sure." His mouth momentarily settled into a firm line. "As you know, Mr. Mason apparently entered the barn that morning with the intention of committing arson, burning Ms. Thornfield's barn and your horse with it. His motive now appears clear. What was less clear at first was why he hadn't escaped. His truck was parked in the barn aisle. He had two packed suitcases in the cab; both escaped damage from the fire. All evidence suggests he had planned to run."

I poured the coffee, which he took black but heavily sugared. As he stirred his cup, the sugar crystals scraped against ceramic. "Ms. Edson, I don't know how to tell you this, but it seems only right that you should know. Mr. Mason must have been very disturbed. He had a pair of bolt cutters with him that morning. The best we can figure is, after starting the fire, he went into the stall and attempted to cut the horse's tail off."

I stared at the detective, unable to process what he was telling me. "You're saying that as if Dave was some kind of sadist. You couldn't have known him. He was a little off kilter at the end, but that's . . . that's . . ." I had no words to finish my thought.

"We don't know if that part was pre-meditated. Being in construction, he may have just had them in his truck, but the marks on the bone match those that the cutters would impart."

I stared at him, wondering if he had told Jenny this. Somehow, the arson seemed believable, but this was too much. Dave said I understood him, but he'd gone beyond me. This made no sense. The Dave I'd known was not so cruel, so hateful.

"At any rate," he continued, "the horse kicked, breaking Mr. Mason's leg. He sustained a segmental comminuted fracture of the femoral shaft, preventing him from making it out. Either pain or smoke inhalation caused him to lose consciousness."

Not "the horse," I thought. *Foxfire.* He should have named him. Foxfire deserved that much. Instead, his identity was erased while Dave's was preserved in formal terms: Mr. Mason. I fought against the story he'd told. Foxy's final moments were horrific enough. "Foxfire has never kicked a soul in his life," I said. Kicking was what Zephyr did.

Detective Watson ignored my comment. "It was unclear to us why Mr. Mason would try to do something so," he stopped and struggled to find the word. Perhaps "sick," "twisted," "depraved" carried too much judgment. He was supposed to be an impartial witness to the facts, merely sorting them into a narrative that explained the evidence. No appropriate word came, and he moved on. "The truth is, we don't understand this part of the crime. From what his wife tells us, Mr. Mason had no documented history of psychological instability. I suppose it will remain a mystery. Human behavior usually is."

"Does she knows Dave's dead then? Jenny?"

"We waited until after we were confirmed the identity to tell her, but yes, now she knows. She, um, she doesn't think much of you right now." The detective moved his hand over his scalp again then smoothed his pant legs.

"It's my fault."

"I'll be writing my report tonight, and there certainly will be no charges against you. I know that doesn't help with guilt, but Ms. Edson, I'm not sure you could have prevented this. You just fell in with a bad character. Mr. Mason was unwell."

My hand shook as I reached for my coffee mug. Dave had cheated me out of a showdown. He'd lassoed the sun and pulled it up to high noon when I couldn't be there to walk my ten paces and face him. Bolt cutters. *Christ.*

The detective swallowed the last of his coffee. "Have you decided what to do with the horse's remains?"

"His name," I said, "was Foxfire."

The silence hung between us. Whatever pain Dave imagined I caused him, I could imagine nothing to match what I felt now. I clenched my teeth, willing myself not to allow even one tear to fall in front of this man.

"I apologize." He was quiet for a moment. "I know how hard this must all be, and I really am sorry to have been the one to share it with you. I'm afraid the question is as painful, but I must ask it. Have you decided what you will do with Foxfire's remains?"

"I'd like to ask Connie if she'll allow him to be buried in her field, but at the moment, I doubt she'd speak to me."

"I'm going to see Ms. Thornfield next; I'll ask. The truth is, we need to get the body taken care of."

"Thank you." The words sounded cold.

The detective stood and shook my hand. "There is no way to say this and sound sincere, but please believe that I am very, very sorry for your loss."

I merely nodded and showed him out, then washed his cup to erase the evidence of his visit and the news it had brought. I remembered burn victims from the ER: the skin boiled away from fat and muscle, the charred flesh, the smell. Every time I shut my eyes, Foxfire burned.

I picked up the jar with Timothy's amaryllis. What a weak symbol it seemed now that he was gone. I wasn't strong. All I had was impotent anger.

My hand squeezed tight around the coldness of that glass, but it didn't break. I turned and moved my arm to pitch it into the wall, but as I did, water from the jar tipped out onto my wrist, cold and pure, and brought me back to a degree of sense. A sob escaped.

I set the jar down as the phone rang. "Are you riding tomorrow?" Eddie asked.

All I wanted to do in the world was ride, feel Foxfire's body again and know his mind. I wanted him to feel the depth of my love for him, like he'd read every other emotion I'd had. Zephyr was the borrowed horse I'd used to betray him. I couldn't ride her now. "I've got work."

"What about after?"

I didn't answer.

"Joannie, this is the one thing I can do for you right now. You need to get back on."

It hadn't been forty-eight hours. I pressed my finger into the scar of my cut and thought of the boy whose life had run out too soon. I began shaking again, and the shaking broke some fissure in the shell of me. My voice broke as I spoke. "Are you going to sell me Zephyr? Because if you won't, then I'm not sure I really see the point of all this."

Eddie paused. "You know as well as I do that riding is more than winning horse shows."

"Riding Foxfire was about more than winning. I'm not sure what riding Zephyr is yet. All I know is, if you sell her, I'll have lost two horses."

"Training has rewards of its own—you know that as well as I do. Don't let what happened to Foxfire erase what you accomplished at Deep Creek."

"Can we talk about this later?"

"Zephyr won't wait."

"It hurts, Eddie."

"I know, Joannie," Eddie's breath rasped across the receiver. "He was a horse in a million." He took a minute to gather himself. "I've moved Zephyr to Ferndean for the rest of the winter. Their indoor isn't as large as Connie's, it's damp, and the footing is not as good, but it will have to do until spring. She needs training for the show."

Tears were in my eyes and I couldn't trust my voice.

"Joannie, I need you to do this. I've got to get the boys to basketball tomorrow night, and Zephyr won't do well if she's in a stall with no work."

"O.K." I hung up before I might have to say one more word.

The phone rang again when I had barely set it in the cradle. I paused a moment and swallowed before lifting it and answering. It was a reporter. Jenny was talking and the guy said he wanted to give me a chance to rebuke her claims. I hung up, but the guy called back at least twice more that evening. By seven, I turned the ringer off.

Tired as I was, sleep wouldn't come. I got on the treadmill, running steady, focusing on rhythm to the exclusion of any other thought. *Tempo, tempo.* I would become a mechanism, a framework of bonemetal, a few clever pumps, some fluid, and well-timed electrical pulses. Machines didn't feel.

When I finally did fall, spent, into bed, I slept fitfully. I dreamed of the monsters we create, I dreamed of Mouse driving me at another brick wall, and, just before dawn, I dreamed Foxfire alive again. I was at Connie's. The black skeleton of the barn still smoldered, and through a ghostly smoke and the cracked black bones, I saw Foxfire running in a back pasture. "We buried him," I said. "He's dead."

Connie appeared at my side, smiling. "We found him out there this morning." She pointed where we'd dug the grave, but it was no longer a neat mound of earth in a pasture corner, but a fresh hole. I looked at him again, and noticed that he no longer moved with the hitching steps. He was fluid as a colt and his copper coat burned with its subtle fire. No, he moved better than a colt—he moved like he had wings on each fetlock, floating across the surface of the earth. Zephyr watched from the next pasture, nickering to him like they were old friends. *This isn't happening,* I thought, and I woke suddenly to yet another new layer of sadness.

Beggars' Horses

Jenny's story ran in the morning newspaper. Cheryl looked smug; she'd been right the whole time, if only anyone had bothered to listen. She leaned to whisper audibly to Doreen. "They did the autopsy downstairs. Kathy said the body was charred so dry that parts kept falling off. A finger nearly rolled off the table." It wasn't true. The autopsy tables had troughs to collect the fluid, but I didn't stop to debate the point.

Jenny emerged a local heroine, the wife who stayed true to her husband even as I seduced him into insanity. Now, the story went, she was back in the loving arms of her family. Her father pushed television reporters away from the pale, young widow. Rumor was he'd bought over-priced tickets to fly his sisters in from Savannah. I pictured her flanked with aunts and said nothing to contradict my own black portrait.

Just after lunch, a thirteen-year-old girl came in, engulfed by an oversized football jersey and jeans. Her pale skin bore the map of her blood vessels, and her left arm hung heavy in a jury-rigged sling. She tipped back a ball cap to reveal her bald scalp. "I have leukemia *and* a broken wrist," she said. "Can you believe that shit?" Her smile was beautiful and proud. Her problems made her special.

I gave her my hand to help her up and she held it with the strong, confident grip of someone who does not doubt she will beat her disease. "Some luck," I said.

"Tell me about it." She settled herself on the table like one experienced in getting radiation. "Hey, you're the one in the paper. The one that guy burned down a barn for."

I focused on positioning the table. "That's me."

"That's so romantic."

"Then I could do with less romance."

The girl laughed. "I know what you mean." Her laughter was amazing, all crocuses pushing through snow.

"What's your name?" I said.

She smiled up into my eyes, glad she would have her own identity here, that who she was mattered, that she was more than a clipboard with a list of symptoms and procedures. "Lily."

"Well, Lily, I'll need you to hold still for a little while so I can get a nice clear shot of that wrist."

"You talk like a doctor," she complained, but she lay still. She was practiced in the art of being a patient, of listening, obeying, hiding pain in smiles. Afterward, she slid from the table and chucked me on the arm with her good hand. "Later, skater," she said, giving me one last wink before she disappeared.

She high-fived Dr. Rivers on his way in. "Meet you in the ER?" she said.

"I'm just off," he told her. "You'll have to settle for Dr. Leonard."

"Drag," she said, letting the door close behind her.

He turned to me and smiled. "I see you met Lily."

"Is she going to make it?"

"Her arm will heal. That's all I know. Her oncologist is the one to ask about the cancer. All I can say is, I hope to be treating her for many broken bones in the future. She loves her skateboard, so if the chemo goes well, we should see her again. This is her third broken bone in two years."

This wasn't the reason he had come. I waited. He straightened the pens in his pocket, only now avoiding my eyes. "I didn't know you rode horses."

He had tried to sound casual and off-hand, but the reference to that morning's article made me defensive. "None of it affects my work."

"No. Your pictures today were excellent as always."

I picked up my bag and moved toward the door.

"I used to ride," he said quickly. "When I was a kid in Iowa. Then one day, a pony bucked me off and I landed in a ditch. I thought I'd broken my neck. I lay there for an hour waiting for someone to save me, but no one ever came. Turned out I had nothing worse than a bruised ego."

"You seem to have made a full recovery."

"You'd never catch me getting on a horse again."

"The thing about riding is that even good horses will throw you eventually." I didn't want to talk about this. "You have to ride knowing that you will get hurt. It's not an if, but a when."

"Mountain bikes are safer," he said.

"I've seen plenty of mountain bikers in this room. There's no such thing as a safe life."

"No, only degrees of danger."

"Riding's not a sport for the faint of heart."

"No, it isn't." He looked at me with a curious expression that seemed to mix understanding and triumph, and I wondered if he was trying to lead me to that confession, like he was the doctor prescribing the necessary thought. "You'll get through this, Joannie. I don't know if everyone could, but you can."

I was supposed to ride Zephyr. Instead, I ran in the last light of early winter, pushing myself hard and fast, needing to be breathless and hurting. Cold burned in my lungs and lactic acid in my muscles, but I ran on, desperate for a physical pain. I ran the long flat of Mountain View Road and on up the base of the mountain. I ran roads I didn't know. When they forked, I chose the steepest route. Evening was falling with brutal cold, and I ran upward to meet its darkness. My face stung against the bitter air.

Out among the fir and pine, the snow began to fall like barn ash, slowly and methodically covering the earth. I fumbled.

My eyes stung with cold, dry air. I turned and looked out over Moscow. From here, it looked so small: a quilt of threadbare trees pulled around houses. It was hard to believe that twenty thousand people lived wrapped there. Bleak wheat fields stretched over the surrounding hills, lined with windbreaks. The Kibbie Dome, pride of the Vandals and the first domed stadium in the country, sat squat and ugly as an airplane hanger at the edge of the university. On its face, the faded pattern of gold and black squares still managed a boldness in the failing light. Water towers and grain elevators reached as high as anything.

It wasn't a postcard town. It wasn't anything people would seek out. I could leave it any time I liked. I already had.

That wasn't true. Even in New Jersey, I'd never left it.

The muscles of my legs tensed, cramping. I took a few tentative steps forward, then broke into a jog. The tears came faster now. No matter how much I wanted to believe otherwise, my heart was no fist of string. It pumped red blood, carrying oxygen, carrying other things. I stretched my stride longer, running back to everything I'd ever wanted to leave.

By the time I arrived at the barn, Zephyr was pacing her stall and striking its wooden door with brutal fury. Hobbes, in the stall next to her, stood calmly eating hay, occasionally flicking his ears toward her antics. Zephyr moved in a contained gyre, exposing the stall mats as she'd shuffled the wood chips into the corners. As soon as she saw me, she charged the stall door, snapping her teeth. I held my breath and a halter, trying to find the moment when I could open the door without getting bitten or struck. "Easy, girl," I said, but easiness was not to be had for the price of small words. She wanted a pound of flesh at the minimum.

I picked my moment and opened the door, my arm raised in defense as she rushed me. She lunged forward and grabbed my arm with her teeth, swinging me up and out of her way. I struck wood and metal. The sound of the stall walls reverberating mingled with her galloping hoof beats. I blinked, trying to clear the clouds away. I felt for my arm. My shirt was torn and my arm was bleeding, but I could still move my fingers. Nothing was broken.

Zephyr had nowhere to run but into the indoor. Even over the ringing in my ears, I could hear a woman shouting. I hoisted myself up on unsteady legs and went after her. In the arena, Zephyr had run the woman and her horse into a corner. She reared and struck at them. I threw the lead rope around her neck and pulled her down to get her haltered.

"That animal is a menace," the lady said. "It should be shot before someone gets hurt."

"I've thought the same thing myself." The world was still hazed with the blow and my head was aching. "She's been abused and we're trying to rehabilitate her."

The woman only glared at me. "If she so much as touches me or my horse, I'm calling my lawyer. You'd better think long and hard about how much that horse is worth to you, especially if you can't control it better than that."

I walked away before I could say something I would regret, Zephyr fighting me every step. One day in, and already we'd be in danger of losing our spot at Ferndean. I popped the halter against Zephyr's nose, hoping to still her, but she merely pinned her ears and lunged for me again, adding another bruise.

I was angry: angry at the woman, angry at Zephyr, angry at the reporters and how they'd told my story. Anger needed to be turned into something functional. I held the show in mind and grabbed Eddie's brush box.

Eddie left a note: *Call me when you're done. Don't worry if it's late.* I snorted and stuffed it in my coat pocket. He was checking up on me. This was a test, and I had nearly failed. My head throbbing, I flicked the dust from Zephyr's coat, trying to avoid her teeth in the front and her hooves behind. I wanted to beat her, to make her the outlet of every aimless frustration, to exhaust my arms with whip strokes as I had exhausted my legs in running. Instead, I slid the crop into my boot and cursed. The bleeding on my arm had nearly stopped, but it throbbed steadily.

When we entered the arena, the women coughed and pointedly dismounted, muttering something I chose not to hear. The field was ours, but Zephyr was no better under saddle. It was like trying to ride a fury. In theory, we were working on flatwork: transitions and circles. In fact, I was doing little more than staying on as she catapulted through a series of acrobatics. She reared and kicked, bucked and lunged. I barely had more than four good trot strides at a stretch, those coming late in the night when she'd exhausted herself.

I returned her to her stall without carrots, slamming the bolt home to show what I thought of this evening's performance. She pinned her ears, struck the walls, and tossed her head as I swept the barn aisle and returned the tack and brushes to Eddie's locker. At least there would be no complaint about my cleanliness. The truck roared to life, and I went home.

Torn and stained with blood, my shirt was fit only for the trash. Everything hurt. I called Eddie.

"How's our girl?" he asked, the same tired question.

"She rode like shit. Worse than shit. She ran me over when I was getting her out and attacked some lady on a Quarter Horse. Rearing and striking. We're wearing out our welcome pretty fast."

Eddie considered this. "She needs more time out of the stall. We could lunge her first thing and turn her out in the bull ring until after you get off work, but I don't have time to get over there in the morning." He was fishing.

I sighed, picking up the Mason jar and turned it round in my hand. The bulb looked like nothing would come of it. "I can do it."

"It'll make an early morning for you."

"What else am I going to do with my time?"

"Good. With the boys' basketball season starting up, I'm going to have a hard time getting over to Ferndean, and Connie's asked me to help her start Bill over some fences. If you have the time, I'd like to turn Zephyr over to you to train exclusively for a while."

"We'll still have our weekly lesson?"

"Yes."

"But other than that, I ride and lunge her every day, almost like she's mine."

"Yes."

I prodded the bulb on the corner. The water level hadn't changed; it had to be dead. "Are you doing this because of Foxfire?"

Eddie considered this a moment before answering. "In part." When I didn't respond to this, he added, "You need to be on a horse, Joannie, and Zephyr needs consistency." He changed the subject. "I've picked your classes for the schooling show. English Pleasure, Hunt Seat Equitation, two-and-a-half foot Hunter, three foot Hunter and three foot Jumper. The two flat classes are early, so if things look bad, we can pull the jumping classes."

"Jesus." Except for the last, the classes worked against Zephyr's strengths. Hunters were judged on form and manners. They were to jump in a clean, round, cadenced style making the trip look effortless and stylish rather than fast, but at least for those, we'd have the ring to ourselves. The flat classes, pleasure and equitation, would put us in amongst other horses and riders, everyone trying to show how well they sat and their horse moved, everyone concentrated on the judge. I hoped they'd stay clear of Zephyr's teeth.

Eddie said, "I want to see if you two can work together."

I rolled back my sleeve and passed my finger over the circle of teeth on my arm. Always circles. "Will you sell her to me if we can?"

"Let's see how the show goes."

"But if it goes well, then the answer is yes?"

Again, he changed the subject. "Jenny called yesterday to say she's planning to show as well. She and Hobbes are doing the flat classes and the two-and-a-half foot with you. I'd been worried after I saw the paper, but she said it won't be a problem for her if it isn't for you."

My jaw clenched and my nails bit into my palm, the fist preparing itself for a fight with no conscious effort on my part. The fences were so small, barely more than a hop.

He tried to laugh lightly. "Two weeks ago, I couldn't convince her to sign up for even one class, and now, she's determined to take the ribbons."

"Huh," I said, not trusting myself to say more.

"You don't have a problem with her showing, do you?"

I ignored the question. "Do you want me to haul Zephyr or Hobbes?"

"We can figure that out later." He paused. "I haven't asked how you're doing, Joan. I'm sorry. That should have been my first question."

"I'm getting by."

"You sure? You need anything?"

"No. I'm O.K."

"You should get some sleep. I'll let you go."

"Eddie?"

"Yes?"

I closed my eyes. "I never said thanks for letting me ride Zephyr. I should have. It means a lot to me."

"None of that now. You're doing me a favor, kiddo."

"Yeah, well, you've done me one as well. Don't think I don't know it."

For a long time after we hung up, I sat and stared at the blank wall, slowly breathing, thinking of Jenny and Hobbes. There would be a showdown after all. Dave had nothing to do with it, and everything.

The Thickness of Blood,
the Thickness of Water

For years, I kidded myself that I'd recovered from Mouse's death. In the days that followed the wreck, it seemed that everyone— the kids at school, my teachers, my parents—expected me to melt into tears at every moment. I hated the way they looked at me, the way they pretended not to look. They pitied me, and even though I understood that their pity was kindly meant, it kept Mouse's loss too fresh. *She* was the one they should be sorry for. *She* was the one who died too soon. I was alive, and I would make my life mean something—not just for myself, but for Mouse, too, since she'd never had a chance. I'd work harder than ever, and if I ever had the chance to hold a gold medal in my hand, I would turn to the reporters and tell them that this one was for Jennifer, my best friend since high school, the girl everyone at home knew only as "Mouse." I'd make her live again. It was the one way I could make up for what I'd done.

I was glad Timothy had gone before he could see me like this. Nights, I'd eat a packet of carrots and ramen noodles, or a frozen burrito, or macaroni and powdered cheese. Stuff I could mostly buy in bulk, avoiding the grocery store. Cheap food, so I could save. I ate only to function, not to taste. What was human could feel pain.

What was human was limited. If I was ever going to hold up that gold and say it was for Mouse, then I needed to be more than just human. I needed to be as strong as Timothy said I was, even if that strength was a lie.

Winter was bitter. The water I used to wash my tack each night was crusted with ice before I finished, and my hands burned with cold. I hung no lights or tinsel. Eddie put away the cavaletti and pulled out fences. Zephyr continued to fight me over striding and angles, head high and attention rapt on fighting me as we rushed toward a fence. Her antics getting no reaction, Zephyr flicked her ears forward at every last moment. Her mouth softened, and she'd reach and stretch in another beautiful arc. Electric, she surged from the pole of before-the-jump to the pole of after.

Eddie raised the fences slowly at first, careful to preserve her confidence, but confidence was never something Zephyr lacked. To test her boldness, Eddie threw blankets over the fences, added fake flowers at the base, hung jackets over the posts. She would look and make a show of spooking, then plunge forward and jump. For Zephyr, it was never about doubt or fear. She had to prove that jumping the fence was *her* decision. The spaces in between the jumps, rather than the obstacles themselves were our challenge. Down an empty line, she skittered in a rebellion of acrobatics that had its own grace. Like me, she needed fences by which to define her best self.

By December's end, Eddie was building oxer combinations, Cheryl had shifted her attention to a suspected affair between a cardiologist and one of the RNs, I was running fifty miles a week on my treadmill, and I hadn't been inside Rosauer's since the barn burned down. To pass time on the treadmill, I rented *Rocky* and *Hoosiers* and every other movie that glorifies training as a valid replacement for life.

The only problem was that I couldn't manipulate time. On film, months of training took minutes, flickering by to inspiring music. The art museum steps aren't run, and then they are. The weight is too heavy and then it isn't. The in-between is only alluded to in jump cuts. As much as I tried to fill my day, training left entirely too many hours.

Like the ghosts of that famous old novel, Dave came to me in a dream three nights before Christmas. I'd been standing alone in my empty white bedroom, when he sidled up in a new white Stetson and dark glasses, a different kind of Jacob Marley altogether.

"Always dressed for the part, aren't you?" I said.

He smiled, revealing a mouth full of flame, fire licking the spaces between his white teeth. Through the dark glass, his pupils blazed. He didn't speak, but reached out a hand and stroked my cheek. I was stunned by the soft coldness of his touch, black velvet in winter. His fingertips slid down my chin, down my neck, between my breasts. I closed my eyes as my breath came shuddering, my body filled with a sexual longing I couldn't suppress.

His hand stopped on my chest. "You know I'd never hurt you," he said, and it was impossible to say whether the words were a statement or a question, only that they burned in my chest where he touched me. A sob escaped and I gritted my teeth against a tide of others. He gazed with fire-filled eyes. Soft fingers pushed through my skin and broke my sternum and ribs to pull the heart from my body.

I stared at it in his flaming hand, the image that hung on the wall of countless childhood memories, the sacred heart. Only, mine was not Jesus red but black. As it beat, charred flakes fell from it. With each throb, it was greyer, diminished.

Dave said, "Nothing is sacred to you, is it?"

The heart, the surrounding fire, the chasm in my chest, the longing, the longing. "I want," I started to say.

"Yes?"

I had no idea how to end the sentence. "I want . . ."

His eyes blazed up. "Exactly," his voice was resonant with sneering. "You are wanting."

He put my heart into his pocket and walked away, leaving only the echo of his footsteps in all that space.

I woke with a start and grabbed my chest. The cotton of my shirt was sweat-soaked. I gritted my teeth and shook the dream away.

On New Year's Eve, my phone rang for the first time in over a month. The ring startled me with its unfamiliarity. It was late. I realized as I listened to it ring that I'd turned off the answering machine weeks before. I stared at the dust that had collected on the receiver, wondering how long it took for a telemarketer to give up: six rings? seven? At ten, I answered.

"Your apartment is not big enough for you to take that long to answer the fucking phone." Only Dawn began phone conversations this way.

"Sorry."

"Yeah, well." I imagined her clicking her nails on the counter, trying to decide whether or not to scold me further. She decided against and said instead. "It's been a while, what with the different barns and all. I thought I'd see if you wanted to grab a beer."

"Sure," I managed.

"Dick's in fifteen minutes then."

But she was pregnant. "You can't drink."

"I never said I was going to." She hung up.

It seemed like something should have changed. I looked around the apartment, but the only difference was the blackness of absent dust where my hand had touched the phone. My mouth was dry and I drank water. Lately, I couldn't drink enough water.

I wore dirty breeches and mud-strewn boots. My hair curled into crisp ringlets, salty with dried sweat, but I wasn't out to impress anyone. I steered my pick-up down the highway to Dick's.

Harold threw down his bar rag when he saw me come in. "Joannie Edson. You still drinking Newcastle Browns?"

"Whenever I can." I smiled. Banter with Harold was easy. No matter how long it'd been, we could do this by rote. Red cardboard letters hung behind him spelling Happy New Year, their metallic sheen long since rubbed dull, the corners of the letters bent with age. Make all the resolutions you want, Dick's was Dick's.

He pulled the cap off a bottle. "You want a glass for this?"

"Nah. Someone might mistake me for someone with class."

"So how come you don't come see me more often? You've been home over a year now, and I've seen you, what, once?"

"You don't flirt with me enough. Hurts my ego."

Harold laughed and picked up his rag again. "You're not my type, lucky for me. You'd break my heart if you were."

"That's my job."

"I know—seen you do it." Harold was smiling, but I couldn't read his tone. "You're a girl that men commit arson for."

The smile fell from my face. "That's not something to joke about."

"No, I guess it isn't." He stopped wiping the counter. The rag was so dirty, that it seemed more likely to wipe on smears than wipe them away. "You're not to blame, Joannie. The guy was crazy. You know that, right?"

I had no answer. I picked up my beer and found a table under the old neon Miller sign. Waiting for Dawn, I watched it now just as I'd watched it over the many years at Dick's. Dormancy, illumination, dormancy. Life was a fucking Miller sign. How was it that so much could have changed—the introduction of Dave and Timothy, the loss of Foxfire—and that I could be sitting in the same place, at the end of another circle, dormant again?

Dawn slapped a tall glass of ice water on the table, startling me out of thought. Her teased hair stood high on her head and glowed in the neon bar light. She could still fit into her turquoise-colored Wranglers, I noticed, but they were now snug over the slight outward curve of her once washboard flat belly. With her pressed Western shirt and her lacquered nails, she still looked like a rodeo queen.

Dawn looked me in the eye, then sighed and leaned forward to pull a piece of hay from my hair. "You look like shit warmed over."

"You know how it is."

"Actually, I *don't* know how it is. What the hell have you been doing with yourself?"

"Working every double shift I can get. Not spending a dime I don't have to. Saving for a horse. Riding." I watched her sip her water. "Everything O.K. with the baby?"

"Peachy. And Timothy?"

"What about him?"

"You haven't called me once. I assume someone's taking up all your time."

"He split."

"When?"

"Day of the fire. He said to call him when I was ready."

"And?"

I shrugged. "I'm not ready."

Dawn stared at me a minute, then laughed and shook her head. "I've known you long enough, I should've seen this coming, but I just don't understand how a smart woman can be so damned stupid." She reached over and stole one sip from my beer. "You always did think you could do it all on your own."

I pulled my Newcastle back. "I *can* do it all on my own."

"Bullshit." Dawn kept her eyes on mine, her gaze as level as a battlefield. "You know, I was pretty damned hurt that you never called me after what happened."

"I didn't think you'd want to hear from me."

"Well, you were wrong. As usual, I might add." She tapped her nails along the edge of the table. "I knew I could call you, but I wanted you to call. It was your turn, damn it. After you didn't tell me about Dave or any of that shit, you owed me that little bit of effort. I wanted just that much faith in our friendship. And instead, you disappeared."

The Miller sign went dark. I said, "I was the last person anyone would want to hear from."

"You don't think any of us needed a friend?"

I was suddenly angry. "What kind of friend was I? A friend who lied, or at least hid the truth? A friend who made a man hate her so much he burned a barn, killed a horse and himself? That's a nice kind of friend. I was a better friend to you by sparing you from me." My anger was short-lived, spending itself out into self-pity. I checked myself.

Dawn drank a long, slow steady sip of her ice water. Her eyes were narrow but unmoving. She said, "We all needed a friend then. Any kind of friend."

"Well, if you still need one, you've got one."

"That's all I need to know." Dawn leaned back in her chair, slumping a little but keeping her eyes, softer now, on me. "You got one, too. Just don't fucking forget it next time."

We were silent for a few moments. The young guys at the bar nudged each other, and one rose to approach, then turned back to his friends. As usual, Dawn and I were the only women under forty.

Dawn's nails were painted with stars and confetti for the new year, but now the polish had already began to chip. "You ditched Timothy and kept Zephyr. Good thinking there, genius."

"We jumped three six yesterday." I didn't add that everything in between fences was uncollected sprawl and fighting. Looking away, I caught the stare of the boy at the bar. I glared, sending the message that I was not a nice girl. "Zephyr didn't even hesitate. If she'll show, she'll be my best prospect."

"If she'll show?"

"You know Zephyr."

The boy was at my elbow.

"Piss off," I said, turning to him. "I'm talking to my friend." My face, dead serious, wiped the shy smile off his face. He blinked twice and turned away.

Dawn spun her paper coaster with the bottom edge of her water glass, waiting for the boy to get out of earshot. "Damn, Joan. Too cold."

"Like you wouldn't have said the same."

"He was just a kid."

"He must not read the paper, or he'd know to stay the hell away."

She gave the coaster three more spins, then slapped the water down to stop it. "What exactly happened with Timothy again?"

I looked away, silent.

"He gave up that easy?"

"I told him about Dave. What I'd done." I dropped my voice. "I told him that I needed him, and he left. He said he didn't want to be the scab I picked when this was over, or something like that. He said I was too strong to need anyone."

"Shit, then. You're both stupid." She sat back and thought about this. "But at least you're stupid along similar lines. He said to find him when you're ready. You realize that he didn't want to be your rebound man. That's promising at least. He wants to be there for the long haul."

"Funny way of showing that. Leaving."

She blew me off. We sat in silence for some minutes before she asked, "So are you ready to call him now?"

"I don't think so."

"Christ. You're in worse shape than I thought. Obviously, you would fall all to shit if it weren't for me."

"I thought you said I didn't need anyone."

"You only hear what you want. I said you *think* you don't need anyone. That's your whole problem in a nutshell."

"Well, I'm glad to know my problem is small enough to fit in a nutshell."

"It's a big fucking shell, Joannie."

The Miller sign blinked on and off. Dormancy, illumination, dormancy. I could make it on my own. "Here's the thing about love," I said. "For love, you have to sacrifice, right? Well, I'm not sacrificing my shot at a grand prix, not even for Timothy. The last month, all I've done is horses, and it's been enough. I haven't caused anyone any pain, and I got Zephyr from barely jumping to clearing oxers over three six in a month because I was there every morning to lunge and every night to ride. That's who I am. If I sacrificed that, I wouldn't know myself anymore."

Dawn closed her eyes. "Where do you get this shit?" Her fingernails tapped again, twice through, then stopped. "Yeah, you've got to sacrifice for love, but not yourself. No one's asked you to throw yourself up on a cross. You think I ever gave up who I am for Russ? You think he ever asked me to? You think it'd be love if he did?"

"That's Russ."

"I never noticed you coming to the barn any less frequently when you were seeing Timothy. Of course, I didn't know you were seeing him. All I knew was that you seemed happier than usual. Did he even once ask you not to ride?"

My silence was answer enough.

"That's what I thought." She sighed, exasperated but caring. "Love *is* sacrifice, Joannie—I won't sell you a false bill of goods—but you choose your sacrifices. I sacrifice my afternoons to shovel shit so that I can keep Sunny without going broke but also so I can get Russ that antique Winchester he had his eye on. D'you know Russ gave up beer while I'm pregnant so he wouldn't make me jealous? And don't even get him started on the Saturday pancakes he's missed for my trail rides. You work out your sacrifices together so that neither of you ends up sacrificing the things that make you who you are, the people who fell in love in the first place. That's love."

Dawn reached out and rubbed my arm. Her voice was softer now than I'd ever heard it. "I saw you ride Foxfire when you were tired, when your mom was sick. You rode him in snow and rain and heat. You sacrificed for him. I know you'll say those days were more for you than him, but they weren't always, Joan. You sacrifice for your parents, working their garden and bringing them shit. You even sacrifice for Zephyr, God knows why. Twice daily trips to the barn for that waste of pasture? The thing about sacrifices for love is that they don't always feel like sacrifices. They just feel like life."

I passed a finger over the sweating brown glass of the bottle and began to peel its label. Cinderella loved, but she had no strength. Snow White, Sleeping Beauty. All they did was fall into nonentity and happily ever after. I needed to be the solitary gunslinger: swaggering, clear-eyed, unencumbered.

On Main Street, the bars were filling with people in spangles and paper hats. They yelled wishes to one another as I drove home. The moon was cloaked in cloud, and the night's darkness seemed to open it to ghosts. I passed a girl walking home, clutching her sweater around her for warmth, and for a moment, it was Mouse. She'd walked in that sweater from many an MHS basketball game, but when I slowed to pick her up, her hair turned grey, and the face was no longer Mouse's. I pulled the truck to the side of the road, needing a moment to gather myself.

When I opened my eyes again, Mouse sat next to me. "We sure fucked up our lives," she said.

"Dave," I said.

She laughed at that. "You still think this is about Dave? You think this is about the guys we did or didn't date? This was never about Dave."

I blinked and was alone. I shook my head to clear it. I needed sleep. "If this isn't about Dave, what is it about?" I asked, but the darkness refused an answer. Christmas lights lit the neighborhoods with their false colors. A hollow Christ waved from his manger, and plaster reindeer froze on rooftops.

Rivals for Possession of the Dead

I'd like to blame Jenny for the disaster at the show, but it was Zephyr who started it. Jenny merely brought Hobbes in range. When Hobbes reacted to Zephyr's vicious bite with a quick kick, my hand was simply in the wrong place at the wrong time. The carpal bones snapped under an egg-bar shoe.

Jenny, too, heard. What else could explain the triumphant smile as she looked back over her shoulder? Before the pain registered, the sound and the smile did. Zephyr had sucked herself back, and dirt and darkness embraced me. Rolling into light, hooves descended like rain, grazing my arms, pinching skin to dirt and skittering away. The world spun, past and present synchronous in that glaring moment of pain.

Early in the day, the show had promised better. Zephyr, washed and braided, scowled like a tomboy in pink frills, but in spite of the pinned ears, she was beautiful. With her round flanks and her muscled neck, she belonged not to Idaho but to the realms of art: European statues, oil portraiture of English hunters, warhorses carved in Japanese jade. Hobbes was a mere fireplug next to her lithe power. Eddie gave me a leg up, and I felt what it was to be regal. In my velvet cap and long black boots, I was a lady on a lady's graceful horse. Land was a distant thing below us, something to float across. We moved among the lesser horses and riders, staying on the inside where the judge could see us. It was no contest after all. Zephyr trotted forward with collected suspension, her liquid stride on display, every eye fixed upon her. At the judge's request, we moved from trot to canter, sharing one mind, scowling together at the meager world. *It's enough, it's enough,* her hooves repeated.

The boundaries between us, the mere flesh, dissolved in the acid of a unified will. The muscles I borrowed filled me with a terrifying knowledge of what was possible: the power to maim, to kill, to fly. Hooves were flint on tinder. Hobbes yielded out to pass a horse, moved into us. Hobbes wasn't being aggressive, but for Zephyr, it was enough. My mind and hers broke as she stretched her teeth forward to find their meat.

From the camp chair, the arena was only present as sound. My shattered hand was full of galaxies, stars exploding in spectacular novas. The show was over. I'd lost my shot at Zephyr. The machine of my body was broken, like my mother's. The old hospital lesson trumped all: Every body can break.

In the arena, the hooves of the cantering horses said, *Jennifer, Jennifer, Jennifer.* My hand had not restrained those teeth, and the dream slipped away in the current of her muscled neck. Eddie, on bended knee, held my hand in his, feeling for bones; a limp and mocking version of a proposal. He shook his head and frowned. "Let's go." Over his shoulder, I watched a blue ribbon flap, hung on the truck mirror, Jenny's first.

I didn't move. Couldn't. Zephyr, tied to the trailer, watched me. Her ears were neither pinned nor relaxed. Without menace closing its aperture, intelligence shown from her soft eye. She waited for me to speak as if she knew how much was balanced on my answer.

The hoof beats from the ring infected my hand with throbbing. All that I'd silenced returned in that primal cadence. I was hardly more, hardly less broken now than I'd always been.

The amaryllis has opened its large red trumpet that morning, heralding an unknown and unknowable future.

"Joan." Eddie was lifting me, hands under the armpits.

I wriggled free. "No."

Eddie stood back and tugged at the strand of hair by his ear. "We need to get that hand taken care of."

"It can wait."

"Wait for what?"

Zephyr stomped a fly away from her pastern, but her eyes never left me. Even without the saddle's telepathy, we were thinking together—or, perhaps, it was her thoughts moving my mouth, my brain too garbled with the fall to act. When my voice came, it was not my own. "For the jumpers."

Eddie stepped back. "You're not thinking of riding with that hand." It wasn't a question.

I turned my gaze on Eddie. My ears rung and my lashes were wet, but most of the shock had drained away, replacing itself with an insistent pain. *If thy hand offend thee.* "You remember back when I first started taking lessons with you on Foxfire all those years ago? The first time you took my stirrups and tied my reins, I was terrified. You said, feet and hands help you communicate, but you can ride without them if you know how to use your weight."

"That was Foxfire. That was flatwork—you were on a lunge line for God's sake."

Zephyr grunted quietly and shook her braids. I said, "I'm only down a hand." It took every effort of thought to make words.

"It's just a schooling show."

"This isn't about the show."

Eddie was quiet.

My face was cold and my hand hot, the blood out of balance, but my voice steadied. "You know what I've got riding on this."

"There will be other chances to show that you and Zephyr can do this."

"When?" I stared at him, willing him to read the determination there. "Months away. I need this, Eddie. I need a way forward."

"The show officials will never let you ride with a broken hand."

"You going to tell them?"

He threw up his hands. "I might." He ran a hand over his cap and looked at Zephyr, who looked at me. "Ah, Christ."

"What's that mean?"

"It means a holding pattern. It means I'm not doing anything yet but watching Jenny get through her rounds, since you won't let me take you to the hospital. Stick your hand in the cooler at least. I'll come back when they've finished the hunters and watch you ride a warm up. We'll see then." He grabbed his hat, beat the dust from it, and crammed it back on his head. "If you come to your senses before then, let me know." He walked off.

I squeezed my eyes because there would not be tears. *No rest for the wicked*: Eddie's words. I dug my hand into the ice between bottles of water, a different kind of pain. "Timothy," I heard myself growl, the word pushing my hand through the coldness. "Fuck." I timed fifteen minutes, and put my slender faith in ice, vet wrap, adrenaline, and Zephyr.

I'd been a fool to see the barn as a temple. Its cinders blown across the hills, mingling with dust, I understood the barn for what it was: a physical marker. My body, like all bodies, was the temple, church, cathedral. The rib bones were rafters. The heart, a nave. The brain, an apse. I wouldn't say I had not been burned, but the flame tempered rather than destroyed. Quenched, the temple of the body was a cold and brutal blade. The cross of cathedrals, the cross of the sword. These things cut both ways.

Jenny rounded the corner with Hobbes, her lip again curling with ill-suppressed glee at my suffering. "Show's over for you, I guess."

The blade in me heated. "I never did shit to you."

"You slept with my husband."

"It had nothing to do with you."

"You think I didn't know? You think I could watch Dave look at you and not understand what was written on his face? I knew him better than you ever did."

"You knew him, did you? You knew he'd burn the barn?"

"Dave didn't do that. You did. That's what you put into him." Her words came quickly. She'd been turning these thoughts for months and now spilled them forth.

It was my turn to sneer. "Is that what you think? Is that the truth you've constructed from all this?"

"You wrecked my life."

"Dave did that."

"And then you blabbed the whole affair in front of everyone, making me look like a fool."

"You did that for yourself, wishing Foxfire dead when he never did a damned thing to you."

Jenny turned and tied Hobbes to the trailer with shaking hands. He stood patiently, so calm he seemed to have seen all this before. "I used to look up to you," she said. "I'd watch you on Foxfire and think you were so great." She pulled a blue ribbon from the last class out of her pocket. "But I guess all sin tells in the end, and the just are rewarded."

Words fought within, each making a case to be voiced, but in the end, I let Jenny have the last word. When she'd gone, I slid *The Count of Monte Cristo* from my glove compartment and put it in her brush box. She could take Dave back. She could keep him.

I guided Zephyr around the warm-up arena, the reins gathered in my left hand, letting her adjust to the pressure coming from the neck rein rather than the direct pressure of hand against bit. Eddie stood at the gate, cursing under his breath.

The fence pattern was an asymmetrical figure eight, then a loop up the center and down the side to the finish. Ten small fences. I repeated the pattern: yellow vertical to square oxer, cross the long diagonal to the wall coming into the short corner, turn again to red triple combination (two verticals and a Swedish oxer) across the opposite diagonal, up the center to a green vertical, the liverpool, back down the side to the square oxer and yellow backward to finish. Repeating the order brought clarity through the fog of pain.

Eddie looked dubious. "Lots of turns. That first diagonal asks for speed, but carry too much and the wall will give you trouble. You'll have to hold back a bit. Can you collect her without hands?"

I didn't reply. The first rider was on course and jumping shallow. Too far from base of the fences, her horse flattened to make the distance. She was clean until the combination, where, predictably, she pulled two rails. Eddie scowled but didn't comment. Zephyr, too, was watching, head high and eyes on the horses, snorting her superiority.

The second two riders jumped clean. Their pinched knees would never win any hunter classes. They were dangerous, ugly rounds, but the times were respectable. The third rider nearly toppled off at the last fence, his knee acting as a pivot, but he clung to the pommel and managed to find his seat again. The forth, riding a palamino, was good and fast. Her blonde hair flew in a pony tail that would have driven Jack Stewart Flaherty into a conniption. I imagined him calling for a hair net or scissors and giving her the option. But though her hair was sloppy, her leg was not. It did not move from the girth as her horse leapt over each fence cleanly.

The fifth rider took a refusal penalty; her horse coming in too fast to the wall, too uncontrolled, dodged the jump. The sixth and last came in deep to the first fence and pulled a rail, then followed with three more pulled rails in the combination. I hung back, letting the others go first.

Eddie sighed. "Well. There's your competition."

I closed my eyes and sustained the vision of a large red bloom. Its phonograph played something faintly, but I couldn't hear it over the volume of pain clamped in my fist.

"That palamino. Jesus, Joannie, even if you *had* two hands."

The words were buzzing flies. I passed through the gate and squeezed Zephyr into a slow canter, sitting well back to maintain collection as we moved through the opening circle.

Jenny scowled from the thinly filled stands. I bent my eyes to the first fence and rose forward in my seat. Zephyr opened her stride, and we crossed the start line; the clock had begun.

Zephyr's hooves beat *Jennifer, Jennifer* to the base of the first fence, but landed *Timothy, Timothy*. We were clear, but the landing rang within my hand, sending shockwaves through my arm. I brought my body slightly upright and she collected herself, deft and sensitive. *Relax.* The reins were bridged in my left hand, where I held them quietly. Fence two, clean. My hand began to drop away from me, lopped out of consciousness. I turned my head and Zephyr turned to the wall, coming in strong and forward to the jump, utterly fearless, and seeming to collect herself in air to make the turn. My heart was beating to the rhythm of her feet, strong and steady. We picked up speed again as we rounded toward the triple with a long, ground-covering stride. Parts one and two were clean, but the rail of that oxer bounced in its cups. We'd come in too fast, too shallow—a rider error—and Zephyr was over-confident, perhaps. I shifted my weight slightly back, maintaining a jumper's halfseat, and gave the reins a slight pressure.

If the rail fell, we'd lost, but to look back now would command a turn. I looked instead to the next obstacle, turning her up the center, eyes trained over the top of the green fence. Zephyr was mad, irked at the fence that clipped her, and threw her legs forward as if striking the air as she galloped through it. "Easy," I said, resting my body weight heavier in the saddle to remind her I was there, then lifting and squeezing hard with my legs as we pushed into air. She took it high, clearing not only the fence but the standards on either side. If anyone ever doubted she could jump grand-prix, that fence ended those doubts. She landed and bucked. Those watching gasped, but Zephyr ignored the noise.

I legged her on: *Timothy, Timothy, Timothy*. If I won this round, if I won Zephyr, I'd be on the phone with him this afternoon. I'd tell him that I needed him. In Zephyr's hoof beats, I discovered that she wasn't the only thing I had riding on this.

Zephyr's ears swiveled toward the liverpool, and she snorted, her head suddenly high. We hadn't practiced water. I growled her forward, clamped my legs to her sides, breathed in deeply, blew away tension. Zephyr pinned her ears flat to her head and jumped long with no sound of splashing water. "That's my girl," I said, as she moved ever faster. I bit my lip, pain screaming through my hand, forcing tears to my eyes. I gritted my teeth and looked to the next fence, allowing her stride to fill me with its hope. Zephyr followed the path of my vision forward to the square oxer. We were moving with some real speed now. The wind carried us forward and over the last fences, its parcel. Zephyr and I breathed in unison, lungs heaving, as we crossed the finish line and circled to slow ourselves. I looked back to the red Swedish. The X of its crossed rails was in place. All that remained was the question of time.

Jenny was gone from the grandstands. Only the ghost of her disgust remained. My hand had become my only thought. Eddie beamed, "My God! She goes better without reins," but his words were distant.

I'd been steadied by the splint of beating hooves; that splint was gone now. The pain in my hand eclipsed the euphoria of finishing. I sagged in the saddle like a sack of grain, split at the corners, pouring out. Blackness closed in at the edges of sight, but I willed it back.

A man's hand lay on my thigh. I studied it: the finger nails jagged and nicked from work, the long lean strength, the spread of bones given movement by muscle, the veins that gave it geography. I couldn't trust my voice to speak or my eyes to travel forth from that one hand I knew, but I felt something latent blooming at its touch. I'd lost a hand; now a hand supplied itself.

"So this is Zephyr," Timothy said.

Zephyr's ears lazed out and her head drooped, recovering from the effort of jumping. She swished her tail at a fly and looked generally unimpressed, but he'd spoken her name with all the notes of appreciation. He'd seen us.

Eddie took Zephyr's reins and turned to Timothy. In a glance, Eddie sized him up: the hand resting on my thigh, the eyes on mine, neither of us flinching. He stroked Zephyr's neck. "Can you give Joannie a lift to the hospital?"

"Hospital?" Timothy's gaze never left mine, but there was a subtle change in its quality. He looked in for all the unsaid things.

"She got kicked in the hand earlier," Eddie said. "Shouldn't have been riding."

I collected. "No one ever died of a broken hand," I said, and swung down from the saddle, but the pain that charged through me as my feet hit the too solid ground caught the words in my throat and stole the strength of my knees. Timothy's arm caught me before I could fall.

Eddie said, "Give me your truck keys. Jenny and I will get the horses home." He shook his head and patted Zephyr's shoulder. Pride lingered in the ill-suppressed smile as he looked into her calm eye. "We'll talk about a price tomorrow."

If Timothy's arm were not around me, the words might again have stolen my knees. Instead, I managed to say, "Don't go raising the price just because we won today."

"Don't push it, Joannie. I'll get your ribbon for you. You go."

Timothy walked me to his borrowed car, an ashy silver bullet-shaped two-seater long familiar to me. I swallowed the coincidence. Small towns only get smaller the longer you live in them.

Timothy spoke softly as we went, like someone telling a time-worn myth. "All week," he said, "I felt like I was forgetting something. Something important. It hung there in the back of my mind, tickling, and I couldn't get to it. Then there I was, trying to sleep in this morning, and I dreamed you were calling me, real clear but quiet. Insistent. And it came to me—the show, New Year's. I kept hearing your voice saying my name the whole way here. Timothy, Timothy. It was like a drum beat, only it was your voice whispering it." He maneuvered me into the car, wiping the tears from my eyes. "You were great today. Really great. There was one fence she jumped like it was eight feet high—"

"—the green vertical—" (my voice barely audible)

"—it was like art, watching two bodies move together like that. Like a horse and animal could be one person. It was like catching the wind by its hair and letting it lift you. I don't think anyone else there could have stayed on for that jump."

"The blonde might've." I couldn't say more. Already a scream was threatening. I shut my eyes as the engine turned over. The car shook, and the fractured bones grinded against each other. Red trumpets. There would always be another horse to beat, another rider, another Mouse, another Jenny. There would always be dormancy; there would always be bloom.

Timothy eased our way forward onto the open road, the old engine shuttering fresh pain. The whole world collapsed into that broken hand. My clenched jaw forbid the scream that threatened to rise, and I trained my eyes on his neck's fish. He'd released me saying I'd always been strong enough, but he'd been wrong. I was and I wasn't. Having walked the border between staying alive and living, it wasn't my need itself that made or moved the mountains in my path, but *how* I needed.

He looked over. "You O.K.?"

My left hand gripped my right, squeezing the bones into a constant but consistent pain. Dark wings fluttered in my throat. If I'd opened my mouth, it was not words that would fly out.

The eye is a kind of hook. If you want to fly, you must look beyond the horizon. Flick your gaze down at the fence, and the hook will catch; your horse will pull a rail. What is this strange gravity? How does it relate to windows of the soul, or the book of the mind a horseman reads in the equine eye? What touches there? What pulls? Is the eye body, mind, or soul?

Timothy cast his glance to mine and pressed the accelerator. We surged forward along a silver thread of the highway that bent through the rolling Palouse, our eyes turned to the western horizon, the way forward, the course.

Acknowledgements

I owe a huge debt of gratitude to the many people who helped me make this book. In particular, I would like to thank:

My children, Gwendolyn and Oliver, for forgiving me those hours I spent staring at my computer into a world you couldn't see, delaying our trips to the park or the library so that I could finish a chapter or write some notes. I love you both more than I can express.

My husband, Nathanael Myers, who took on parenting and meal cooking and countless other duties to give me the time and space to write, and whose constructive but unflinching commentary helped me revise this novel through its most dramatic redrafting.

My dissertation committee at the University of Georgia, including Richard Menke, Roxanne Eberle, Judith Cofer, and most especially to Reg McKnight, whose faith in me never flagged. Any draft not inscribed with your insightful comments ("needs more pepper") seems to be missing a little something.

The members of Reg McKnight's graduate fiction workshop, but most particularly to Kirsten Kaschock and Jeff Newberry, who continued to read drafts long after we'd all been hooded. I am lucky indeed to count two such talented poets and novelists among my dearest friends.

My parents, for your unwavering belief in me, and to my talented sister, Megan Griffiths, who is always up for a good long talk about art and what it should do—and whose humor keeps the conversation from ever getting too stuffy.

My fact checkers: Sara Steger for making sure I got my Southern women right, and Jerry Cummings, former program director of radiography at Athens Technical College, for teaching me how to take an x-ray. Any mistakes in here are mine alone.

Tom Ordway, who, for so many years, taught me how to bend the bow and let the arrow fly.

My agent, John Talbot, for taking this book on and finding it a home, and my book team at New Rivers Press, including Alan

Davis, Suzzanne Kelley, David Binkard, Megan Bartholomay, and Jenna Galstad, for your belief and support and for making this book happen.

Josh Ritter and Rural Songs for permission to reprint the lyrics from the song "To the Dogs or Whoever."

Killian, inspiration for both Foxfire and Zephyr, who forever set the bar by which all great horses must be judged. You will forever be my grey old gentleman. I miss you every day.

And to all the many, many others—too numerous to list—who helped me along the way.

About the Author

Dr. Siân Griffiths lives in Ogden, Utah, where she serves as assistant professor of English at Weber State University. Her work is published in *Quarterly West, Ninth Letter, Cave Wall, River Teeth: A Journal of Nonfiction Narrative, Clackamas Literary Review, Oregon Literary Review, The Sow's Ear Poetry Review, Permafrost, Versal, Court Green,* and *The Georgia Review,* among other publications. Her story "What Is Solid" was nominated for a Pushcart Prize, and Janet Burroway included her poem, "Fistful," in the third edition of *Imaginative Writing.*